THE HOUSE OF THE WOLF

# The House of the Wolf

by Alison Baird

edited by Judy Diehl

**Salon Books**

**ONTARIO ARTS COUNCIL**
**CONSEIL DES ARTS DE L'ONTARIO**

an Ontario government agency
un organisme du gouvernement de l'Ontario

The author wishes to thank the Ontario Arts Council for its assistance in the writing of this book.

In memory of Josepha

**Canadian Cataloguing in Publication Data**
Baird, Alison Elaine
*The House of the Wolf*

© Alison Baird 2017
All rights reserved
ISBN 978-0-9698031-6-4
Published by Salon Books

Cover © Y. Nikolova at Ammonia Book Covers
Frontispiece: © Alison Baird 2016

You may hear their hurried breathing,
You may see their fleeting forms,
At the pallid polar midnight,
When the north is gathering storms;
When the arctic frosts are flaming,
And the ice-field thunders roll;
These demon-haunted werewolves,
Who circle round the Pole.


from *The Werewolves*
by Wilfred Campbell
(1858-1918)

# THE HOUSE OF THE WOLF

*Hunter*

The wolf made his way along the riverbank, moving warily.

His pack, ravenous for meat, was tracking a herd of caribou farther up the canyon, but he was focused on a solitary chase of his own. He dropped his nose to the barren ground, breathing in the scent trail. The men were very close. He had tracked them for nearly an hour and was closing the gap: before long he would be upon them. He had first caught sight of them on the far side of the river, and waited for them to move on before swimming across. Since then he had lost sight of his quarry, but he could see their footprints in the softer earth near the river: peculiar marks, oblong and toeless, like the tracks of no other living thing; and their scent lingered. It too was unlike any other animal odor.

They must, he thought, be looking for a way up the side of the canyon. Yes, here was their scent again amongst the stones, moving upward and away from the water. That spur of rock jutting from the canyon wall obscured his view. He followed the trail, nose to the ground, up and across the spur to its far side.

There they were – on the slope, just above him.

Men were scarce here in the arctic, and in his brief life he had encountered only a few. But there was no doubt as to the identity of these creatures. No other mammal walked thus, using the hind limbs only. Even on this steep and stony slope they did not make use of their forelimbs. The wolf stood staring up at the creatures.

They had not seen him. Good. His pure white colouring was a disadvantage, he knew. Against drifts of arctic snow it made him all but invisible, but against the dull brown of exposed earth he stood out clearly.

Fortunately human senses were weaker than his; even had he not been downwind of them they still would not have been able to smell him. He went on up the side of the canyon, picking his way with care amongst treacherous stones that could announce his presence with a clink or long rattling fall. The men meanwhile had nearly reached the top of the slope. One was clearly a tundra-man, but the other three men looked different: paler in the face, longer in the nose, and their scent was subtly different too. He pressed ever closer, excited and eager.

Too eager. A small stone dislodged by his foot went clattering downhill. His first careless move. One of the pale-faced men turned sharply, pointed at him and shouted. Two of his companions raised their guns, pointing them directly at the wolf as he froze in alarm. But the tundra-man stood still. He shouted to the others.

*"Non, non! Ce n'est pas nécessaire!"*

The three other men stared at him. *"Êtes-vous fou?"* one southern man barked back. *"Il va nous tuer!"*

*"Non! Observez-moi!"*

The southerners stared as the tundra-man lay down in the sparse sedge. He lay on his back: the submissive posture adopted by lower-caste wolves in the presence of their betters. *"Lentement – comme ça,"* the tundra-man said in a softer voice. *"Soyez calme!"*

Slowly, the other men put their weapons on the ground and lay down too.

The white wolf approached them, cautious still yet unable to resist his fascination. He went right up to the prone bodies, stared at them, then stretched out his neck and sniffed at their toeless feet. But *were* these their actual feet, after all? They seemed to be casings of something like loose animal-hide. Men were not then, as he had conjectured, toeless: they merely covered their feet up to protect them, as they covered the rest of their

2

bodies. The discovery brought a sense of relief: these were not strange unnatural monsters, but kindred beings, sharing some anatomical similarities with his own kind.

The tundra-man spoke in a soft voice. *"Bonjour, Monsieur Amaroq."*

These strange guttural vocalizations were almost certainly their equivalent of language. The white wolf dared to look at their faces, turning from one to the other. Though he could not understand the peculiar sounds they made, he had the distinct impression that these men bore him no ill will. One man held up a small object, pointing it at him. But there was no aggression in his body language, and the object made no threatening sound. His gaze moved to the tundra-man, and for an instant the man's eyes locked with his. They were dark brown eyes, very deep-set in his furless face, benign and profoundly intelligent.

No wild animal can meet another's gaze in comfort: a protracted stare is an indication of belligerent intent. Though he saw no hostility here, irrational panic surged suddenly through the white wolf's brain. With a high-pitched whine of anxiety he recoiled, whirled around and bolted. Soil and pebbles sprayed from his paws as he fled back down to the river. He now wanted only to put as much distance as possible between him and these alien creatures. He raced down into the valley and slipped and slithered down its side, falling twice in his haste, fleeing even as something else within him yearned to remain.

Farther up the valley the river had met another, and melded with it: a brown-and-white heaving torrent, formed not of water but thousands of living bodies. The great caribou herd of Ungava was at long last beginning to migrate south from its summer calving-grounds.

3

They were woodland caribou, the males at this time of year bearing luxuriant white manes and antlers whose long sloping beams ended in palmate tines like splay-fingered hands. The does, mild-eyed and more delicately antlered, were accompanied by their young. The animals looked around them as they approached the riverbank, but seeing nothing in the canyon save for a small group of shaggy musk oxen cropping the tundra on its northern bank, they continued on their way: less a multitude than a single creature formed out of many parts, all ruled by a common need. It was not unusual for caribou to drown in rivers during migration time, sometimes in great numbers. But this one did not flow so fiercely here as it did farther to the west, where it descended in foaming rapids; the lead animals' hooves soon touched its graveled bottom again. They emerged soaked and chilled and sneezing water out of their nostrils, but scarcely paused in their onward movement – continuous and nearly as mindless as the river's, an extension of a larger life-force.

Like a mighty tide that force rose and ebbed. For now its energies were waning with the sun: it had begun to seep away southward, following migratory routes in earth and air. The caribou exodus was one of many undertaken in advance of the arctic autumn. Flocks of snow geese and eiders flew overhead at intervals, departing their coastal nesting grounds. Lands to the south still basked in August's warmth, but here the sunlight was growing paler, the winds colder. The air had a bitter clarity, drawing out details from the distant canyon walls.

All the herd had now crossed over save for a small number of weaker and slower animals that took up the rear. The smallest of the calves was amongst these: birthed only in June, he still walked close by his dam's side and his legs were stick-thin and uncertain. He

4

thrust his head forward and snuffed at the unfamiliar scent of the river. It flowed so swiftly, unlike the still waters of the little northern lakes he knew. There were strange gushing and gurgling sounds along its margin, and the sun sparked uncounted points of fiery light upon its restless surface. But unease at the sight of this unfamiliar, glittering, plangent thing was overruled by the greater need to remain close to the security of his mother's warm body. When she headed in the direction of the water he hurried after her.

But even as these last stragglers approached the river, from the brow of the northern slope behind them burst a dozen lean forms, white and black and grey-brown in colour. The lagging caribou stopped and snorted in alarm, and their warning passed forward in a rippling pattern to those at the front. The river of flesh swirled and eddied, streaming away from the attackers. The musk oxen meanwhile encircled their young, rumps pointing inward and heads outward, presenting to the encroaching hunters their formidable helmets of horn. But the wolves paid no attention. Another time they might have challenged the musk oxen's defenses, but just now they were after easier prey. As the last of the caribou plunged towards the river the hunters split into two separate groups, one racing along the bank to try and cut the animals off from the water, the other charging at the stragglers still on land.

The smallest calf strove to keep up with his mother. He saw terror in her rolling eyes and heard it in her ragged gasping breaths. No rudimentary caution spurred him now: his brain, small and undeveloped as it was, understood his mortal peril. Without thought, he fled. But the wolves had their eyes on him, recognizing in him their best chance of success. An old or lame animal would have suited their purposes just as well: it was weakness they targeted. Four wolves divided doe and

5

calf from the rest of the herd; three more leaped in as the doe turned her antlers in desperation on the first attackers, and separated mother from offspring. One of these seized the calf by the neck as the other knocked its legs out from under it. Followed by a third they dragged their prey, still kicking and bleating, away over the tundra.

His mother, powerless to save him, bawled a brief protest before wheeling about to flee her pursuers. The four wolves followed her, but drew back again as she merged once more into the moving mass of legs and bobbing antlers. The sounds of the stricken calf's distress now came to the attackers' ears: their pack-mates had secured food for them all. They turned back, racing to rejoin the others while the caribou herd slowed and moved on. A life had been taken from them, but many more remained. With the predators' bellies filled they would be able to continue their journey in peace.

The wolves settled down to feed. As they exchanged growls and glares over the still-thrashing prey, the lone white wolf came loping into their midst. His pack mates ignored him, save for one large grey-furred male that eyed him with open dislike.

"You! Where have you been?" he snarled in the wolf-language.

The white wolf skidded to a halt. "Nowhere, Fore-wolf," he said evasively, tucking his tail between his hindquarters.

The higher-ranking wolf was not appeased. "If you keep going off without permission the Head-wolf will run you out of the pack. What is the matter with you, Hunter?" He called the white wolf not by his name, for he had none: "Hunter" was the title assigned him by the male head-wolf of the pack, a description of his function within their group. Other wolves of low rank went by such descriptive handles as Scout or Spotter. The Head-

6

wolves were addressed always as "Father" and "Mother", in part because they were the biological parents of most of the pack, but also because they alone enjoyed the right to breed.

The white wolf made no reply. He watched the other wolves tear at the young caribou's flanks and belly. It kicked and bleated, and for an instant the calf's large dark-brown eye stared straight into his. He saw in it fear and pain, and beneath both a blank incomprehension as the world, so new and wondrous, began to fade from view. Moved by a sudden impulse – too swift and thoughtless to analyze – the white wolf lunged forward, right into the melee. Seizing the throat of the calf, he severed it with a snap of his teeth. In the next moment the glinting spark of torment was gone: the eye was dull and empty of expression as a stone, reduced to the realm of inanimate things.

The other wolves reacted with instant outrage, turning their gored fangs upon him. The largest wolf charged him, knocking him over, and stood over his sprawled body bristling with rage. "How dare you approach the kill? You know the rules. Head-wolves eat first, then fore-wolves. Hind-wolves last of all." A savage, deep-throated growl accompanied the last words.

"I did not take any meat, Father," Hunter gasped. "I only meant – I just –" He glanced at the dead calf, and continued confusedly: "I had to do that. It – it was in pain."

"What?" The Head-wolf looked down at him in blank incomprehension. All the wolves were staring at him now, the indignant anger in their eyes replaced by a similar bewilderment.

"Mad," muttered the grey Fore-wolf to his pack-mates. "He's gone stark, foaming mad."

The Head-wolf glowered. "Keep your place, Hind-wolf, and we'll leave you a bone – perhaps. But try again to snatch food out of turn, and you're out of the Lake Pack for good. Now get out of my sight!"

The white wolf at once ducked his head in submission, then sprang up and darted away as the dominant wolves continued to feed. He ran up to the top of the slope. Another wolf lay there in the sun, his thin face overlaid with the silver mask of age. He looked up as the younger wolf joined him and gave a long lupine grin, showing worn and yellowed teeth. He was the oldest member of the pack, a former Father-wolf from days long gone. Mother-wolf was his daughter, and she and Father-wolf allowed him to remain with the pack since he could not now hunt alone.

"Good hunting, hey?" he said to Hunter. "Hope there'll be some pickings for us later, young one."

"It was only a calf. What would be left? You can go dine on scraps with the ravens if you like. I'm not hungry." This was a lie: hunger ravaged him as though he himself were being devoured from within. Hunter threw himself down beside the old grey wolf. In his mind the caribou calf's eye seemed still to stare at him, with its pitiful glint of dwindling life – and what else? What had he seen there? Not a plea for mercy: the calf had expected none. Its eye had seemed, rather, to hold in its fading depths a question, posed not to him or his pack-mates but to something else. It seemed to ask why such a thing need happen; how it was that the world permitted it. A question for which the young wolf had no answer.

Hunter could not articulate this strange new thought. Instead he said, pointing with his muzzle at the caribou herd retreating up the gorge, "There were so many of them, and so few of us. They could have trampled us to death, and saved that calf. But they didn't – they never

8

do. They endure our kills, and just move on. Why is that, Old One?"

"Because they are only plant-eaters, and have no intelligence or courage. Also, one calf is a small thing to lose when the whole of the herd is in peril. It could have been worse. They are content to let us fill our bellies while the rest escape. They can always breed more calves."

The white wolf fell silent. In his wild animal's mind he saw perfect sense in what his elder said. The life that had left the calf had merely transmuted, flowing into the feeding wolves to fuel their own bodies. He gazed out across the river valley and its surrounding plateau. The low-circling arctic sun sent long and mellow rays across plains whose heaths and sedges thrummed with activity. Insects swarmed about the leaves and stalks of Labrador tea and bearberry in thick droning clouds, and through their midst swooped snow buntings, horned larks and Lapland longspurs with gaping beaks, feasting on the wing. Higher up a circling gyrfalcon drew in its wings and stooped, plunging into the tundra. It rose with the small brown shape of a lemming dangling lifeless from its claws. The whole land teemed with a diverse, tumultuous life that thrived and grew and fed upon itself. Before day's end countless individual lives would be sacrificed, their losses unmarked and unmourned. The white wolf was aware of a new feeling, a restlessness within him that rose up in rebellion against this uncompromising reality. He felt the cruelty of the world like the first chill of winter in his bones.

"So some kill and some are killed," he said, "and we are fortunate to eat without being eaten in turn."

"The earth eats us," said the older wolf. "When we die it takes us into itself again. In the end all are consumed."

Hunter turned to look at him: at his silvered muzzle, the ribs that were beginning to show through his thinning fur, and he wondered if the old one would make it through another winter. "I wonder sometimes whether all this was meant to be. If this suffering is all there truly is to our existence."

"What else should there be? We live a little, hunt a little, eat a little – mate, if we're lucky – and then we die. It has always been so. There is nothing else." The old wolf rose to all fours and went to Hunter, nuzzling the side of his face. "There, enough of that. Where did you go today, young one? You were gone a long time."

Hunter took a moment to answer. "I swam to the other side of the river."

The old one stared. "What on earth were you doing *there?* You know the river's the border of our territory! We may hunt the lake-lands north of it, but everything to the south – "

"Belongs to the Stone Pack. I know, I know! But I didn't go very far. Just a little way up their side of the canyon. I wasn't really in any danger."

"You young fool, you know those wolves will kill anyone who strays onto their hunting grounds. They killed your parents."

"What?" It was Hunter's turn to stare. "How do you know that?"

"I'm old. I know a lot of things." The old wolf's eyes softened as he spoke. "I remember your mother well. She was my daughter, too. Swift and savage in the hunt she was, but gentle and patient with her sister's pups. So she kept her place in the Lake Pack for four seasons, and hoped to do so for many more years. But her sister failed to produce a litter one spring, and she grew jealous and insecure, unwilling even to tolerate her as a hind-wolf. She turned on your mother, and chased her away from the pack. The poor creature was forced to fend for herself, far away from their territory. She went as far as the Lake of the Owl, where she found a mate and raised her own pups.

"It didn't last long. Your father and mother raised their litter close to the Stone Pack's land, and strayed into it seeking food for their pups – as far as the Lake of the White Bear. There the Stone Pack killed your father for trespassing, and then they hunted your mother down and killed her too."

"So that is what became of them," said Hunter softly. "We never knew – my brother and my sister and I. We just found ourselves alone, with no one to look after us."

"Well, now you know. I'd have told you long ago, but I didn't want to distress you. I tell you now only to warn you. Don't cross the river again, or you'll surely share your parents' fate."

Hunter made no reply. He gazed at the landscape below, picturing it as it would be in a few short months: a waste of wind-scoured snow under unending night. Late in the winter would come mating time and its attendant tensions. There had been no litter last spring. With their fertility in doubt, the head-wolves would grow insecure about their status and the family would begin to fall apart. Mother-wolf would harass the younger females, her daughters, so that stress would prevent them from going into oestrus; she did not want them to depart and mate with outsiders, raising new litters that would compete with her pack for scant resources. Father-wolf would do the opposite: bully and dominate the males, forcing them to depart the family group for other territories. Hunter, as a hind-wolf and not even his own offspring, would likely be the first to feel his wrath. Hunter had earned respect from this pack over the years, hunting food for them and helping to care for and watch over their pups. But without a litter he had no role in their extended family.

"Why *did* you go off alone anyway?" asked the old one presently. "Looking for food?"

Hunter looked away. "No. I was after – something else."

"You're not following men again?" Hunter's silence signaled affirmation, and the aged wolf looked perplexed. "If the Head-wolves catch you at it one more time they'll expel you – or worse. You know it's against our laws. Men are dangerous, young one."

"Not to us. They kill mostly hoofed beasts, as we do."

"True. But they have also slain many a wolf that ventured too close to them. I would give them a wide berth even if it weren't for pack law. Why this fascination with the creatures, Hunter?"

"I don't know. I have always been fascinated by humans, ever since I first heard about them. I even dream sometimes of *being* a human. I am standing up on my hind legs in these dreams, and I can feel that my front paws have changed: their toes grown longer, their pads replaced by soft flesh... It is so strange – I can't explain it."

The old wolf looked thoughtful. "Perhaps I can. Do you not know the old tale of the wolf-men?"

"The tale of what?" Hunter asked.

"You really don't know? That's interesting. Makes me wonder if it might all be true..."

Hunter's mother had told him and his litter-mates many stories to while the time away in their snug den. The memory filled him with reawakened grief, for of that little family he alone survived. But it also brought with it images of warmth and security. "Tell me then, while you wait your turn at meat."

"Very well." The Old One sat back down, his movements awkward and slow. "They do say that men and wolves were one, long ago. In a past so ancient we

12

can't recall it, and in a land so distant no one knows now where it lies, we became kin. And these wolf-men, or man-wolves, had the power to look like one or the other – being in their blood both at once, as you might say."

"I don't understand." How could such strange beings as men be considered kindred to wolf-kind? Was it because they too were hunters? But the polar bears and arctic foxes were also eaters of meat, and no wolf called them kin.

"They were two in one, wolves and men. Like the water that becomes ice and then thaws to water again, each had two forms, and could assume either one at will. Man into wolf, wolf into man. You see?"

Hunter stared. "But that isn't possible."

"Who can say what's possible and what isn't? I'm in my tenth year, and even I haven't seen all that there is to see in the world."

"Of course not. Pardon my interruption, Old One."

"Well, down in the southlands where the trees grow tall there are all manner of strange things, or so they tell me. The men there are not like the ones that live here. They also go on two legs, but they don't make their dens out of snow or hides. They build them out of dead tree-trunks or stones. Enormous dens they are, big enough to hold a whole pack of men with room to spare. In these dens they live lives of ease and comfort, eating their fill every single day."

"But no one eats every *day!*"

"Men do. And those with the power of changing their bodies used to have the best of both lives, safe and wild."

"Wolves," said Hunter, "lived in man-dens?"

"So it's said. But the man-wolf people became divided in the end, with some preferring one form and some the other. Those that wished to be men stayed down in the tree-lands, and those that wished to be

13

wolves went to live in the forest – moving farther and farther north, as their man-kin outnumbered them and took all the land. Now few of us can assume the other's shape any more. But we are still kin for all that, which is why we don't eat men. Most wolves don't believe this tale nowadays. But my father told it to me, and he heard it from his father's father."

"So they're our blood-kin – "

"If they are, though, they've forgotten it just as most wolves have. If you seek out men, you seek your own death. Did you actually find any down in the canyon?"

"Yes." He recalled again the terrifying and exhilarating encounter. "I sensed something in them that I've never experienced in any animal save for other wolves. An intelligence. They could not speak my language, but one of them knew the right body position to take in order to avoid violence. At his prompting the other men also adopted submissive postures. They had weapons and could easily have slain me, but they didn't. They spared me, and even allowed me to approach them. They were as interested in me as I was in them, Old One. I'm sure of it!"

The old one grunted. "If you say so. But they're done for, those men of yours. The Stone Pack will kill them."

"Kill them!" Hunter stared. "Why? No wolf kills men!"

"*They* do. They've killed many in their time, and they'll do it again. I told you, the Stone Pack tolerates no trespass on their territory – not by wolves or men." He yawned again, showing his ruined teeth. "Well, it looks as though the heads and fores are done gorging. I'm off to take my turn. There's got to be something left of that calf worth fighting a raven over."

He rose stiffly and made off down the slope to where the other wolves lay huddled together, glutted with

14

meat. But Hunter remained where he was. His eyes turned to the sere and stony plateau beyond the far side of the river valley. Its dun-coloured, rolling folds of land were forbidden to all but the pack that claimed them: to walk there meant death. The Lake Pack wolves knew this well.

*But the men don't know. They've no notion of what they are walking into.*

They would die. The savage wolves would kill them, and that glint of curiosity and warmth and intelligence he had seen in their eyes would be annihilated forever, just as the spark of awareness had vanished from the caribou calf's. The life force would reabsorb them and return them to the earth, their destruction making no more impression on the implacable landscape than would the death of a lark or lemming. Once more his wolf nature understood and accepted this inevitability. Once more that second, inner voice rose up in rebellion against it. As he sat listening to its silent urgings, a strange thought took shape within his mind. *This must not happen.* The thought floated before him, oddly abstract to his animal mind, a denial of all that was. Even as he pondered it a second, stranger thought arose to take its place.

*I must not let this happen.*

Father Wolf looked up, baring bloodied teeth at Hunter as the white wolf ran down the slope towards the canyon floor. "Hind-wolf! " he snarled, rearing up. "You may take what you need from the pickings, now. But break the rules again and it will mean expulsion from the pack! Do you understand me, Hunter?"

But the young wolf seemed not to hear him. He was heading away from the kill site, away from his pack; racing at full speed along the riverbank as if his life depended on it.

Returning to the point in the canyon where he had first spied the men, Hunter once more plunged into the river. Even in summer its water was cold as ice and made him shiver and gasp, but he persisted. Once safe on the far bank, he shook the water out of his thick coat and stood still a moment, filled with a deep foreboding. It increased as he struggled on up the steep slope, then smote him with full force, like a storm-blast, as he hauled himself over the top. The desolate landscape of the Stone Plain stretched before him, with its long low ridges that could conceal any number of enemy wolves in their shadowed and secret folds. For all he knew he was being watched already. He felt utterly exposed and defenseless.

There was no sign of the men anywhere, and only the faintest traces of their scent. Around him the immense solitude of rock-strewn earth and dull overcast sky seemed altogether empty of life: he might have been all alone in the entire world. That in itself was a terrifying feeling for one born to run with a pack, living always in the company of his own kind. For an instant as he stood there in the forbidden territory he wrestled with himself. Perhaps Father Wolf would *not* expel him after all; if he returned and begged forgiveness for leaving the pack without permission he might yet be forgiven... He struggled to quell these craven thoughts, but it became ever more difficult as he forced himself slowly onward, one paw after the other, head lowered as though walking into a wind.

He came across the tracks of the caribou, freshly trampled into the tundra: they had laid down a broad path leading south across the plateau. The scent-trail of the men also led in that direction. As Hunter stood there a flock of snow geese flew overhead, vast and clamorous, commencing their own long autumnal migration. The whole world seemed to be rushing precipitately southward. He loped on again, following the flock's flying shadows across the plain.

A wolf can travel fifty kilometres in a single day, and go for many days without feeding. But Hunter had not gorged of late, and after only a few hours he was so famished that he would have eaten anything that showed itself on the seemingly endless plateau. "I am a fool," he said to himself. "A sentimental fool. If that caribou calf were in front of me now I would eat it to the bone, and not care in the least what it suffered." Prey was scarce here, but he finally routed a couple of lemmings out of their burrows and snapped them up, bones and all, in his starving jaws. In a sheltered place underneath a glacial boulder he surprised a rock ptarmigan and killed her with one swift bite to the neck, mourning only that at this season she had no eggs or chicks for him to eat as well.

A little further on he found a shallow pond, and took a long drink of its ice-cold water. With a little food in his stomach and his thirst eased, he felt his morale improve. It is difficult for a wolf to tear himself free of his comrades and wander the wilderness alone. Loneliness and hunger and increased danger – from other wolves as well as other predators – are but a few of the consequences that await the lone wolf. Although younger wolves may choose to break away from the main pack and seek new hunting grounds, they usually do so in small groups or pairs. Lone wolves do not normally choose a life of solitude. It is thrust upon them, and they endure it because they have no other option. Hunter recalled well his relief on finding the Lake Pack as a young pup, submitting with humility to their occasional bites and blows as the price for inclusion. That even such treatment was preferable to lonely roaming was a lesson he could not easily forget.

Yet as he rested on the plain he was surprised to feel a sense of release. Perhaps before many days he would be overwhelmed by loneliness and uncertainty. For now, though, his newfound freedom made him feel almost giddy. "No more snarling and biting, no more turning up my belly to bullies," he said to himself as he lay down again for a brief rest. "I'm my *own* head-wolf now. My head leads, my body follows: I am a pack of one!"

Lying flat the ground, he was struck by the change in his perspective. Dwarf birch and willow and creeping black spruce grew around the edges of the pond, forming a thick mat that would not have reached Hunter's shoulder when he stood upright. It was a forest in miniature, of a type common to arctic regions where trees, mutated by the bitter cold environment, never grow to more than thirty centimetres in height. But with his head level with the ground he seemed to look up through colossal branches to an over-arching canopy of foliage. He could almost imagine that he had stumbled into the legendary southern woods, where trees grew many times higher than one's head. Of course, he realized, to the lemmings and other small creatures inhabiting it this *was* a mighty forest. A rodent would view itself as normal-sized, and most other living things as giants. How terrifying must the thunderous passage of a musk ox herd be, down here in this lower world! And how a lemming would cower at the predations of hawk and owl – terrifying winged monsters from the unimaginable realms of the upper air. He thought of how he, too, would seem to lemming-kind. He pictured himself looming above that sheltering canopy, immense, ruthless, lunging down with gigantic teeth –

He sat up again sharply, disturbed by the peculiar vision. Shaking the dirt and leaf-debris from his coat, he ran on.

As he moved deeper into their domain his mind dwelled more and more upon the Stone Pack wolves. His one hope was that they had left the immediate area, following the migrating caribou herd to the southernmost border of their territory. Near day's end, Hunter paused again to rest on a rise of land that offered a clear view of what lay before him. A few kilometres distant a colossal shape rose high above the plain, a grey-brown slope all strewn with rocky rubble like an esker, but he had never seen an esker as tall as this. The vast feature seemed to him sinister and somehow threatening, appearing to brood over the whole landscape. But the scent of the men – ever fainter on ground that grew harder and rockier as he went – led towards it. As he drew closer to the stony slope his eyes picked out a tiny object perched high upon it. It would not have been visible at all but for its colour, a bright unnatural orange that stood out loud as a shout against the dull brown rock and the grey clouds.

It was a tent.

The Stone Plain was the wolf-name for the stretch of barren land in the midst of the Ungava Peninsula, where the naked granite of the Canadian Shield lies bared to the sky. One can spend many days in this region without seeing more than the occasional fox, or a few waterfowl – loons, gulls, sandpipers – visiting the lonely lakes. From the air one perceives nothing but a barren waste. It might be a landscape from a more ancient epoch before animals arose upon our world, or from some alien and lifeless planet. And there is in the middle of that plain a place that might as well belong to another world.

19

Into its midst there fell, more than a million years ago, a meteor of great size. Its impact – the equivalent of eight thousand Hiroshimas – blasted a tremendous crater into the granite crust of the plateau. From space it appears as a giant hole, perfectly round, as though bored into the rock by a celestial bullet. This is the New Quebec Crater, or as it is called by the Inuit, *Pingualuit.* The wolves called it simply The Land That Rises, and anyone who sees the site from the ground will understand the reason for the name. The land around the meteor's point of impact welled up like a wound, raising a round rim of stone one hundred and fifty metres high that dominates the surrounding plain.

Hunter found the crater rim a daunting challenge. It was almost sheer in places, and everywhere covered in loose talus and tumbled, broken boulders. The only advantage it offered was the chance to conceal himself amid the rocks, both from the Stone wolves and from the men themselves. They had been friendly during the last encounter, but if they realized he was deliberately pursuing them they might assume his intentions had become hostile and react with fear and violence. He must get as close to them as possible without their seeing him, he decided, then approach them in a way that could not possibly be misunderstood. They knew the language of submission; he could speak to them in that language, reassuring them that he meant no harm. And then – somehow – communicate to them that they were in danger here. How he was going to accomplish that he did not yet know. He was still puzzling over the problem when he topped the ridge.

The tent was right in front of him, pitched on a stretch of ground that was slightly flatter and less rocky than the rest. In olden times these makeshift dwellings had been constructed out of caribou-hide; nowadays they were made of some curious substance that no wolf could identify. The white wolf approached the tent and sniffed around the base of the structure. The orange material had a strange odour. If it was some kind of animal hide, then it was not like any creature he knew. He peered cautiously into the opening. No one was inside, but the man-scent was fresh, there was a burning campfire out front and various unidentifiable objects were strewn about the place as if their owners expected to return soon and reclaim them. Hunter made a couple of circuits of the campsite, and then went to look over the other side of the stony ridge. There he stopped in his tracks, forgetting all else as he gazed astounded at the view spread out below him.

The Pingualuit Crater is remarkable not only for its great collar of stone. Within its walls there lies a lake some three kilometers across, and more than two hundred and sixty metres deep. Lake Pingualuk is fed only by the sky, snow and rain replenishing what it loses to the sun, and its water in consequence is among the purest and clearest in the world. In winter a sheet of ice covers it, white and round and fitted to the crater as a lid to a pot; but during the brief arctic summer the colour of Pingualuk's waters is a blue as deep and lucid as sapphire. Strangely, arctic char may be seen swimming in those translucent depths. How fish came to be here, in a crater-lake with neither inlet nor outlet, is an enigma and may forever remain so.

The men were down there. Hunter could see them, scrambling about on the rocks near the water's edge and throwing small stones into the lake. His heart stirred to see them: it was comforting to know there were other thinking beings in this strange and forbidding place. Floating on the water close to shore was a strange-looking object, bright yellow in colour: it resembled an enormous bird with stiff wide-spread wings, but it did not appear to be alive. He guessed that it was some sort of man-made thing, but he could not imagine what it might be. A conveyance of some sort, perhaps? It did not resemble the water-skimming "boats" described in stories.

Hunter turned back and looked at the sinking sun, and the lengthening shadow of the crater wall advancing over the stony plain below. It would be dark before long; the men would have to climb back up the slope again to be safe in their tent before nightfall. In the meantime he would conceal himself, and wait.

Three ravens flew above him, croaking in their harsh guttural voices. They spoke no language that he could understand, but ravens and wolves shared an affinity born of need, and their meaning was plain to him. They had found some carrion. Even their great stabbing beaks were not equal to the task of penetrating a caribou or musk ox's hide, so these birds flying over him were inviting him to a feast. When his sharp fangs did their work, the birds would alight and wait to scavenge whatever he left them. This was the curious symbiosis of their kind and his.

Hunger was raging within him again, and since the men still showed no sign of coming back up he decided to satisfy his needs while he could. He followed the flying ravens back down the outer side of the crater, until he came upon the carrion they had found lying amid the rocks on the plain. It was a bull caribou, one antler jutting up like the branch of a dead tree. There was already a wolf feeding on the carcass – he could see its white-furred back and hindquarters protruding behind the curve of the animal's flank. He feared for a moment that this was a Stone Pack member, but closer inspection showed him that it was much smaller and lighter of build than he. This animal was not, then, a high-wolf like himself but merely a low-wolf. He was not surprised to see it here. Low-wolves tended to follow the caribou on their long southward migration, unlike the high-wolves who kept to their established territories during both winter and summer. The attachment of the latter to their ancestral lands ran deep; they also respected the territorial boundaries of other high-wolf packs, which unlike those of low-wolves did not shift in size from season to season but forever retained the same unalterable boundaries. Though their winter diet was meagre in comparison with the bounty of summer months, there were usually enough musk ox, lemmings and arctic hares to keep high-wolves alive until the caribou returned with the spring.

Hunter advanced confidently towards the carcass. Low-wolves possessed only a rudimentary animal intelligence and could not speak, so there was no point in addressing this one. He merely gave a warning snarl, pulling back his lips from his fangs, in a message any wild thing understood: *Go now, or I will fight you.* He knew from bitter experience that food in the arctic is life, and any attempt to plunder it from another may mean a duel to the death. His superior size and strength gave him the advantage here, but he still felt some relief when the low-wolf did not rise and meet his challenge. It did not move at all, in fact, but remained draped across the carrion. Was it taking a rest after gorging? As he rounded the carcass he noticed that the wolf's eyes – a fierce yellow colour like those of all low-wolves – were open, but glazed and unseeing. As he got closer he saw why. The wolf's neck was darkly matted with blood, showing clearly against the white fur. This animal had been killed by another carnivore, in the very act of scavenging meat from the kill…

Even as he looked with distaste at the unpleasant sight he heard another sound, one that set all the fur on his hackles upright: the deep full-chested roar of an enraged wolf. Swinging around, he saw to his horror the lean dark shapes of three high-wolves not thirty metres distant.

They were charging straight at him.

A wolf pack functions like a single animal with many eyes and ears and nostrils, constantly alert and aware. While some of its members sleep others keep watch, turn and turn about; and so Hunter had let down his guard by habit, where a lone wolf accustomed to solitude would have been more wary. His inattentiveness, it seemed, would now prove his undoing: still weary from his exertions on the crater rim, he could not hope to outrun his fleet-footed pursuers. Looking back as he fled, he saw with panic that they were gaining on him. He put on a last frantic burst of speed, his lungs labouring and his tongue hanging from the side of his mouth. But it was no use. They were upon him in moments, cutting him off, surrounding him on all sides with snarling teeth.

Had he fought them, or even attempted to defend himself, he would have been set upon and torn to pieces. But this time his pack experience stood him in good stead. As a hind-wolf his instant reaction to another wolf's aggression was to adopt a submissive posture. Without thinking, he dropped and rolled over onto his back. The other wolves closed in on him, and the largest one set his great wide paw on Hunter's heaving chest. But their quarry's passivity appeared to mollify them: at any rate, they did not immediately go for his exposed throat.

"Intruder!" raged the big wolf. "How dare you come here? This land is the Stone Pack's: to stray on our hunting-ground is forbidden! And to steal our meat – "

"I took no meat!" Hunter gasped. "I seek no game – I am only passing through this place. Let me go, and I swear I will leave now!"

Three pairs of hostile eyes glared down upon him. They were a peculiar colour: not blue or grey like those of the high-wolves in his own pack, but feral yellow like the eyes of the low-wolf. Two of them – the big brute holding him down, and a smaller leaner animal that held back behind the others – had black pelts, and the third a coat of dark brown: this made the strange pale hue of their irises stand out all the more. The eyes of wild beasts, set in the faces of creatures that could reason and speak…

The smaller black wolf whined: "Why waste time talking to this fool? We've better things to do."

"Yes," said the brown-furred wolf. "Kill him now and be done with it. He invaded our territory; let him pay the price, like that wretched low-wolf."

"No," argued the smaller one. "I meant, why bother with him at all? We came to kill men, not wolves!"

They glared at each other for a moment. Then both of them turned and looked to the biggest wolf. He had a grey-flecked muzzle and a commanding air, clearly the head-wolf of this pack.

"And so we will," he rumbled. "Be patient, my sons."

"Plenty of time to kill men later, Father," the brown wolf replied, "after we have dealt with this little interloper." His lips pulled back from his fangs, exposing them right to the gums, as he leaned over Hunter's upturned and vulnerable throat.

"Wait," the head-wolf said. He pulled back slightly from Hunter, though his paw remained on the young wolf's chest, and regarded him with eyes that were cool and steady despite their feral hue. "This one may know something useful, if he's been here a while. Tell me, stranger, have you seen any men here?"

Hunter thought fast, as the brown fore-wolf stood over him with teeth still bared. It was possible his own

25

life would be spared if he provided useful information about the men. Self-preservation was the first duty of any living creature. For an instant, in which his own life hung in the balance, he wavered. Then with relief he recalled the deadly weapons that the men carried. They were not defenseless, after all...

"I have seen their tent," he confessed. "It sits atop the – the big ridge – "

"The Land That Rises?" All three turned and looked at the crater.

"Yes. You can see it for yourselves, if you approach from the north. But I would not go too close if I were you," Hunter added quickly. "Those men carry with them the weapons that kill from a distance. Best to stay far away from them!"

The brown wolf was unimpressed by his admonitions. "Night is near. They need to sleep like all other creatures. We can take them unawares."

"And so we will," said the head-wolf.

"But why?" Hunter dared to ask. "Wolves don't kill men. And most of these are strangers, from the far south. They will not remain here long."

The big black wolf looked down at Hunter. "You don't understand. It's because they are southerners that they must die. Those men will try to make this place *their* territory, run it and rule it according to their own desires. They will drive us out in the end, and we will have no hunting-grounds left to call our own. These ones *must* be destroyed. That will put fear in all the others."

"Enough! Kill the miserable creature now!" cried the brown wolf. His tail was held low, indicating subservience to his father, but his teeth remained bared — an oddly conflicting set of signals. The head-wolf turned and met his son's savage gaze.

"Save your strength for later, and your teeth for human throats," he said, on a low growl. "For now, we wait and rest. At nightfall, we kill!" He removed his paw from Hunter's chest and spun away across the plain, heading for the crater. The thin black wolf followed him at once, but the other continued to glower at Hunter.

"You are spared – for the moment," he said in a soft low voice, filled with menace. "But trespass on our territory again, and I will rip your throat out. Now go!"

Hunter rolled onto his feet. He remained crouching low, though, literally crawling before the other wolf. *If we do meet again,* he thought, *let it be when you're alone as I am, and we can fight it out one-on-one.* His enemy was not much bigger than he: on his own, Hunter thought, he could surely take him. The other wolf's arrogant confidence came only from the security of being in a group.

But that was a matter to be dealt with in future. Hunter's most pressing concern was the present, and as he ran away he tried to shape a plan. His survival instinct warred with the new emerging emotion within him – that thing to which he could not put a name, but which had lately roused at the sight of the suffering caribou calf. He *had* to help them – those gentle beings who were, even now, preparing for their night's rest completely unaware of their danger. He had betrayed their location, putting them in mortal peril. Would they think to post a watch? He doubted it. Wolves were not known to make unprovoked attacks on humankind, and they had already had one perfectly harmless encounter with Hunter himself. By approaching them with benign intent, he had put them off their guard. He *must* warn them somehow – but without being caught by the three high-wolves, who would certainly carry through on their threat to kill him.

Darkness was creeping over the plateau as he climbed the northern face of the crater. He could just make out the pale shape of the tent atop the western rim. He swung his muzzle, questing for another scent: the musk of the wolves, dreading the thought of their tearing fangs. But then he imagined those fangs ripping into the soft defenseless throats and bellies of the four men inside the tent, and he set aside his fears for himself and ran on along the crater rim.

When he reached the tent he found its flap was closed. The structure now glowed with an inner light, like a cloud incandesced with lightning – but this illumination was steady, the strange fireless light of men. It showed their shadows as they moved about within the tent's confines, talking to one another in their odd language. They must *not* fall asleep. If they did, they were doomed. He sat down and whined shrilly. They did not hear. He dared not make too much noise, for fear of being heard by the killer wolves. He pawed at the thin wall of the tent, whining more loudly. His claws could make no impression on the strange orange stuff, which was soft and simply yielded to his touch. He reared up and put all his weight upon it.

Suddenly there was a sound like ripping animal-hide, and he felt the wall give way. Underestimating either its strength or his own, he had accidentally torn it right open. Taken by surprise, he lost his balance and fell forward – right inside the tent.

At once there was a confusion of cries and struggling bodies. Light blazed in his eyes, dazzling and disorienting him. Something hit him hard in the nose, and he yelped in pain. Hunter lurched back to his feet as the startled men flailed, bellowed and groped about them, no doubt looking for their weapons. He whirled – a manouevre not easily achieved in the tiny enclosed space, amid the men's thrashing limbs – and leaped back

28

through the ragged opening he had made, fleeing for his life.

At least he had succeeded in alerting them. But it remained to be seen if they would stay alarmed and vigilant.

Aware that his white pelt would make him a highly visible target for their weapons, the wolf made haste to put distance between himself and the tent. The moon was out: three-quarters full, it showed all the plain below, casting black shadows under the rocks and making the surrounding lakes and ponds glimmer. He concealed himself amid some boulders and waited. He could see no signs of activity from the men, and presently the light went out in their tent. Surely they were not going to sleep after all? Could they truly be so foolish? For all they knew, he might have broken into their sleeping place with hostile intent. He debated whether or not to approach them again. It would be dangerous, if they were awake still and watching out for him. But what if they were not – if his warning had not been heeded?

Then his heart began to pound as he saw three dark figures slink across the moonlit plain towards the crater. The wolves had come to kill the men. He stood up, in an agony of fear and indecision, wondering what to do. Might a loud howl wake the men and alert them to their peril? But it would also alert the wolves to his presence…

The Stone wolves raced up the slope, swift and silent. Hunter opened his jaws to howl.

But before he could make a sound there was a thunderous crack, and the largest wolf, who was in the lead, dropped to the ground as if knocked over by an invisible assailant. He tumbled over and over, struggled to his feet again and fled back downhill, but he limped and staggered as he went, as though he were wounded.

The fore-wolves turned tail as well and ran after him. More shots rang out, but the wolves dodged behind an outcrop of tall rocks and vanished from view.

Hunter saw the shape of a man emerge from the tent's mouth, a weapon at his shoulder.

His clumsy intrusion had worked, after all. They had posted a guard! But his jubilation was short-lived. The Stone wolves would be enraged, with their plan thwarted and one of them hurt. They would not likely dare attack the men again, but they might well take out their anger on Hunter if they found him. He must flee this area at once, using what cover he could find until he was safely off the Stone Pack's territory.

He scrambled back down the north face of the crater, heading for the river canyon and safety.

## 3

The howling started not long after he set out. These were not the usual deep and melodious vocalizations with which wolves communicate amongst themselves, remaining in touch with others of their pack. They were discordant, piercing cries of distress, and even from a long distance Hunter could feel the anguish throbbing through them. He knew at once what had happened. The big head-wolf must have died of his gun wound. A jolt of pure terror ran through him.

"No! They couldn't possibly know *I* warned the men," he tried to reassure himself as he ran. "The fore-wolves didn't see me enter the men's tent. They only know that their Father was shot by a man and died." But he increased his speed all the same, from a lope to a full-out sprint, until his tongue lolled out of his gasping mouth. All he could think of was the cold savagery in the big fore-wolf's eyes, and the disdain in his younger brother's. If they caught Hunter a second time, lingering on their land even after their warning, they would need no other reason to kill him. But their fresh grief would make them all the fiercer. Killing him might even help to ease their pain.

Spurred by this fear, he continued his headlong flight northward, attempting to put as much distance as possible between himself and the mourning wolves. He could no longer hear any howls. Had they faded with distance, or had the wolves ceased their lamentations? Were they even now tracking his scent through the tundra? If it came to a fight he had little chance of surviving. Even with their numbers reduced they still held the advantage.

Suddenly he stumbled as a shock of pain jolted through him. He gave a shrill yelp of terror. Something had seized his right foreleg – something hidden in the tundra, with great jaws that snapped shut upon his limb and held it. For a mad moment he thought the fore-wolves had ambushed him and that one had bitten his leg. But the sparse ground-cover gave no hiding place to anything as large as a wolf. He smelled nothing, no odour of wolf or bear or any other animal. Yet he could not move: the strange unseen jaws held him with a grip stronger than stone. It was as if the earth itself had taken hold of him.

Whimpering, he scrabbled with his free paw in the soil and touched something cold. Not stone, but something smooth and hard that gleamed dully. It had the shape of an animal's jaws, with two halves that came together to grip their prey. But it was lifeless as a rock, half-buried in the soil. He sniffed and gnawed at it, and it did not react.

A man-thing of some sort – another of their inventions? He had heard of such things. Devices that trapped animals, keeping them pinned in place until the men could come and kill them. It was part of the terrifying cleverness that made them the most feared of all creatures. He forgot all the elation of his earlier encounter. A human had caught him – a human whose intentions might not be as benevolent as those of the men in the crater. He would die as the head-wolf had, at a man's hands, in a strange form of unintended justice.

Provided the two fore-wolves did not find him first.

As he lay there in a state somewhere between sleep and a swoon, memories came back to him. Of his sister and brother, whose voices he could almost hear... He relived his last days with them: saw again the polar bear, enraged at their thievery of its food, strike the life from his brother with one swipe of its paw, and tear a great gash in his sister's side. He saw her collapse even as they fled together, and sat whining at her side as the life faded from her eyes. He heard her say, between whimpers of pain, "You must find more of our kind, brother. You remember what Mamma told us: *The world is harsh for wolves that walk alone.*"

The remembered words rang in his ears as if newly spoken. Half asleep, not quite understanding that she was not really there, he whispered back, "I know it, sister. But it is harsh among wolves, too."

At long last he slept from sheer exhaustion. But within his mind he continued his journey, in the form of dark dreams. He ran across endless barren plains, some covered in the unrelenting snows of winter; he climbed eskers, and swam across great rivers and endless lakes. In every dream he could just glimpse, like a faint low-lying cloud on the horizon, the land of giant trees that lay to the south. No matter how far and fast he ran he could never seem to reach it. At times he thought that he could see shapes moving among the huge trunks of those dim and distant trees: men or wolves, he could not say which; for before his eyes they shifted like shadows, altering their forms. Then his own body changed, and he was a man himself: striding along on two legs with his head high in the air. Then he was a lemming crawling through the undergrowth; then a caribou calf, lying wounded and helpless as its life drained away... He felt as though he had left his own body behind, yielding his selfhood to merge with the wider world. Was he dying, or already dead? Was this how it felt?

*No!* Hunter woke with a start, and struggled to get up. The hard jaws that still gripped his foreleg limited his movement, but he found that he could stand, albeit stiffly and awkwardly. He shook the loose leaves and soil from his coat and looked down, relieved to see the familiar white fur of his chest and legs, the claws jutting out from the broad pads of his paws. "I am alive, and myself still. I am a wolf," he reassured himself. "A wolf, and nothing else."

He looked up, and spied on the southern horizon dark and distant figures. They were human forms, walking upright – walking towards him. Hunter collapsed to the ground again. At least he would not perish at the fangs of the outraged Stone wolves. This way might well be swifter and less painful. The men drew closer with agonizing slowness as he lay there, hampered by their awkward two-legged gait and the difficult terrain. In a dull disconnected way he took note of their appearance: two men of the tundra species, it looked like. The hunters, come to claim their prey. If only he *could* take their shape, stand before them as one of their own kind and plead for his life! But it was no use. He closed his eyes, listening to their approaching footfalls. To the approach of death…

"*Monsieur Amaroq!*" said a low voice. "*C'est vous, mon ami…*"

Hunter's eyelids flew open and he stared up at the man bending over him. In the growing light the facial features were clearly defined. It was the same tundra-man he had encountered before. But Hunter did not recognize the other man with him. It was not one of the southerners, nor did it look quite like a tundra-man. The figure seemed like a cross between the two, golden-skinned and dark of hair but with sharper features, and a short slight build. Hunter kept his eyes on the bigger man, disregarding the other. He felt hope stir in him again.

The tundra-man drew closer. Hunter could not help giving out a little whine of anxiety as the man reached for his pinned leg. The unreasoning fear of a trapped animal, the instinctive terror of physical harm, overpowered his mind and made his body shrink from the other's touch. He struggled to his feet, and sought to pull away.

The smaller man touched the larger one's shoulder and spoke softly. The latter nodded, and without another glance at Hunter he turned and strode away across the plain. Again a whine escaped the wolf's throat. Now he was alone with a strange human, one whose intentions could not be fathomed. Had the gentler and kinder tundra-man abandoned Hunter to some terrible fate?

The strange man spoke again in a quiet voice, not meeting Hunter's eyes directly. Then he knelt down. Slowly he removed his outer layer of coverings, making no sudden or startling movements, tossing them into a heap. Then the underlying layers were removed, both those that clad the lower and upper portion of the body. Hunter was too fascinated to be afraid. The human anatomy now exposed was disturbingly different, the hide nearly hairless. Only the top of the head was luxuriantly clad, in very long grey-streaked black hair that hung down around the face. And it was not a man after all, but a female. She possessed mammary glands, though there were only two of them: they had an oddly swollen and udder-like appearance, and were situated between her upper limbs instead of her hind ones.

The creature bent her head low and, reaching down with her forelimbs, crouched upon the ground on all fours. Was she trying to reassure him by looking more like an ordinary animal? She began to rock back and forth, making a curious crooning sound – whether to soothe him, or for her own comfort he did not know. He felt faint and his eyes were blurring, deceiving him: how else to account for the way her naked form wavered before his vision, seeming to flow and change, to reshape itself? The dark hair of her head appeared to be spreading all over her body, covering up the exposed

35

skin with a pelt of thick dark fur. Her head grew longer, her ears pricked up into points, and the whites of her eyeballs receded and only the deep brown irises showed.

He blinked. A small, dark brown she-wolf stood where the human had been. She waved her furry tail and then sat back upon her haunches, regarding him with friendly eyes.

"There!' she said in the high-wolf tongue. "That's better!"

He thought that he must be unconscious again, and dreaming. But this did not feel like the passing visions of the night. He raised his muzzle and sniffed: she smelled of wolf. And yet the scent of human also lingered in the air.

The she-wolf seemed amused by his bewilderment. "Oh, I am real, my friend! Your eyes, they do not lie to you." She spoke in an odd dialect of the wolf-speech, pronouncing her words in an unfamiliar way. She got up and advanced towards him, and he could not help pulling back, though the jaws in the earth held him fast. "Here, let me help you. I can spring this trap." She touched something with her forepaw, and the jaws abruptly released their hold. Hunter staggered and almost fell over. "There, there! You are free now. It was not a killer-trap, the kind with terrible teeth; it was only made to hold you in one place. The men of the south placed it here so they could study your kind more closely. They'd have set you free eventually, you know."

Hunter broke in: "But you *have* saved my life. There are vicious high-wolves in this place who will kill me if they find me on their territory. You are in danger too, if you stay."

"The Stone Pack won't meddle with me. They know I am here with my good friend, the man of the tundra.

Noah Aglukkaq. It was you who broke into his tent last night, wasn't it?"

"The men – the Stone Pack wolves were planning to kill them. I – I warned them as best I could."

"You saved their lives. They owe you a debt, and Aglukkaq will not forget."

"You say you and this man are friends? Then I did not dream what I saw, just now? You *were* with him, in a human form?"

She trotted over to the spot where the woman had knelt, and pawed at the tundra. He followed her, limping a little – though his leg was not hurt it was very stiff – and he saw there the pile of discarded clothing. The strange scent of human emanated from it. "Wolf and woman: I am both."

He still could scarcely believe it. "But then it is all true! There *are* wolves that can take human form."

"It is the other way around, my young friend. I am human, but can take a wolf's form. I am a shape-changer. A *rugaru.*"

"A what? What is that?" he queried. "How can one being have *two* bodies?"

"The answer to that is lost in time, friend. Suffice it to say that once upon a time, our forms were not so... fixed."

"Your friend: is he a wolf-man too?" Hunter asked.

"He? No, he is just human. There are a few ordinary humans who know about us shape-changers, and are not afraid." She looked at him thoughtfully. "You are a *rugaru* too, you know that? There's human blood in you."

"There is?"

"But of course! Did you never wonder why the high-wolves are so much larger than the low-wolves, and so much more intelligent? The low-wolves are true wolves, descended from beasts that lived here in ancient times. No real wolf has beautiful blue eyes like yours, pup. Many humans have them, though; and high-wolves take after their human ancestors in many ways. You are descended from human shape-changers who came here long ago, from another land far across the sea."

"Came here? How?"

"On boats: objects that float on water. Men can do such things. Over sea and under sea they go. They fly on wings they craft for themselves. They have even," she dropped her voice and paused for effect, "walked upon the moon."

He continued to gaze at her in blank disbelief. Was she lying, or mad – or just making things up for fun?

"We are both of us descended from *rugaru,*" she said. "So we are kin, even if you are wolf and I am human."

"You are not of the tundra-people?" he asked. "You look – different."

"My tribe lives to the south of here, in the land of trees. But I have visited many different places, over the long years. I am an old lady."

"You don't seem old to me," he said. She had only a few silver hairs on her muzzle.

"No, I was just making a little joke. I am only fifty-six."

"Fifty-six?" Hunter stared at her. "In years? Impossible! No wolf could live so long."

She grinned a lupine grin. "No, but humans can. My mother, she is seventy-nine. And *her* mother lived to ninety. How old are you, friend? You look young to me."

"I am not so very young. I already have seen two winters; this will be my third."

"Three years! You are a mere babe in human terms. A pup! What is your name, pup?"

"Name?"

"What they call you."

"My – my designation is Hunter, hind-wolf to the Lake Pack."

"Ah, of course: I'd forgotten the wolf-people up here have no names," she said. "It wasn't always that way. Your Lake wolves are the last remnant of an old human family, and every human being is given a special name at birth. Mine was given me by my mother: Josephine." She cocked her head to one side, gazing at him. "There is a man inside you, pup, deep down. I can see him in my mind: he is young and tall, with keen far-seeing eyes and fine strong features. That is what you would look like today, had your forerunners not discarded their human heritage. You are a descendant of bold brave men from lands beyond the sea who came here, not to settle the land, but to explore it. Whose desire was not just for beaver pelts and the wealth these would bring, but for adventures and for the love of woods and wildness. The wolf-within brought them to these lands.

"So they journeyed deep into the forests. Some wed native women, and raised half-breed children – my ancestors. Others journeyed further still, into the nameless regions, and dwelled among low-wolves. But they could never be true animals, for they still had men and women inside of them. Have you not at times heard a voice inside you that seemed at odds with your wolf-self?"

It was as if she read his inmost thoughts. As she spoke, he once again envisioned himself in a new and different body: standing upon his hind feet alone, his protective pelt diminished to a few fine hairs and one thick patch on the top of his head. He seemed to *feel* on his denuded hide the warmth of the sun and the wind's cold caress. It was like his persistent dreams, but more vivid. Was this some kind of ancestral memory, passed down by human forebears able to take either shape at will? Did that old memory run stronger in some than in others, and was this why he could never find a place with other wolves?

He reared up and attempted to stand on his hind legs, but quickly overbalanced and toppled forward, landing hard on his front paws. Humans must have a different sort of spine, he thought, designed to distribute their weight more evenly in an erect position. He ached to know all that she could tell him.

The wolf-woman Josephine watched all this with amusement. But before she say anything, a piercing howl arose on the chill morning air. Hunter started, coming back to himself and to their dire situation.

"The Stone wolves! We can't stay here. Run!" he cried.

His foreleg was still stiff and he stumbled as he fled. The she-wolf appeared at his side, adjusting her pace to his. "Don't slow down for me!" he gasped. "Save yourself! Woman or wolf, they will kill you if they catch you. They fear nothing and no one." He looked back, and saw the two dark pursuing shapes. The young fore-wolves were running at top speed, seeming almost to float like flying shadows over the ground, closing the distance with ease.

"There's no need to panic!" she said. "Stop! Ah, what a nuisance. Those are perfectly good clothes I've left behind on the plain. Slow down, pup."

He had to stop, but not because of her command. Directly ahead of them a vast expanse of water appeared. A lake, larger than any he had yet seen. Deep and wide it spread before them, completely cutting off their escape.

As they drew up to its shore the two Stone wolves cut in front of them and faced them head-on, confronting them with bared fangs. Hunter could feel all four of his legs quivering with stress, but Josephine sat down looking utterly at ease.

"I thought it was you lot causing all this trouble. Where is your father?" she asked them.

The larger fore-wolf growled low in his throat. "Our father is dead, murdered by those intruders Aglukkaq brought here. If you had anything to do with it, wolf-woman – "

"I'm sorry for your loss," she said, cutting off his threat, "but I think you lot had murder on your minds too last night, so who is really to blame? Those men were not allowed to defend themselves? In any case," she added, idly raising a hind paw to scratch at her neck, "I wasn't there."

The fore-wolf turned to Hunter. "This one is fair game. He trespassed on our territory and ignored our warnings. For that he must be killed. It is the wolf's law."

"Just try it," she replied. "He is with me. It's two against two." The fore-wolves did not move.

Hunter said looked at her, incredulous. "What are you doing? We can't fight them! They're bigger than we are."

"We won't have to fight, pup. Aglukkaq is coming, and he has a weapon."

"He would not dare to shoot at us," retorted the black fore-wolf. "He is not like the southern men. *He* knows there are... consequences... for angering the Stone Pack."

"You think so? We shall see. I tell you, my friend will help me at any cost."

"He is not here!" interrupted Hunter. "He can't save us."

"He is coming. Do you not hear?"

A drone like the roll of distant thunder filled the sky behind them. Distracted by his immediate danger,

41

Hunter had not taken note of it at first. The noise grew louder, nearer. He cowered as a shape – winged, but larger than any bird – plunged out of the lowering clouds, then dived low over the lake. It was the same giant yellow thing he had previously seen floating on the crater lake. Eider ducks took off in terror as it swooped down and settled with a burst of spray on the water's surface.

"You see? I said he would come!" Josephine said. And as their enemies hesitated she added softly, "Bang, bang!"

They backed off, tails lowered, eyes burning with hate. She turned to Hunter again. "To the water now, hurry!"

They hastened to the lake where the stiff-winged thing floated on its huge flat feet, not far from the rocky shore. As he stared at it Hunter saw something like a mouth open in the object's side, gaping with out-flung jaw: inside was a dark cavity, and in it he saw the familiar shape of the tundra-man. He waved an arm at them.

"It is an airplane," the she-wolf said as they paused on the shore. "Just as I told you. Men make these things to carry them through the air." She leaped into the water and began to swim towards the floating object.

Hunter glanced back. His enemies stood not far away, menacing but also motionless. They clearly feared the man, or whatever weapon he bore. But when Josephine and her friend departed in their flying conveyance the Stone wolves would lose that fear. And Hunter would be left all alone to face their wrath.

He watched as the she-wolf scrambled up onto the broad floating foot of the flying craft and shook the water from her fur. "I won't leave you, pup," she called across the water. "You must come with us. We'll set you down in a safe place, far from here. They'll never find you. Hurry now!"

She sprang nimbly up the set of metal steps affixed to the pontoon, and into the craft's interior. Her human companion took her in his arms, wrapping a piece of soft brown material around her body. Hunter followed, splashing through the shallows until he reached the deeps of the frigid lake. He struck out, swimming as best he could with his sore leg. Behind him his enemies growled low in fury, but did not follow him into the water. In a few moments he was gasping and scrabbling for a foothold on the rocking surface of the floatplane's pontoon as Josephine called down to him encouragingly.

"Can I not go with you all the way?" he asked as soon as he had breath.

"All the way where?" she asked.

He set his paw upon the lowest step. "Now that you have told me of my ancestors, I want to see the land of men. Will you take me there?"

Her brown eyes sparkled. "Ah, you're a creature of impulse, I see. I like that: it reminds me of me. Yes, why not? You shall see where your people came from!" she said.

Before Hunter's eyes she changed again. It was not the wolf's but the woman's face that beamed down at him through locks of grizzled black hair; it was a human arm that beckoned to him from the folds of the brown blanket. She spoke in the human tongue he could not understand, but her meaning was plain: *Come!*

He sprang up, wet and shivering, into her warm embrace. Then the mouth-like opening closed upon them. There was a terrible roar and vibration, and the strange vehicle rushed forward. Like a waterfowl it skimmed across the lake, gathering speed before launching itself once more into the air.

The thunderous din drowned the frenzied howls of Hunter's foes as he was swept away, up into the sky and out of their reach.

*Chantal*

# 4

"I still can't believe she's gone," a voice said.

Whose voice, Chantal neither noticed nor cared. She stood apart, drained and listless, as family and friends talked together in low voices. Uncle Hank and Aunt Ginny had come up from Nebraska, and Uncle Nate from South Carolina with his new girlfriend whose name Chantal could never remember; Uncle Phil was there of course, and most of her cousins too. Katharine had come all the way from Oregon with her new husband Walter, Liz from Boston where she was attending college. It was like a grim shadow of former Vandusen clan gatherings. Full mourning was no longer required for such occasions, but it happened that Chantal's one good dress was black: a sleeveless sheath, originally bought for parties at college. She'd never had a chance to wear it – until now. With her old black blazer on top, it struck the right blend of formality and somberness. And reflected her mood of utter misery.

Another voice rose above the subdued murmuring. "Well, it could be worse I suppose. There was poor Sally, now, wastin' away with the Alzheimer's. And old Henry West, now that was just awful…"

The voice belonged to Mavis Dooley, from Nana's bridge group. Chantal's cousin Liz called her Mrs Ghouley behind her back, and the name was well earned. On being told that one was going to have surgery, she could be relied upon to mention an acquaintance who had died of the very same procedure; any announcement of travel plans invariably produced grisly accounts of train and plane accidents. When she spoke she always sounded as though she were munching with gruesome relish on her own words. *At least I'll never have to hear that voice again*, Chantal thought. It was the only positive thing to come out of her loss: the idea that her life now would belong to her alone, and contain only those people she wanted to have in it.

"...and when they opened him up it'd spread everywhere, no use tryin' to do anything about it, so they just sewed him up again. They're doin' a nerve block on him to stop the pain, but he's down to a hundred pounds, last I heard."

"And him just left a widower the year before!"

"That's right. He woke up one morning and there was his wife, stone cold dead beside him. Must've been her heart, but they never did... Oh, would you excuse me a moment, Doreen? Just saw someone I need to talk to –"

*Oh no,* Chantal thought. Mrs. Dooley had spotted her standing alone. She tried to head for the door, but the old woman intercepted her, moving with alacrity, an eager look in her small close-set eyes. "Chantal honey! How're you doin'?" she asked. "So sad losin' your gran like that. Very sudden, wasn't it?"

*Yes, a horrible slow lingering death would have been* so *much better,* Chantal thought in distaste, and barely restrained herself from saying it aloud. Mrs. Dooley was fishing for details with which to regale her friends later. She was like a monstrous leech, battening on the misery of others, and Chantal was determined to yield her nothing. "Yes," she said, snapping her lips shut on the word.

"So what're you goin' to do now?"

"I don't know." This was true. She had left college mere weeks into the first term of her freshman year. Her uncles had been urging Nana for some time to go into a nursing home, but her grandmother had fiercely resisted the idea of leaving the house Gramps built for her as a bride. It was too dangerous for her to live there alone, the uncles argued. She was over eighty now. What if she had another stroke, or fell on the staircase and broke a leg?  She might lie alone and helpless for hours... Chantal had finally intervened, leaving her first term of college so Nana could have company and stay on in the house.  But she had not been back home for more than a month when the second, fatal stroke hit.

*And now what do I do?  I got permission to take the year off so I could be with Nana.  There's no point in staying here anymore.  I should really go back and ask to finish my year, but...*

Suddenly she could not stand it any longer.  She had to get out of the house – this big old house that, with Nana gone, had ceased to be *home.*  Even filled with people, there was an achingly empty feel to it already.  As soon as they had all gone, these friends and neighbours and relatives, that emptiness would become more acute.

"Excuse me," she mumbled, and disentangling herself from Mrs Dooley's clutches she fled the room.

She caught a fleeting glimpse of her cousin Katharine's face looking towards her in concern, but she did not stop.  Out the front door she hastened, past the umbrella-stand that still held Nana's assortment of canes.  How her grandmother had hated using them: she had been so proud of her posture, compensating for her lack of height by always holding herself rigidly erect.  Stooping and relying on a prop had made her irritable, and so had Chantal's presence which she had insisted was not necessary.

"Think I need company, do you?" she had said.  "But it wasn't you, was it: those sons of mine sent you here.  They need their heads read.  I'm perfectly fine.  So stay if you like, but don't you give me any nonsense either.  I won't stand for it."  Such had been Chantal's welcome.  Nana had been poor company throughout the following days, constantly complaining of her arthritis and other ailments. Even her silences had been punctuated with deep sighs and groans. It had been torment for both of them.

But Nana was gone now.

It was hard to believe. Losing Nana was like the sun burning out: you knew it would happen one day but you could not imagine it. Around her the lives of two generations of Vandusens had revolved, orderly as a little solar system. Each year at Thanksgiving her children and grandchildren dutifully returned to the old homestead for the great family feast, and often for Christmas and summer vacations as well. But with Nana dead these mandated gatherings would cease. The Vandusens would all drift away into their own separate lives: planets no longer bound together by a common centre of gravity. *This is how it will be from now on,* Chantal thought. She would have to grow used to it, like living in a world without light.

Half-way down the front path she paused and looked back at the old wooden frame house. Its dark green paint was peeling, shingles were missing from its roof, and weeds sprouted from the gutters. In the old days Nana had kept it in perfect order: its deterioration was a sad sign of her own decline. Uncle Phil would fix the place up, no doubt, now that the house was his. At least it would still be in the family. But Chantal and her uncle had never gotten along; and his second wife would want to make the place her own, as any woman would. The house would endure, but furnishings and décor would change, every trace of Norman and Martha Vandusen and the life they had built together completely erased.

Chantal turned her back on the house and walked on, hunching her shoulders against the wind. October was cold this year, and the overcast sky made even the autumn colours look dull. She had just begun to adjust to Los Angeles with its brilliant desert sun; to be thrust

50

into the grey chill of mid-October in Vermont added to her depression. She walked on up the street, passing the big red brick house that had been Uncle Phil's in the old days. She'd spent nearly as much time at her cousins' home as she had at her own, until Uncle Phil got his job transfer and moved his family to Burlington when she was thirteen. Everything had gone downhill from that point. Not long after the move, news came that Aunt Fran had succumbed at last to her chronic illness; then Gramps had his first heart attack, and had to live very quietly, sleeping much of the day, until the next attack ended his life. After that Chantal and Nana had been left in the old house – the large home that at one time had held a family of six – to grate on each other's nerves, until Chantal's graduation from high school this past spring set her free.

She paused to look at Uncle Phil's house. It had changed little: the new owner had painted the white trim beige and replaced the rose trellis, but that was all. Standing by the mailbox and looking up the drive, she could almost imagine that she was a little girl again, and could run up that driveway and open the front door. Aunt Fran would be there in the kitchen, plump and jolly with her beaming freckled face and curly red hair, stirring a big pot on the stove or perhaps baking cookies. Her cousins would be gathered in the sun porch at the back of the house: Liz who was closest to her in age, and Katharine and Tammy and Amanda...

The door opened suddenly and two small children ran out into the yard, pausing to stare at the stranger standing by their gate. The spell was shattered. Chantal turned quickly away from the house and walked on.

The red brick house was the last one on this street, which ended not in a cul-de-sac but rather with a curious abruptness, giving way to a muddy track worn by many feet through a vacant field. In the middle of the field the track too ended, as if the countless feet that had trodden it into the earth had retreated before an unseen but impassible barrier. In the field some children were tossing a ball to and fro: they might almost have been the ghosts of Chantal and her cousins who had also played Border-ball when they were little, much to the annoyance of their elders.

Chantal's hometown was an unusual one. Located at the extreme northern limit of Vermont, Derby comprised a number of smaller villages, including North Derby, Derby Center, and this community of Derby Line, a tiny place with a population of less than a thousand. The northernmost of the Derby villages, it was literally built on the border with Canada. That is to say, the border ran right through it, bisecting its main street and even some of its buildings. On the other side lay the Canadian village of Stanstead, the two forming what functioned very much like a single community, though ruled by two different governments and two separate sets of laws. All who lived there were constantly aware of the divide that ran, unseen, through their towns and their lives. Part of one street in Stanstead, called "Canusa" after the two nations, had Canadian homes on one side and American ones on the other; merely crossing the street required a passport. There was even an apartment complex where American and Canadian nationals lived across the hall from each other, and in some homes it was possible to have dinner in one country and go to bed in another without ever going out of doors.

At times Chantal felt as though that invisible divide ran through her, too. As a child she would sometimes place a foot on both sides of the border, claiming that her Canadian birth certificate entitled her to be in both countries simultaneously. Her friends and cousins took advantage of this supposed immunity to have her retrieve stray balls and kites from the Stanstead half of the playing field. Admonished continually by their elders to respect the international border, they still delighted in pushing its limits. Derby Line children would toss paper planes over it, boasting that they were violating Canadian airspace; the children of Stanstead would retaliate by brazenly sticking their fingers and toes into Vermont. The American children also picked up a few French words from their neighbours, for their state bordered the province of Quebec: these words included some interesting profanities which they could use without fear in front of their parents, who had no idea what they were saying. But for Chantal Boisvert it had never been enough merely to pick up a few words here and there. Like her mother before her she had learnt the language, taking classes and joining the French club at school.

Her eyes drifted from the children playing in the muddy field to the houses on its far side. Everything that set her apart from her community, her family and friends came from *up there,* that place beyond the border. Her French Canadian name for instance, which no one in her hometown seemed able to say: *"Chan-*dle *Boyz-*vurt" was always the preferred pronunciation at her school, much to her annoyance. The Québecois children across the border line, none of them her friends, always said it correctly – *"Shahn-tahl* Bwah-*vair" –* even when exchanging insults with her. Then there was her equally alien appearance. The Vandusens were rosy and fair with green or blue eyes, while Chantal was brunette with an almost olive-tinged complexion. Her brows were thick and black, her eyes golden-brown: dark at the borders, they lightened almost to amber at the centre. The Vandusens were short, and tended to a comfortable roundness of figure; Chantal was tall, gawky and angular. All of these things were the gifts of her Québecois father. He had left her nothing else, not even a memory of his face or voice.

Nana and Gramps had expected a quiet uneventful life following retirement, with the occasional visit from their grown children and grandchildren. They had not been prepared for Chantal, thrust on their hands eighteen years ago after her mother – their youngest child and only daughter – died in a car accident. Helen's husband had also died not long afterwards, in a hiking accident that some blamed on his blinding grief. Aunt Fran would have taken the baby in, but she had a houseful of her own offspring to deal with and chronic health troubles too. So Nana had resigned herself to her duty.

*Yes, that's what I was: a duty...*

Of her father's family, presumably still living in Montreal, Chantal knew nothing. They had never attempted to contact her once in all these years. Nana told her the Boisvert clan had feuded with her father: "He married a girl who wasn't one of their kind, and they never forgave him for it. That's why he had to bring you here, to be raised by your mother's family." Chantal often pondered those words. Not "one of their kind" – did that mean they hadn't liked her mother because she was not French? The separatist element within Québecois society was notoriously obsessed with maintaining French-only bloodlines. Or was it a question of religion? The French Canadians were Roman Catholic, weren't they, like the continental French? She had the impression that Catholics were not so strict these days about marrying "out of the faith", but perhaps the Boisverts were old-fashioned. Whatever the reason, it was serious enough to alienate them forever from their own granddaughter.

The wind whipped her hair about her face as she left the field and she pushed it back. Long, thick and wavy, it was prone to mat and snarl, so much so that as a small child she had been forced to wear it short: practical Nana, tired of the tears that came whenever she brushed her granddaughter's hair, had simply lopped it off. Vandusen hair did not tangle: with the sole exception of Katharine, who had inherited her mother's red curls, Chantal's cousins had tresses that always lay silken-smooth upon their heads, when not bound up in neat plaits or ponytails. Even when Chantal plaited hers it rebelled, seeking to escape its confinement in little untidy wisps and flyaway hairs. Nana had often commented on this in disapproving tones, as though Chantal's unruly mane were a sort of moral defect. Right now it seemed like an outward manifestation of her mental state, dark and tangled as her thoughts.

She looked up presently and saw that she was on Caswell Road. She had been wandering aimlessly, but her feet had taken over for her mind and brought her to another favourite haunt: a grand old building with a façade built of the local granite, its one majestic conical turret rearing up against the grey sky. She stood gazing at it, awash in memory.

Of all the oddities created by Derby Line's unique location, the strangest and most famous was this structure, the Haskell Free Library and Opera House. A blend of public library and concert hall executed in turn-of-the-century neoclassical style, it straddled the border by the deliberate intent of its long-dead owners, American businessman Carlos Haskell and his Canadian-born wife. They had built it in 1904 as a monument to the friendly relations between Canada and the United States, and for the enjoyment of citizens in both Derby Line and Stanstead. The opera house was located on the second floor: though the main auditorium with its lavish baroque décor was technically in Vermont, the stage – equally magnificent, with its painted drop curtain – lay within the province of

55

Quebec. Americans here could attend a concert in a foreign country without ever needing to leave their own. The international boundary was marked outside by a grey granite marker next to the sidewalk – something like a miniature obelisk, with the names of the two countries engraved on each side; inside the building it was represented by black lines, one running across the floor of the concert hall and another dividing the library on the lower level. There were poignant (and possibly apocryphal) tales told in Derby Line of draft dodgers who, after fleeing to Canada, arranged at times to meet with their families in the Haskell library – not daring, under the hawk-like gaze of US officials, to step over that painted line and return home with their loved ones.

Here Chantal had taken on her very first job: since many library patrons came from the Quebec side, her ability to understand and speak French had been an asset. She had also come here often to read and escape. Sometimes, to her delight, Russell Gordon had been there too, sitting at a desk with his glossy auburn head bowed over a book...

*No. Get out of my head. Get out get out get out....* With an effort Chantal wrenched her mind back to the present. She was *not* going to think about Russell. Her present troubles were more than enough.

She marched up the path and into the building's grand arched entrance, which was on her side of the border. (Another entrance on the other side was used by the Canadian patrons; using the other country's doorway meant you had to report to customs.) Hardly anyone was inside at this time of day; the supper hour was always quiet. Chantal wandered into the reading room and sat down at a desk not far from the black line on the floor. Cold grey light seeped in through the tall windows, a light too weak to bring out the delicate tints of the stained glass in their topmost panes. Opening up one of the books lying on the desk she pretended to read it. But nearly an hour passed without her seeing a word printed on its pages. They seemed to blur and swim before her eyes.

"I thought I'd find you here."

Chantal looked up at the voice. Katharine was standing in the doorway. She had always been Chantal's favourite cousin – quarrelsome Liz had really been more of an adversary than a companion, but Katharine had inherited much of her mother's wisdom along with her red hair. And in defiance of all redhead conventions, she never lost her temper. She came and sat down next to Chantal. "What're you reading?"

Chantal stared at the book in her hands. "Um..."

"*Agricultural Practices of Sixteenth-Century Europe,*" Katharine read the title aloud. She took the volume gently from Chantal's hands and closed it. "Everyone's gone home, it's just family there now. You can come back to the house."

"I'm okay, Kath." Chantal got up. "You know, in a way I think Nana is better off. She'd have hated living in a nursing home. And she was never the same after Gramps passed away. Remember how well he used to handle her?"

Katharine smiled. "I remember all right. I'll never forget when he called her My Little Cabbage."

The trace of a smile touched Chantal's face, for the first time in weeks. Gramps had responded to Nana's frequent upbraidings with ludicrous endearments. "Did you call me, my sweet?" he'd say with a wink at the sound of her raised voice in house or yard. "I'm coming, my angel!" But only the "cabbage" remark had provoked a real reaction. Nana had turned beet-red, as if with rage – then she had laughed – then had looked vexed with herself for laughing – and finally had just exclaimed "Oh, *you!*" and walked away, utterly defeated.

"Liz and I used to keep score cards and check off points when they yelled at each other over dinner," Chantal said. "I think they enjoyed it, really. They were sparring partners. But Nana and I just got on each other's nerves." Her smile faded. "Anyway, it's all over now. My life here's over. Your stepmom will have the house, and I don't want to be in her way."

"Oh, Lorraine wouldn't mind if you stayed, Chantal," Kath said. "She's really very sweet, you know."

Uncle Phil had shocked the family by remarrying scarcely a year after Aunt Fran died, choosing of all people one of his former wife's nurses. Plump, fair and thirty-five, Lorraine Hillman had given up all hope of finding a husband and starting a family, and resigned herself instead to lavishing her maternal instincts on her patients. She had pounced on Phil's offer of marriage, and lost no time in bearing children – very sensibly producing twins, and boys at that. So Uncle Phil at long last had his male heir, plus an extra. "I wanted to resent that woman, really I did," Kath said, looking rueful, "but how can you resent someone as nice as Lorraine? And she's made Dad happy, and since she's a nurse she can take good care of him – with this family's heart and stroke history, that's something to think about."

"Please don't," begged Chantal as they left the library together. "I've had to listen to Mrs. Ghouley go on like that for hours."

Kath grinned, then turned serious once more. "Ghouley Dooley is right about one thing: life is short. Mom once told me her multiple sclerosis made every day seem like a blessing. She was just so glad to be alive. So *carpe* that *diem,* girl." Kath sighed. "You wouldn't believe how fast time goes. I'm going to be thirty my next birthday – thirty, Chantal, just think of it!"

Chantal's eyes strayed to the gold wedding band on her cousin's left hand. "Kath – do you love Warren? Really love him?" she asked.

"Warren and I understand each other: that's enough for me. We both want to have a family, and I want to have my kids when I'm still young and energetic enough to enjoy them. This may be my only opportunity. Face it, kiddo, women don't get second chances. My father got to be a dad again when he was nearly fifty; that can't happen for me. Don't you wait forever, either. You've only got one more year to be a teenager, and you'll find each decade passes faster than the one before it. If you wait for the perfect guy, you may find he never shows up – because he ever existed anywhere but here." Kath tapped her own forehead.

Chantal looked away. "Maybe I don't want a guy."

"Liz said she thought that you and Russell Gordon were going to be an item."

"So did I."

"Oh." Kath, like her late mother, was the soul of tact.

But suddenly Chantal wanted to talk, to get it all out of her head and into the open. "I was such an idiot," she burst out. "Russ never contacted me, or answered my calls when I got to L.A. A little summertime romance, that's all it was to him."

Russell had been one grade ahead of her in high school. They'd had friends in common and known one another quite well, but she had longed to be more than a friend to him. When he left Derby Line for Los Angeles after graduation to study film, she had shed many bitter tears in secret, fearing that she would never see him again. Through the long and dreary winter that followed she had pined for him, and slaved over her homework so that she too could get into UCLA and be near him once more. When Russell returned home for a brief visit this past summer she had been ecstatic to see him and to give him the good news of her acceptance. And he had seemed truly pleased. "But that's great! We'll see lots of each other! And I can show you all over the place," he promised. "I'll give you a tour of Hollywood." And he'd kissed her full on the lips for the first time ever, and flirted with her while their other friends winked at one another...

"I was so sure we'd be a couple by year's end, or dating at least. Everyone else thought so too. But it didn't mean a thing. He was just bored, amusing himself with me until he could go back – to *her,*" she said to her cousin.

"Her who?"

Chantal explained. "I went to a party on campus with my roommate, and – and Russ showed up. He never told me he was going to be there. And he was with the most gorgeous girl I ever saw outside of a magazine cover."

Her cousin raised her eyebrows. "So that was it? You just surrendered the field without a fight?"

"Kath, you didn't see her! She was just so perfect, with the most amazing blonde hair –"

"Extensions, I bet."

" – and the straightest, whitest teeth – "

"Capped."

She knew what Kath was doing with these playful interruptions. It was supposed to make her laugh when she only wanted to feel tragic. "Well," Chantal continued, "I haven't even mentioned her top assets. *They* were out to here – " she held both hands, fingers rounded, inches in front of her own more modest endowments.

"Isn't it amazing," Kath said, "what silicone can do?"

Chantal gave up and allowed herself to laugh. "Okay. So I learned afterwards they'd been together for a year. And I went all the way to L.A. because of *him!* I majored in Spanish just so I could settle down some day and live in California with *him.* I had my whole life planned out: I'd get my teaching license, teach Spanish to English-speaking people and English to Spanish-speaking people... But it was all based on me being with Russ. I guess I forgot to live for myself."

"Well, now you have your own life back again. Are you going to return to L.A. and do your degree?" her cousin asked.

Evening was setting in, and a cold wind blew from the north under a clearing sky. Chantal huddled into her jacket and thought of Los Angeles. How exotic and alluring it had seemed mere months ago; but so much of that allure had come from the fact that Russ was there. No: not L.A., not ever again. But there was nothing for her in Derby Line either, not with Nana and Gramps both gone, and her high school friends all attending college in far-flung states. Her mind swung to and fro, from California to Vermont and back again, directionless.

Realizing that her cousin was still waiting for an answer, Chantal cleared her throat. "Actually, I was thinking of taking a year off. Some of the kids in my grad class were planning to do that: work, travel, live in the real world for a while before going to college. I can afford it – now." Unlike her cousins, Chantal inherited her late mother's full share of Nana's legacy. It was not a fortune, but it would look after her needs while she decided what to do.

"So where will you go?" asked Katharine.

Chantal's mind wavered again. She turned and looked up the street to where the unseen border ran. The field itself was invisible now too, lost in the darkness:

beyond that shadowy terminus lay the undiscovered north, and the birthplace that she had never seen. Above it Polaris burned diamond-white and steady. Her heart yearned suddenly northwards, like the needle of a compass answering the pull of the pole.

"To a place I've never been," she answered. "Home."

## 5

She decided to drive to Montreal. Train or bus would get her there faster, but she could take the famed scenic route through the Eastern Townships and still be in Montreal by nightfall. Chantal had flown to California, and now regretted not having driven there and seen the sights of the Midwest along the way. In any case, traveling by car was cheaper.

"I'll take Minnie," she told Katharine.

"That old wreck?" her cousin replied. "Better you than me."

"Minnie" was Chantal's second-hand Mini-Cooper from her high school days, still sitting in the family garage. Kath's playful jibe aside, the car was in very good condition and Chantal had intended to sell it before she went to college, using the money to buy herself a new one in Los Angeles. She was glad now that she had not succeeded. Minnie had taken her on many a road trip and seemed to her like an old and trusted companion. Chantal cleaned the vehicle inside and out, checked that the radio was working, and packed the glove compartment with her road maps, flashlight and cell phone. She always kept everything in the same place: it gave her a sense of reassurance, like having her own little home away from home.

"Chantal dear," Aunt Lorraine said as she watched her niece load her luggage into the trunk, "we don't want you to feel you have to leave. You're welcome to stay here as long as you like – even live with us after we move in. You're much too young to be on your own."

"I understand, Aunt Lorraine. And thanks." Much as she appreciated her aunt's kindness, Chantal could not endure the thought of remaining in the house. It was so desolate now, so haunted with loss and memory. Uncle Phil's family would not be moving in for at least a month, so she would be all alone during that time. The road trip to her birthplace was as much a timely escape as a sentimental journey.

Despite living within a literal stone's throw of her home province she had never actually visited it. Her grandparents had allowed her to travel to France with her school French club, but when she wanted to attend a summer course in Quebec Nana had put her foot down. There had been quite a scene about it. Disappointingly, even Gramps had not supported Chantal: he just couldn't understand why anyone would bother to learn French. "Hardly anyone speaks it this side of the Atlantic," he said. "Why don't you learn Spanish instead? That'd be more useful to you in the long run."

"It's her French temperament coming out," Nana sniffed, forgetting her own famously short fuse, and the stubborn streak that ran through all the Vandusens. Everything that aggravated Nana about her wayward granddaughter got blamed on Chantal's Québecois ancestry.

Chantal shoved those memories to the back of her mind. There was no use dwelling on past grievances. She was eighteen now: not yet fully adult, but at the magic threshold when authority at last loosens its constraining grip. No more "legal guardians', or sitting in classrooms because the law demanded it. Any courses she took now she would choose for herself, and attend only if she wanted to. No more eating what was put before her, or being scolded for not squeezing the tube of toothpaste from the bottom up or for being out after curfew. As for Russell, his removal from the picture only expanded her freedom. The future was no longer pre-set, but stretched before her wide and unknown as the northern horizon. She was like a fledgling on its first tentative tumble from the safety of its nest, fear and elation intermingling as its wings embraced the air; or like a salmon departing the quiet pool of its hatching to rush headlong down streams and rapids in search of the unseen ocean. As she got into her car she felt the last of her bonds finally fall away.

She drove past the modest stone marker at the border, and the large sign reading "Welcome to Quebec". In the checkpoint booth a middle-aged border guard sat looking affable and not terribly vigilant. "Shahn-*tahl* Bwah-*vair,*" he said on seeing her passport, pronouncing the name correctly in his thick Québecois accent. "You are French Canadian, *hein?* And where are you headed, Ms. Boisvert – to see relatives, *peut-être?*"

"I'm just traveling for pleasure." She had no intention of seeking out her father's family. If the Boisverts wanted nothing to do with her, what would be the point? She would not impose on them. That was not why she was making this trip.

She switched on the radio as she drove. Music always buoyed her spirits, and soon she was humming along, then singing aloud in her high clear soprano. For some time she was conscious of nothing but the songs and the road unscrolling before her. Then gradually she became aware of, and finally entranced by, the scenery. Under patches of alternating clear sky and light drizzle town after town arose, emerging from enfolding hills and undulating fields: little clumps of houses with a pointed steeple or two sheltered by groves of autumn-touched trees. Some of the homes and places of business, she noticed, flew the Canadian flag with its red maple leaf, but many more sported the blue flag of Quebec with its French fleur-de-lys. The *Cantons de L'Est,* or Eastern Townships of Quebec, were not at all what she had expected. On the maps many of the villages and towns had sturdy English names, the legacy of Empire Loyalist founders: Granby, Sherbrooke,

Drummondville. She had thought that their inhabitants, like the people of Stanstead, would be mainly bilingual; but as she journeyed deeper into the *Cantons* she found that many of the residents spoke little or no English and all of the posters and billboards – even the highway signs along the way – were in the French language.

Before long the songs on the radio were all in French, too.

She need hardly have traveled to the Continent to experience French culture, Chantal thought in surprise. All this time it had awaited her, not so very far from home. France had not merely established a colony here: it had transported itself to this side of the Atlantic intact and entire, rooting itself in the foreign soil. When she stopped for gas and food she was obliged to put her neglected French-speaking skills to use. Store: *magasin;* money: *l'argent;* the words came back to her, springing up unbidden from remote recesses of her mind. As she drove on everything came into her head with a doubled name, like an echo. Town: *ville.* Road: *rue…*

As the day drew to its close the clouds grew heavier, the intermittent showers replaced by a steady and determined rain. When she reached Montreal at dusk the city was only a blur of light through her watery windshield: bright-lit high rises glowing behind veils of rain, neon signs reflecting in wet streets. The famed Mountain was invisible. She located her small hotel and hastened inside with her bags, recollecting that among the things she had forgotten to bring was an umbrella. The lobby was adorned with grinning jack o' lanterns and dangling bats, reminding her sharply of school. Back home kids would be decorating the gym for the Halloween dance; her former classmates would be attending costume parties at their colleges. She felt terribly isolated and out of place.

*What am I doing here anyway?* she asked herself as she rode the elevator upstairs. *It's probably just going to be a huge waste of money and time...*

It seemed strange to have a hotel room all to herself instead of sharing it with friends. She unpacked right away and scattered her things about, trying to make the space seem more homelike. She piled the desk with magazines, and propped up her elderly teddy bear on the bed. She had always preferred stuffed animals to dolls – it felt nicer to hold something covered in soft cushy fur – and this toy had been her first and favourite. He was so old and threadbare from cuddling that he looked as though he had a bad case of mange, and his eyes had long since fallen out and been replaced by buttons, sewn on by Nana. They gave him a somewhat blank expression. But Mr. Bear had gone with her everywhere, on overnight trips and even to her college dorm in Los Angeles.

On the nightstand she put the wedding portrait of her parents and sat for a while gazing at it, deep in thought. Her mother had been a typical Vandusen, small and fair, her blonde hair worn in a short fluffy cut, her bright blue-grey eyes matched by a radiant smile. This much Chantal knew from this photo and others, and the brief video taken of the wedding. Helen Vandusen did not exist for her as her grandparents did, preserved in memory. She had never had a chance to know her, just as Helen had never had a chance to become a Mom, to grow wise and maternal. Chantal saw only a young woman forever frozen in time. And as she herself grew older, that woman seemed to grow younger; someday, she realized, she would look on her mother as a mere girl, their roles strangely reversed.

"I envy you for being old enough to remember my mom," she had told Katharine.

Kath replied, "I don't actually remember a lot about her. I was usually out playing with the other kids when the grownups gathered. I do remember how pretty Aunt Helen was, and how sad Gran seemed when she finally left home. After that she only came back for short visits. And then she met your dad, and we hardly saw her at all. I remember her telling us that he thought her name was Ellen at first because the French don't pronounce the letter H. She thought that was pretty funny. And that's about it. I didn't get to her wedding in Montreal: none of us kids was invited. The grownups told us all about it, and the glamorous reception they had afterwards. I never saw her with you, either, because she died so soon after you were born."

At least Chantal knew a few things about her mother. The broad strokes of her personality were laid out in family anecdotes and reminiscences. Of her father Chantal knew virtually nothing. The Vandusens had seen little of Édouard Boisvert beyond the initial engagement visit, the wedding in Montreal, and his final appearance with baby Chantal in Derby Line. He was to her an image only: the darkly handsome young man in this photograph, with strong black brows like her own, and the tall lean build that she had inherited. What had Helen Vandusen so loved about this man that she had been willing to leave family and country behind to stay with him forever?

Her gaze strayed to her cell phone on the night table. "At least," she said aloud to her stuffed bear, "I don't have to report in." Nana had always nagged her to call home every night when she was away, even on Spring Break with friends; she would phone repeatedly if Chantal did not comply, filling up her voicemail with scolding messages. It had been an aggravation when she only wanted to relax and forget about home. But now as she checked her phone for texts or missed calls she was a little disconcerted to find that there were none: no one had thought to check up on her. Perversely, this made her feel abandoned and unloved. Knowing that she was being self-contradictory did not improve her mood.

She was somewhat cheered when she switched on her old laptop and found an email from Katharine, who was now back in Oregon. "Chantal: You can run but you can't hide! Hope you're having fun. But stay in touch, or I'll report you to the Missing Persons Bureau."

Chantal sat down and typed a reply. "Hi Kath! I arrived safe and sound. Montreal looks just like any other city really, lots of office buildings and high-rise apartments. Of course there's the Mountain which isn't really a mountain, but a sort of rocky ridge right in the middle of the city. That's how the place got its name (*Montréal* = Mount Royal, get it?). The people here speak both English and French. Actually they speak a sort of regional dialect of French called *Joual*, with flatter vowels and special slang words. It's a little hard to follow at times, but I can understand it. Anyway, I'm really looking forward to exploring this place, walking in my mom's footsteps."

But it doesn't feel like *home,* she thought as she clicked Send.

She turned to her web browser and pulled up the McGill University website. She had already searched through it and made the discovery that the Nature Club her parents both attended as students – the group that had brought them together – still existed. In fact an annual meeting was scheduled for the very next day, and she had timed her trip to coincide with it. Maybe someone in this group remembered her parents, or knew someone else who did. Some old, tenured professor perhaps, who could share memories of the young Édouard Boisvert with her. This could be her last chance, she thought as she switched off the laptop and prepared for bed. A few more years, and they might all be retired and gone.

The rain ended by the following morning, but the sky was still overcast and dull as she set out for the university. Since it was within the city limits, she went on foot. As a country girl she had always been fascinated by urban centres and enjoyed exploring them: the crowds, the traffic, the vast scale of the buildings were simultaneously alienating and alluring, spiced with just the faintest hint of danger. Life was larger here, more urgent and passionate. Montreal still looked to her like any mid-sized American city, with glassy storefronts and steel and concrete office towers, but she was struck by the appearance of the women here. They reminded her of the women she had seen in Paris. They were all so – *chic,* that was the word: slim and fashionably dressed in little short coats nipped in at the waist with wide belts. Chantal was wearing her old red plaid jacket, which was loose and boxy and long out of style: she had not bothered to buy herself a new one since she had not expected to need it in southern California. Now she felt frumpy and out of place – *A hick from the sticks,* she thought, catching a glimpse of her reflection in a store window. *I look like a lumberjack at a fashion show.* She found herself hunching her shoulders and lowering her head as she walked, an old habit from her school days to try and make her tall gangly figure less conspicuous.

She was relieved to arrive on the downtown campus and find the students there all clad in the usual uniform of blue jeans, track shoes and windbreakers. Her bowed shoulders came up again, and she looked around her with interest. McGill had an attractive campus for a city university, not huge but with plenty of green space, set against the backdrop of Mount Royal's forested slopes.

All the structures seemed to be built of the same grey stone, and their architecture was mainly Gothic in style: spires and turrets and medieval-style stone tracery dominated. The building that was her goal was the sole exception to this theme: it had the imitation Greek-temple façade with pillared pediment that seems universal in older museums. And the Redpath Museum, according to its website, was among the oldest in this country.

Once inside, she found it to be a well-preserved Victorian relic. The foyer's paneled walls were adorned with fossils, specimens in glass cases, and a dark oil portrait of the museum's founder in a gilded frame. A grand banistered wooden staircase rose with an air of importance to the second floor. Directly ahead of her a short hallway, hung with more dangling animal skeletons, led to a small auditorium. This too was a perfect piece of Victoriana with its circular design, round ranks of cushioned benches set one above the other at a steep angle. The floor space in the centre was set up with a podium and some computer equipment; it was so small that no microphone was necessary. A large video screen dominated the wall to the right.

The room was already filling up with club members. Most were speaking in English, she noticed: according to its website McGill was an anglophone institution for the most part, though some French-speaking students attended. As she took a seat in one of the higher, less crowded tiers Chantal saw initials of countless generations of students scratched into the wooden back of the bench in front of her. No doubt all the benches were similarly decorated. Might her mother's or father's be amongst them, somewhere? She sat taking in the atmosphere of the place, trying to picture her mother walking up the narrow wooden steps, sitting in one of the rows of seats – perhaps this very one; chatting with friends, or with her husband-to-be. But the hoped-for feeling of connection did not come. Chantal only felt like an intruder in these unfamiliar surroundings, vaguely guilty and ill at ease.

Most of the members were already seated, but as she sat down two boys came into the room. They were both dark-eyed with glossy dark-brown hair, alike enough to be brothers, and looked to be in their late teens. As they climbed the narrow stairs to look for a seat the taller of the two glanced at Chantal, looked again, and whispered something to his companion. The other boy shrugged. The tall one went to Chantal's row and sat down right beside her. His eyes were an unusual shade of pale amber-brown, almost yellow, and bright with friendly interest.

"Hello there!" he said, flashing a smile at her. "Haven't we met before?"

It was such an obvious pickup line that she nearly laughed. Since he spoke in heavily-accented English, she answered him in French. *"Pas possible...* You see, I'm not a member, I'm a total impostor. I just wanted to sit in on your club meeting, if that's all right." It was something of a relief, really, to confess to her intrusion. She hoped he wouldn't tell her to leave.

He did not. His smile only broadened. "But of course, this isn't a private club. Anyone on campus may join," he said in the same language.

She switched back to English. "Actually, I'm not even from your campus. I'm a foreign visitor, from the States. As I said, an impostor."

"From America! How wonderful! And completely bilingual – *c'est formidable!* Please do stay for the lectures, no one will mind." The boy held out a slim long-fingered hand. "I'm Yves, and this is my brother Jules. We're both students here. I'm just starting my second year – I'm nineteen. My brother's a year behind me. What's your name?"

"Chantal," she replied. "Well, if you're sure it's okay…"

"Absolutely. We *want* the public to know about our conservation projects."

The other boy came and joined them. He was not as good-looking as his older brother, thin and lanky, and his face wore a sullen expression. He sat a little distance away with his shoulders slumped, letting Yves do all the talking.

"Nice to meet you both," Chantal said. She was about to explain her reason for coming here and ask if they could help her, but at that moment a young red-haired woman went up to the podium and the auditorium fell silent. She made a few announcements in both English and French, concerning nature hikes and registration for some special trips: one was to "the steppe-desert of Osoyoos", wherever that might be, and another to Pelee National Park in Ontario to observe migrating birds. There was also a petition concerning an undersea canyon off the coast of Nova Scotia. "We're trying our best to keep the oil and fishing industries out of the area," the redheaded girl said to murmurs of approval from her listeners, "and have the government declare it a wildlife sanctuary. There are beautiful deep sea corals in the canyon, as well as endangered swordfish, dolphins and whales. We'll keep you updated about our petition. But right now it's time for our guest speakers. With Halloween right around the corner, we've got two very appropriate topics for our annual lectures: Spirit Bears and Monster Wolves!"

There was a round of enthusiastic applause. Chantal sat in silence as the first speaker, a graduate student in McGill's biology programme, took the podium. "Spirit bears" sounded like a rather mystical subject for a nature club, but it turned out that they were real animals, a rare colour variant of the black bear found only on the coast of British Columbia. As images of snow-white animals roaming through emerald-green rainforest filled the screen, Chantal's attention shifted to the audience. Despair filled her as she scanned the rows of heads before her. Most of the people here looked her age or just slightly older: graduate and undergraduate students, none of them old enough to remember her father. There were only a few with grey hair; even the guest speaker looked to be in his thirties at most.

All this time Chantal was aware of Yves moving closer and closer to her in a slow, not obviously intrusive way. She hadn't been imagining things, then: this boy had his own, obvious reasons for wishing her to remain. Still smarting from Russell's treachery, she was unsure whether to feel flattered or not. She thought about moving to another seat, but it occurred to her that if Yves was really attracted that might make him more helpful and useful to her. *You're not the only one with an ulterior motive, Yves,* she thought to herself wryly, and stayed put.

The grad speaker meanwhile concluded his presentation and was replaced by three men who stood in a row behind the podium. The eldest looked to be in early middle age, with glasses and a neat beard just starting to turn grey. He introduced himself as Dr. Marc Hébert, a biologist connected to the museum; the other two, much younger, were his students.

"Those of you who attended last year's meeting," Dr. Hébert began, "know that for the past two years I've been making trips to the arctic territories of our country, to study wolf populations. When my research team and I went up to the Nunavik region in northern Quebec last year we heard rumours of the so-called Monster Wolves, which have never been studied or photographed. The scientific community has been very divided on this subject, as you may know. Most biologists dismiss the reports as just another blend of native myth and local tall tales – something like the *waheela,* the giant wolf-monster of the Northwest Territories. But we were intrigued by the accounts we heard, and decided to come back the following summer to see if there was some truth to them. Now we can tell you what we found."

A buzz of excitement ran through the room as the researchers ran a video on the big screen. It showed a green-brown arctic plain with steep-sided mountains rising in the distance, barren but majestic. In the foreground a small group of wolves could be seen loping across the plain. "We took this footage on Ellesmere Island a couple of years back. The animals you see in this shot are common arctic wolves, a regional variant of *Canis lupus.* We spent some time observing this pack. Ellesmere is so far north and so sparsely populated that the local wildlife has virtually no fear of humans, which made our job much easier! These wolves didn't mind our presence in the least. In fact they would come up and watch us with interest, until at times we felt *they* were studying *us*." A warm ripple of laughter ran through the audience. The lecturer smiled. "You may have heard about the social structure of this species, with a dominant mated pair – the 'alpha wolves'– ruling the pack, while a couple of 'beta wolves' occupy a subordinate position to them in the hierarchy and a so-called 'omega wolf' has the lowest status of all. This omega, we've been told, is the designated scapegoat or 'whipping boy', who eats last and often takes the brunt of his or her pack mates' frustration or anger. I see your heads nodding. This concept of a rigid hierarchy among wild wolves has been widely disseminated in our culture ever since it was first proposed back in the nineteen-forties. Would it surprise you to learn it isn't true?"

There was stunned silence in the audience. He paused the film and continued: "Those earlier studies were based on captive wolves, none of them related, all around the same age. The pecking order these animals established among themselves was a result of their unnatural confinement and the tensions it brought. Our studies in the field have shown that this hierarchy is not really present among wild wolves. While there is a breeding pair that leads the pack, these are in fact the parents of all the other wolves. The patriarch and matriarch of the clan. What we called 'betas' are simply older pups who have not yet departed the pack to begin families of their own. As for omega wolves, they do exist but are usually blood relatives too. The runts of the litters, perhaps, or elderly relatives. Wolf packs are simply extended families.

"The alpha male isn't even necessarily the 'top dog'. It's his mate, the alpha female, who bears the young, so she decides where to make her den, which determines where the rest of the pack will hunt and live for that entire season. In the world of wolves, it's Mom who calls the shots!

"Now, I'm showing you these pictures for the purpose of comparison. After studying the wolves of Ellesmere we decided to shift our attention to a different part of the country, to see if pack behavior was the same everywhere. We moved south, to Pingualuit National Park in the Ungava Peninsula of Quebec. And there we first learned of the Monster Wolves. Some lone Inuit hunters had supposedly been killed by these animals, and the park rangers were worried for the safety of the tourists. Healthy wolves don't normally attack humans, and we thought it likely that there was just one sick or injured individual responsible for the killings. But we promised to do a thorough investigation.

76

"In Pingualuit we were joined by Inuit park ranger Noah Aglukkaq, who insisted on accompanying us on our expedition. In addition to guiding us and supplying us with meals of caribou meat and *muktuk* – that's whale blubber to the uninitiated – Noah was a mine of useful information. He said that the tales of outsized wolves were true, and that there was a very fierce pack of these that made the park their territory. But he claimed he knew how to deal with the creatures, having encountered them on previous occasions. We asked him why we never heard anything from the local Inuit of these unusual animals, and he replied that the elders think it's unlucky to talk about them. The older generation is a bit superstitious still, according to Noah. Some believe that these aren't wolves at all, but *angakuit:* sorcerers that can transform themselves into animal shape."

"I'm telling you, before the end I was half believing it was true," added one of Hébert's graduate students with a laugh. "It really seemed as if those brutes had human intelligence! We put out cages with fresh meat for bait and we set dozens of snares – humane ones, you understand, just to immobilize the animals until we could arrive with a tranquilizer gun and take a DNA sample. But not a single wolf was caught. We sometimes found their tracks right next to the snares, as if they were taunting us!"

He advanced the video and then paused it to show dog-like prints in the damp soil along the margin of a lake, with a human hand next to them to show the scale. "Look! These prints are nearly twice normal size. Most wolves run about 40 to 150 pounds at most. But we estimated the weight of these individuals to be about 180 to 200 pounds – as big as a grown man!"

Dr. Hébert continued: "Our colleagues here at the Redpath have advanced various theories about our findings. One rather romantic idea is that the Monster

Wolves are surviving members of a prehistoric species, the dire wolf. But that's not very likely. *Canis dirus* became extinct around ten thousand years ago, the same time as the mammoth and the sabre-toothed cat. And though it was in fact bigger than the modern wolf, it was also more heavily built and probably not a very efficient hunter. These giant wolves, by contrast, are fast and deadly. A more convincing theory is that they're the result of cross-breeding between wolves and Inuit dogs. Hybrid vigour might account for their unusual size, and possibly for their fearlessness around humans."

"What did your Inuit guide think?" another audience member asked.

"Mr. Aglukkaq didn't seem to want to discuss the subject much. He only joined our expedition to protect us, he said. And a good thing, too, as we found out later." He paused, as if for effect. "We finally caught one of the wolves – on film, anyway."

There was an audible intake of breath from everyone in the audience. Yves and his brother were leaning forward – literally on the edges of their seats, their expressions intent. Even Chantal could not help staring at the screen in fascination.

"Yes, you heard me correctly," Dr. Hébert added with a smile. "And apart from a few experts, you're the first ones to view this footage. We haven't even shown it to the news media yet." He turned and made a dramatic gesture towards the screen. "Ladies and gentlemen of the club, I give you an exclusive look at – the Monster Wolf!"

## 6

A view of another arctic landscape appeared on the screen, not a flat plain this time but a broad deep gorge with towering cliffs to either side and a river at the bottom. Dr. Hébert and one of his students were climbing over the top of the nearer slope – the other student was presumably filming them – behind their guide, a much older man with the distinctive Asiatic features of the Inuit. Suddenly all three men stopped dead and stood staring and pointing at something behind them. The video jumped around, then zoomed in and focused on the shape of a wolf advancing up the steep treeless slope towards them. The student raised a rifle and took aim.

"No, no! That's not necessary!" shouted the Inuit man in French, waving his arms.

"Are you crazy? It'll kill us!" objected the student in the same language.

"No! Watch me!" returned the Inuit man.

The audience in the lecture hall gazed in rapt silence as he lay down on the steep slope, positioning himself on his back: "Slowly – like this. Stay calm." Dr. Hébert followed suit, and then the others did the same, the cameraman still filming. Closer and closer the great wolf came, muzzle thrust forward. Its coat was pure white in colour, making it stand out clearly against the dun-coloured background. When it was within a few yards of the men the staggering size of the animal become apparent. It came right up to them, thrust out its head on its thick ruffed neck – and slowly, delicately, sniffed at their feet.

As the camera zoomed in close Dr. Hébert paused the video. "Notice the colour of this animal's eyes," he said. "They're blue. Every wolf species we know has yellow eyes. This could support the argument that we're dealing with a new, unknown species.   Or it could simply mean that it's a wolf-dog hybrid, since some huskies have blue eyes.   But it doesn't look like any wolf-dog I've ever seen."

He pressed Play again.   The Inuit man seemed to be talking to the animal, though his voice was low and the words scarcely audible.   The great white beast stood with ears pricked, its strange sky-blue eyes intent on his face.   Then it suddenly wheeled away from him and galloped off downhill.   The audience expelled a collective, audible breath.   Chantal was surprised to find she had been holding hers too.

"Noah Aglukkaq was right. That is the correct thing to do in any encounter with a wild wolf," Dr. Hébert continued, switching off the video.   "Take a submissive posture, belly up, and don't make any sudden moves. That way the wolf won't view you as a threat.   It worked here, but our next encounter was more alarming, and happened so fast that we have no footage of it.

"That valley you saw was the Puvirnituq River canyon, at the northern border of Pingualuit National Park.   That same day we hiked back to the northeastern shore of Lake Laflamme, where Noah had left the floatplane, and he flew us the remaining distance to the meteor crater.   He said it would be best to be up high where we could see if anything was coming, and also suggested that one of us keep watch while the others slept. He seemed very uneasy, and he volunteered for the first shift.   We set up our camp atop the crater rim and had a good look around before the light failed, walking along the shores of the lake inside and tasting the water, which is incredibly pure and clear.   We also caught some arctic char for dinner.   But before we even got around to settling down to sleep that night we were attacked – right inside our tent!   It was another huge white wolf, exactly like the one we'd seen in the canyon.

"We yelled and flailed around, and the wolf turned and ran out of the tent again, through a hole it had ripped into the side. There was no question of us sleeping after that! Barely an hour later, three more monster wolves charged straight at our campsite, in what seemed almost like a coordinated attack. This left us no choice but to defend ourselves. I fired my rifle, hitting one of the animals."

There was a curious growling sound, like someone barely repressing an angry interjection, to Chantal's left. She glanced around to see Yves tapping his brother on the shoulder. *"Non! Pas maintenant!"* he whispered sharply, in French.

*Not now.* Apparently Yves was trying to calm Jules who, like many animal-lovers, was easily upset by stories like this. Chantal turned her attention back to the lecture. "That scared them off," Hébert said. "We never did manage to find the wolf we'd wounded, though we searched for it next morning. Noah flew us out on his floatplane that same day. He said it was too dangerous for us to stay in the park any longer. He only seemed worried on our account though, not his own. I believe he went back to Pingualuit shortly afterwards."

"Mr. Aglukkaq had kind of an odd take on the whole business," added the second student. "He suggested that since the wolf in the tent didn't do us any harm, it might actually have been trying to warn us about the other wolves. But he's not a scientist of course, and he tends to anthropomorphize when he talks about animals."

"Anyway, to conclude," said Dr. Hébert, "we can announce that we are able to confirm the existence of this apparent new subspecies of *Canis lupus*, but detailed DNA studies will have to wait for our next trip up north. We'll keep you posted!"

They sat down to enthusiastic applause, and the red-haired girl returned to the podium. "That's it for today," she said. "Please feel free to join us at our next annual meeting, when we'll have our promised report on the endangered wild horses of Alberta, as well as the eagerly awaited update on Dr. Hébert's Monster Wolves! But before we go I would just like to thank our speakers again – and also all of you, for supporting our various programmes. But most especially I want to thank our generous benefactor and founder of the McGill Nature Club, Monsieur Honoré Dubois. *Merci beaucoup,* Honoré." More applause followed, mingled with a few cheers, and a silver-haired gentleman stood up to take a bow. Chantal had not noticed him before as he was sitting in the front row and a pillar had partially blocked her view. She sat up straight, staring.

The club's founder? If anyone here remembered Édouard, it would be this older man. She *must* speak to him!

At that same moment Yves spoke in her ear, startling her: she had almost forgotten he was there. "Chantal, I know it sounds strange but I just can't help feeling I know you from somewhere," he said. "Perhaps we could go and have lunch together somewhere?"

He really was very persistent, and maybe she should take it as a compliment, but she needed to get to Monsieur Dubois before the old man left the building. "I doubt we've met, unless you've been to Derby Line – which hardly anyone has," she said, getting up and grabbing her handbag. "I'm so sorry, but there's someone here I'd really like to speak to – so I have to run and catch him now – "

The audience was already flowing away through the doors. She could not see the silver-haired head anywhere, and swore under her breath as she jostled her way down the cramped wooden stairs which had filled up with slow-moving bodies. *"Excusez moi, excusez moi,"* she muttered.

There was no sign of M. Dubois in the main lobby either, but when she looked out the front door he was nowhere to be seen on the green lawns of the campus. Surely an older man could not walk so fast. Was he still inside then? She turned back and ran for the main staircase.

The museum's principal display space was on the second floor, a large roughly ovoid-shaped hall with a wooden-railed gallery encircling it. A huge cast of an Albertosaurus skeleton dominated the exhibits, which featured everything from fossils to stuffed birds and animals. But her eyes went straight to a figure standing at the far end of the hall, where it ended in a curved wall of windows looking out on Mount Royal. It was M. Dubois. He and Dr. Hébert were standing beside a stuffed timber wolf, talking together in French.

"I hope my little incident won't put you off wolves altogether, Honoré," she overheard Hébert say to Dubois as she drew closer. "Most are quite harmless. And they have their place in the scheme of things." He pointed to the mounted wolf on its plinth and a sign next to it. "You see, it says right here: when men killed off the wolves of Anticosti Island, the deer there multiplied in such numbers that they starved. And I have very much appreciated your contributions to my funding."

"It is my pleasure. I just beg that you will take more precautions if you go up north again, Marc. You are not going back there just yet?"

"No, I am off to Ontario – to Algonquin Park for the winter, doing field studies. You should visit there someday, Honoré. Thousands of tourists come to the Wolf Call every August, some from as far away as Europe. You should see their faces when the ranger imitates a wolf-howl, and the wolves in the forest howl back in answer! I'd be delighted to show you over the park."

"Perhaps I will, *mon vieux*. Until then, *à bientôt.*"

As Dr Hébert walked away Chantal edged closer and cleared her throat. "*Pardonnez-moi.* I – I wondered if I might have a word, Monsieur Dubois."

Dubois turned to her: she saw the puzzlement in his hazel eyes, but the fine lines at their corners fanned out as he smiled. "But of course, *mademoiselle.* How may I help you? Are you a student here?"

"No, I'm a visitor from the United States. But I was born in Montreal. I – I wondered if you might have known my father, Édouard Boisvert. He was a student here, a biology major."

At once the old man's eyes sparked with interest. "Édouard? Can it be true? But this is amazing! Édouard's daughter! Of course I knew him: he was a brilliant student. I am delighted to meet you, Mademoiselle Boisvert."

"My name's Chantal."

"So he gave you a French name. *C'est charmante!* It suits you well, Chantal."

"Uh… thanks." Chantal had never really felt that her name fit her. It sounded too soft and dainty, too *feminine,* for a big tomboyish girl like herself. But at least it sounded better when pronounced correctly, and in this old man's voice it was like music. "I never knew my father, of course – "

"My poor child, that is right: the … hiking accident. I am so sorry. And you would like to hear more about him, *n'est-ce pas?* I will be most happy to oblige you. I am here all this month. My wife and I, we live in the capital, in Quebec City; but we maintain in Montreal a small *pied à terre.* We would be delighted to show you around and share with you our recollections of Édouard Boisvert. He was a very dear friend of ours. We miss him still, all these years later. Here, I will give you my card – "

"Boisvert!" exclaimed a voice behind her as M. Dubois searched his wallet. She whirled, startled, to see Yves and his brother Jules standing there. They had been tailing her without her knowledge, and eavesdropped on the whole exchange. "No wonder I thought you looked familiar, Chantal! I know the Boisverts. So *you're* the lost granddaughter!" exclaimed Yves, striding forward. *"C'est incroyable!"*

She stared. *"You* knew my father? But – that's impossible – " Yves was much too young ever to have met Édouard.

Yves looked amused. "Your papa knew my papa. Guy Lapierre. The Boisverts and my family are good friends. It's true, I tell you," he added, seeing her doubtful look, "but you don't have to take my word for it. Why don't you just go look up your family here in Montreal? They can tell you anything you want to know."

She stiffened. "I don't want to intrude where I'm not wanted. The Boisverts have never had anything to do with me."

It was his turn to stare. "What? That's not true! The Boisverts have been longing to meet you for years. They thought it was *you* who refused to see *them*. You must visit them before you go."

She stared back at him, dumbfounded. Eighteen years of silence – just a simple misunderstanding? Was it possible? But a kindly voice spoke before she could say anything herself: "Perhaps, Yves, we should leave it to Mademoiselle Chantal to decide what she wants to do."

The voice was that of Honoré Dubois, and she turned to him in gratitude. "I didn't come here to force myself on anyone. Honestly! I just want to learn about my dad, and see the place where he lived. Where I was born."

"But of course!" Dubois took her very gently by the elbow and steered her towards the entrance. "And so you shall."

The two brothers continued to shadow them, Yves still protesting, Jules still silent. There was something in the younger boy's fixed stare that she did not like. His eyes were a pale amber colour like his brother's, but looked darker because their pupils were vastly dilated. They seemed curiously dull and expressionless, almost like the eyes of a shark or a spider. She wondered uneasily if Jules might be on drugs.

Dubois paid no attention to either of the boys. He kept up a light patter as they headed for the stairs. "I am so glad you came here, *mademoiselle* – "

"Chantal. Please."

He made her a little bow, a courtly Old World gesture. "If you want to see where your father lived, Édouard spent more time in this museum than anywhere else. As a graduate student he had access to the labs and specimens. I remember your mother coming here to meet him when her classes were over for the day. How pretty she was! Can it be so long ago? To me it seems like yesterday!" He sighed and shook his head.

She glanced up as they headed for the stairs, then glanced again. "There's a gorilla on the staircase," she remarked. The enormous stuffed ape stood atop a wooden ledge on the landing, sharing the small area with a lion and a large antelope.

He smiled. "Space is at a premium here. The Redpath is a small antique museum, which is part of its charm; but they run out of places to put their many treasures. You must come back for a proper look, and see the rest of the campus too. You have explored the city, have you?"

"Not much of it. I only arrived yesterday."

"There is a great deal to see." They were at the main door now, the boys still dogging their heels. "A lot of history. There are more museums, and some beautiful old churches. Notre Dame is the most famous, with its interior all decorated in real gold. The Seminaire de Saint-Sulpice next door to it dates back to the 1600s, the oldest building in the city. And you should go to Île Ste Helene and have a look at the Biosphere. As an American, it is an important part of your national heritage. It was the American Pavilion originally, for the great World Exposition of 1967 – "

Jules suddenly roused. "That old ruin!" he burst out as they walked down the stone steps to the front path. "Why should she care about that? Yesterday's naïve idea of some perfect future civilization! It might as well sink into the river, along with all the other wreckage of Expo '67. There *is* no future any more. Humans are doomed! The planet is being destroyed by industry, by deforestation – "

Chantal was surprised to hear him speak; she had begun to wonder if Yves's brother was mute. The words seemed to pour out of him, a furious spate all the more violent for being pent up. She was a little alarmed, but Dubois seemed quite unruffled by the mad outburst.

"Naïve it may seem, in retrospect," he replied in a mild tone. "But I was there; I witnessed it all. It was more than a world fair: it was both a paean to civilization, and a brave embrace of the new. The young people of the day explored the exotic foreign pavilions, and developed a hunger to travel and see the world. The Cold War was on, but at Expo the US and Soviet Union rivaled each other not with weapons, but displays showcasing their culture and technology. For one summer the human race came together and faced the future without fear."

"And see what came of it," Jules sneered.

"Say what you will," Dubois replied, still without rancour, "but the spirit of that time must be kept alive – especially for those who do not remember. Lose it, and we lose everything."

"Come along, Jules," said Yves in a brusque voice. "It's time we left."

Jules, who had been opening his mouth to argue, shut it again suddenly. The two brothers strode away across the campus without so much as a backward glance. Chantal was relieved to see them go, and Dubois sighed again as he watched them. "They mean well, the Lapierre boys, but you must not let them push you into anything for which you are not ready."

"Do they really know my family?"

"Oh yes, the Lapierres and the Boisverts have always been close, but especially so since the boys' father died earlier this year. They spend a lot of time at your grandmother's house." Dubois turned back to her. "Here is my card as promised, Chantal. My wife would be enchanted to meet you, and talk of dear Édouard. Feel free to call us at any time, my dear. *À bientôt.*"

And with another courtly little bow, he left her.

Chantal stood clutching the card in unsteady hands as he walked away. She wanted to yell, and dance with joy, and weep, all at the same moment. Her plan had succeeded beyond her wildest hopes.

*At last I'll know who you were... Daddy.*

It was the first time she had ever called him that in her thoughts.

## 7

Chantal stood inside the Biosphere, gazing at the steel latticework that webbed the sky above her and cast a net of shadow on the ground beneath. A near-perfect sphere, the huge structure had been cutting-edge architecture for its time: the masterpiece of its American designer, Buckminster Fuller. The gleaming transparent bubble of a building had dominated Expo '67 much as the Eiffel Tower had the World Fair in Paris. This much the Internet showed her, and she had found some old archival footage showing the attraction at its height. But while the old Parisian tower still stood tall and proud, time had ravaged the erstwhile American Pavilion. Its acrylic skin was gone, apparently burnt off long ago in a fire, leaving only its stark steel framework; the cultural exhibits within were long gone. On her cell phone's screen a monorail carried excited tourists on an elevated track that passed right through the centre of the sphere; in the empty shell surrounding her two wide and purposeless holes were all that remained to reveal where the track had once run.

Chantal stopped the video and put her phone away. Far from inspiring her, this place made her feel depressed. Was there anything more sad and pathetic than the site of a former world fair? Most of the structures had been razed. The fabulous inverted pyramid of the Canada pavilion was no more. The great glass box of the Quebec pavilion still stood on Île Notre Dame, but together with the neighbouring France pavilion – a surreal structure of outlandish curves and angles, yesterday's idea of the future – it had been turned into a casino. The aquarium that had once featured tropical fish and performing dolphins was long since closed and empty. The sole surviving element of

Expo that maintained its original purpose was an aged amusement park.

The idealism that had so inspired the young Honoré Dubois had vanished with the passing years, replaced by a mundane commercialism. There was nothing here for her, not even nostalgia. If she could not dwell in her own past, still less could she inhabit someone else's.

At least the weather had cleared. About noon the clouds had rolled away eastward, and the sky above was now a flawless blue, the sun hot; many of the casual strollers she encountered wore only light jackets, or none at all. A large segment of the city's populace had taken advantage of the warm spell to come over to the islands which, connected to the larger Île de Montreal by bridges, were easily accessible by car and by foot. But they made Chantal think of the happy Expo crowds from the Internet footage, which had begun to haunt her like legions of ghosts. No doubt many of those people were now ghosts indeed, dead for decades...

Oppressed by these dismal thoughts she sought out the less-peopled areas of the island. Île Ste. Helene was still maintained as a park, but some parts of it had been allowed to go wild: around the streams and artificial ponds of the island's southern end thick greenery grew, and over the years trees had matured and planted their own saplings. Weeping willows trailed their fronds above still water where fountains had once played. They were turning golden, and many of the other trees were clad in yellow and red. Chantal followed the main path through this wilder area, and began to feel better. She might almost have been walking through a wooded trail at home.

Presently she heard her name being called. After a frozen moment of astonishment, she laughed at herself; of course, it was some other Chantal being summoned. Such a mistake had never happened back in Derby Line, but for all she knew hers was a popular name in Quebec. She walked on. But the hails did not stop, and in fact grew louder and nearer. At last she turned in perplexity, to see two young men in jeans and long-sleeved tees approaching.

*The Lapierres,* she thought. *Now how in the world did they find me?* Despite the bright daylight, she felt a tiny twinge of unease. There was no one else around on this wooded path… Then she scolded herself for being paranoid. As Yves rushed up to her, she returned his smile.

"Well! Imagine meeting you here!" she said, with just a slight note of query in her voice.

"Oh, everybody comes over to the islands in the good weather," laughed Yves.

Jules scowled. "There are too many people here today. I prefer the parks when they are empty. Not so many… strangers." His cold eyes looked directly at Chantal.

"Now, now, Jules," said Yves through his tightening smile. "Why don't you go back to the house? You know you're expected. I'll meet you there later." As his brother slouched off, Yves turned back to Chantal. "Since it's such a nice day, why don't you let me show you the city?"

"Uh, thanks, but M. Dubois told me he and his wife would – "

"Them! They're not from here. I was born and raised in Montreal; you couldn't have a better guide. Please, Chantal. Let me do this one thing for you."

She gave in. There was really no polite reason to refuse. On learning that she had come by car, Yves walked her back to the parking lot where she had left Minnie. He was enchanted by the little red car, and by the teddy bear that sat bolt upright in the passenger seat like a copilot, button eyes blandly staring.

"He's a sort of mascot," she explained, embarrassed. "I've had him since I was four. I call him Mr. Bear. I wasn't too original with names as a kid." She picked up the stuffed animal and tossed it into the back seat, trying to appear casual.

He chuckled. "Isn't it bizarre that children turn for comfort to the image of an animal that in real life would eat them alive? Believe me, there is nothing cute about a bear." He got into the driver's seat and she handed him the keys. "I've hunted grizzlies in British Columbia. Not mountain bears, mind you, but the giant ones that live along the sea-coast. They grow huge from eating so much salmon."

So Yves did not share his brother's sentimentality about animals, Chantal thought. She said nothing, and he looked sidelong at her as he backed Minnie out of the parking spot. "Now please don't tell me you're one of those girls who get all judgmental about hunting."

Chantal shook her head. "There are lots of hunters where I live. My part of Vermont's very rural. No one in my family hunts, but we had a neighbor once who used to bring us wild ducks for dinner." She did not tell him of her deep distaste for hunters who targeted animals just for trophies, and took pleasure in the act of killing. There was no point in antagonizing someone who clearly wanted to be helpful.

His brows rose. "So you're a country girl! Well, that makes sense: all the Boisverts love the outdoors – "

"I guess I do. But it could be pretty boring too. Nowhere much to go on a Saturday night."

"Then you will enjoy Montreal. There is plenty to do here every night of the week! Lots of entertainment and culture."

They crossed the bridge over the river and reentered the city. "There are so many churches here," she noted. "Everywhere I look there's a dome or a steeple."

He chuckled. *"La ville aux cents clochers,* we call Montreal. 'The city of a hundred bell towers'. With such a large population of Catholics there had to be lots of churches in the old days. Some have been converted into condos, what with secularization and our falling birth rate. A lot are still in use though, and several are world famous: Notre Dame for instance, and that huge church downtown with the green dome, Marie Reine du Monde. It was inspired by St Peter's in Rome. Then there is the Bonsecours chapel in the old harbour that dates to the 1600s. And up on top of the Mountain is St Joseph's Oratory, the biggest church in the whole country. But that is not the Oratory's only claim to fame: millions of pilgrims go there each year to pray for miracle cures. Do you belong to a church, Chantal?"

"Not really." Her grandparents had both been raised in the Methodist church, but neither they nor any of their descendants had attended in many years. "My family only goes for weddings and – and funerals."

"My family has not gone to mass in years, not since my mother died when I was a little boy," said Yves. "And the Boisverts never go. They are not … believers."

So religion was *not* the reason her father's family had resented his marriage. Chantal filed that thought away in her head. Perhaps the Boisverts just didn't like Americans? But why would that lead to such a bitter rift? To cut off relations with your own grandchild was a terrible thing. Unless Yves was right, and the bitterness had all been on Édouard's side?

"Now where would you like to go first?" he asked.

"You mentioned a church on Mount Royal. Is there anything else up there, or is it just wilderness?" she asked.

93

"People live there, and there is a park on the summit. Shall we go see it? You get a wonderful view of the city."

Yves drove up a steep street that led them northwards, weaving back and forth in wide curves up the side of the Mountain. "McGill is below us. You see those grey towers and battlements? That is the university hospital, which was designed to look like a medieval castle. We were all of us born there. You too, of course. There is something to brag about when you go home! You were born in a castle on a hill, just like a fairytale princess!"

He was, as Nana would say, "laying it on a bit thick", but Chantal realized she didn't care. Nor did it matter to her whether he was seriously attracted, or merely flirting with her. At his flattering attentions the sting of Russell's betrayal had begun to subside, and at the back of her mind she couldn't help thinking it might be rather nice to have a sophisticated Québecois boyfriend. Word might even get back to Russ... Yves was certainly attractive. She stole surreptitious glances at his face as he drove. He was so very different from freckled, ginger-haired Russell Gordon; like some people of Gallic extraction he looked almost Hispanic, with clear olive skin and that thick brown-black hair. But where one would expect dark brown eyes with that colouring, Yves had those unexpectedly light amber irises. His mouth confirmed a pet theory she had long had, namely that the French had more expressive and mobile mouths than any other people. His was certainly generous, with full dark-red lips, and its corners were always twisted slightly upwards as though he were on the verge of a sly grin. *He'd be a good kisser,* she found herself thinking suddenly. *Much better than Russ.* For a moment she imagined the warm pressure of his mouth on hers, and his voice murmuring endearments into her ear in

94

mellifluous and seductive French. *Je t'aime, chérie... je t'aime.*

He glanced sideways at her suddenly, his lips curving into a full smile, and she wondered if he had guessed her thoughts. After all, a boy this good-looking had to be aware of the effect he had on girls. Feeling slightly embarrassed by her own obviousness she attempted to make conversation. "This city has such a castle complex! Just about everything here has turrets and battlements on it. Schools, colleges, hospitals – "

"I suppose it must seem rather quaint to American eyes."

"No, I like it – it's very Old World. Reminds me of France." She proceeded to tell him about her French Club trip as they drove on uphill. There were houses on the hillside too, she saw, rows of elegant mansions tucked into the groves of trees.

"This is a very wealthy neighborhood we're in now," he said. "Rich people live in those houses, most of them Anglos – English Canadians, that is. Westmount, it's called. The wealthy old Francophone families live mostly in Outremont, on the far side of the Mountain."

Westmount, Outremont: the very names, one English, the other French, testified to the fundamental divide in this two-tongued land. The Mountain rose up between them like its visible embodiment. And to which side of that divide did Chantal herself belong? It seemed that no matter where she went she would always be pulled in two directions.

The road continued to climb. They drove past a vast sprawling cemetery, and then through a park-like space, a place of lawns interspersed with dense woods. The road led them on in long sweeping curves, past a small lake in a hollow – "The Lac aux Castors, or Beaver Lake as the English would say" – and then up again. "We are in Mount Royal Park now, right on top of the Mountain.

Not far away from here is the famous giant cross that lights up at night, and can be seen from the city below. It marks the spot where Maisonneuve – the founder of Montreal – first raised up a cross of wood in 1642."

"I read somewhere that the Mountain is really a volcano. Is that true?" she asked.

"Not exactly, but it is a volcanic feature. You see how dark the rock is?" He pointed to the roadside, where the layers of underlying rock beneath the roots of the trees were exposed.

"Yes – almost black, as if it was burnt."

"That's because it's solidified lava. This is a huge extrusion of magma that thrust up through the planet's crust and hardened. Later the earth all eroded away and left the hard part to stand on its own as the Mountain. So don't worry, it won't erupt and blow us up!"

He stopped at last at the lookout where a crowd of people stood, leaning on the iron railings to admire the view. It was breathtaking. Wave upon wave of maple and birch and oak billowed beneath them, and in the sunlight their scarlet and vermilion and gold blazed as if the Mountain had reverted to the molten fire of its beginnings. Far below the city stretched out in grey and white grids, with the wide blue expanse of the St. Lawrence to the south; beyond the river the countryside swept on, hilly and green, to meet the sky. Chantal imagined the changes that had unfolded in Mount Royal's shadow, from the legendary Iroquois fortress of Hochelaga with its wooden palisades to the first tiny French colony of Ville-Marie, on up to the modern city that lay spread out before her. But it did not give her any sense of belonging: its long pageant of history only made her feel small and insignificant.

"It's like the lookout in L.A.," she said, forcing a cheerful tone. "You can see the entire city!"

"Not all of it – just the eastern end. There is a better view of downtown at the southern lookout. But from here the *Laurentides* – the Laurentian Mountains – are visible on a clear day like this. You see them? They are not tall mountains, like the Rockies out west; but they were once just as big. They are so old that time has worn them down to stubs. And look over there to your right: do you see those other mountains way over there, against the horizon?" He pointed to the extreme south, where a distant range of rounded peaks undulated against the sky.

"Yes, I see them."

"Those are the Green Mountains of Vermont. You can actually see your home state from here."

"Wow. I didn't realize we were that close," she said. Chantal had spent little time in the Green Mountains, but the sight of their distant summits gave her a surprisingly strong twinge. It was impossible to keep a slight tremor out of her voice.

"Homesick?" Yves said. "But this country is your home too, you know. You belong here as much as I do."

And there was nothing in her home state for her now. What she yearned for was not the Vermont of the present, but that of the distant past. With a slow deliberate motion Chantal turned her back on the far-off mountains, and smiled at Yves. "Thanks. You make me feel so welcome."

They returned to the car, and he opened the door for her. No boy had ever done this for her, and she could not help being impressed by his show of chivalry. "So whereabouts do you live in Montreal?" she asked. "In Outremont?"

"We did, for many years, but my brother and I have sold the house and moved to a downtown flat near the university."

"Oh – M. Dubois told me your father died. I'm so sorry. Was it very recent?"

He nodded. "This summer past. We were on a hunting expedition up north and someone shot my Papa and fatally wounded him. He... mistook him for an animal. These accidents do happen, unfortunately. There were no medical facilities anywhere near, so there was nothing Jules and I could do for him."

She could think of nothing to say, so she murmured "Sorry" again and fell silent. He drove on, back through the park, and then drove over to the side of the road. "What is it?" she asked as he switched off the engine and turned to face her. Was he making a move? She decided she didn't object at all if that was his intent and she sat still, expectant.

But he just gazed steadily at her for a moment before speaking. His tone was quiet and serious. "Chantal," he said, "I wish so much that you would consider meeting your family."

She looked away form him, down at her hands. "Yves, I just don't want to intrude on them. That's all."

"Don't tell me you believe all that nonsense about them not wanting to see you! I phoned them to say I'd met you and they were just wild with excitement. They begged me to bring you to the house, the girls especially. Did you even know that you have cousins, Chantal?" he persisted as she sat saying nothing. She had not known, and the desire to meet them – this never-before-seen family – rose within her.

"If you're... sure they really want to," she said, hesitating still.

"Of course I'm sure. I told you, I'm a close friend of the family." He reached over and placed his hand under her chin, gently forcing her to look up. "Come with me now, Chantal. Please. Come home."

She looked, unwilling, into the depths of his eyes – in this light the irises were limpid gold, the shade of liquid honey – and she felt the last of her resistance slip away.

The Boisvert house was a large and impressive dwelling, located on one of Outremont's quieter and shadier streets and set well back from the road. It too had castle pretensions, with a proud pointed turret at one end and walls of carved sandstone. Yves led her up the path and pressed the doorbell. After what seemed a long wait to Chantal the big oaken door finally opened to reveal a middle-aged woman, dressed in a somewhat dowdy fashion in a plain high-collared blouse and navy skirt. Her mouse-brown hair was drawn back into a plain knot. There was something subdued and deferential in her attitude as well, as she stood there holding the door. She must be a housemaid of some kind, Chantal thought. Did people still have maids? No doubt people like the Boisverts did.

"Ah, Genevieve!" Yves greeted her in a casual tone. "Would you tell Madame Thérèse that I have brought her granddaughter to see her?"

The woman stared at Chantal for a moment with a kind of dull astonishment in her brown eyes. *"Dieu,"* she murmured. *"C'est vrai?"*

"Of course it is true," said Yves, this time with a touch of sharpness in his tone. "I told you she was in town. Now she wants to meet her family. Please tell Thérèse at once."

The woman scurried away down the entrance hall, disappearing through a door to the left. Yves strode right in, as if he were accustomed to having the run of the place. Chantal hung back a little. The hall was so very grand, with its varnished paneling and oaken staircase, and framed oil paintings on the walls. She had expected nothing like this. The odd reaction of

Genevieve unsettled her, too. Beneath the woman's surprise there had been something else – dismay, displeasure? Certainly not the delighted welcome that Yves had promised her.

"Um, are you sure it's okay?" Chantal asked. "Maybe we came at a bad time – "

"Don't be silly," said Yves. "This is your family *home*. Come on!" He took her arm and led her down the hall and into the left-hand doorway.

Inside was a magnificent sitting room. Window draperies, paintings, ornaments, all were in impeccable taste. An immense Persian carpet covered the floor, gold and wine-coloured, complementing the antique furnishings. The wood paneling on the walls was exquisite, with a design of leaves and flowers carved in bas relief on the arched lintel of the doorway, and the stone mantelpiece bore the sculpted head of an animal: a fox, or was it a wolf? Above the mantel hung a huge dark oil portrait in a heavy gilded frame, depicting a seventeenth-century gentleman in resplendent lace ruff and doublet. An ancestor, perhaps.

In a graceful upholstered wing chair by the fireplace sat another woman, much older than Genevieve. The latter went to stand beside her, hands clasped and head lowered. "Yves, *mon chèr!* You have done it, you have brought her to me!" exclaimed the old woman, rising to her feet.

"Yes, Thérèse. Here she is at last."

Chantal gazed at her grandmother with something akin to awe. Thérèse Boisvert had a striking face, with sharp pronounced features: high-bridged nose, pointed chin, and deep-set eyes of a light amber colour, much like Yves's own. Her thick grey hair was swept up in a style almost like a pompadour, framing her face, with two streaks of its original black curving away from her temples. She wore a tight black skirt reaching to mid-calf, and her ivory silk blouse had lace ruffles all down the front and was pinned at the neck with a cameo. Frilly blouses were the fashion, and Mme. Boisvert's no doubt came from some stylish Montreal boutique. But in that antique setting it gave her a curiously anachronistic appearance, an effect heightened by her severe hairstyle and erect posture. She might have been some upper-class Victorian matron, exuding regal self-assurance as she received guests in her parlour. A formidable woman, one whom even the redoubtable Nana might have hesitated to cross.

But at the sight of Chantal a smile softened the angular face. Mme. Boisvert stretched out both hands and kissed her granddaughter on each cheek, European-fashion. "Ah, *ma chère enfant!* How wonderful that you have come to us. If only your Grandpère could have lived to see you!"

"I – I'm sorry. I'd have come sooner," Chantal stammered, "but – I wasn't sure you wanted to see me. I've never heard from any of you – "

"Édouard forbade it. And when we heard nothing from you or your guardians over the years, well, we thought you did not wish to be reunited with us. We did not even know your name; you were not yet christened when he took you away. Such a waste of time over such a foolish little quarrel! Édouard never forgave us; I can barely forgive myself." She did not say what the quarrel had been about, and Chantal decided not to press her. There would be time for such delicate inquiries later.

Thérèse gestured to the dowdy woman who still stood beside her chair. "Genevieve, go fetch Francine and Lysette. We must celebrate!"

"Yes, *Maman.*" The woman left in swift obedience.

Chantal stared after her. *Maman?* That meant "Mother". Then that was Thérèse's daughter, not her maid! The woman's drab attire and air of servility had

101

misled her. By the look of things Genevieve's mother had her thoroughly cowed, and again Chantal reflected that Thérèse Boisvert was not a woman to be trifled with. But the matriarch was all smiles as she took Chantal's arm and led her about the room. "You come from a proud lineage, my dear. Your ancestors here in New France were *Seigneurs* – landowners. That is one of them, Jean-Paul Boisvert, in the portrait over the mantel. The old Manoir Boisvert is long gone, *hélas,* burned down during the war with the British. This is our only home now."

"It – it's a beautiful house."

"Thank you. The paneling in this room, you know, is by a local woodcarver of the nineteenth century. He is rumoured to have been apprenticed to none other than Louis-Amable Quévillon."

"The famous church sculptor," Yves whispered in Chantal's ear, seeing her blank look.

"But you are not here to talk about the décor, *ma chère!*" exclaimed Mme. Boisvert. "You are here to meet your family – and here they are! Francine is the eldest, she is fourteen; and Lysette is nine. Come and meet your cousin, girls!"

Genevieve – *my aunt,* thought Chantal – ushered her two daughters into the sitting-room. The sisters were so like Chantal with their straight black brows, golden-brown eyes and wavy brown hair, that she understood at once why Yves had experienced déjà vu when he first saw her in the auditorium. It was almost uncanny – like seeing two life-sized pictures of herself, one from childhood and one from early adolescence, placed side by side.

Lysette rushed forward. "At last you've come! The Lost Cousin from America! I always hoped you'd come back to us one day – I used to make up stories about it, and tell them to my friends –" The little girl beamed and danced with delight, her mop of brown curls bobbing around her face. Her teenage sister was aloof though, almost hostile, her eyes peering out from under a drooping forelock of unruly hair. She mumbled *"B'jour,"* and quickly withdrew her hand from Chantal's. But Chantal was not offended. She recalled herself at fourteen: wary, insecure, oppressed by a domineering grandmother, forever feeling awkward at social occasions. And what could be more awkward – discombobulating, even – than meeting a long-lost relative?

"You will stay for dinner, of course," said Mme. Boisvert.

*No, not Mme. Boisvert,* Chantal corrected herself again. *Grandmère.*

"I'd love to," she said.


Dinner was a very formal affair, held in a dining room twice the size of the sitting room and just as grand. The food was equally superb. Nana had been a good cook – her Thanksgiving turkey in particular had been a thing of magnificence – but she had disdained what she called "fancy cooking". Beef and pork she had served in great plain slabs, without any sauce save for the thick beige gravy with which Nana smothered everything. It was not until Chantal visited Paris with the French club that she discovered the delights of herbs, spices and other seasonings that enhanced flavour and tantalized the palate. The Québecois, if her grandmother's table was anything to go by, were as devoted to cuisine as the continental French. The main course was venison, which despite her country upbringing Chantal had never tasted; it came, her hostess explained, from a wild deer Yves and Jules had brought back from a recent hunting trip.

"Jules hunts, too?" she said, surprised. She recalled the younger boy's seeming anger over Dr. Hebert's shooting of the Monster Wolf.

"Of course he does," said Yves. "Why not? Part of loving nature is understanding how it works. In the natural world you kill, or you are killed. Jules and I both respect that."

Perhaps, Chantal thought, Jules was simply more sentimental about some animals than others. The rich red meat was served with wild rice and oven-roasted vegetables, and followed by a homemade sorbet as light on the tongue as lemon-scented mist. Wine accompanied the meal, a vintage Merlot; she demurred at first, explaining that she was not yet of drinking age, but Yves and Thérèse overruled her: "This is a special celebration! We must have a toast!"

Even Francine had a small amount, Chantal noticed, though the indignant Lysette was denied. "But I want some too, *Mémé*!" the little girl protested, watching the others drink.

"*Non, non,* Lysette," said her grandmother firmly. "You already had your *apéritif* before Chantal came, and you know you will want the liqueur afterwards so you cannot have wine as well."

Chantal nearly choked on her own wine at that. She had forgotten that in France it was common practice to let young children drink alcohol at home.

She had another surprise when Jules Lapierre himself joined them for the main course, appearing as if out of nowhere and without so much as a greeting. She had not heard the doorbell ring. Thérèse merely nodded at him as he slid into one of the carved mahogany chairs at the vast table. "Jules has been here all the afternoon painting," she said. "So I forgive him for being late. Such a hard worker he is! And Yves, I do not know what I would do without you. It is so good to have men around in this household of women. Like a nunnery it is here, at times!"

She did not explain the absence of her daughter's husband. Was he deceased, or had he divorced Genevieve? *Tante* Genevieve herself said little during the meal, staring down at her plate; with the sullen Francine seated to her right and the equally moody Jules to her left, there was a little pool of silence at that end of the table. Almost as if to counter this, Thérèse in the hostess's seat bantered in a lively animated fashion with Yves, with frequent excited interruptions from Lysette.

"Is Chantal going to live with us, *Mémé*?" she exclaimed. "I hope so!"

"That is up to Chantal," replied the matriarch, smiling at her youngest granddaughter. "We must remember that she has a home in America."

"Well – not so much, any more," admitted Chantal, who was feeling a little giddy with the wine and trying not to show it. "I mean, I have relatives there, but my American grandparents are dead."

"No grandparents – and you an orphan, too! My poor child!" cried Thérèse. "You *must* stay here, as long as you wish. We have plenty of spare rooms; you shall choose one for your very own. And do not talk to me again about imposition! You are my own grandchild, and I have been deprived of you for eighteen years!" She reached out a thin hand, heavy and glittering with rings, and laid it on Chantal's.

"That's – that's very kind of you," she began.

"Not kind, *ma chère enfant!* My duty, and my pleasure also. Indulge your old grandmother, won't you, and let me make amends for the past."

To Chantal this seemed a perfectly reasonable request, especially through the warm rosy haze of Merlot. That she had just met these people, and knew next to nothing about them, seemed a trifling detail.

105

They were her blood relatives, and they were offering her a chance to mend an old family feud. "I guess I could extend my visit for a while longer," she said.

Lysette clapped her hands with delight, and Yves and her grandmother exchanged looks of satisfaction. Yet she still heard nothing from the other end of the dinner table. Turning, she was suddenly aware of Jules Lapierre's eyes watching her. They were expressionless as before and their pupils were still oddly dilated, but their gaze was sharp and somewhat unsettling. Her aunt, who had barely touched her food, was also staring at Chantal with – what was it? Unease? *No, more like fear. But fear of what?* The elder daughter's sulky demeanour meanwhile had flared into what looked like outright fury. Francine's eyes burned under her tumbled locks and her hands gripped her linen napkin until the knuckles blanched.

Thérèse noticed. "Francine *ma chère,*" she said, "you're very quiet today. This is a very special time for us all; are you not happy?"

"*Non!*"

The word seemed to burst from Francine, an eruption of emotion she could no longer hold in. It shocked everyone else into silence. Then before anyone could speak or move the girl sprang up from the table, kicked her chair aside, and stormed out of the room.

## 8

"Don't mind Francine," said Yves. "She will get over it."

Upstairs, Genevieve could be heard remonstrating with her daughter, apparently through Francine's locked bedroom door. The rest of the group had retired discreetly to the sitting room. "Get over what? Was it something I said?" whispered Chantal to Yves.

"No, no! It is just that she is a little bit spoiled, you know? And now she has a cousin who is getting all the attention, so her nose – as you say in English – is a little out of joint."

This did not seem quite adequate as an explanation – she was sure it was not mere resentment, but pure hatred she had seen in the girl's eyes – but Chantal was prepared to accept it for now.

"Come sit by me, my dear," invited her grandmother, and Chantal complied. Thérèse had a leather-bound family album on her knee and was leafing through its stiff pages. "I want you to see these… Look, there is your father as a little boy! Isn't he adorable? And here he is with little sister Genevieve playing in the garden. And there is your Grandpère – my poor Émile! How I miss him still!" She sighed over the photograph, which showed a stout man with heavy black brows that made him look as though he were scowling. There was a picture of Genevieve, much younger and slimmer, resplendent in a wedding gown complete with long train and a veil with a tiara. On her arm was a pleasant-faced young man with light brown hair. "My daughter on her wedding day. She looks so happy, doesn't she? If she only knew then what would happen!" Thérèse sighed again.

"Did her husband die?" Chantal asked.

"He? No! He lives still – with another woman. His Church gave him an annulment so he can remarry." Thérèse shook her head. "I tried to warn her. I told Genevieve that Henri was wrong for her, that it could not last. But she was in love, the foolish girl, and would not listen to her *maman*. Now she is left alone with two children. Fortunately I took them all in."

Chantal glanced at Lysette, playing happily in a far corner of the room with a pair of dolls. "Oh, that's a shame. But at least you have your granddaughters."

"Yes, some good came of it. But not without a great deal of pain which could have been avoided." Thérèse turned the album page with a swift dismissive movement. Chantal wondered what it had cost the wayward daughter to return home after the collapse of her marriage, eating humble pie so that her children could have a roof over their heads. And what of Édouard? He had never come back at all after *his* wedding. What words could be so bitter as to be unforgivable? Thérèse and Genevieve had reconciled, after a fashion; but both Édouard and his father had a stubborn and unbending look in their pictures, their eyes keen and confident beneath the heavy black brows. She could only imagine what clashes they might have had.

Suddenly she felt uncomfortable. The glow of the wine had worn off, and she felt out of place here again. "Well, I really should get back to my hotel, I guess," she said, rising from her seat.

"I'll drive you back," Yves offered.

"Oh, I'll be fine."

"But you do not know your way about the city, and I took you a long distance from downtown. Please, let me drive you: I would feel terrible if you got lost."

She gave in and let him go with her to the door. Thérèse accompanied them. "Tell me what hotel you are staying in, Chantal dear, and I will be in touch.

Perhaps you and I can do a little shopping together tomorrow, or meet for lunch?" She kissed Chantal on both cheeks again.

Feeling oddly reluctant, Chantal supplied the information to her grandmother. As Yves led her outside, her aunt came down the staircase with an expression of utter despair. *"Maman,* it is no use, she will not listen to reason –"

*"Pas maintenant,* Genevieve," interrupted Thérèse, her tone sharp. "Goodbye for now, Chantal my love. *À demain."*

She closed the great oaken door, but not before Chantal heard the sound of raised voices within.

In the end it all went just as Thérèse wanted. Chantal was to learn that her grandmother invariably got her own way in everything. The very next morning the phone in her hotel room rang before she was fully awake, and in a brisk voice Thérèse laid out her plans for the day, not seeming to care if her granddaughter had made plans of her own. And why should she? It was not unreasonable to assume a long-lost family member would prefer to spend time with her relatives. Chantal took out Honoré Dubois's card and looked at it, debating with herself. Was there really any point in accepting his offer now that she had been reunited with the Boisverts? What, after all, could he tell her that they could not? And perhaps he was just being courteous with his invitation. She, after all, had approached him and not the other way around. She phoned the number on the card and got a recorded message, to which she replied with the explanation that his assistance was not after all required, and thanked him for his kindness. Then she tossed the card in the waste basket, and went to shower and wash her hair.

She had spent a restless night, her mind too busy for sleep, and her unruly mane as a consequence of all the tossing and turning was a matted mess. She could barely get her hairbrush through the snarled locks. She slipped on a clean pair of jeans and a linen shirt – she had brought no dressy clothes for what she had assumed would be a casual trip – and went down to the lobby to wait for her grandmother.

Thérèse arrived, punctual to the last second. She looked Chantal over, and the latter hoped the more recalcitrant tangles in her hair were not too noticeable, and her outfit not too inappropriate. Perhaps it was only a coincidence that her grandmother offered to take her clothes-shopping first. They walked up to St Catherine Street where the major fashion stores were located, and spent a busy morning perusing and buying outfits. When Chantal politely protested her grandmother giving her such expensive gifts, Thérèse countered: "But think of all the presents I have not been able to give you over the years! All the birthdays and holidays missed! I am just making it up to you, *ma chère.*" And Chantal let her have her way, overwhelmed by a guilty gratitude.

They had lunch at the grand old Ritz hotel on Sherbrooke, on the outdoor *terrasse* since it was a mild day. The waiter gave Chantal an odd look as they entered the restaurant, but when he saw Thérèse Boisvert he immediately ushered them to one of the best tables. The curtains under the awning were drawn back and tied, giving a good view of the garden's flowerbeds. In the midst was a pool with a bridge, an artificial waterfall and a flotilla of white-feathered ducks. Chantal tried to keep her face from registering shock at the menu prices, but once again her grandmother insisted on paying. Still, Chantal opted for the least expensive item, Montreal smoked meat served on a bun and accompanied by a garden salad. The conversation

110

was mainly about Chantal herself; Thérèse was anxious to know about her life, her upbringing, the closeness of her ties to the Vandusens. *"Ma pauvre petite,* you are all alone in America now," she said. "Why not come here to live? You speak the language so beautifully, and you can live in my house. If you wish to study, there is McGill or the Université de Montreal. What do you say?"

"Well – I hardly know what I feel, yet," Chantal temporized. "This is wonderful, but I just expected to be here a short time, I'm still discovering the place – "

"I will show you Montreal," her grandmother offered, taking both of Chantal's hands in her own. "And you must come with us to our cottage in the *Laurentides* – the Laurentian Mountains. We'd planned to go there this week. It is so beautiful there this time of year! As a child of the country you would perhaps feel at home there, *hein?* Later you can decide for yourself what it is you wish to do."

She released Chantal's hands and turned to peruse the dessert menu, while Chantal pretended to watch the ducks preening and bobbing about on the pond as she tried to sort out her conflicted feelings. *Everything's moving so fast,* she thought. *I should be happy – I am happy really – I guess it's just hard to take it all in...*

She wanted some quiet time to herself, to sit and think; but her grandmother had other plans. After lunch she swept Chantal off on a tour of the oldest parts of the city. "Look, here is Rue St. Jacques: it used to be our Wall Street, back in olden days, but now it's full of restaurants and shops," she said, pointing as they drove along. "You can see that it was once a wealthy bankers' street though. Some of these buildings go back to Victorian times."

Façades of limestone, red sandstone, or grey granite sported Roman columns; walls burst into flower and foliage, pillars were twined with spiraling vines. Each edifice seemed to be trying to outdo the others in flights of baroque fantasy, in chimeras and grotesques. There were Greek gods, and caryatids, and grinning satyrs; medieval-looking dragons and griffins; plump cherubs and heraldic dolphins with leafy tails. Bat-winged gargoyles perched on high ledges, like prehistoric reptiles poised to take flight from cliff-tops. Glancing up one side-street, she caught a glimpse of the immense pillared front of Notre Dame basilica, with its stone statues of saints in tall niches. Again Chantal felt a curious sense of displacement: surely she was back in Paris, or in some other ancient European city. This did not feel like North America at all.

They drove on to the port district, with its antique cobbled pavements and old stone houses transformed into boutiques and restaurants. Here they stopped at the Marché Bonsecours with its gleaming silver dome, and got out of the car. The old market hall inside was now divided into ateliers showcasing the work of Quebec artisans. "You must see Jules's work," Thérèse said as they entered a gallery full of paintings and Inuit sculpture. "The boy is very talented. I have become his patroness."

"Oh – you mentioned he'd been painting. I thought you meant house painting," said Chantal. "So he's an artist?"

"Indeed, yes – already exhibiting in galleries, and he only eighteen years old!"

Chantal couldn't help wondering whether the influence of his wealthy patroness had something to do with that, but when she saw the work itself there was no denying the boy's talent. Jules himself was there, framing a new picture at the back of the gallery, and he showed them his new exhibit. In one painting, titled simply "Biosphere", the skeletal geodesic dome was depicted as overgrown, with trees and rambling vines growing both within and around its empty frame. In the foreground roamed a herd of deer. Another, "Temple of Gaia", showed Notre Dame Basilica as a roofless ruin where animals ran about the abandoned sanctuary, and birds nested amid the rood screen's gilded carvings and statuary.

"Those are older works. This is my latest," he said, propping up the unframed painting on a chair. It showed Habitat '67, the futuristic apartment complex that had been designed for Expo: a set of cube-shaped modular structures resting one upon the other in seeming haphazard fashion like a child's set of toy bricks abandoned in mid-play. The complex still existed, Chantal knew, and was considered a prestigious address. But in Jules's painted vision its concrete walls were crumbling and filled with gaping holes, home only to crows and raccoons and a family of black bears. "The title of this work is 'Habitat', which is the actual name of those apartments," he explained to Chantal. "But in this case it is an intentional irony: here it is the future, and the complex is now a habitat for wildlife. 'Biosphere' is an ironic title also."

"Yeah, I got that," said Chantal in a dry tone.

"Some find these works depressing. Others think they are a warning of our possible future, if we continue to waste the word's resources. But to me, these paintings are a celebration of life."

"You mean, the idea that some life will survive even if humans die out?" she asked. "I guess that's *kind of* a comforting thought, in a way – "

"No." His eyes glowered, looking blacker than ever: their pupils, she noticed, were hugely distended, and she was convinced now he must be on drugs. "You don't understand. I mean that these are visions of a future that I *hope* for. Not the future imagined by Expo, where humanity dominates the Earth, but a future when humans have ceased to be. When their final extinction finally frees the world from pollution and development, and nature purifies and renews itself."

"You actually *want* that to happen?" she asked, repelled.

"Of course. All right-thinking people should. The human race has been disaster for the planet."

"But the environmental movement – "

Jules snorted his disdain. "Too little, too late. If people truly cared about the Earth they would stop having children altogether, and let humanity disappear for the good of other living things."

His words were as disturbing as his works, and her jangling nerves made her irritable. "So how are sales?" she asked in a pointed tone.

The sarcasm was lost on Jules. "Oh, the *bourgeoisie* do not hang such things on their living room walls. My art is intended to make a statement, one they would not want to contemplate."

Thérèse intervened. "Jules dear, I was thinking that you and Chantal might like to join the rest of us up at the cottage this week. You can work on your art there in peace, and we can show Chantal the *Laurentides*. What do you say, my dear?" she asked, turning to Chantal. "Will you come with us?"

Again Chantal had that sense of being rushed and pressured, but she also feared that if she showed any more hesitancy it might offend her grandmother. Who would not be insulted by such obvious manifestations of distrust, when there was no sane reason for it? She herself could not explain her feelings of unease around the Boisverts. Perhaps it was rooted in years of believing they wanted no contact with her, and she still could not quite believe they did. But she had received nothing but kindness from them (with one sole exception), and really ought to return their affections. She had already been welcomed into their home. This new invitation to their cherished private refuge in the countryside was yet another offer of acceptance into their family circle. She could not help but say yes: anything else would be churlish.

"*Bien!* We depart tomorrow, then," said Thérèse.

The cottage of the Boisverts was a considerable distance from Montreal, and even from most city-dwellers' Laurentian retreats; it was located not on a lake or river but deep in the forest, on the fringes of the vast national park that neighboured Mont Tremblant. They all went in one car, the Boisverts' huge SUV which seated up to eight. Yves drove, with Thérèse sitting next to him. It was a long exhausting drive of many hours, and after a while it became tedious too. The countryside north of Montreal was certainly scenic, with its rolling hills and lakes, but up here the autumn colours were past their peak. They passed mountains that must have been a wonder to behold even a few days ago, but were now dun-grey and austere under the late October sun. Thérèse directed Yves to stop for lunch at a restaurant on the outskirts of St. Sauveur, where they sat at outdoor tables and ate sandwiches on homemade bread, and then bought some more bread, cold meat and fruit for supper. After this brief respite they drove on.

The signs of civilization became ever more scattered and scarce. Soon they passed only the occasional house or cottage on a lonely lake, sometimes with a floatplane parked at a dock. It was growing dark when Yves turned off the main highway, driving straight into the forest down a long track – one could not call it a road – that consisted merely of two overgrown earthen ruts. Weeds and branches rattled against the sides of the car as it lurched along, following the bends in the track, until at last the trees drew back to form a clearing, and the Boisvert cottage loomed in the headlights.

Chantal had expected a summer cabin of the type city people maintained in rural Vermont, a simple structure of wood or even logs. This place was more like a proper house, with a sloping roof sheltering a wide veranda at the front and gabled windows; it looked as though it must contain a generous number of rooms. Yves turned off the engine but left the headlights on so they could find their way up the steps to the door. Inside, a cavernous main room ran the full width of the house, and wooden stairs beyond led up to a second floor. This was, her hostess explained, a former hunting lodge that had been in the family for more than a century. Over the fieldstone fireplace hung a mounted moose head with a majestic spread of antlers, and other hunting trophies adorned the walls to either side: elk, antelopes, a mountain lion baring its savage leopard-like teeth. Two bearskin rugs, a grizzly and a polar bear, reposed on the wooden floor. From a central beam above hung a chandelier made of deer antlers.

"Your *grandpère* killed the moose here years ago," Jules told her. "He got that pronghorn antelope on a hunting trip to Alberta. My father went with him. They got the bighorn sheep in the Rockies, and the mountain lion too." He pointed to the head of the great cat. "Your father didn't much care for hunting, so M. Boisvert used to take Papa with him on his trips. Later Papa took Jules and me along. We bagged the grizzly in British Columbia and gave the hide to Mme. Boisvert as a gift. And here's the bear Papa and Jules and I killed in Nunavik." Yves set his foot on the polar bear rug. "Huge, isn't he? He put up a real fight. We were lucky he didn't get one of *us.*"

The bear's head was still attached to its pelt, the bared fangs still seeming to rage and threaten. The great

116

claws on its forepaws were longer than her fingers and it was not hard to imagine what horrific injuries they would have inflicted in life. She gave a little shudder and looked away.

"*Ma pauvre!* It is cold in here, isn't it?" said Thérèse, taking her arm.

Yves and Jules set to work lighting a fire in the stone fireplace. They ate their cold sandwiches, cheese and fruit sitting around the fire, and heated water for tea over the flames. Chantal was glad of the hot drink; it was in fact quite chilly in the cottage. There was no electricity here, and no land line; she suspected there was no indoor plumbing either. There seemed to be no food in the cottage, and she wondered what they were going to eat with no supermarkets anywhere near. "So," she said, forcing a cheerful tone with some difficulty, "what do you folks do when you're up here? Are we going to go see Mont Tremblant?" It would be fun to see the famous resort, with its Alpine-style village nestled between mountain and lake.

Thérèse looked at her as though she had committed a mild *faux pas.* "No, *ma chère enfant,* one does not go to Mont Tremblant this time of year. The shops are all closed up; even the scenic cable car is not running. The time for summer sport is past, and skiing season is still far off."

*Then why come all the way out here?* Chantal wondered. The Boisverts had brought with them no guns or other equipment for hunting; they were nowhere near any water, so there could be no chance of fishing or boating. Even the trees were bared of their autumn beauty, their leaves lying in heaps on the ground. What were these people planning to do all week long?

Thérèse seemed to guess her thoughts; perhaps her puzzlement showed in her face. "We come out here for a change, my dear, to escape civilization. One can have too much of modern conveniences: it makes one pampered and soft. There is very little real wilderness left, even in the *Laurentides*. It is all being built up, especially wherever there is water. The Lac des Sables used to be such a lovely place, but now the lake is completely surrounded by cottages and condominiums. People do spoil things! But the Parc du Tremblant is a conservation area, so it is still wild. There are not only rabbits and deer here but bears, lynx, even wolves. Do not be surprised if you hear the wolves tonight: autumn is the time when they howl the most."

Wolves! She recalled the video lecture at McGill and shivered a little. *Tante* Genevieve noticed. "You must have wolves in Vermont, dear, surely?" she asked in a timid voice.

Chantal shook her head. "No, just the occasional coyote."

"Wolves lived there once," said Jules. "Your ancestors killed them off, as they did most of the wolves in America. Some would like to reintroduce the wolf to Vermont, but most of you have such a prejudice against it that no one dares try – "

"Leave off, Jules, *je vous en prie,*" said Yves in a weary tone. "You talk as if it were Chantal's fault."

"She's an American. They are all – "

"Jules! *Ta gueule!*" his brother snapped.

Chantal recognized the French for *Shut up* from her Derby Line days. It was the rudest form too, like saying "Muzzle it" in English. She could feel a tension in the room, not only between the Lapierre brothers but everyone else as well, as if invisible wires were strung taut from person to person. *We're all tired and cranky from the long car trip, that's all,* she tried to convince herself. But Genevieve seemed even more depressed than usual, and Thérèse's face wore a preoccupied expression, as though her thoughts were engaged

118

elsewhere. Francine had not said a word to anyone all day, though in her case that was normal. Chantal glanced up to see the younger teen's eyes fixed on her, a simmering hostility in their brown depths. Only Lysette seemed happy, chattering as she carried her small bag up the stairs. "Shall we go for a walk in the woods tomorrow, Maman? Shall we see a deer?"

*"Peut-être, ma chère,"* replied her mother with a tired smile, going up with her.

"Well," said Thérèse, "perhaps we should all go to bed. It has been a long day, *n'est-ce pas?"*

Chantal was quite grateful to retire to her small room and the first privacy she had known all day. Once she was alone, however, her mood worsened. There was something oppressive about the cottage. She went to the window, pulled back the faded print curtain and looked outside. There was nothing to be seen but the black outlines of trees against a dark sky. Even in Derby Line there had been other houses, the sounds of children at play, dogs barking. Here there was nothing but the faint creak of the night breeze in bare branches. The fact of their isolation made her still more uneasy. She could understand why the Boisvert women wanted to take some male friends along with them to such a lonely place.

She looked at the SUV sitting on the grass at the front of the house, and suddenly felt a surge almost of panic to realize that she didn't even have her car with her, the homely sense of security that Minnie gave her. And for the first time it occurred to her that in accepting her relatives' invitation and leaving her own vehicle behind, she had deprived herself of a ready escape should there be a problem or falling-out of some kind between herself and her newfound kin. Given the Boisverts' frequent family quarrels this seemed more than a theoretical possibility. Her cell phone did not work out here in the wilderness. There was no electricity for her laptop. All lines of communication were closed off. She was, in a very literal sense, a prisoner here... There was that absurd paranoia again! Her mind seemed to split into two separate voices:

*I'm with strangers, in a strange place.*

*Not strangers! Blood relatives. The whole point about strangers is that they might harm you. Your own family wouldn't do that.*

Tired of arguing with herself, Chantal prepared for bed. She had just pulled on her warm flannel tee and sleep pants when the sound of a knock on the door made her jump. She opened it to find Thérèse standing there, a steaming mug in her hand. "Here is a hot *tisane* for you to drink, love; it will warm you and help you to sleep. Are you comfortable? There are extra blankets in the closet if you need them."

Chantal thanked her, feeling guilty for all of her baseless and (it suddenly seemed to her) neurotic misgivings. The herbal tea, sweet and aromatic, soothed her nerves and warmed her body all over, with a pleasurable tingling sensation that went right down to her toes. She drained the mug, then got into bed and turned down the wick of her oil lantern, plunging the room into absolute darkness. Sleep took her almost as soon as she laid down her head.

It was the wolves that woke her.

At some indeterminate point between sleep and waking she became conscious of a sound. It insinuated itself subtly and delicately first into her ears, and then her mind, becoming part of her dreams: a sound she had never heard before, composed of multiple high-pitched cries. She visualized these in her head as intertwining silver threads, weaving in and out of the darkness as if it were a backing of black velvet: each strand clear and shimmering and pure. They reminded her of birdsong or whale-music. But birds and whales are solitary singers: this was a whole chorus of ethereal voices raised, not in perfect harmony, but in a kind of counterpoint. One voice would begin, soft and low, rising to a thin quaver; then the rest would join in. Trying drowsily to analyze what she was hearing, Chantal moved at last from fragmented semi-consciousness into full waking awareness.

*Wolves – it's a wolf pack!*

She had never heard wolves howl in the wild, only in movies where the sound effect used was a single long wail like a lonely dog's. Never had she imagined anything like this. The sound was beautiful, but also unearthly. She had heard of things that could make one's hair stand on end; as she listened, she swore she could actually feel the fine hairs on her arms and the nape of her neck pricking up. It must be her imagination though, for the odd sensation extended even to where she had no hair, on her cheeks and the backs of her hands and along her spine. She alternately shivered as though cold, and then flushed as if with a fever. Opening her eyes, she saw the moon at the window: full, round, tinged with gold; a "hunter's moon".

Springing out of bed, she went to the window and opened it, letting in the chill night air. She breathed it in, in deep hungry gulps. But she still felt sweaty and flushed. She tore off her pants and tee shirt and tossed them aside. Now the night breeze blew upon her entire body, and her hot prickling skin responded to its icy caress as if to a physical touch. A brief giddiness made her reel and clutch at the windowsill for support. Chantal looked down at her hands resting on the sill.

But they were no longer hands.

They had become two grey-brown furred limbs ended in broad, clawed pads. It was the fur that made her feel

121

so hot, she realized. Her tongue lolled, panting, from her mouth, its soft length spilling over teeth and jaws that now had a different shape…

With understanding came not fear, but relief and joy. She was not feverish after all, nor was she in any kind of danger. This was obviously just a dream. She would wake from it soon, as she did from every dream, and then everything would be all right. But now the wolf-voices called again, and the dream-body she wore yearned for the freedom of the outdoors, for the cool scent-laden air and the exhilaration of running through the forest. She glimpsed indistinct, shadowy shapes flitting through the blackness under the trees, and eyes like glimmering stars turned towards her in invitation.

In one light easy motion, Chantal sprang out of the window and into the night.

## 9

"Wake up, pup!" called Josephine.

Hunter opened his eyes and looked around him.

Since parting company with her friend the tundra-man, who had set them down at a considerable distance from Pingualuit, the white wolf and his new companion had travelled southwards. Josephine had worn her wolf-form most of the time, needing its superior stamina. Hunter for his part was amazed: he had never dreamed the world was so large. As the moon slowly changed its phases high above them, the land around them also changed. Tundra gave way to taiga, where clumps of birch and willow higher than their heads reared up from the heath. Then they passed through the vast region of the tree line, where at last they saw true forests: conifers whose dark-green tips rose to impossible heights, or so it seemed to Hunter's eyes: he wondered that these monstrous plants did not topple over from their own vast unwieldy size. Yet Josephine told him the trees further to the south were taller still. "These are just little baby trees up here," she had laughed. "You haven't seen anything yet, pup!"

As they journeyed southwards food became more plentiful. There were many hares, and deer too: smaller than caribou and lighter of build, and very swift of foot. He and Josephine had to find older ones to chase down. Hunter was unaccustomed to being first to eat at a kill, savouring the rich taste of entrails and muscle meat that were still warm and steaming instead of chewing at cold bony remnants after others had had their fill.

It was at this point that isolated cabins built of felled tree-trunks began to appear deep in the forest. They had not yet come to the true domain of men, Josephine explained; any they encountered here would be loners living far from the rest of their kind. The wolf-woman returned more frequently to human form now, appealing to the native trappers and woodsmen in the log cabins to lend her clothing and a bed for the night. Some of these humans were shape-changers too; others were friends of the *rugaru* who did not fear them. A few had to be kept in the dark however; she approached those ones always in woman form, clad in borrowed garments, and instructed Hunter to hide himself out of doors while she stayed in the cabins. One elderly man allowed him to come in and sit in a warm corner by the hearth.

"I told him you were a dog," said Josephine after they had left and she resumed wolf-shape.

"What!" Hunter was indignant and astonished at once. "Is his eyesight failing him? How could he mistake me for a dog?"

"I told him you've got wolf blood. Which is true, after all." She grinned at her own joke, showing all her wolf-teeth, as they set out again.

At the next lonely dwelling Josephine borrowed a vehicle from another old friend: not a flying machine, but one that ran on round limbs along a rough track trodden into the earth. Hunter rode with her at first in the front seat, but he could not stand it for long. The land-vehicle bounced up and down in the ruts, making him feel dizzy and sick, and its speed was alarming. Everything – trees, boulders – seemed to be rushing straight at him, making him duck and cringe. Finally Josephine stopped the vehicle, and he rode for the rest of that trip in its flat open back, watching things race away from him into the distance. The track grew wider, and not so rough, and he did not get jostled about quite so much. This man-made object was not as swift as the thunder-wing, but it was still far faster than walking. With each day that passed he drew ever closer to the lands of men, yet he still had the company of Josephine and her *rugaru* friends. He had it both ways: he had left the wolf-lands behind, but not the companionship of his kind.

Now after many days they had stopped again. Before him Hunter saw a large structure, hewn out of tree-trunks and blazing through the dusk with unnatural lights. This was apparently a safe-house for *rugaru*. There were several native humans sitting on the front porch, black-haired and tawny-skinned like Josephine; when they saw her emerge from the vehicle they ran down the steps in a gleeful mass and hugged her. Out of the woods at the back several *rugaru* in wolf form came running, some transforming back to humans even as they ran. It was very apparent that Josephine was well-known here, and greatly loved. At last she gestured to Hunter, who had jumped out of the truck but stayed close to it, shy and hesitant to join the joyful gathering. He was not afraid of the humans; it was the wolves that made him feel edgy and defensive. But when several of those in wolf-form approached him, he began to relax. Their body language – broad grins, lowered ears and tails – indicated non-hostile intent.

"Greetings," said one in the high-wolf language. "Any friend of Josephine's is welcome here." He touched noses with Hunter, a reassuring gesture.

"Thank you," Hunter said. "I'm afraid I cannot assume your human form, but I would gladly be your friend."

"Come and join us in the man-lair," said another. "There is nothing to fear. We are all friends here."

The *rugaru* kept their lupine forms as they led him into the house. Here the others were gathered, some in human and some in wolf shape, lying about on the furnishings or on the floor. The place was hung with the furred hides of animals and with cloth hangings that the wolf-men told him showed the shapes of living creatures, though Hunter could not make them out.

"They are made by our people in the native style," one wolf explained. "It is an art we have. We are descended from the forest-men who have lived in these lands since ancient times."

Josephine was deep in discussion with a group of the human-shaped *rugaru;* though he could not comprehend their language it was clear to Hunter that they were discussing things of grave concern. The *rugaru* who were in wolf form translated some of it for him.

"There is some trouble brewing down south, among the wolf-folk that live there," explained the one who had first greeted him. "In particular, there are two families that are being extra troublesome. It's an affectation of some wolf-men to organize themselves in packs like their wild kin, with male and female heads, and fores and hinds. These two human packs are planning to join together as one, and raise up more offspring with the shape-changing gift."

"Why does that trouble you? Are they not free to do as they please?" asked Hunter.

"So long as they harm no one, yes. But the *Lapierres,* the Stone Pack, you have met before. Josephine says you encountered them on the plain near the Land That Rises."

He stiffened. "*Those* wolves! But I thought we had left them behind in the north? How can they be down here in the tree-country, too?"

"Because they are not merely high-wolves. They are *rugaru* like us: their true form is human, and their home is in the south. When their hunting season up north is done, the Stone Pack returns to the south lands."

Hunter stared. "But they said they hated humans. They tried to kill some men that were in their territory."

"They resent the presence of other humans in the wilderness – particularly the lands they think of as theirs, though they have no more claim to them than any other creature. And so they have been murdering men: hunters, tundra-people, all in the hope of frightening them away from their hunting grounds. It was the pack father who began this, and his offspring follow his ways."

"The father-wolf has been killed, though. Did Josephine tell you?"

"Yes. That pack is now diminished to just two members, the natural sons of the head-wolf. Once the Stone Pack was a great and powerful family, but no longer. So the new, young head-wolf has had to ingratiate himself with another human pack, the *Boisverts* or Greenwoods, who have also fallen on hard times: all their male members are dead or gone. He plans to mate with one of them, and raise up a new brood. That will be a terrible thing."

"How so?" Hunter asked.

"Most of us *rugaru* are harmless, but there are... some... that abuse their powers. They like the fact that they can do things ordinary humans can't, that they are able to run free and wild in another form, and hunt and kill whenever they choose. It makes them arrogant and superior, contemptuous of other humans."

"Like the way the high-wolves look down on the low-wolves?"

"Exactly."

"There is another danger, pup," put in Josephine, speaking in Hunter's ear. He turned, to see that she had reverted to wolf form. "The young Greenwood female he has chosen does not yet know she is a wolf-woman, able to take another form. She has been long separated from her family and only just reunited with them. How will she react when she learns the truth? If she is unwilling to cooperate, I fear the pack may kill her."

"But why?" asked Hunter, bewildered. "I thought they needed her."

"They may fear that she will reveal the secret of the *rugaru* to other humans. It is always a risk with new shape-changers. Other humans would be afraid of us if they knew about us."

"And I for one would not blame them for being afraid," said the first *rugaru,* "knowing what I know of the Stone Pack and their ilk."

"True enough, Jean-Louis," Josephine agreed, turning to him. "So you see, Hunter, good and evil *rugaru* both have kept our secret for centuries. Oh, there have been little slips: tales are told of us among humans still, though most dismiss these as nonsense nowadays. Still, think of the damage were a *rugaru* to transform in plain sight, by design or by accident, revealing to all humans that we really do exist! To prevent her from doing that, they would destroy this young wolf-woman, blood kin though she be. She is in terrible danger if she does not do as they command."

"You seem sure of this," Hunter noted.

"I am sure because they have done it to others before now," she replied. "They killed her father and mother."

"Chantal! Chantal!"

The voice penetrated the thick darkness of her drowsy mind. Images still flitted through that darkness: tree-boughs spreading above her like black cracks in the sky, a golden moon swimming in luminous cloud, eyes shining like stars through the shadows, lean furred shapes running ahead of her... always far ahead, leading her into the dark. Chantal groaned and rolled over, rubbing her eyes. They felt gritty and the lashes were stuck together, reluctant to open, while her head pounded as though she were hung over. With an effort she sat up. The bedclothes were lying on the floor. When her bare feet touched the floorboards they felt like ice, and she shivered even in her flannel pants and shirt.

128

"Chantal, are you awake? It is time for *petit déjeuner.*"

It was the voice of *Tante* Genevieve, summoning Chantal to breakfast.

She glanced out the window and saw to her bemusement that the sun already stood high in a clear blue sky. She picked up her watch. A quarter after ten! She never slept in this late. She stood, still feeling light-headed and a little unsteady on her feet, and got dressed in haste. When she went out into the main room she saw only Thérèse and Genevieve sitting at the table, steaming mugs before them. Gratefully Chantal accepted some coffee and took a seat, noting all the used plates scattered on its wooden surface. "The others are finished eating," Thérèse told her. "What would you like to eat? We brought croissants and jam and some fruit, and you can make toast over the fire."

Chantal accepted one of the croissants and buttered it. She had forgotten the meagreness of the Continental style breakfast, and was glad that she was not more hungry. In fact her stomach felt slightly queasy. She hoped she was not coming down with something.

"How did you sleep, *ma chère?*" Thérèse asked.

"I – fairly well, I think." Her memory of the previous night was blurred and chaotic, like a fever-dream. She remembered feeling uncomfortably hot despite the lack of central heating, and tearing off her sleepwear – but no, that couldn't really have happened because she'd still been wearing her tee and pajama pants when she woke. Was that all just a part of her nightmare? The one in which she had seemed to be not herself, but some wild thing running through shadows under autumn trees...

"I think I heard the wolves last night," she murmured, finishing off her slim breakfast. "I'm not sure though; I was sort of half-asleep."

Thérèse smiled. "Oh, they were howling last night all right! I heard them too." She turned to her daughter. "Genevieve, will you wash the plates please?"

Genevieve always seemed to get stuck with the chores, Chantal thought. "I'll help," she offered as her aunt got up in voiceless obedience and began to collect the dirty plates. But Thérèse raised an admonishing hand.

"No, no, you are our guest! Go out now and enjoy the morning before it passes. The weather is beautiful today. The rest of us have been out already."

Outside, her cousins were sitting on the front step in the autumn sun, Lysette playing with a handful of red-and-yellow maple leaves, Francine gazing ahead of her with her chin on the heels of her hands. When the latter saw Chantal come out, she sprang up and walked back into the house without a word or a backward glance. Chantal realized she was going to have to have a talk with Francine, but now was not the time for confrontations – not with everyone confined to one small building. Instead she went and sat down by Lysette. "Good morning," she said.

The little girl looked up at her. "You mustn't mind Francine, it isn't your fault she hates you," she said.

"What?" Chantal said, startled.

"You have to understand, she is in love with Yves. She has been for such a long time, and she hoped he would wait for her to grow up. But now you have come, so he will marry you instead."

"Marry!" Chantal looked her little cousin in the face, incredulous. "I'm not marrying anybody. I'm only eighteen!"

"Oh, but that is very old!" Lysette's eyes widened. "You're a grown up lady. Anyway you are older than Francine. So Yves can marry you; he doesn't have to wait for my sister now." She explained it slowly and

130

patiently, as if she were talking to a younger child. "He cannot marry Maman or *Mémé*, they are too old for him. And I am too little."

Chantal returned her stare. "Where are you getting all this from? How do you know Yves wants to marry into your family?"

Lysette twirled a leaf in one hand. "Everybody knows he wants it. Because that is the only way he can become head of our family, and lead us. Besides, why else would he be courting you?"

The question as posed was unflattering, but there was no malice in it. The little girl's face was open and guileless. Chantal could not doubt Lysette was speaking the truth, or something that she sincerely believed. It was not the sort of thing a child her age would invent. As for that comment about "head of the family" and "leading", it seemed oddly archaic. Wasn't Quebec a modern society like the rest of Canada, with full equality for women? Why should the Boisverts need a man to "lead" them? "I thought Grandmère Thérèse was head of our family," she said.

"Only back when our Grandpère was alive. They were the heads, together. But now he is gone, and always a man *and* a woman must head the family. Not just one or the other. *Vous savez?*" Again Lysette spoke as if explaining something to a much younger child.

Chantal was still struggling to make sense of this when the little girl suddenly sprang up, tossing her leaves aside, and waved. "Look, there he is! And Jules is with him."

From out of the depths of the forest two figures appeared: the Lapierre brothers. Each was carrying over his shoulder a brace of fresh-killed rabbits, hind feet tied and heads hanging. Lysette's face fell at the sight of the dangling prey. *"Oh, les pauvres lapins!* They were so pretty, so furry and soft, and now – "

131

Yves grinned. "Little hypocrite! You know you will eat them for supper tonight like everybody else, and bawl if you don't get your share." He tousled her curly hair, and smiled at Chantal. "Have you ever had wild rabbit? No? Well, you are in for a treat."

She looked the two men over in puzzlement. Neither one carried a gun. Perhaps they had used snares? She could not help feeling a little squeamish at the sight of the rabbits: they looked somewhat torn and mangled and blood stained their fur. But no doubt when they were cooked – over an open fire, yet – they would be much more appealing.

"Take these in, Jules," Yves said, tossing his catch to his brother. "I'll come give you a hand with the cleaning later."

"No need." Thérèse had appeared in the doorway, a benign smile on her face. "Genevieve can help him. Why don't you take Chantal for a walk, Yves, and show her the woods?"

"I want to go too," said Lysette.

Thérèse took her granddaughter by the shoulder in a gentle but firm grip, and steered her back inside. "Not this time, *ma petite.* Come inside and keep your old Grandmère company."

It was rather obvious, Chantal thought, that she and Yves were being thrown together. As they set out on their walk she was not quite sure whether to feel flattered or manipulated. Lysette's naïve confidences, true or not, filled her with a deep unease.

132

## 10

There was no path. They walked through the undergrowth, over a floor of fallen leaves as brilliant in hue as any oriental carpet. It crunched and rustled underfoot, giving off a sweetly pungent scent that went to her head like wine. The autumn breeze was cool, the sun on her back pleasantly warm; Chantal was reminded of country hikes with friends back in Vermont. She had already begun to miss autumn during her first week in evergreen Los Angeles: the chill air that seemed to cleanse and invigorate her lungs with every breath, its poignant sting of frost that hinted of winter to come. She loved that time of year when the sadness of summer's decay gave way to a new beauty; when the trees incandesced, the fiery reds and golds of their leaves rivaling the vanished wildflowers. As sunlight pierced the thinning canopy and fallen leaves brightened the forest floor the dim green caverns of summer transformed into light and airy chambers. Then you could walk through colonnades of birches, silver-pillared and golden-roofed; through red rooms of sumac and maple woods vaulted with amber.

A squirrel scolded them as they passed a centuries-old oak, secure and confident as any baron on his fortified tower. At the familiar sound Chantal smiled. This was, she thought, a place where she could belong... one she could call home. And then she recalled that Thérèse had used that very word. *At home.* Had this just been thoughtfulness on her Grandmère's part, or was she trying to make Chantal feel at ease for another reason? It felt a little bit like being seduced – which would be all right if it were being done for the sake of love, but what if it were something else? Some kind of secretive manipulation...

When Yves took her hand she started, and almost withdrew it, but he winked at her. "The footing is a little difficult here," he explained, tightening his grip. They scrambled down into a little gulley and hopped across a stony stream. Down here the fallen maple leaves were piled so thick that they waded through them as if through water. Out of the golden ankle-deep drifts there rose great shoulders of grey granite, thrusting up from the earth.

"Here we are," Yves said when they reached the far side, where a massive cliff-wall of solid rock confronted them. But he did not release her hand.

She should have been pleased, flattered. Wasn't this exactly what she wanted? She'd given up on her fantasy of true love. All she wished for now was to feel a boy's arms around her again, to know the comfort of closeness. She felt a physical attraction to Yves and clearly he felt the same about her. Wasn't that enough? But instead of moving closer to him she kept on talking, as if building a barrier of words between them. "You Québecois really love your country, don't you?" she babbled.

"*Mais bien sûr.* It's a fact that our ancestors were the first to call themselves *Canadiens*. The English did not use the word until much later." He led her to a natural shelf of rock, and they sat down. He let go of her hand, but put his arm around her shoulders. That started her talking again.

"That reminds me: are my family separatists or federalists?" she asked. "I guess I should know, before I go putting my foot in my mouth."

"The Boisverts are neither. They are proud of their heritage, but they are not interested in politics." He moved closer to her, and put his other hand on her knee. If only she had not heard Lysette's foolish remarks!

They had her questioning the motives of everyone, Yves especially.

"And – you?" she asked. "Do you think Quebec should secede, or stay part of Canada?"

He said nothing for a moment. Then he pointed to the grey rock face. "That is Laurentian rock, four billion years old. There are no fossils in it because it is older than life itself. Some call this a 'young' country, but that's only in terms of its human history. The land itself is very ancient – older, perhaps, than any other part of the planet's surface. We can claim this land, name it, fight over it, but the fact remains that it was here long before any of us. And it will be here long after all of us are gone."

She shuddered a little. "That sounds like something your brother would say – or paint."

"Oh, you mustn't mind Jules! He is gifted, yes, but he thinks too much – more than is really good for him, you know? Anyway, enough of him." His voice changed, becoming low and husky. "Tell me what you think of Quebec, Chantal. Do you think you could stay here? Make it your home?"

Yves leaned in towards her as he spoke. There was no mistaking his intent, and she told herself sternly to stop being foolish. What was wrong with being wanted by somebody? Hadn't she yearned for this her entire life? She made herself sit still and smile at him encouragingly. He smiled back. With one hand he reached out and stroked her cheek, while with the other he cupped the back of her head, gently but firmly bringing her face up to his. She closed her eyes as his mouth met hers, reveling in the warm moist pressure of his lips. With her eyes shut she seemed to feel everything more, every nerve coming to life in her skin. *Yes – he's a better kisser than Russell. Way better...* His hands shifted to either side of her head, fingers lightly stroking her hair, then kneading the sensitive muscles of her neck behind her ears – moving on down to her shoulders, still massaging, and down again...

She shifted in response to his caresses, moving closer to him, and as she did so her eyelids fluttered open. His eyes too were open, and something about the look in them gave her pause. There was neither warmth nor softness in their pale amber gaze; they were steady, intense, and – it suddenly seemed to her – calculating. She pulled back sharply, breaking his hold on her.

"What's wrong?" he asked, frowning.

She wondered if she imagined a trace of impatience in his voice, and she took a deep breath before answering. "I'm sorry, Yves, but – everything's so new and strange to me. I'm still adjusting to it all. I'm not really ready for... for..."

"Whatever you like." He shrugged, feigning indifference, but this time she was sure she saw irritation in his eyes as he pulled away from her.

They rose and walked back through the woods in near-silence, and she was relieved when they drew close to the cottage. As always when she was uncomfortable she could feel her shoulders hunching up and her head drooping, as her tall lean body tried to make itself less conspicuous. She was unable to meet his eyes, and cast her gaze down at her feet instead. And so it was that she noticed the tracks, imprinted in the soil of the front yard: great prints of broad pads and clawed toes, like a dog's only larger.

Much larger. She halted, staring down at them.

"So close!" she gasped. "No wonder I heard them in the night."

"What's that?" Yves stared at her.

She pointed at the paw-prints. "The wolves – do they always come this close to the house?"

He shrugged again, but said nothing in reply.  She followed him into the cottage, equally silent.

As the day progressed the feeling of tension inside the cottage increased.  It was harder to persuade herself that it was just her imagination: the air felt as charged as the atmosphere before a thunderstorm.  Yves seemed to avoid her company.  He and Thérèse exchanged many looks and whispered words, while Genevieve was visibly nervous, dropping things and wringing her hands continually.  Jules ignored Chantal too, but that at least was perfectly normal for him.  He paid no attention to anyone, but sat in a corner by himself, busily attaching a hanger to the back of a painting. Executed in dark and gloomy acrylics, it depicted a landscape with pillared ruins like those of ancient Greece; only when she moved closer did Chantal recognize the shattered remnants of St Jacques Street, the grand façades of Montreal's once-mighty banks and businesses reduced to crumbled fragments. Trees surrounded them, ivy twined round broken pillars in an ironic echo of their carved stone foliage, and in the middle of the grass-grown street there stood a pack of black-furred wolves. It was a sinister work, yet also oddly compelling and brilliantly conceived: the wolves seemed to stare straight out of the painting at the viewer, a look of challenge in their luminous yellow eyes. This former hub of human power was now the animals' rightful territory, while the viewer was made to feel like an unwanted – and endangered – trespasser. Chantal could scarcely tear her eyes from the canvas.

Taped to the front of the wooden frame was a small paper label, evidently the title of the piece. "What does that mean: *'Arcadie'?"* Chantal asked, fascinated despite herself.  But Jules merely scowled at her and went on working on the back of the frame.

137

Dinner was delicious, as Yves had promised, the roasted rabbits tender and savoury, but Chantal could not really enjoy any of it. The meal was full of awkward silences. As soon as dinner was over Francine strode from the room and slammed her door. Even Lysette seemed at last to sense that something was wrong: she stopped hovering and chattering around the adults, and went and lay down on the grizzly bear rug, patting its head and pretending to talk into its ears.

Chantal also retreated, sitting on the couch and pretending to read a stack of old magazines. She could not help reliving in memory that scene with Yves in the forest, and puzzling over her own reaction to it. She had not in the least minded being kissed; for a fleeting moment she had truly enjoyed it. But it had left her with an uneasy feeling, a lingering aftertaste of – what? She struggled to sort out her feelings. There was guilt, perhaps, for using Yves in an attempt to rebound from Russell. Had she imagined that Yves might be using her in turn as a sort of self-defense, a way to appease her own guilty conscience? *No, that's not it,* she thought. *I don't think I imagined that look in his eyes. The guy's not in love with me. So why do I feel so bad?*

More than anything, she was uncomfortably reminded of an occasion this past summer when Nana had caught her and Russell kissing deeply and passionately under the big elm tree in the backyard. "Like a couple of dogs in a hedge. You're a bit young for such goings-on," Nana said to her after Russ had left in a hurry. "Must be the French in you coming out."

Chantal had taken refuge in insolence. "What else is there to do around here?" she retorted, waving a disparaging hand at the sparse scattering of houses in the surrounding fields.

"Plenty. You don't have to make yourself cheap."

Chantal rolled her eyes. "Things have changed, Nana. This stuff isn't such a big deal nowadays," she said, words and tone relegating her grandmother to a primordial past. "And anyway Russ loves me. He told me so."

"Did he now? And you believed him? That's what they all say, girl. They'll say anything to get what they want." Nana was looking at her with a kind of sardonic amusement. "You think the boys were any different in my day? There were always some who figured if they paid for your dinner they'd bought *you*, too. But we always told 'em where to go if they got fresh. That's the only difference between your generation and mine, missy – *we* were too proud to let ourselves be used."

Chantal had made no reply to this. But she never forgot it either. Russell had never gotten any farther than kissing – and remembering her later humiliation at the fraternity party she was now grateful for that. *At least I got out of that business with my self-respect intact,* she conceded to herself, and added grudgingly: *Thanks to Nana.*

The memory raised another disagreeable thought. Was Francine's love for Yves really just an unrequited teen crush? Or had Yves by any chance led the girl on, underage as she was – given her false hope? Was he another Russell? Worse still, had Lysette been correct about his wanting to marry into the wealthy Boisvert clan, and was Chantal now replacing Francine as his formal ticket of admission into the family? Had his apparent annoyance in the woods been merely the result of a bruised ego – or the anger of one whose well-laid scheme has gone unexpectedly awry? But at that point she rebelled against her own thoughts. She was being ridiculous, she told herself; her imagination did not usually run to such Gothic fantasies. Nana's slurs against her heritage notwithstanding, she had always been a practical, down-to-earth kind of person.

She longed to go for a walk and clear her head, but she was afraid to go alone into the pathless forest with night coming on. She might get lost; and there were the paw-prints too, a reminder that this was no tame stretch of rural woodland but a teeming and dangerous wilderness. In addition to wolves, there were bears in the vicinity. Black bears, not as large and deadly as their West Coast cousins, but still perfectly capable of killing a lone human hiker – especially a young woman, groping and stumbling through unfamiliar surroundings in the dark... No, it was not worth the risk.

Chantal withdrew to her room instead. For a long time she sat gazing listlessly out of the window. As evening came on the grey twilight under the trees thickened like mist, and an almost menacing stillness descended. With all the birds flown south or roosting for the night, crickets and tree-frogs banished by the frost, and fewer leaves to make a silken rustle in the breeze, the forest was voiceless, sullen, withdrawn into itself. The spaces between the tree-trunks grew darker, until they gaped black as cave-mouths, no longer disclosing their depths. Soon the whole mass of the woods had become a single looming shadow. She recalled suddenly that in French the term for wild forest was *"la forêt sauvage"*. A savage place... In its depths furtive things would be stirring now: night creatures crawling out of holes and lairs, creeping or fluttering, darting or stalking. At the thought Chantal felt the stirrings of a new and very different terror, a kind of primal dread. She recalled her dream of the night before, in which she had seemed to run free and unafraid through those very groves. But that had been a fantasy in which she wore an animal's form instead of her own. No human being could move through a forest without fear once the sun had set. Out of that living darkness humanity's earliest ancestors had fled; later they had learnt to fend it off with fire, and with walls of wattle and mud. It belonged not to them, but to the fanged things that lurked within its shadows: the reason that her species feared the dark.

She jumped, startled out of her contemplation by a voice behind her. "Here's your *tisane,* my dear," said Thérèse.

Chantal fought to compose herself. "Thank you," she said, accepting the mug.

"I hope it will help you to sleep tonight," said her grandmother. "A pity it did not work last night, but perhaps you did not drink it all?"

"No, I guess I didn't finish the whole thing," admitted Chantal.

Thérèse said nothing, but she lingered at the door. Did she want to make sure her granddaughter drank the draught? "Is there something wrong, Grandmère?" Chantal asked, still cradling the mug in her hands.

"No. That is… I am just afraid it is a little dull for you here, after all," said Thérèse. "Tomorrow perhaps Yves can take you for a proper hike, and show you the Parc National du Tremblant?"

Alone with Yves, in a vast trackless forest… Was this another set-up, a way to force intimacy on him and her? Whether it was or not, she didn't care for the idea at all. "Oh, I don't want to put him to any trouble."

"No, he has offered to do it. He is very taken with you, my dear. I think the two of you are going to be good friends."

Was there something of a command in that last sentence? "I'm sure we are," Chantal replied, keeping her own voice neutral.

"Do drink up your tea, dear, it doesn't work as well if it's cold," said Thérèse.

"Yes. Yes, I will. Well, good night, Grandmère," said Chantal. She too could turn a statement into an order, she thought.

As soon as Thérèse had retreated, Chantal opened the window and emptied the contents of the mug into the grass. There was no way to know if the concoction had caused her bad dream the night before, but she was taking no chances. Whatever was in the drink was probably quite potent and could have given her a bad reaction, and she needed a proper rest tonight in order to sort out her thoughts.

But try as she might, she could not relax. She kept tossing and turning, restive as a ship on a storm-lashed sea. Lysette's unsettling confidences; the quick flash of anger in Yves's pale amber eyes; Thérèse's subtle manipulations – all the things that could be dismissed by daylight as her own imagination seemed more compelling when she was alone in the dark.

When at last she slipped into a shallow doze, it was only to be awakened once more by a noise.

It was not the howling of wolves that disturbed her this time, but the sound of footsteps inside the house. She lay listening for a moment, her heart beating unaccountably fast. It was one of the boys, no doubt, going late to bed. Or someone getting up to go to the outhouse. The luminous face of her wristwatch told her it was 1 AM. She laid her head down on the pillow again.

Then she heard the voices.

Just whispers, with the hissing sibilants dominating as they do when voices are purposely lowered. Again she could not say why this unnerved her. Of course people talking late at night would whisper, so as not to disturb others. There was nothing sinister about that, nothing at all...

And then her door began to creak open.

Her heart skipped a beat. She felt it, the stumbling contraction followed by a breathless pause before the next heartbeat. Her whole body went rigid under the bedclothes, but she dared not open her eyes.

*"Rien!"* whispered a voice.

*Rien:* that meant *Nothing.* But what did the speaker mean by that? She wondered if she imagined a tone of disappointment in the whispered comment. And whose voice was it? It sounded like one of the women. Thérèse or Genevieve?

The door closed and the footsteps retreated. She sat up in bed. What on earth was going on? She could hear two sets of footsteps at least, walking down the hall – softly, so as not to wait those sleeping. Or... was there something sly and furtive about those faint creaking treads? As of people moving with caution, in the hope of avoiding notice?

She heard the front door open and close, and voices talking outside. At one in the morning! Suddenly she could not bear it any longer. Her overworked brain would not be still. What were they doing out there, stargazing? Or was there some emergency – sickness, prowlers, fire? She leaped up, and scuffed on her shoes and flung her jacket on over her T-shirt and pajama pants. Then she went to the door – without lighting the lamp, so as not to dazzle her eyes – and easing it open, she slipped out of the room.

The first thing she noticed was that all the bedroom doors were wide open: Thérèse's, Genevieve's, both the Lapierres', and the one the girls shared. She peered into that one and saw Lysette curled up in bed with her doll, fast asleep. But Francine's bed was empty. So were the other beds in all the other rooms. Her heart was pounding now. If it really were an emergency they would not have left Lysette asleep alone, and their guest too. So what was the matter?

143

When she entered the main room *Tante* Genevieve was there, sitting next to the one lit lamp. At the sight of Chantal she gave a violent start and put a hand to her breast.

"What's going on?" demanded Chantal. "I heard voices." She could still hear them, murmuring outside. At least three, perhaps four people talking together in the front yard.

Her aunt turned so pale that for a moment Chantal thought she would faint. She said nothing by way of reply, but stood up and made feeble shooing gestures with her hands as Chantal strode towards the front door. "No, no! You mustn't go out there!"

"Why not?" Chantal demanded. Her alarm and increasing mystification made her irritable. The voices outside had ceased.

"You *can't!*" It was almost a wail. Genevieve tried to block the door, but Chantal shoved her aside and ran into the front yard.

There was no one there. But in the darkness the light from the open doorway reflected back from multiple sets of eyes, glowing like living flame. The four enormous wolves in the yard turned their heads and stared straight at her.

## 11

"The Greenwoods are in their summer lair," the *rugaru* had said. "South of here, in the forest near the Trembling Mountain."

"Then that is where we must go," Josephine replied.

They went in human form, in human vehicles, because the distance was so great – not too great for the wheeled machines to travel, however. These made what would have been a journey of days on wolf-foot into one night's ride. Hunter was puzzled by their quest, and the fact that it was taking him and Josephine off their planned route. If these human "packs" were so dangerous and defensive of their lairs and family members, surely it was a mistake to confront them? And what was the point? None of them knew this young human female, they had never even met her. She was not their kin. But for some reason they were willing to risk all to intervene in her pack's plans for her.

"You will understand one day," was all Josephine would say to him.

At last the vehicles halted. The *rugaru* jumped out and stripped off their clothing before taking lupine form. The night was dark and still, with no man-made lights showing anywhere and no traffic on the road. "This is a wilderness area," said Josephine. "The humans have set this forest aside, reserved it for the use of beasts and birds." He wondered why they would do such a thing. Had not the Stone pack wolves said that humans always destroyed wilderness?

The tawny-brown wolf who was called Jean-Louis turned to look at Josephine. "Did you hear that?" The whole pack of transformed *rugaru* raised their heads, wolf-ears pricked. They all heard the noise: the sound of wolves' cries carrying through the clear autumn night. The voices of wolves are as distinctive and individual as those of human beings. These members of the other pack were saying to each other as they raced through the thick dark forest: *"This is I, here I am!"*

"It is the Stone brothers, and the Greenwoods," said Josephine listening.

"They're hunting," said Jean-Louis. "Do you hear? One just said to the other, *There she goes, follow her!"*

"She?" repeated Josephine, her tone sharp.

"They're coming closer," said another wolf.

"Then move towards them! Cut them off!"

"Is that wise?" said Hunter. He remembered the viciousness of the wolf-brothers on the Stone Plain, the older one in particular. "They're in full cry after whatever it is. They will be angry if they're thwarted of their prey – "

"Not prey, Hunter. *She,"* muttered Josephine again. "The young female, it must be…"

She broke into a loping run, and they all ran to keep up with her. They burst into a glade, wide and open under the stars. They were just in time to see a pale figure emerge from the dark beneath the trees. It was a human form, female. She did not see them. She had run so hard she had cast off one of her shoes, and as they watched she tore off the other and attempted to run on in her bare feet. But she tripped on something and fell to her hands and knees. The pursuing wolves burst from the wood. He saw a grey-muzzled she-wolf at their head, another younger female, and then with a raising of his hackles he recognized the two brother wolves from the Stone Plain. The woman cowered as the pack encircled her, and she screamed – a scream that became an unnatural rasping howl. She tore at the outer layer of her clothing, ripped it away with hands that changed their shape even as she raised them. She was turning into a wolf and she was not yet out of her clothes. She whirled, rending the fabric that enclosed her into strips

146

with her teeth and claws. It fell away and she struggled free of the tattered remnants as her form changed completely from woman to wolf.

The pack did not attack her. They merely stood confronting her with bared teeth and menacing glares. She spun about, snarling and snapping at each of her tormentors in turn. At last she made an opening by lunging at the youngest wolf, knocking it over on its side. She fled through the gap, heading for the wood. But like a very young pup unaccustomed to running she stumbled, tripping over her own paws, and almost fell. The pack watched her awkward, lurching flight across the meadow. They followed her, this time at a more leisurely pace, confident that she could not escape.

Josephine growled. "You see?" she said to Hunter. "Their work is done. They woke the wolf in her by force of fear, threatening her until she had to defend herself by transforming. There is a potion they administer that puts the human half to sleep, and wakes the wolf. But sometimes it is not quite strong enough, if the wolf is buried deep. Then they do this instead: terrify the human until the old instinct awakens, and she or he reverts to wolf form. This poor child probably does not understand what is happening to her. Such a wicked, cruel custom!"

Josephine ran after the pack, and after a brief hesitation Hunter followed her. The Stone and Greenwood wolves scented them, and turned and closed ranks at Josephine's approach.

"You!" snarled the elder, silver-muzzled female. "What are you doing here?"

"This is not your territory," retorted Josephine. "This is the free forest of the Trembling Mountain. Why should I not be here? And since I am, I would like to know what you are doing to that poor girl."

"She is one of ours, a Greenwood," returned the matriarch. "What we do with our own is none of your affair. This is pack business. Go back to your wilderness, lone wolf."

Josephine's friends now drew up and quiet as shadows made a semi-circle around her. "Not as 'lone' as you think," she said. "And if you harm any human you make it our business."

The Stone wolves had spotted Hunter in the midst of the group. The elder brother stalked towards him. "You! So you have come here, to our lands? You stupid brute, I promised I would kill you if I ever saw you again."

Hunter met his gaze steadily. "On your territory, you said. This is not your land, and I have broken no law."

"Oh, haven't you? It was you in the film, wasn't it?"

"In the what?" said Hunter, bewildered.

"The film that was made by the men."

His brother joined in: "Fool! Being seen by humans is bad enough, but to let yourself be filmed – ! For that alone you should be killed. Why do you think high-wolves are forbidden to go near humans? You broke the rules, and now men know for a fact that we exist. What secret will you betray to them next? That we are shape-changers, and walk in their midst?"

"Not if we put an end to him first." The larger wolf glared at Hunter. "It was you who broke into the men's tent that night, and alerted them to our presence – wasn't it?" His lips drew up to show his front teeth – the curved fangs made for slashing and tearing.

Hunter backed up, completely baffled now. "How? How could you know these things?"

"So you admit it!" raged the other. "It *was* you!"

The lean black wolf went to stand beside his brother. "If this is true, then you owe us your blood in exchange for our father's," he threatened.

They both advanced on him. With an effort, Hunter held his ground this time and offered no submission. "It was your pack that killed my father and mother," he returned, "so you owe me a blood-debt, too. All they did was stray onto your land – "

"Then they deserved to die," snarled the bigger he-wolf. "That is the penalty for trespass under the high-wolf law. But my father walked as a man, and a man's killing must be avenged..."

His voice faded as he looked around him. Josephine and her friends had slowly fanned out to surround the Stone brothers, and the Greenwoods too. Seeing that they were outnumbered, they clumped together. The youngest wolf whined and leaned against her grand-dam's flank. The old she-wolf's eyes smouldered, but she could do nothing.

"Go!" said Josephine. "There'll be no fighting tonight – as long as you go quietly."

"We will remember this," grunted the old wolf as she turned away, the young female cowering at her side.

"So will we," Josephine replied, undaunted.

The Greenwood wolves and the two Stone brothers fled back into the forest and were swallowed up in its shadows. Only the newly-transformed female wolf remained, but she was lying on her side in the field and her eyes were half-shut. Her flank heaved, so she must be alive, but she did not move or react even when they went right up to her and nudged her with their noses. Hunter thought her eye flickered briefly as he gazed into it, but her breathing was slow and shallow.

Josephine looked at Jean-Louis. "She is in shock. I have seen this before, in wild animals. When they are in a state of extreme terror and stress, they do this: shut themselves off from the world. Sometimes they never wake again."

"What can we do?" said Jean-Louis.

"There is another safe house near here, yes? We will take her there, and see what we can do for her."

Two of the biggest male *rugaru* took their human forms, and making a cradle of their arms they gently lifted the limp body of the catatonic wolf and carried her back towards the road where their vehicles waited. They placed her inside the van. Hunter jumped in too, and stood beside the she-wolf. He put his paw upon her flank, feeling her breath, her heartbeats: they were weak, the tenuous rhythms of a fading life. He had felt this once before, as he had lain at the side of his dying sister upon the blood-stained tundra. Then, as now, the life-signs seemed to throb within his own body, mingling and blending into it as though she and he had become one creature. He drew away, at once intrigued and disturbed.

Josephine watched him. "What do you feel, pup?"

"I feel... her weakness. I feel ... Do you remember what I told you about the little caribou calf?"

"You looked into its eye as it was dying, and felt for an instant what it felt."

"And that time when I lay half asleep in the tundra and imagined I had become a lemming... I was almost afraid – as if I somehow wasn't *myself* anymore. It was as if I were dying, dissolving away to become part of everything, ceasing to be *me*. But I'm still myself."

"Of course you are. Look at me, pup, with my two bodies. Am I not always *me,* no matter what shape I walk in?" He inclined his head in assent. She continued: "Some *rugaru* blame their wolf-forms for the evil that they do, but the truth is that they are evil when they are in human form, too. Were you to change your form all of a sudden and become human, you would still be yourself, Hunter my friend. The inner self does not change."

"So what does it mean, then, when we look at another creature and feel we have become that creature? Is that not the inner self changing?"

"Not changing completely, merely growing. What you feel is empathy, compassion. But of course, you do not know these *rugaru* words, do you? They are words for a kind of love, Hunter: a love that knows no limits. A wolf loves his pack, his dam, his brothers and sisters, his mate. A human feels all of these loves, but does not stop there. We are taught to love and respect all humans, even all animals. Of course it is a tall order, and not all of us can do it. But no wild animal could ever even imagine such a love. Animal bonds are only of blood, desire, or convenience. Humans have compassion. Many of us have come to believe that there should be no more suffering in the world than is necessary. When my friends trap, I urge them to use methods that are humane. Would a bear, or a lynx – or a low-wolf – worry about such a thing?"

Hunter looked down at the still grey-brown form lying between them. "Then that is what you feel for this young female – compassion? Even though she is a Greenwood, and no kin of yours? A member of an enemy pack, in fact?"

"Yes," she said simply.

So like him, this young female *rugaru* had lost both parents to the savagery of wolf-kind, and then sought out the pack of her blood-kin only to be cruelly used by them. "I think I feel it, too. For she is no kin of mine either, not even a true wolf, and yet ... I do not wish to see her die."

Josephine touched her nose to his. "You are growing wise, pup. Too wise for a wolf. You cannot live as a beast in the wilderness when you think such things. That is the trouble with wisdom: once you've got it, you can never be rid of it."

151

"Then how much wiser might I become, were I able to live for tens of tens of years like a human!" Hunter said.

She looked at him, her gaze intent. "There is someone you should meet, pup. An old friend of mine. I think I must introduce you to him, when we go to the country of men. But for now, we have this poor creature to care for. She *must* live. If she perishes now her body will remain in wolf form, and we won't be able return it to her family. They will never know what became of her: to them, it will be as if she vanished from the Earth. And she is so young – only eighteen."

Hunter looked down at the she-wolf, filled with awe to think that she was so old – twice the average lifespan of a high-wolf. And yet in human terms she was still considered young. It was a wonderful gift, this enormously extended life expectancy. It should not be taken away from her.

*It should not be taken away from her.*

Again he felt that curious sensation, as of thought seeking to shape reality. Slowly and gently Hunter lay down next to the unconscious wolf and rested his head upon her heaving flank. If only his own strength could somehow pass into this failing body! "Do not be afraid," he said to her softly.

Once more he thought her eyelid fluttered slightly, but in the poor light he could not be sure. He moved his muzzle closer to her ear.

"You are safe with us. Hear me," he urged. "We will not let you die."

## 12

Chantal came back to herself slowly. Waking seemed an act of will, a slow reassembling of her sleep-fragmented self. She'd been having a dream – a bad dream, about being pursued through the woods by wolves. Yet another rousing from yet another nightmare, she thought. But was it truly over? As her eyes opened she saw bared fangs surrounding her still, and eyes that glimmered coldly through the dark.

She gasped and struggled to rise, and as she did so her bleary vision refocused. The animals were still there, and real; but they were lifeless and harmless. A coyote's teeth snarled at her from its dead mouth, its hide flat and empty on the floor behind it. Shaggy pelts of bear, fox and lynx were piled on some rough furnishings and hanging on the wooden walls, along with snowshoes and other outdoor gear. The eyes that had seemed to gaze at her were glass, given the illusion of life by the sole source of light in the strange room: the flickering glow of fire. Flames burned on a primitive stone hearth and candles were everywhere, from small tapers to votive candles in glass holders adorned with the Virgin and other Catholic saints. A smaller fire burned in a brazier set up on the floor. In front of it, seated upon a fur pelt, was a woman swathed in a patterned shawl. She had long, draggled, greying black hair; her skin was weathered and brownish, with fine wrinkles raying from the corners of her eyes, which were deep-set and dark. The firelight cast strong shadows in her face, highlighting her prominent nose and high cheekbones.

Chantal sat up. Looking down, she saw that she was clad in an unfamiliar flannel nightgown at least a size too large for her. The blankets of the bed in which she had lain were worn and threadbare. It had apparently served as a dog's bed too in the not-so-distant past: the blankets smelled rank and were covered in loose brown hairs.

"Where am I?" she rasped. "How did I get here?"

The woman answered with a question of her own. "Do you remember what happened?"

"I..." Chantal frowned. "I thought I was dreaming, but now I'm not sure. I think it really happened... I ran into some wolves. I was outside looking for my family, but they weren't there, just this pack of huge wolves standing and staring at me. I – I was terrified. They got between me and the cottage. I could hear Genevieve – my aunt – screaming, and I tried to get into the SUV but it was locked. So I ran towards the road..." Dirt and stones flying under her feet, her heart pounding in time to her strides, the gaping darkness under the trees, the howls of her pursuers ... "There was no traffic, no one to flag down and ask for help. No houses anywhere near. I knew there wouldn't be. I was just running in a panic, not thinking at all. And they – the wolves – kept chasing me." Driving her, like sheep dogs with a sheep, forcing her off the road and into the forest... Fangs snapping at her legs, steamy breath hot on her skin, dark furred forms blocking off all escape routes but one: the one that led into the darkness... "They do that, don't they – herd their prey, hunting together in a team? I was in the dark then, among the trees. I kept bumping into things, I couldn't see where to go. But I could hear the wolves: the howling, the panting. They were all around me then, and I – " She broke off.

"And then – ?" the woman prompted.

Screaming, twisting, tearing at her own clothing, to pull it off and free herself – free the fanged and savage self confined inside the cloth. To fight her attackers as wolf against wolf... No, that part was clearly a dream.

154

But what *had* happened to her then? All she remembered after that was another wolf appearing, confronting those that pursued her: a white wolf, fur like snow under the moon, blue eyes that gazed steadily into her own – not with hostility, but comfort and reassurance. The white wolf stood over her protectively as she lay helpless on the ground…

No, wait: that last part couldn't be real. It was just a displaced memory. The white Monster wolf, from the Redpath video…

"I guess – I must have fainted," she said at last. "It's all kind of a blur. How did I get here – wherever here is? And who are you?"

"My name is Josephine Legris."

"I'm Chantal Boisvert."

"I know that, love."

"What – ? How could you know my name? I don't have any ID on me – "

"I will explain. But first, to answer your other question: this is a place that my trapper friends use when they're up here in the north, for storing skins. It's just a little cabin, no water or electricity I'm afraid. A group of us were out walking in the Parc National du Tremblant, and we found you lying on the ground, uninjured but out cold. So we carried you here. No doctor to take you to. I'm glad you're awake at last. You were unconscious for nearly two whole days."

"Days!" she cried. "But then I – uhh, what are you doing?"

The woman was pouring handfuls of something into the fire. "This is a smudging ceremony. I burn sweetgrass and sage for spiritual cleansing, to drive away evil influences." As the thick pungent smoke coiled up from the bowl the woman fanned it with a large white feather, sending it towards Chantal, who coughed and backed away.

155

"You're Native American then?" she asked, flapping at the smoke with one hand. "I mean, Native Canadian?"

"I'm part Cree and part French Canadian. They would call me a half-breed, in the olden days. Very rude. My people's own word for ourselves is *Métis* – that is French for 'mixed'. A much more accurate term. I am not half-and-half, you see, with a line down my middle! My heritages are mixed together, blended: like coffee and cream. Once they're stirred together, who can say which is coffee and which is cream? It's all one thing. And so I am Aboriginal and French, a good Catholic who prays to the Holy Virgin but also respects the spirits in the wild places." She gave a secretive smile. "And I am – other things, as well. Oh, I'm very mixed-up, *moi!"*

"But how did you know my name?"

"Your family is well-known around here. We heard about your return, Chantal; and you have a strong resemblance to the Boisverts."

"Then you know I have to go back to them. They'll be worried, out looking for me – "

The woman shook her head vehemently. "No! Do not go back to them. The Boisverts are bad people. Our finding you wasn't altogether an accident, you see. We came here on purpose to look for you. To protect you from them."

Again she had that feeling of lurking menace. She swallowed. "Why? Are they criminals? My family?"

"They do… bad things. Not necessarily criminal, but still bad."

"Well, I think they may have drugged me. They gave me some kind of herbal drink that first night, at bedtime, and – "

"And you had dreams afterwards?" The woman nodded, a knowing expression on her face.

"That's right. Are they into illegal drugs, then? Is that it?" She remembered the strange taste of the drink; also Jules's distended pupils and strange behaviour. "Please, tell me!"

Josephine appeared to hesitate, as if on the verge of making some important disclosure. Then she shook her head. "No, not now," she said. "You must leave this place, tonight. Have nothing more to do with the Boisverts, they are not good people. Go and see Honoré Dubois instead. You've heard of him?"

"I – I've met him. Once."

"He's a good man, Honoré; you can trust him with your life. He was very fond of your father, and a great support when Édouard was on the outs with his family. Do go visit him; you'll be glad that you did."

"Thanks, but the only place I want to go now is home. Only they've got all my stuff – and my car's back at their place in Montreal…" Awareness of her solitude and helplessness struck Chantal with the force of a physical blow, threatening to overwhelm her.

"I will lend you whatever you may need: money, clothes. I will drive you to Montreal in my van. You can fetch your car and return home." The dark eyes dwelled on her, thoughtful and intent. "But you may not be safe from them even there. I am worried about you, Chantal."

Since the van had an enclosed rear section, Hunter could not see where they were going. Inside the dark metal box he lay, sensing the curves of the road they followed (a road far smoother than those of the north, so that he felt not a bump nor a jolt) and the increasing noise of traffic all around him. There were many more vehicles in the country of men, it seemed from the continuous roar.

He fell asleep at last, only to be awakened some time later – not by a noise, but rather by its absence. The van had stopped. He heard voices outside, and then the sound of another vehicle's engine starting up and fading away. The van began to move again. He sensed the ground sloping steeply upwards; then it leveled out again, and after a while the vehicle stopped once more. The back of the van was opened up, and he saw Josephine standing there. She jumped into the back with him, divested herself of her clothing, and took her lupine shape.

"She is gone, the young Greenwood female," Josephine told him.

"Will she be safe?" he asked.

"For now. At least she lives. But she does not understand what happened to her in Tremblant. She believes it was only a dream, and if I say otherwise she will only think I am mad. So she is still in danger, because she won't be on her guard."

He jumped down and looked around him. They had come to a place where there were trees and grassy lawns but no houses anywhere to be seen. "We are safe to run free here?" he asked.

"We should be. It is very late," said Josephine. "Humans are day-creatures, and not many live on this part of the mountain-top. No one is around to see us. We must go up to the park, to Beaver Lake. It is a lake that was made by men."

"Humans can *make* lakes?" Hunter was amazed. "Did they make the beavers also?"

She laughed. "There are no beavers there, it's just a name. Humans like to be reminded of the natural world even though they have left it behind. Anyway, my friend is there waiting for me – and for you."

"Who is this friend? Another *rugaru?*"

158

"Yes, but like you he was born a wolf. As a high-wolf he dwelt once in the wild woods north of here, but he learned over time to become a man. Or as he would say, to find the man that was concealed inside of him."

There were many small structures of stone here, solid and most no higher than a wolf's head. They were clearly man-made, not natural. Hunter asked what they were.

"These stones mark the place where a dead human lies," said Josephine as Hunter sniffed at one in puzzlement. "They bury their dead in the earth, and then mark the place so they can return to it."

"Return? Why?" Hunter could never endure to revisit the place where his sister and brother died. It still was full of pain and horror for him.

"Because they have hope," said Josephine. "They remember their lost ones with sorrow, but also many of them believe that death is but a passage, like being born. That though the body fails, the spirit goes on into eternity."

"Spirit?" queried the wolf.

"Ah, so many things to explain! It is the belief of many humans, pup, that there is an invisible world beyond this one, everlasting as this is transitory. One of the tribal Elders explained it to me this way: he said that the other world intrudes into this one in the forms of living things: beasts, humans, plants. When their mortal part dies, the spirits return to where they came from." She looked up at a stone: atop it reared the carved shape of a human with the wings of a bird. "And there are other spirits that never take bodily form, but dwell unseen in earth and water and air, watching over our world. So the Elder said, and he was a shaman so he had given much thought to the subject. Myself, I do not know what the truth is. But I feel there is more to the world than what we can see and touch and smell."

They walked on through the thronged monuments of the Cimetière Côte de Neiges. "You see that stone thing, like a small house, over there? It is the Greenwoods' ancestral tomb. They are aristocrats, you know, and are too good to lie in the earth like other humans. Oh no, *their* dead must have a proper house! Even in death the class structures must be observed." Josephine laughed.

As he turned to look, eyes appeared in the shadows of the mausoleum, glowing fierce as fire. Dark shapes darted between the standing stones.

"Something is there!" whispered Hunter. He scented the air. "Wolves!"

"Confound it! The Greenwoods are out – and their allies too," said Josephine. "Move on: hopefully they won't spot us."

They slunk between the tombstones, heads low. "Why are they here?" he whispered.

"*Rugaru* often gather in the places of the dead, for the living will never go there by night. That is why some humans accused our kind of being eaters of the dead – ugh! – in the olden days. But truly, we only go to graveyards for the privacy."

"They saw us! They're coming after us!" he cried as the shadowy shapes raced out into the open.

"So I see. I guess we'd better run! Come on, pup!"

They fled out of the Cimetière and into a broad space of parkland. Ahead of them water glinted through tree trunks: the Lac aux Castors. Far away above the trees the dome of the Oratoire Saint Joseph rose, illuminated and majestic, like a second moon. But there was no other sign of humanity's presence here save for a small empty pavilion at the far end of the lake.

Hunter looked back and saw their pursuers gaining on them: two males and three females, one of the latter only half-grown. *Yes: it is they, the same wolves...* They came on in eerie silence, for even here in the uninhabited part of the Mountain's top they dared not howl aloud.

"At last!" snarled the matriarch as they caught up to Josephine and Hunter. "We have *you* out-numbered now. How dare you trespass on our territory? This is Greenwood land and always has been."

"You don't say? And here I thought it was a public park," responded Josephine. But for the first time her bravado sounded a bit hollow. The enemy wolves leered at her. "We are leaving now," she added, "so there's no need for a fight. We only came to drop off the girl at your house. She has taken her car and gone home to America."

"Good riddance!" growled the youngest wolf. But the pack matriarch silenced her with a glare before turning on Josephine again.

"You think you can keep her from us forever? You are fools, you and your friends. We will have her yet."

"So sure of that, you are. Would you like to bet on it?"

The old she-wolf advanced, her yellowed front-teeth bared for tearing. "I have had enough of your insolence."

She sprang at Josephine, going for the throat. But Hunter, not stopping to think – there was no time for thought – launched himself at her flank, knocking her aside, and her teeth snapped on air. The youngest wolf gave a shrill whine of fear as her grand-dam fell sprawling on the grass.

At once the two Stone wolves were upon him. The elder charged with a howl of rage, giving Hunter just enough warning to whirl and take him head-on. But the younger brother, black and silent as a shadow, whipped around and came at him from the rear, sinking his fangs into Hunter's hind leg. Hunter yelped and released his hold on the head-wolf's ruff, turning to confront his second attacker. Immediately the head-wolf moved in from the side. So they kept him swinging back and forth, intending no doubt to wear him out until both could rush in and get a good hold.

Josephine darted in and flung herself on the black wolf's back, biting at his neck.

As the two of them scuffled and mauled one another, Hunter and the head-wolf circled, their eyes locked. The young she-wolf moved in to nip at Hunter's legs, but the male said, "No, leave him to me."

"I want to help you!" she whined.

"No! Go to your mother. He is mine, I say!"

The third Greenwood female had not joined the fight, but was watching the melee at a distance, yelping her distress. Her daughter ran back to her with seeming reluctance, glancing back at Hunter and the head-wolf. Josephine and the black wolf meanwhile were rolling over on the grass, biting and clawing. The matriarch moved in and bit Josephine's flank. She bit back, and the three of them became one snarling, struggling mass of flesh and fur, jaws and limbs interlocked and entwined.

"Now you're on your own," said Hunter to his adversary. "You must fight me all by yourself."

The other wasted no more words but rushed at him, eyes and teeth flashing in the subdued light.

Hunter knew he had no chance of winning, for all his bravado. His wolf-sense told him this affair could end only in one way: with himself and Josephine lying torn and lifeless upon the grass. Their enemies had the advantage of numbers, and were on their home turf: they would defend their territory as any wolves would. So he fought on merely as a means of delaying the bloody and inevitable end, and for the slim chance of leaving his slayer with some permanent injury by way of revenge.

162

Something came leaping out of the darkness, and fell upon his foe.

It was another wolf, a great grey male whose muzzle shone silver-white in the moon. It did not growl as it came, but instead gave the deep roar that only a very large and enraged wolf can utter. The Stone wolf, taken by surprise, staggered and fell on his side, inadvertently assuming submissive posture.

"Watch him," said the old wolf, briefly, to Hunter. Still feeling somewhat dazed, Hunter straddled the head-wolf with his jaws closed on the other's neck, pinning him in place. The head-wolf growled but dared not move with his opponent's fangs so close to his vulnerable throat.

The newcomer meanwhile hurled himself upon the three struggling wolves, who had rolled into the shallows of the lake but still remained twined together. He seized the black male by the scruff of the neck and pulled him off Josephine. The Greenwood matriarch backed away, eyes wide and startled.

"What are you doing here?" she demanded. "This is none of your business!"

The old he-wolf met her menace with a pose of confidence, head held high and tail straight and steady. "Thérèse, is it to be war between us? I have no wish to harm any of you."

"Then why do you intrude on our territory, and meddle in our affairs? That means death in the world of wolves," the old she-wolf said.

"But here we are in the world of men. Can we not reason with one another, as humans do?"

"Humans – reason! They destroy everything they touch! We are *not* human, we are wolf-people!" raged the matriarch.

"If you live like beasts then beasts you are. Now let these two go, if you do not truly want open war. Your

163

clan is much diminished, Thérèse, in numbers and in influence."

"So is yours, Honoré. If mine is diminished, then your Dubois pack is all but extinct."

"Perhaps. But I have a great many friends."

The matriarch snarled. "Go, then! Take these two mongrels and go!"

The old male turned and looked at Josephine and Hunter, who hastened to his side. The three of them loped away together into the depths of the park.

It was wilder here: the trees, almost all deciduous, had been allowed to grow in a thick natural tangle. Hunter smelled traces of rabbit in the undergrowth, and the pungent musk of a fox. There were other animal odors he could not identify at all.

"Where to, Honoré?" asked Josephine of her friend, pausing to lick a hurt paw.

"The lookout." The old male led them on.

They emerged into a cleared space. A chalet, dark and vacant at this hour, sat surrounded by pavement that dropped in terraces to a stone balustrade. It was not the iron-railed lookout at which Chantal and Yves had stood, but the much larger belvedere that looked to the south. The old wolf led them to the edge and stood gazing out on the prospect below. "Come and see," he said to Hunter.

Hunter stared at the view beyond the balustrade. It was as if he had come to the very edge of the world. The ground before him plunged down in a long, tree-covered slope that vanished into darkness, and beyond that there was nothing but a sea of stars. He could hardly believe his dazzled eyes, but when he shut and opened them again it was still there: a vast sprawl of light lay *below,* composed of many points of different hues and grades of brightness.

"That, Hunter," said Josephine, "is a city – a great habitation of men."

Then he realized there *was* land down there, after all. The true stars shone overhead, thinly scattered across the night sky, high and remote. But these earthly lights were nearer: were in fact the illuminated windows of dwellings. They clustered on the ground, as thick as flowers in a meadow. Some were piled up into great glowing towering shapes, the highest of these nearly as tall as the hilltop on which he stood.

"So many," he whispered.

"As many as the stars." The old silver-muzzled wolf had moved to stand beside him.

"It is – it is… I don't know how to say it. I have not the words."

"It is beautiful," said the old one. "Very beautiful, the habitation of men; but it is dangerous too. Light and dark, as humanity itself is light and dark, good and evil. Still it is no more perilous than the world that you have left behind, young one, and it has much to offer you. Would you enter this new world? It is hard to live in both, you see; one or the other must claim you in the end. You must decide."

Hunter imagined the young she-wolf Chantal, now restored to her human form, making her way through that vast place of light and dark. All alone, without anyone to comfort and guide her… Pity and tenderness filled him at the thought. He yearned to help her, to tell her that she had many friends, that she need not be afraid. But then he remembered that the city of men was her own familiar ground, to which she returned with relief and joy. It was her wolf nature that filled her with fear. Josephine and the others would have to monitor her progress, assist and instruct her in the days to come.

He could join in their efforts – but not while he wore his present form.

"I have decided!" he said. "I want to live as a man among men."

The old one touched noses with him. "I am glad to hear that. But first you must come with me, so I can teach you their ways."

"I'll be there too, pup," Josephine reassured him. "Don't be afraid."

"I'm not. Now that I see the country of men, I want to know more of it. Those creatures down there are my own people." He felt pulled towards that city, that scattering of light in the darkness: it was as if the human blood in his veins cried out to his lost kindred, as a lone wolf howls for admission into a pack.

The older wolf reared up on his hind legs and placed his forepaws on the stone barrier. As Hunter watched, he changed his shape: limbs lengthening, fur wisping away to nothingness... A man now leaned upon the balustrade, old and stooped and pale of skin. In the city's glow the hair atop his head shone silvery-grey.

"Indeed they are," said Honoré Dubois, speaking softly as he gazed down upon the heart of old Montreal. "And you shall come to know them better, as you desire. But we must proceed with caution. Like their cities, they are wonderful and terrible."

## 13

It was not far to the dwelling place of Honoré Dubois, which lay in a section of the city between the Mountain and the eastern end of the McGill campus. But short as the trip was, Hunter was nearly asleep by the time they arrived, lulled by the swift-rushing, forward motion that not too long ago had made him feel anxious and uneasy. He had grown used to the sensation of being swept along, submissive and unresisting, as a leaf rides the surface of a fast-flowing stream. Like the leaf he was content to be carried, giving no thought to his final destination or whatever fate awaited him there. The night's events had left him exhausted and he wanted only to rest. But before he could drift away completely there came a sudden quick swerve, the motion of the vehicle ceased, and the throb of its engine was stilled. His ears pricked up and his nose strained, as his eyes still showed him nothing but the impenetrable darkness in the back of the van. He heard approaching footsteps, smelled a soothing familiar scent: then Josephine Legris, in her human form, swung open the back doors of the van. With her was Dubois, his man's body now clad in clothes that he had retrieved from a hiding place in the park.

"We're here, pup!" said Josephine, smiling in at him. "Come on out."

Hunter looked around him with interest as he leaped out onto the pavement. The van was parked in the driveway of a building in an unfamiliar part of the city. A yellowish, artificial glow came from rows of tall street lamps: this light, not that of moon or stars, lit the scene. There were no gigantic towers here: all the surrounding structures had only two or three levels at most. But they were also far larger than the humble huts and cabins that he and Josephine had visited in the north. Those on the nearer side of the street had elaborate decorated fronts, while those on the opposite side were plainer in appearance, their separate floors joined by external staircases. There were also many more trees in this neighbourhood.

Due to the lateness of the hour there was no one about on the quiet residential street, but it would not have mattered if there had been any witnesses. Josephine and Dubois appeared to be perfectly ordinary human beings, returning home from a late-night drive, while Hunter could easily pass for their pet dog.

"I've never quite understood why you two picked this neighbourhood for your *pied à terre*," Josephine said to Dubois, walking with him towards the nearest house, a tall structure with a carved sandstone façade. "You could easily afford a nice place in Westmount or Outremont."

"We love the McGill Ghetto," Dubois replied. "The area has its charm. This street, now, such a study in contrasts! The houses on our side date to Victorian times when wealthy and influential people lived here. See all the fancy gingerbread trim, the gables and balconies and bay windows. And they are as elegant inside as out. Most are being turned into condos now that the area is being gentrified again. But those newer buildings on the far side are all divided into apartments, and McGill students and young immigrant families live in them. It makes her feel young again, Angélique says, to live in such a vibrant and varied neighbourhood."

"Why on earth do Montrealers put staircases on the outside of their apartment buildings?" Josephine asked him, pointing to the buildings on the far side. The wrought iron stairs were painted in bright colours, and some zigzagged sharply on their way down to street level while others descended in sedate and graceful curves. "It looks so funny. You never see that anyplace else."

"To conserve heat in the long winters. A heated internal stairwell costs more. But the exterior staircase has also become a cultural motif of this city. The residents help each other to clear snow off them in wintertime, and in summer they use the landings as balconies, sitting out on them, calling greetings to one another. Angélique has made many friends here, on both sides of the street."

"Who is this other person you speak of?" Hunter inquired, padding up to stand at Dubois's side.

"Angélique is my wife," explained Dubois.

"Wife – that means mate, does it not?" said Hunter.

"That and more," said Dubois. "It has a meaning beyond what wolves mean by the word."

"Is she here with you, your mate?" the wolf asked.

"She was, but she left when we got Josephine's call." He turned to the Métis woman. "Angélique has appointments to keep back in Quebec City. Also she felt that Hunter doesn't need too many unfamiliar faces around him at first."

"Ah, that is so like her! She is always so thoughtful. And she's right, of course. But you will enjoy meeting her later, pup," Josephine added to Hunter. "Angélique is a lovely person."

"And here we are." Dubois led them up the sandstone steps and unlocked the door. The house had been divided in two: in its front hallway a second door to the right led to the Dubois apartment. "Welcome to my home, Hunter," he added as he ushered them in. "Or rather, my home away from home. My wife and I come here when we visit this city; our permanent home is far away from here. I will take you there tomorrow. It is too long a journey to make at night."

The building was light and airy, with high ceilings and many windows. Hunter padded about, sniffing curiously at its furnishings and the rugs on its wooden floors. The scent of Dubois was much in evidence throughout the rooms, along with traces of another, unfamiliar person which Hunter's keen sense of smell identified as a human female. The mate of Honoré Dubois... Her scent had a touch of sweetness to it, like the fragrance of flowers.

"We can't keep calling him Hunter," said Josephine to Dubois. "It's not a real name."

Her host nodded, taking a seat on a large comfortable couch and beckoning to her to join him. "I agree. He can choose a human name once he is ready."

"How did you come to choose yours?" she asked, sitting next to him. "You've never said."

"It was the name of one of my ancestors. I chose it when I began to learn about my family history. I liked the sound of it."

Her face softened. "It must have been so hard. I was human from the first; but you had to learn to read, to use money, to interact with others..."

"My family had not forgotten altogether how to be human," Dubois replied. "They were not like Hunter's pack, content to be nothing more than animals in the wild. But I was always curious about my two-legged ancestors. Their oral record concerning humans was incomplete, not having been updated in centuries. I was convinced that much must have changed in the intervening time, and I discovered I was right."

Hunter lay down on the carpet at their feet. "I am curious also," he told them. "I have dreams about being human at times. Other wolves dream of everyday things: chasing prey across the tundra, running with the pack. I asked my pack members if anyone else ever dreamed of

170

being human, and they only stared at me. My dreams were yet another thing that set me apart."

"Dreams, you say? That's interesting. Almost like an ancestral memory," said Dubois. "*Eh bien,* you can now make your dreams into reality, *mon ami.* As did I. But not yet. First we rest."

"I have waited this long," said Hunter. "I can wait one more night."

They ate a simple meal of sliced meat and bread, the two in human form sitting at a table in the kitchen while Hunter sprawled on the hardwood floor. He declined the bread, which did not smell at all like food to him, but accepted some slices of meat. It was cold, chilled by the special preserving cabinet in which it was kept, and the taste was strange, but he was too hungry to care about such things and bolted it straight down. Then, replete, he lay thoughtfully licking his chops while the other two talked together.

"So tell us, Honoré," said Josephine, "why did you decide to remain in the human world? Perhaps Hunter would like to hear about that. What was the one thing that decided you?"

"It was not a thing, but a person," said Dubois.

"Ah," said Josephine.

"A person?" said Hunter, looking up.

"I believe Dubois means his wife," said Josephine.

"Yes," said Dubois. "I met Angélique for the first time at the winter carnival in Quebec City. I had gone there with some of my new human friends, who told me it would be a wonderful experience. A carnival, Hunter, is a great gathering of humans for the purpose of play and leisure. It takes place in the winter time here."

"Is that the mating season for humans then?" asked Hunter. "The same as for wolves?"

For some reason both Josephine and Dubois laughed at that. "I'm sure that some—mating—goes on at

*Carnaval*," said Josephine. "But humans have no set season for such things. They breed all year round."

"Yes, it was only a coincidence that I met my future wife there," said Dubois. "I was not looking for love, only for knowledge. But of course that is when love finds you: right at the moment you least expect it. While I was in Quebec with my human friends I made contact with the *loups garous* of that city. It is a very old werewolf community, the oldest in the whole country save one. I paid a call on a family—what you would describe as a pack—that was descended from some of the city's first settlers. The *famille* De la Roche. They were a noble family as well as an old one: their ancestors were aristocrats in the Old World. I knew about them because the Dubois and De la Roche clans came together from the land across the sea, exiles in a time of persecution. These *loups garous* introduced me in turn to the *famille* Bernier, humans whom my ancestors had entrusted to look after their house, the Maison Dubois, until an heir came to claim it. I have lived in that house ever since.

"Angélique De la Roche was the youngest daughter of that clan, and she took pity on me when she heard of my humble origins in the wild. She became my constant companion and helper, taking it upon herself to teach me all about civilization, about music and art. Her love for these things impressed me so much that I came to love them also. I desired greatly to remain in the world of men, to become a part of it so that I might continue to enjoy its beauty and wonder. Angélique was my inspiration, the embodiment of all that was good and true in this new life."

"A lovely story," said Josephine. "So often when we are first learning how to navigate these two worlds there is one special person who helps and inspires us. For you it was your wife. For me, a young Inuit man who looked beyond my double nature to the inner person and helped me to accept who and what I was. Angélique and Noah were there for us, Honoré, when we needed confidence and guidance. And we will be here for you, Hunter. Have no fear: from this moment on you will never be truly alone."

How kind they both were, Hunter thought in gratitude. The love of Josephine truly knew no bounds. He had learnt that during the time they spent in the cabin in the woods, watching over the young wolf-girl as she lay between life and death. Josephine had spoken soothing words into her ears while Hunter had lain next to her, comforting her wolf-fashion with his own body. When at long last Chantal had changed her form beneath the blankets, shifting from wolf back to woman even as she slept, he was surprised to find himself feeling just as relieved as Josephine. It no longer seemed strange to him that Josephine cared deeply about a person whom she barely knew. He too felt a stirring of emotion at the thought that Chantal would be able to return home, to her own place and people.

*Josephine and Honoré Dubois have already begun to alter me,* he thought. *I may have a wolf's form still, but I am not at all the same person I was.*

"Well, I will retire now," said Dubois at last, getting up from his chair. "The bed in the spare room is made up, Josephine. But I'm afraid Hunter will have to sleep on the floor, though I will put down some blankets to make him comfortable."

They made up the makeshift "bed" for him on the sitting room floor before retreating to their separate rooms. Hunter curled up on the pile of blankets. It still seemed odd to him to sleep in places that had walls and a ceiling, instead of outdoors under the stars. But he recalled his earliest days as a pup, sleeping in an underground den with his mother and siblings, all of them snuggled together in the shared warmth of their own bodies. The comfort and security of those times came back to him now: for not since his earliest days as a pup had he felt this safe and loved. Two older wolves, a male and a female, were taking care of him. This, his lupine instinct said, was as it should be. He could safely leave everything to these two new protectors, trusting them even with his life. He heaved a deep contented sigh and then curled up in a ball, tucking his tail under his nose. Sleep came upon him almost instantly.

He had not been slumbering long, however, when he was startled by a noise – or so he thought; he was not entirely sure what he had heard, filtered through the gauzy layers of sleep. Was it a voice calling out? He believed so; but whether lupine or human he could not say. He recalled no words, only the impression of a cry and with it a sense of urgency. Hunter sat up and looked around him. All was dark and still in the apartment. He got up and padded down the short passageway to the room where Josephine was, pushing the door open with his nose. She was fast asleep in her bed, so it could not have been she who called. So, too, was Dubois when Hunter checked. Then whose voice had it been? There was no one else in the apartment. Had he heard someone calling out in the street, perhaps? Hunter went to one of the front windows and peered out.

And then he saw her, standing alone at the foot of the front steps. It was the female human, Chantal.

He could see her face clearly by the light of the street lamps. She was looking up at Dubois's dwelling, one hand resting on the side railing of the front steps as if she were debating whether or not to ascend them. Hadn't Dubois said he'd given Chantal the information on how to find him? She must have changed her mind about going home, and come to seek his aid after all.

The hand on the railing fell back to her side as she stood there, irresolute.

Hunter pulled back from the window. He must wake the others at once and tell them of this – quickly, before the girl lost her resolve and went away again. Why did she waver? What was wrong? Was she not sure she had come to the right place, or was she afraid? Hunter went back to the window. She was still there, standing on the pavement.

And then as he watched she changed.

Not in the usual way of wolf-people, gradually exchanging one form for another, but in the blink of an eye. She was simply gone, and in her place there was a wolf. Hunter stared in amazement. How had she done it? She had not even shed her clothing; it had just disappeared along with her human form. Now the brown she-wolf was whining softly as she paced back and forth in front of the house.

The window had been left open at the bottom, as the night air was mild, and he was able to thrust his head out through the opening. Instantly he regretted the impulse. Before he could call out to her she gave a loud yelp of alarm and backed away, bristling and showing her teeth.

She had also attracted the attention of some passers-by on the far side of the street: a small, straggling group of young men, all of whom stopped short and pointed at the wild animal that had so inexplicably appeared in their quiet urban neighbourhood. She cringed and cowered at the sound of their raised voices, and then with a last agonized cry she broke and ran.

Hunter watched aghast. She didn't know what she was doing. He must follow her – there was no time to try and wake the others now; she would be long gone by the time he roused them and he would not know in what direction she'd fled. Hunter shoved his head and forelegs through the open window, wriggling and pawing wildly at the sill in the effort to squeeze his entire body through the gap. After a few moments' struggle he managed to force the sash up just far enough to let his shoulders and hindquarters through. He half-fell, half-leaped the six-foot drop to the ground, landing awkwardly but without injury on the hard pavement.

Chantal meanwhile had fled westward. He could see the she-wolf in the distance, still running down the middle of the road: she was heading towards an intersection at its far end. At once he gave chase. The artificial light at the busy crossroads was much brighter, dazzling to his eyes. Clearly it had the same effect on Chantal, who after a brief hesitation dashed madly out into the street. There was a lot more traffic here: horns blared and brakes screeched as she dodged the vehicles, then doubled back and returned to the sidewalk. By some miracle she reached it unharmed, scattering a few pedestrians who cried out in terror. Hunter strove to catch up with her, his heart swelling with alarm and pity. This cityscape should have been like home to her, but she was now an object of fear and loathing to her fellow humans. She would come to grief soon if she didn't transform back to a woman. But she didn't seem to know how to do so, and was opting for flight instead, the panicked reaction of an animal. He put on a spurt of speed until he was running alongside her. He took care not to come too close. She must not think that he too was pursuing her.

"Don't be afraid!" he cried. "Don't run from me, please; I'm not an enemy! I can help you. I know who you really are. I can show you how to return to your human shape –"

But his words were in vain. She couldn't understand them, not having been raised as he was by speakers of the wolf-tongue. She shot him a frantic glance out of the corner of her eye, and did not slow her pace for even a moment. To her he was just another threat in a world that had become a nightmare.

There were shouts behind them: he could not understand the human speech, but he had no need to. Fear and anger blazed through the raised voices. He risked a quick backward look – and what he saw nearly made him stumble. A pair of men with long-barrelled guns had appeared in the midst of the crowd, and the other humans were talking to them, waving their arms in the direction of Hunter and Chantal. *Telling the huntsmen where the dangerous wolves are...* The two of them would be shot, like any potentially harmful animal that strayed into human territory. Josephine had feared that Chantal's double nature would destroy her before she had a chance to grasp and comprehend it. And he was a target, too. Hunter looked around him desperately, and his gaze fell on the opening to an alleyway up ahead and to his right. It was narrow and dark, and with any luck would lead away from this harsh-lit city street to a less populated area.

"There!" he shouted to the other wolf. "Do you see that dark place? We must both get off this road now!"

His speech might be incomprehensible to her, but if she too saw the alley she might get the gist of what he was saying. He ran faster, to get ahead of her, then glanced back to see if she was still behind him. She was, and it looked as if she was trying to keep up. She must have realized at last that he was not an enemy and was in fact trying to help her.

Unfortunately the two men with the guns were behind as well, and running as fast as they could. Experience with humans in the north had taught him that they tended not to fire their weapons while running; perhaps it was too hard to take proper aim at speed. He ran on towards the alley, leading the way for Chantal. A shot was fired as he tore down the opening of the dim-lit, walled-in lane, but it went wide. The she-wolf followed him and closed the gap between them. They ran together now, almost neck-and-neck, dodging around the heaps of trash that littered the alley.

His relief was short-lived. To his despair he saw that the alley ended in a brick wall, too high for either one of them to jump even had they not been utterly spent. He stood panting for breath, his tongue lolling from his jaws. Had he not been winded he would have howled. There was no escape here after all. Far from helping her, he had doomed them both.

The she-wolf halted at the sight of the wall and looked straight at him. Something passed between them, something stronger than speech: a shared wordless understanding. It was too late for him; the men were coming, he could hear their voices and their footsteps echoing between the brick walls. But she at least might still be saved if only she could transform. "Change back!" he pleaded again.

She only stood there, panting and wild-eyed. He began to nudge her towards the heap of rusty bins and cardboard boxes piled up by the wall. "Hide behind these, then, if you can't make the change. I will try to find a way to stop them."

Hunter had no idea what he was going to do. He wanted to call out to the men, "I am not what I appear to be! I'm not an animal, I'm human like you!" But it would be a wasted effort: like Chantal, they would not understand his speech. *So it ends for me here,* he thought. *But perhaps they will not find her... or perhaps if I delay the men long enough she will be able to transform before they see her...*

He crumpled to the ground, waiting for the fatal shot to ring out. But the two men stopped short and just stood looking down at him. "What are you doing here?" one asked.

He could understand what they were saying! But why were they talking to him? Didn't they believe him to be a beast? Then he glanced down at himself, and stared in stunned disbelief.

He was a wolf no longer. His body was human: a young man's, long-legged and lean, and clad in clothes much like those of the two men. He huddled on the ground, on all fours, blinking in confusion. Slowly he eased back on his haunches and raised his forelimbs, staring at the hands on the ends of them, flexing the long slender fingers.

The men glanced at each other, then back at him again. "Hey, it's all right, kid," said one, lowering his weapon. "You can put your hands down. We won't shoot you. We're not police, just wildlife control. We were after a couple of wild animals. Wolves we think, or coyotes maybe."

"I was sure they went this way," said his partner, sounding puzzled.

"He'd have seen them," replied the first man. "Did you notice any big animals running through here?" he asked Hunter.

"N-no," Hunter stammered. His own voice sounded strange to him.

"Told you so," said the second man to the first. "Let's go. I doubt they jumped that wall. Way too high. They must've run back down this alley when they found it was a dead end. We missed 'em, that's all."

He watched them walk away, filled with joy and relief. He tried to get to his feet – his human feet – but could not balance on two limbs. So he sank back to all fours and crawled on his hands and knees over to the heap of rubbish. "You're safe," he called out, feeling sure now that Chantal would understand him as the men had done.

Then he saw that she too had changed. She crouched before him in human form, and like him she was fully clothed: the very same clothes he had seen her wear earlier. How that could possibly be he could not understand. But it didn't matter; what was important was that they were both alive and unhurt. There was a smile on her face, he saw, and no longer any trace of fear on her features. She reached out, took his hands in hers, and slowly rose to her feet without releasing her hold. He was pulled up with her, until he too stood on his feet facing her. When he swayed she steadied him, moving her hands to his shoulders. "Thank you," she said. "You saved me, didn't you? You saved my life just now."

"I – tried," he stammered.

She released her hold and turned away, walking back down the alley towards the street. "Wait!" he called, staggering after her. "Please, could you help me now? I want to be truly human, as you are. Please, help me learn how to live in your world..."

He followed her out onto the sidewalk, noticing how the pedestrians passed them both without a second glance. No one feared him or wished to harm him. He was a man now – truly a man! He belonged here. The city beckoned to him with its looming towers of glittering light. He glanced up at the vast luminous structures, filled anew with wonder now that his own fear was gone and he had the leisure to observe his surroundings. Had these tremendous things really been constructed by human hands? It hardly seemed possible. If human beings could create such things then there was clearly no limit to what they could achieve.

All this was available to him now, with his change of form, to explore and to claim. He had been incorporated into the world that Chantal already navigated with ease, having known it from her birth. But where *was*

Chantal? Tearing his eyes away from the towers he glanced around him and realized that he could no longer see her in the milling crowd, nor could he track her scent with his human nose.

"Chantal?" he called out. There was no reply.

He must find her. He wanted to join her, to help her understand what she truly was, and also to thank her: for it was the impulse to protect her that had made him fully human at last. As he walked on, still feeling a little unsteady on his two long spindly legs, he realized that he also felt strangely cold even with the clothes draped over his body. Was it the lack of fur? He shivered, his elation giving way to unease. There was no sign of Chantal anywhere, nor could he see the street that led back to the apartment of Honoré Dubois. Hunter stood still. He was lost and alone in this strange place. How could he ever hope to find his way back to his friends, without Chantal's help or a wolf's ability to follow a scent?

He counseled himself not to give in to his fear. *I have only to take my own shape again, and my friends will be able to find me. In the meantime, I can enjoy this new form – or I could enjoy it, if only I were not so cold...*

And then, with another violent shiver, he woke.

He was still in the flat. He was shivering, Hunter realized, because he had rolled off the heap of blankets onto the bare wooden floor, which felt cold as a slab of ice. He looked around him in bewilderment, still half-expecting to see the city all around him, with its traffic and its towers, and the night sky above. Instead he saw the light of morning streaming in through the windows, and Honoré Dubois and Josephine standing and gazing down at him. Dubois stooped to pick up a blanket and drape it over his body.

181

"There! Is that more comfortable, *mon ami?"* he asked, kneeling down next to him.

Hunter was too devastated to reply. *It was only another dream!* he thought, anguished. But of course it was. So much of what had happened was clearly impossible: the instantaneous shape-shifts, his sudden inexplicable ability to understand human speech... Yes, clearly it had only been a dream. The new freedom that had seemed to be his was snatched away, as had happened so many times before on so many other awakenings.

*"C'est absolument incroyable!"* marveled Dubois, shaking his head. "I never saw the like."

"But – how?" Josephine asked. "We've given him no instructions, no potions... nothing. What triggered this?'

"He was dreaming," suggested Dubois. "You heard him thrashing about and howling. Something happened to him then, right after that. Something, perhaps, on a subconscious level?"

"Well, he can tell us himself what happened – later." Josephine knelt down beside Dubois. "There, pup, it's all right!"

Only a dream, though the most vivid to come to him yet... He felt a howl of protest build in his chest, but it could not seem to burst forth – all that escaped his mouth was a faint, breathy sound. Josephine said, "Easy, Hunter, easy."

The two concerned faces hovered above him, and he struggled to get up, but his limbs would not obey him either. He fell back, feeling strangely disconnected from himself. *What is wrong? Why do you look at me like that?* he wanted to ask, but his voice still would not come. At last, with an effort, he stretched out his forelegs, in a gesture of desperate appeal.

182

His forelegs: what was wrong with them? Was he dreaming still, after all? He stared at the limbs, now strangely elongated and seemingly stripped of all their fur; and at the long jointed fingers that splayed out, so that the light fanned around them in beams.

*Oh*, he thought. *That is why...*

*Raoul*

## 14

Derby Line was sunk deep in the grey gloom of winter. Christmas had passed, and New Year's Eve; nothing remained but snow-bound, cloud-dulled dreariness. As Chantal drove through the streets of her hometown her thoughts were shrouded in a corresponding gloom.

She had driven to the town of Newport that morning, in hope that getting out of the house would lighten her mood. But the storefronts looked forlorn now that they were stripped of their festive decorations, and the lake was bleak and cold under the grey sky. It was hard to picture it blue and scattered with white sails, the sun high and hot, the trees green. Recalling last summer was like looking back on an irrecoverable golden age. Nana had still been alive then, Chantal still living at home; she had been in love with Russell Gordon, and looking forward to college... She had heard of people's lives "falling apart", and always imagined it to be a poetic exaggeration. Now she knew otherwise. Her own existence had utterly fragmented: it had no shape or centre to it any more.

She pulled into the Vandusen driveway, past the discarded Christmas tree that lay sprawled at its foot, looking pathetic with its few bits of clinging tinsel. By the twenty-sixth of December most of the neighbourhood trees had been thrown out; her aunt and uncle had kept theirs up until New Year's Eve, following Nana's tradition, but now it had joined the rest. She paused for a moment, engine running, as she gazed at the old homestead. Repainted creamy-white, with new blue shutters, it was brightly lit and the driveway was full of her cousins' cars. She squeezed Minnie in next to Liz's second-hand Toyota and behind Amanda's blue Honda. Inside the house there were more disconcerting alterations. It felt strange to look into the kitchen and see, not the old red wallpaper and wooden countertops, but stark white walls and grey granite. Even the pictures in the hall were gone: framed photos of Uncle Phil and his family had taken the place of her grandparents' murky oil landscapes. Objectively the changes in décor could only be seen as an improvement, but her heart still ached at the loss of the familiar things she had known since childhood.

As she entered the front hall and kicked her boots off the twins' wheaten terrier puppy barked at her furiously from his basket. Chantal liked dogs – her grandparents had owned a variety of Labrador retrievers over the years – and dogs usually liked her. But Terry the terrier had clearly decided that Chantal was an enemy, and greeted all her attempts at friendship with hostility. It was a little thing, but one of many that made her feel distanced from her former home. She eased past the dog and hung her coat up in the hall closet. Jesse and Norman were in the kitchen baking with their mother – brownies, by the warm chocolatey smell – and her uncle and her visiting cousins were lounging by the fire in the living room. Amanda was on the couch, knitting a snowflake-patterned sweater; Liz sat next to her, thin and pinch-faced as Amanda was plump and jolly – she'd been dieting again. Tammy lolled on the hearth reading a magazine.

"Hey, Chantal! Did you see this flyer from the library?" Amanda asked as Chantal entered, setting down her knitting needles and holding out a piece of green-tinted paper. "They're having some kind of free concert there, all French Canadian music. Thought you might be interested, since you've traveled there now and everything." Chantal took the flyer, but averted her gaze from it. "How *was* your trip? You haven't said much about it," Amanda pursued. "How are things up in America's attic?"

"Great. In fact I now think of America as Canada's basement."

Tammy looked up, grinning. "Uh-oh, she's turned Canuck! Look out everyone, we've got a spy in our midst! She probably works for the Royal Mounted Police now."

"Royal *Canadian* Mounted Police," Chantal corrected.

"Yup, she's gone native!" Tammy laughed. "I always pictured Canada as kind of like an enormous Alaska. Am I right?"

Liz smirked. "Sure, if everyone in Alaska spoke French."

"Not everyone." Uncle Phil spoke without glancing up from his newspaper. "I've been to Ontario on business trips, and they all speak English there. You'd hardly know you weren't in America."

"That's English Canada, though," said Chantal. "French Canada is… different. The people are different."

"Different? How?" Liz was in full know-it-all mode. "Just because they speak another language doesn't mean they aren't the same as we are, Fifi."

*Knock it off with the nickname, Liz.* "It's more than just their language," said Chantal. "It's their culture, their history… everything. You'd understand if you really got to know them. They're pretty unique."

Liz tossed her silky blonde hair back over her shoulders and shrugged. "If you say so."

Uncle Phil put down his paper and looked at Chantal. "So tell me, when are you going to get back to your studies?" he asked.

"I *am* studying," said Chantal, nettled. "Going to Quebec helped me improve my French. Like an immersion programme. I could probably teach it now."

"Not without a degree you couldn't. If you're not going back to UCLA then you'll have to apply to another college soon, won't you?"

"I *will,* Uncle! I just haven't had time to go over all the literature yet."

"Come and sit down, Chantal," said Amanda, patting the seat of the couch. "Move over, Liz. There's lots of room."

But Chantal did not want to join them, tempting as the hot fire was on that bitter day. Her uncle's queries about her future plans grew more pointed every day. And Liz and Tammy in the absence of their eldest sister could be aggravating; despite her geniality Amanda did not seem able to manage her sisters as Katharine did.

It was a pity Kath had not been able to join them this Christmas. She had come for Thanksgiving with Warren, beaming and happy, a gentle swelling now visible at her waistline. "So, are things looking up a bit, now you've had your trip?" Kath had asked her, using a light tone. But her clear blue eyes looked straight into her cousin's. "You Found Yourself, and all that?"

"I'm fine," Chantal replied, her voice resolute. She did not want to worry Kath at this delicate time. When she said goodbye to her cousin on the last day of her visit, it had felt almost like a permanent farewell. Katharine had always been caring and protective of the younger girls in her family, but that maternal streak now had a new focus in the life burgeoning within her. She and Chantal would grow farther apart in the coming years, the younger girl sensed.

There was no longer anyone to whom she could turn.

She went up to her bedroom and shut the door. Aunt Lorraine had changed everything else in the house, but thoughtfully left Chantal's personal space untouched. She was grateful on the one hand, but looking around the room – the same old wooden chest of drawers,

190

nightstand and desk, the bed on which Mr. Bear sat slumped over, looking as though he had never left – she suddenly felt like a coward. Retreating into the safety of her childhood was like regressing, admitting defeat. Yet there was no real alternative, for she was afraid to be on her own. Ever since her return from Quebec her sleep had been troubled by dark and stressful dreams. Interspersed throughout these nightmares were images of a white wolf with blue eyes, standing over and gazing down at her. She felt no fear of it, oddly enough; in the dreams it even seemed to her that the animal was protecting her somehow. She could not say why her subconscious mind had turned the wolf from the Nature Club footage into a sort of personal totem. Was it because the scientist's Inuit friend had claimed that this wolf was trying to warn him and his companions about the other monster wolves? That had been nonsense, of course – but the idea had been planted in her mind, all the same. That might explain why she turned repeatedly to the wolf's image in her sleep, as a symbol of reassurance and protection.

Because the nightmares were terrifying. In every one of them she transformed into some kind of beast, with coarse black hairs sprouting all over her limbs, face and body. She would wake shuddering with fear and disgust, to find her sleepwear and blankets lying in a heap on the floor. She could never remember discarding them. And now she was sleepwalking too. Her bedroom door was often open in the morning, even though she was always sure she had closed it the night before. Things downstairs got disarranged. Uncle Phil blamed the dog, though the indignant twins pointed out that Terry was too small to knock over floor lamps and chairs. When Chantal confided in her cousins, they did not seem overly concerned. Tammy even thought it was funny. "I have a classmate at college who sleepwalks," she said. "She lives alone and every morning she has to go around her apartment cleaning up after herself. She says it's like being your own roommate."

Chantal was not amused. She recalled what Aunt Fran had said about how *distancing* it was to have a chronic illness – how it had made her feel cut off, not only from the rest of normal healthy humanity, but from her own body. Chantal understood now what she had meant. She felt alienated from her own flesh, betrayed by it; even afraid of it. Her family doctor laughed at her fears, saying that any drug given her back in October should have cleared her system by now, and suggesting her problem was simply stress.

Chantal did not agree. She believed she knew what was wrong with her.

She sat down at her desk and turned on her laptop, pulling up a page from a psychiatry website. Re-reading this page had become a kind of nervous compulsion ever since she first found it, but she could not stop herself:

> **Lycanthropy**: This disorder is rare, but well documented. It is believed to affect the region of the brain associated with self-image, and those who suffer from it experience delusions of transforming into wolves or other animals, to the point where they have been known to adopt animalistic behaviours: growling, crawling on all fours, and even biting people. Most patients have other underlying disorders such as schizophrenia. At least one sufferer was known to use hallucinogenic drugs in a deliberate effort to bring on his delusions, which he found enjoyable.

So her affliction had a name; but some mysteries remained. What exactly had she been given to bring it on? Thérèse must have given her some illicit concoction in that mug of herbal tea, awakening the latent psychosis. That strange woman Josephine had spoken of the Boisverts engaging in dubious activities; though she had not gone into detail, these could well include drug smuggling. Quebec was apparently notorious for organized crime. The Boisverts might have a gang affiliation, or be in the drug business on their own as a way to keep the family fortunes alive.

Did clinical lycanthropy run in their family, and had it become itself a form of addiction? If they succeeded in making Chantal an addict too, would she be more like "one of them" – and, perhaps, more compliant to their desires as the drugs took hold? Compliance in such matters as marrying a man whom Thérèse Boisvert favoured, and desired as the father of her great-grandchildren…

*I'm going crazy,* she thought, groaning aloud. *Completely, totally, no-holds-barred insane. I'm going to end up in a psych ward, flailing around and chewing on the furniture*… She felt almost dizzy from following her own restless thoughts. With an effort she switched off the computer, and found herself staring at Amanda's library flyer, which she had tossed down on the desk. A French Canadian concert, had she said? Chantal loved music and often found it soothing when she was going through a crisis of some kind. But the last thing she wanted right now was to be reminded of Quebec and the disturbing things that had happened to her there. She seized the paper and was in the act of crumpling it when the wording caught her eye. Below the title "A Québecois Concert: Folk Music from La Belle Province" she saw printed in smaller lettering: "with host Honoré Dubois".

Her fingers froze. Then, trembling, they smoothed the paper out again.

Honoré Dubois? Was it – could it be the same man? She'd lost his contact information when she tossed out his card, and she had not been able to find him again on the Internet. But if this concert host was indeed the same man she'd met in Montreal then she could catch him after the show, just as she had done at the McGill lecture. She could tell him her theory and beg for his advice.

Her brief spurt of independence had long vanished. She now wanted only to be guided and protected from her fears, and this little piece of paper offered her hope. It was as if a friendly hand had been extended to her.

The Haskell Opera House was nearly full when she got there. Evidently lots of other Derby residents had the post-holiday blues and were looking for some light entertainment. She had hoped for a seat close to the stage but had to settle for one in the front row of the high baroque gallery. As the lights dimmed and the drop curtain with its painted Venetian scene slowly rose, she saw Honoré Dubois walk out on the stage and at the sight of his gleaming silver hair her heart leaped. She longed to run down the aisle and speak to her father's old friend right away. But she could only sit and wait as he addressed the audience.

"*Bienvenue, mes amis!* Welcome, and thank you all for coming out on such a cold night! I am here as an ambassador of sorts for my home province of Quebec. Tonight we come as neighbours, to share with you our French Canadian culture. First, some *chansons* – the songs beloved by many generations of francophones. Please welcome René Leblanc and his Acadian Accordion!"

Out of the wings came a little man with a lean, dark, Gallic-looking face, resplendent in red-striped shirt, black trousers and beret. "The *Acadiens* settled not in Quebec but in Canada's Atlantic provinces, where they developed a unique French culture all their own," said Dubois. "Some of them went back to France after their expulsion by the British, but some also went to Quebec,

194

especially to the region of Gaspé where our René was raised."

Leblanc sang some traditional Acadian folksongs while accompanying himself on the accordion, then switched to Québecois songs like *"Alouette"* and *"Vive la Canadienne"*, encouraging the audience to sing along to the simple choruses. These were not at all like the songs of continental France, thought Chantal in fascination. The French Canadians were a breed apart, descendants of hardy settlers who had hewn out a home from a harsh wilderness. Born survivors, who worked and revelled with a will. Not for them the indolent strains of *La Vie en Rose;* their songs were jaunty and robust, and through them all ran the fierce love of the country they had made.

Leblanc bowed and retreated into the wings, giving way to three girls who looked to be in their early twenties, costumed in eighteenth-century gowns and mob-caps. They sang a capella, their sweet sopranos higher and more pure than any human voice Chantal had ever heard, intertwining like three strands of a silver cord. The audience which had been laughing and clapping moments ago fell into a rapt silence as they listened. The girls sang French carols – "Because," Honoré Dubois explained, "for us it is Christmas still. In Quebec, *Noël* – the celebration of the Nativity – does not end on the twenty-sixth, but is merely the start of a longer festival: *le Temps de Fêtes.* We begin with the *Reveillon,* the Christmas Eve feast and family gathering that follows midnight mass and lasts all night long. Then throughout the following weeks we visit friends and have more parties. It all ends on January 6 with *la Fête des Rois,* the feast of the Three Kings."

After the trio finally gathered up their skirts, curtseyed and swept off the stage, they were followed by a young man with long flowing black hair, also in period clothing with a red sash at his waist. "Now, the Métis of Quebec enjoy a double heritage, both European and Aboriginal," said Dubois, "but they are recognized by the government as a distinct people. The costume that Jean-Louis wears is the antique garb of the Métis man, European clothing with native touches like moccasins. He sports also the red *ceinture flechée* that was worn by the *voyageurs*, the French explorers of olden days, many of whom the Métis count among their ancestors. And one of the many things they learned from their European forebears was the art of playing the fiddle."

Chantal sat back, expecting tedium. She loathed the violin as a solo instrument, finding it shrill and grating to the nerves. But the first sweep of the bow across the fiddle's strings felt like a jolt of electricity through her veins. This music was more than lively; fast and fiery, it got into the blood and heart, made you want to get up and dance along with the youth as he leaped and spun around the stage. *He's playing us too,* she thought, fascinated. *As if our bodies were musical instruments...* All around her she saw tapping toes and nodding heads. She half-expected the balcony's plump plaster cupids to take up their own sculpted mandolins and join in.

At the fiddler's final bow there was a breathless silence, followed by a storm of applause that filled the auditorium. M. Dubois took the stage again. "*Merci, mesdames et messieurs!* That is all we have for you tonight. I urge all of you who have not traveled beyond your neighbours' homes in Stanstead to come and explore La Belle Province some day. Until then, thank you all for coming out in such nasty weather and I wish you all *bonne nuit. Au revoir!*"

The cheering and clapping faded at last, and the other audience members in the balcony began to drain away towards the exit. Chantal sprang up from her seat and joined them, making for the lower level of the concert hall. Once there she had to move against the flow of departing patrons, struggling towards the stage. She could see Dubois standing in the middle of the aisle, surrounded by audience members and performers. He was talking to a tall, denim-clad youth – not a local, for she would surely have noticed him before: the boy had the lean but muscular build of an athlete and a striking face, strong-boned and framed within thick fair hair of a silvery platinum-blond shade. Another time she might have tried to speak to this handsome stranger, to learn his name and find out where he came from. But not tonight. She strove desperately to catch the eye of the older man.

"Hello! M. Dubois! Do you remember me?" she called out, waving.

He swung around. "But of course, Mlle. Boisvert! How could I forget?"

The good-looking boy turned away to join the group of performers, and Dubois came towards her. His face was beaming with pleasure. "M. Dubois," she said, "I'm so sorry I didn't meet up with you in Montreal. I would still really like to, though, and talk to you about my dad." *And a whole lot of other things,* she added silently to herself.

He smiled. "I would talk to you now, but my friends and I have to drive to Montreal tonight, and then on to Quebec City early tomorrow."

"Oh." Her heart plummeted. "I – see."

"But perhaps you'd like to come for a visit sometime? It is the Winter Carnival in Quebec next month, and Angélique and I will be at home. Say that you will come, and be our guest!"

"Thanks, but I wouldn't dream of imposing on you. I could stay at a hostel or something – "

"No, no! You will not be able to find a room at a hostel during Carnival time, they are booked up months in advance. But you are very welcome to join us. You have my card still?"

"I – I lost it," she lied, embarrassed. "Sorry."

"No matter, I shall give it to you again. Here."

She clutched the precious little square of cardboard to her and stammered her thanks. Then she watched as the old man and his performers began to move away towards the stage, disappearing behind its curtain – back into Canada. As she made her own way back through the now-deserted auditorium and down to the main floor she felt almost giddy with renewed hope. It would be all right, after all. Here was an adult and friend, someone who knew all about the Boisverts, who could comfort and advise her, tell her what she should do –

"Chantal! Well, well, what a bit of luck finding you here!"

The voice spoke in French. Chantal started and looked wildly around her. For an instant she half-thought she had imagined it, but there in the half-light of the empty library stood a tall figure. Yes, it was really he...

"What are *you* doing here?" she cried. "No – stay away from me – " as Yves stepped towards her. There was no one else around here on the lower floor either, no one to whom she could cry for help. All the concert-goers had left for home.

Yves stood still. "What's wrong, Chantal? Why did you run away from us like that? Your Grandmère is very hurt."

At that Chantal's short temper came to her defense, rising up hot and fierce within her. "My Grandmère! Did you know she was putting drugs in my tea? What kind of a grandmother does that?" Energized by her anger, she moved towards him. "You *did* know, didn't you? What exactly did she give me?"

198

His amber eyes did not meet hers. "Thérèse would give you nothing that would harm you."

"So you don't deny it! What was it, some kind of acid? I had horrible dreams and – and *trips,* afterwards. Just like something you'd get from LSD. The people who found me in the forest said I was out cold, lying on the ground. I could have *died!* And I've been having problems ever since – hallucinations, and – and –"

"Hallucinations?" Yves stared at her. Suddenly he began to laugh. "Is that what you think? That you're just reacting to a drug?" He moved towards her again. "Tell me. These... dreams of yours: would they by any chance be about turning into an animal? A wolf, *par exemple?"*

It was chilly in the room, yet she was sweating heavily. Her fury had abated, leaving her feeling drained and fearful once more. She took a step back. "I said stay away."

He pointed downwards, to the black line of the border running across the floorboards between their feet. "Stay away? I'm not even in your country! I'm still in Quebec. Don't panic*, chérie,* I will keep to my own side of the line. I just ask you to listen." His tone grew more serious. "Chantal, you can't trust Honoré Dubois. He's the one you should want to stay away from you. Do you think it's a coincidence that he and his merry little troupe showed up here, in your tiny little hometown? That they have no other engagements elsewhere in the county? Strange, *non?* The truth is, he's after you. Trying to lure you out of hiding, so he can make you one of his pack."

*Pack?* "I don't know what you're talking about. And what are *you* doing here anyway?" she threw over her shoulder as she headed for the door.

"I came here as soon as I heard Dubois was on his way. I wanted to warn you about him." True to his word, he did not step over the border line, but he shadowed her along his side of it – *stalking me,* she thought – as she made her way towards the entrance. "Once you are in his hands he will try to tame you and change you. To make you into what *he* wants you to be. We cannot let that happen to you." Yves reached out suddenly, across the border, and for an instant she thought he was going to try and grab her arm. But he merely held his open hand out to her and spoke again, using a softer tone this time. "You're so alone in this place," he said, looking straight into her eyes. "You should be with *us*, Chantal. With your own kind."

"My own kind?" Again she felt that hot, prickling sensation down her back, and with it came a spurt of anxiety. "What do you mean exactly? What's 'our' kind?"

"Instead of telling you, can I not show you? Come back to Quebec with me. There's going to be a special gathering next month, just family and friends, and I'd love for you to be there with me. To meet all the people I care about." His voice took on an imploring tone. "We want to protect you, to help you. One day, you may even learn to accept what you are, not to fear it – "

She had been determined not to run away from him, not to let him see any sign of fear in her. But at those words her nerve broke, and she fled: through the door and out of the building in one frantic burst of speed, desperate to be out of reach of his voice.

She slept poorly again that night, and woke up to the familiar hot, itching sensation. Nana had looked on central heating as a shameful luxury and indulgence, keeping the house so cold that in the daytime Chantal had sometimes fled down the street to the cozy warmth of her aunt's home. But apparently Uncle Phil and Aunt Lorraine had no such compunctions about sparing heating oil. She threw off the covers and her sweaty T-shirt and sleep pants, and reached for her terrycloth robe. Since sleep was impossible, she would just go watch television downstairs until she was too tired to sit up any longer.

The terrier puppy growled at her as she went by his basket at the foot of the stairs, but she ignored him. She poured herself a glass of cold water in the kitchen and filled it with ice, then went to sit and drink it in the family room. She glanced out the window as she turned on a lamp, and then she started, splashing water on herself.

*Why am I so jumpy? It's nothing: just the lamplight reflecting off something outdoors...*

A small pale light glimmered through the shadows under the fir trees at the back of the property. Surely it was only her strained nerves that made her imagine a second glimmer right next to it? No – there really *was* another one. They did look uncannily like eyes –

The lights moved.

As Chantal stared out the window a dark, furtive shape slunk out from under the trees. It looked towards the house, and now she saw, unmistakably, a pair of pale eyes glowing like twin moons in the light from the window. She lurched backwards with a strangled cry.

*It's a coyote. Or maybe a neighbour's dog has gotten loose. That's all. There are no wolves in Vermont. There are no wolves....*

The glass slipped from her fingers and crashed to the floor. She had not released her hold; rather, her fingers had grown strangely stiff and could not seem to grasp it. Her pounding heart seemed to shake her entire body with each beat, and the adrenaline racing through her veins made her light-headed. Then she began again to feel the strange sensation, like the sprouting of fur – she could *see* it, darkening her arms and her bare feet.

201

She threw off the heavy encumbering bathrobe, panting. It was happening again: the half-waking recurrent nightmare. The illusion of fur, of paws that replaced her hands and feet; in a moment she would be crawling about on the floor, snapping and snarling, in the manner of lycanthropy patients. She could hear Terry barking and whining hysterically, terrified no doubt by her odd, animalistic behaviour. Somebody upstairs would hear; they would come down and find her, unclothed, groveling and growling on the floor. Gasping, she struggled to pull her robe back on again, but her hands still stubbornly insisted they were paws, and her eyes conspired in the lie. She could not seem to get any grip on the robe, only claw and rend its fabric.

Then pain needled through her leg. Teeth bit her foot – *hind paw?* – below the ankle, tearing a cry from her throat: a hoarse wordless howl of hurt and rage. She whirled in surprise and fear to confront her attacker. It was the terrier. She advanced on him, her own fangs bared in fury, and he bolted in panic behind the couch. She lunged after him, shoving her head as far as it would go into the narrow space. The smell of him filled her nostrils, maddening her. She wanted to seize him in her jaws – tear his flesh – feel his warm pulsing life ebb away between her teeth. The little dog cowered back, whimpering, all aggression gone as she sought to force her shoulders between couch and wall.

Feet thumped across the ceiling, heading for the stairs. Voices were calling out. At the noise Chantal pulled back, startled. Her hands came back to her: she could feel her fingers again, and saw that they had lengthened and lost their coat of imaginary fur. She grabbed for her robe and yanked it on, then flung herself onto the couch cushions even as her relatives ran into the room en masse. Lights flashed on, dazzling her eyes.

202

"Chantal! What happened? You're hurt!" cried Aunt Lorraine. "Tammy, run and get the first aid kit in the bathroom cupboard upstairs."

Blood was smeared on her bitten ankle. "Terry bit me. And there was – I thought I saw – " She threw a quick glance out the window. The ground outside was hard, the snow trampled to slush and re-frozen into glassy ice: it showed no trace of footprints. Impossible to say if the lupine shape she had seen was real, or only another delusion.

"She was sleepwalking again," Liz said. "Look, stuff's scattered all over the place!"

"We *told* you it wasn't Terry!" said Jesse, triumphant.

"Boys, go back to bed please. And take Terry with you."

The dog emerged from underneath the couch and, recovering his courage, lunged towards Chantal. He barked wildly, his brown button eyes filled with fear and furious accusation. Jesse snatched the dog up and carried him out, followed by Norman.

"You've got to do something about this sleepwalking, Chantal," said Amanda, sitting beside her on the couch.

Tammy returned with the kit. "Here, Lorraine."

Under the light of the lamp Lorraine studied the wound with a nurse's practiced eye. "It's not too bad, his teeth didn't do much more than graze the skin. But let's just go down the hall to the powder-room and get this washed properly, and I'll put some antibiotic ointment on it."

"What she needs is a shrink," said Liz.

Chantal rounded on her. "Shut your mouth, Liz! I've had it with you and your snide remarks! If you push me one more – "

"Chantal!" cried Amanda.

203

The shock in her older cousin's voice forced Chantal to attention. She realized that she had been practically screaming, and baring her teeth as she yelled. She'd lost her temper many times in the past, but never like this. They were all staring at her in open-mouthed disbelief – even alarm. Liz had turned pale, the smug insouciance completely wiped away from her face.

"What am I saying?" Chantal rasped. "I don't know why I said that. What's the matter with me?"

Aunt Lorraine stood up. "Come along, Chantal," she said, quietly but firmly. "Let's go wash that graze. And how about I give you something to help you to sleep?"

Shaking, Chantal let her aunt lead her from the room. Her breath was still coming in ragged gasps and her legs were unsteady as she walked the short distance to the downstairs bathroom. She could almost feel everyone's eyes following her down the hallway.

*What's the matter with me?*

## 15

For those who first come upon it by road, the Old City of Quebec is a complete surprise. From that direction the profile Quebec first presents might be any urban skyline: high-rises, office towers, a hotel with discoid revolving top floor: all aggressively modern. But driving on down the Grande Allée, past the cafes and bistros and the rows of town houses and condominiums, one is confronted by the St Louis Gate. With its arched entrance and little watchtower it resembles a relic of the Middle Ages, as does the grey stone wall into which it is set. Once past this guardian portal one is in Old Quebec, and time like a retreating tide appears to reverse its flow.

The Old City is the original settlement of Quebec. Its grey stone houses are guarded by grey stone fortifications, some still sporting mounted cannons: the oldest of these walls date to the sixteen-hundreds, when Samuel de Champlain built the first fort. It is the only walled city that survives in North America, and its inner citadel to this day remains an active army base. Outside its ramparts the urban landscape has sprawled and raised its upstart towers, but for the most part Old Quebec remains impervious to modernity. By some inexplicable oversight a wealthy and powerful family in the 1930's was allowed to erect a skyscraper within the old city's walls, the *Edifice Price*. But it is modest in scale compared to other high-rises of the period, and remains a unique exception. After four centuries Quebec looks very much as it did in its early days. So it will appear, at least, to those who approach it from the opposite direction, by ferry across the St. Lawrence River. From that perspective it is a walled bastion looming atop sheer cliffs, dark and imposing against the sky. "The impression made upon the visitor by this Gibraltar of America: its giddy heights; its citadel suspended, as it were, in the air; its picturesque steep streets and frowning gateways; and the splendid views which burst upon the eye at every turn: is at once unique and lasting," wrote Charles Dickens after his visit there. "It is a place not to be forgotten or mixed up in the mind with other places, or altered for a moment in the crowd of scenes a traveller can recall."

It was by road that Chantal made her first approach. As she drove her car down the Grande Allée she could see evidence of the Winter Carnival all around her. The affable visage of Bonhomme, the carnival's snowman mascot, smiled down from banners and posters all over the city. Opposite the parliament building stood a fabulous construction: a frozen palace, built not of snow like the "forts" Chantal and her friends had built as children, but from solid blocks of clear ice. The pseudo-medieval design of its turrets and battlements mimicked Quebec City's own fortifications. Within moments the real city wall rose before her: she guided Minnie through the narrow stone passage of the Porte Saint Louis, and found herself in the inner precinct. Here were houses much like those of Montreal's old port district: sturdily made of solid and well-weathered stone, with small windows and doors that opened right onto the street. Many of these were shops and restaurants now, or small *pension*-style hotels such as she and the other students had stayed in on their trip to France. Beyond rose the largest and grandest hotel of all, the Château Frontenac, designed in imitation of the old aristocratic *châteaux* of France. In the gathering dusk, with its high red-brick walls and its copper turrets reflecting the last lingering glow of sunset, it looked to Chantal like a palace in a fairytale.

As she passed the grand arched gateway leading to its inner court she saw that a dog sled race was in progress. Dozens of over-excited huskies yelped and lunged in

206

their harness, barely restrained by their masters. She watched as they took off down the snowy street, hurtling their drivers right through the heart of town. It seemed an unusual venue for this kind of sport, but the crowds gathered in the public square before the Château and on the Terrasse Dufferin opposite were loudly enthusiastic. Adding to the festive air, an enormous cut fir tree dominated the terrace, secured by cables. It must have been quite a sight when it was lit for Christmas, she thought wistfully as she drove by. She recalled Honoré Dubois's description of the *Temps de Fêtes*. But Christmas was now long over, even for the Québecois.

She found her own hotel, a modest *pension* on the Avenue Genevieve which ran alongside the small public park behind the Château. The "Maison Diamant" was a historic house of rough grey masonry, early-nineteenth century according to the website of the owner who had inherited it from her ancestors. Inside it was full of quaint Victorian bric-a-brac: old framed prints of hunting scenes, china vases, lamps topped by glass globes and supported by gilded cupids. Chantal obtained her key at the front desk from the owner herself, a tiny bird-boned woman who smiled at her and said: "Chantal Boisvert – you are Honoré's friend, no?"

"I – yes," she stammered, startled. "How –"

"I thought I recognized the name. They have mentioned you, he and his wife. They are good friends of mine, and live only a few doors away from here in the Rue St Denis. You will pay them a visit while you are here?"

"Oh, definitely." It was why she had chosen this place, so close to the Dubois residence.

There was no elevator, but she refused to let little Madame Bernier lug her suitcase up the two steep flights, and arrived at her room puffing and out of breath. The chamber was small, but not without charm:

the far wall was of rough grey stone like the house's exterior, and its small lace-curtained window looked out over the street with a fine view of the Château's towers rising over the distant roofs. A horse-drawn *calèche* passed along the street below, clopping and rattling as it carried tourists to some festivity or other. It completed the illusion of being transported to some bygone era.

As she stood there she heard feminine voices tittering and chattering in French in the hallway outside. To her surprise, they came right up to her door and knocked. Chantal went to open it, and saw three young women standing there.

"Um, hello?" she said in English, thinking they must have accidentally knocked on the wrong door.

"Chantal! We heard you'd come at last!" one of the girls, a pert redhead, replied in French. "We were afraid you were going to miss everything."

Now Chantal recognized them. It was their modern dress that had confused her momentarily. These were the three French girls who had sung on stage at the Haskell.

The redhead continued: "I'm Suzette Lafontaine, and these are Hyacinthe and Manon Lafontaine" – indicating her companions, who smiled. "We're cousins. We came here to welcome you."

"Thanks very much." Chantal felt herself begin to relax. Friends of Dubois would be friends to her also; that was plain to see in their smiling faces.

"But why did you not stay with Honoré and Angélique, like us?" asked the blonde girl. "They would have you too, there is lots of room at their place."

"I – uh – I walk in my sleep. A lot. And I have nightmares, too. I've been seeing a specialist and I'm taking some meds, and they seem to be working, but I didn't want to disturb everyone else's sleep – "

Suzette laughed. "Who sleeps during *Carnaval?*"

"Anyway, here I am. So, uh, what sort of things do you do at this carnival?" she asked, trying to sound as if this were her sole reason for coming.

The dark-haired Manon replied. "Many things. Dog sledding, sleigh rides, tobogganing. There is a canoe race on the river. The teams must drag their canoes over the ice floes when there is no open water."

"That sounds kind of dangerous – "

Hyacinthe broke in. "Oh, it is – and so exciting! And there is a parade every weekend, at night; and an ice hotel, like the ones in Scandinavia. You should go see it: the rooms, the furniture, the bar, even the artwork on the walls is all carved out of ice! There are lots of things to do here. Just don't try the Caribou!"

She stared. "Caribou? Isn't that like reindeer? Why shouldn't you eat it?"

The girls giggled. "Oh, there's nothing wrong with caribou *meat,"* said Hyacinthe. "I meant the drink called Caribou, that people here make. It's supposed to keep you warm when you're out of doors. It has vodka in it, and sherry, and port wine, and brandy – oh, it's powerful stuff!"

It sounded positively lethal to Chantal. "Don't worry, I'll steer clear of the Caribou. I'm too young to drink anyway."

"You don't have to drink to have fun," said Hyacinthe. "Millions of people come to *Carnaval* every year. It is the biggest winter carnival in the world. And it has been going on ever since the 1800's – imagine that!"

"We're just heading out to dinner," added Suzette. "A whole bunch of us are going to Aux Anciens Canadiens to celebrate. Honoré's husky team just won *le Grand Viree* – the big dogsled race, you know. It starts here, at the gate of the Château Frontenac, and goes all the way through the city and out over the Plains of Abraham."

"Yes, I saw part of it.  Will M. Dubois be there himself, then?"

"Of course!  Honoré is paying!" laughed Suzette. "Come on!"

Night had fallen.  The sky was black above the roofs and the air cut like a knife; Chantal could almost feel her breath flash-freezing into crystals as it left her lips.  But in the streets all was light, colour and gaiety. *Carnaval* looked to her like a cross between Christmas and Mardi Gras, with a little bit of New Year's Eve thrown in. Many of the revelers in the streets wore the bright red "carnival sash" – another form of the *ceinture flechée* – and carried red plastic carnival horns as long as their arms that made a sonorous but cheerful noise when blown.  The blatting of these horns came from all quarters of the city, like the calls of lovesick moose. People stood together in groups, stamping their feet in the cold, drinking hot drinks, and chattering in both official languages.  It would all have been delightful if she were another tourist like them, come here for pleasure only.  If she were not constantly looking over her shoulder, afraid to see a familiar but unwanted figure following her… She had delayed this trip for some time, for that very reason: the fear of running into the Boisverts or the Lapierres. What if they were here also, partaking in the annual celebrations…?

Well, in crowds like these it should surely be easy to avoid them.

The three girls led her through the Parc des Gouverneurs and on past the Château, onto the Terrasse Dufferin.  Ahead of them a great pyramid of lights in vivid jewel colors reared up out of the blackness.

Chantal remembered the giant fir tree on the terrace. "Uh, the Christmas tree's lit," she said.

"Of course!" said Hyacinthe.

"A Christmas tree," repeated Chantal, "in February?" Hadn't Dubois said the *Temps de Fêtes* ended on January 6?

*"Mais bien sûr!"* said Suzette, laughing. "Up here the winter is so long and so cold, we leave our outdoor decorations up for months. They're so pretty and cheerful. They've become part of *Carnaval*."

Chantal, remembering the grey gloom of January evenings back at home, thought that Americans might do well to adopt this custom.

There were more Christmas trees along the streets around the Château Frontenac, set up in front of shops. And there were outdoor ice carvings too, rather like the ones that adorn fancy buffet tables in restaurants but very much larger. Backlit by spotlights, they glowed through the night like statues of illuminated glass: a leaping swordfish in front of a seafood restaurant; a pink-lit pig next to a bistro called Le Cochon Rose. At the doorway of Aux Anciens Canadiens stood a fiddler whose icy limbs seemed to caper along to the recording of Québecois folksongs blaring out of a loudspeaker.

This restaurant had once been a residence, the Maison Jacquet, dating back to 1675: oldest of all the Upper Town's surviving houses. Its exterior was painted white, with a steep gabled roof painted bright red; inside the rooms were small, with low beamed ceilings and walls of rough-hewn mortared stones. The wait staff were costumed like old-style *habitants,* or settlers: the women in long dresses with white aprons, the men in linen shirts and breeches. The three Lafontaine girls, after a quick consultation with the hostess, led Chantal up the narrow wooden staircase to the upper room Dubois had rented for his party. It was cozy and dim, lit only by the flickering lamps on the tables, but she could see that the low roof slanted steeply at the south end, where the deep embrasures of the dormer windows looked down onto the street.

A large group stood in the middle of the room, talking and laughing. Honoré Dubois was indeed there, at the centre of the gathering; at the sight of him Chantal's heart seemed about to burst. She wanted to run to the old man and beg for his help, for reassurance, for advice. But of course she could do no such thing, not in front of everyone. Some of his friends she recognized. René Leblanc, the Acadian man who had played the accordion at the concert, was there; according to Suzette he was a physics professor at Laval University, and only a musician in his spare time. She was also surprised to recognize the Inuit man Aglukkaq from the McGill "Monster Wolf" video: his sharp-chiseled features were unmistakable. It gave her a strange feeling to behold him in the flesh. Beside him she saw the tall youth with the platinum hair who had talked to Dubois at the concert. Though he was plainly and casually dressed in a dark-grey turtleneck and black jeans, the boy's strong sculpted features and unusual pale colouring made him stand out in the group. She had been too distracted at the time to notice whether he left the concert hall along with Dubois's company or not. It was a pleasant surprise to find that he was, in fact, a friend of theirs.

"Who's that?" she whispered, making a surreptitious gesture towards him.

Hyacinthe grinned and dug an elbow in her ribs. "Cute, isn't he? That's Raoul Dulac. I hoped he'd come tonight."

Suzette added, "I should warn you Chantal, despite his name Raoul speaks very little French. But like you he wants to learn how to speak it. You must talk slowly to him, and use simple words."

The boy did look uncomfortable, she thought, standing there in silence while the others talked. Stray tufts of pale hair shaded his eyes, and his hands hung loose at his sides as if he did not quite know what to do with them. As she and the other girls drew closer he looked up, and she saw that his eyes were a striking shade of deep blue, glinting like sapphire in the lamplight. It added to his oddly ethereal appearance.

"*Salut, Raoul!*" Suzette greeted the youth as they passed him on their way to Dubois.

"*Mesdemoiselles,*" he murmured, bobbing his head slightly.

Hyacinthe nodded to their guest. "*Voici notre nouvelle amie, Chantal.*"

"Hello," said Chantal in English, to put him at ease. "Nice to meet you." But Raoul made no reply, and the sapphire-blue eyes quickly shifted away from hers.

What was wrong? Hadn't the girls said he couldn't speak much French? She looked away too, feeling snubbed. But there was no time to dwell on it, for Honoré Dubois and his wife came and placed themselves to either side of her. Madame Dubois embraced Chantal, kissing her on each cheek; there was a warmth and spontaneity to the gesture that had been entirely missing from her grandmother's more formal greeting. Angélique Dubois was no less elegant than Thérèse: her silver hair haloed her head in a mass of perfectly-coiffed curls and her dark eyes and fine-boned face held the same exotic Gallic beauty. "*Ma chère Chantal!* At last I get to meet you! You have such a look of your dear father – hasn't she, Honoré? I am so glad you came!"

"As am I," added her husband, beaming at Chantal. "*Bienvenue a Québec!*"

213

Several tables had been put together and set for the dozen or so diners, and the party began to drift towards them. Gently placing his hand on her shoulder, Dubois guided her to a seat and pulled it out for her. She felt a little shy still, but with the notable exception of Raoul everyone at the table was very friendly, shaking hands and complimenting her on her French. Someone passed her a menu: she did not need to read its English translations, and she knew that "entrée", often misused in English to mean the main course, was in fact the appetizer. The main dishes all seemed to reflect the provincial culture: wild salmon, caribou steak, bison. "It is farmed bison," Dubois told her, "but it is very good. It comes from the Île d'Orléans."

"From where?" Chantal asked.

"The big island out in the middle of the river, just east of here. It is covered in very fertile farmland and supplies our city with fresh produce and other foods. The owner of the bison farm, Bernard Lavallée, is a good friend of mine."

Costumed waitresses bustled in and out of their room, along with young women bearing baskets of red and pink roses for sale. M. Dubois purchased two red roses, handing one to his wife and the other, with a playful flourish, to Chantal. *"Pour vous mademoiselle,* to thank you for joining our company tonight," he said with a smile. Chantal stammered something by way of thanks, and when he turned away again she held the dewy bud to her cheek, feeling the silken softness of the scarlet petals and breathing in the sweet aroma. It meant nothing, of course: just a kindly gesture from an older man to a young woman, a faux-flirtation aimed at building up her self-confidence. Even so must elderly gentlemen of a previous era have flattered timid debutantes at their first coming-out balls. But it still filled her with an almost absurd happiness.

No man had ever given her a rose before.

Most of the guests opted for the bison; Chantal, feeling a little self-conscious, chose the much less expensive *tourtière,* the traditional Québecois meat-pie. It came with golden fried potatoes and red cabbage on the side, and had a savoury filling of ground beef and pork mixed with onions and herbs. It was as different from Parisian cuisine as French Canadian music differed from that of continental France: heavier and heartier. It was very much to the taste of Chantal, who had always had a healthy appetite.

Much of the conversation around the table was centred on Aglukkaq and Dubois, who were apparently partners in a husky breeding programme; Dubois provided the funds and Aglukkaq supplied pure-bred Inuit dogs from his home town in Nunavik. It appeared their sled team had performed exceptionally well in the race, not only winning but leaving their competitors far behind, and there was much cheering and raising of wineglasses. But Chantal couldn't help noticing that Raoul Dulac was still saying little. Perhaps he was hampered by his poor French; or was he simply shy? She hoped that was the explanation for his earlier snub. It was foolish of her to care, really; she must not let her experiences with Russ and Yves make her hypersensitive around boys. And it wasn't as if she were pursuing a relationship.

*Besides, any boy this cute most likely has a girlfriend already.* Chantal instantly pictured the girlfriend in her head: she would be French Canadian, with a sophisticated-sounding name like Monique or Françoise; his age or slightly older, about twenty or so, smart and cultured and confident. She would wear little black dresses that showed off her petite figure, and her hair would never tangle but always lie helmet-smooth on her head. She and Raoul would dine together by candlelight in fashionable bistros – but here Chantal had to rein in her thoughts, as she was working up a surprisingly intense hatred for Monique-or-Françoise.

For dessert Mme. Dubois urged her to try the *tarte au sucre,* another Québecois favourite.  It reminded her of pecan pie, and came with a drizzle of real maple syrup on the side.  "I think I'm going to like it here," she told M. and Mme. Dubois.  "I love the way you French Canadians do food."

Mme. Dubois smiled.  "Then I take it you have not encountered *poutine.*"

"What is that?"

"A most lamentable dish," put in M. Dubois.  "It consists of a bowl of *patates frites,* what in English you call the French fries, smothered in gravy – "

"Oh, no!"

"It gets worse: atop this crime against cuisine are poured melted cheese curds."

Chantal grimaced.  "It sounds to me like a coronary in a bowl."

They all roared with laughter.  "They should put that on the menu in French," said Suzette.  "The Anglo tourists will all want to order the *'crise cardiaque dans une cuvette'!*"

Chantal laughed along with them.  The warm friendliness these people showed her, their *bonhomie,* was exactly what she had longed for from her blood relatives.  She could feel their love for her late father, now naturally extended to her.  For a time she was content merely to relax in that encompassing warmth, leaning back in her chair and listening to the others talk over their dessert and coffee.

Hyacinthe suddenly sprang up from the table, pointing to her wristwatch.  "*Dieu,* the parade!" she cried.  "Hurry or we will miss it!  Come on, Chantal!"

216

Chantal had just enough time to tuck the rose into her purse and grab her coat before the three girls literally dragged her out of the restaurant and into the icy darkness outside.

Tonight's was the first of the two official Night Parades, held in the Haute-Ville or Upper Town. There were marching bands, and fire dancers whirling flaming poles. But the stars of the show were of course the floats, which were illuminated from within like Chinese lanterns. One was shaped like a giant igloo, glowing blue-white through the night: men and women in Inuit parkas danced and strolled around it, some leading over-excited yelping huskies on leashes. Another was apparently based on Québecois folklore. At its centre was a huge canoe containing half a dozen or so costumed men who wielded wooden paddles, pretending to row. The canoe perched atop a gilded pedestal shaped like a Gothic spire.

*"La Chasse Galerie,"* said Manon, seeing her staring at it in puzzlement. "The magic Flying Canoe from the old story. It belonged to the Devil."

"So what's it doing on a steeple?"

"It's supposed to be crashing into it. You see, the Devil's magic won't work near anything holy. If you hit a church tower while you're flying in his canoe, it stops and plunges straight to the ground! That's what happened in the story."

Dancing around the float were more costumed performers, led by a witch-like figure with long flowing black hair, shrieking and laughing diabolically. Manon pointed to her. "That is La Corriveau, the most famous ghost of Quebec City," she told Chantal. "She was a wicked murderess when she was alive, and after she was executed she haunted the city. Sometimes she's a horrible skeleton in an iron cage, sometimes a beautiful woman. She leads an army of ghosts and demons.

217

There's a story that a young man met her once on the bank of the St. Lawrence River at night, and she tried to get him to take her to the Île d'Orléans in his boat."

"That's the island with the farms on it, right?"

"*Oui.* But in the old stories l'Île d'Orléans is also where the Devil was supposed to gather his witches and goblins to dance the night away. Evil spirits cannot cross water on their own, though, especially a river named for a saint. So the young man wisely refused La Corriveau's request and ran away from her."

Behind La Corriveau cavorted her army of supernatural minions, horned devils and cackling witches. One man was costumed in *habitant* dress with a furry wolf's head hiding his face. Suzette and Hyacinthe shrieked with laughter as he lunged and pretended to bite them, and Manon rolled her eyes. "And that is the *loup garou* – what in English you call the werewolf. This one is part-way through transforming, see. By day he's a man like any other, but by night he becomes a wolf." Manon gave a wry little smile. "It's a curse on him because he hasn't been to mass in seven years."

"How long since *you* last went to mass, Manon?" teased Hyacinthe.

"*Mon Dieu,* who can remember back that far?" giggled Suzette.

Manon scooped up a mittful of snow and hurled it at her squealing cousins. But Chantal could not summon a smile. She did not want to think about werewolves and unholy transformations. It came too close to her own terrifying delusions.

The parade ended with an ornate float on which Bonhomme the snowman stood waving and greeting the crowd. The carnival mascot was not the usual carrot-nosed, globular snowman figure, but was more anthropomorphic in design with a broad smile, black

218

eyes puckered with laughter, a jaunty red cap on his head and a striped *ceinture* at his waist. Once he had passed on the parade crowds began to disperse. Chantal was cold and tired, but the three other girls were still full of energy and enthusiasm. "Let's show Chantal the Ice Palace!" Hyacinthe said.

Chantal did not want to seem like a spoilsport, so she followed the girls through the Porte St. Louis. The ice structure glimmered through the dark like the aurora borealis, lit from within by floodlights in shifting hues. One could walk right inside it, following a path of well-trodden snow between its luminous walls. In earlier times, Manon told her, these ice palaces had included a "dungeon" for carnival-goers who did not show the proper festive spirit. Chantal wasn't sure whether to believe this or not. At any rate, nothing of the sort was to be found within the frozen fortifications. At their centre rose a domed tent, showcasing more ice sculptures: swans, snowmen, a carousel with prancing horses. In the flickering light they glittered as if they were carved out of crystal. The crowds inside this central pavilion were thick, almost shoulder-to-shoulder. As Chantal and her companions exited again she lost sight of the other girls. She looked everywhere for them, her eyes sweeping from face to unfamiliar face in the shimmering glow of the icy walls.

The floodlights cycled from blue to green to gold, and then to a blazing red. Chantal's shifting gaze fastened suddenly upon a single face in the crowd, its features clearly revealed in the bright glow. Recognition turned quickly to disbelief, and then flared into full panic.

It was Yves Lapierre.

## 16

No, it couldn't be. Not Yves, not here. She'd been thinking a lot about him, and having him on her mind had led her to mistake some other boy for him. It was only her imagination, she told herself desperately, working overtime... But then the youth in front of her turned again, and his profile showed in the fiery light, sharp and unmistakable: the thick dark hair springing back from the high forehead, the straight-bridged nose and jutting chin. Her heart began to pound uncontrollably. *Is he looking for me? Does he know I'm in Quebec City?*

Of one thing she was certain: he did not know that she was there in the Ice Palace, only a few paces behind him. He was not looking directly at her, but talking to some other person she could not see in the crowd. The lights had dimmed to purple again, but as they changed and brightened she would be plainly visible to him. Abandoning her search for her companions, Chantal turned around, fighting against the flow of the crowds, not daring to risk even a glance over her shoulder. She must get out of the Palace now. With every step she feared that she would hear his voice shouting her name.

Once she was free of the ice structure she ran like a hunted thing for the gate to the old city.

Even after she entered her hotel, slamming the door behind her, she still shivered with fear. The proprietress noticed. "It is very cold here when you are not used to it," she tutted. "Especially at night. You must dress more warmly."

"I'm all right, Madame Bernier. Thank you." Chantal mumbled as she made for the stairs.

"Please, call me Marguerite," the woman called after her. "I can bring you up some hot tea if you are chilled, or coffee if you prefer. It is no trouble."

"No thanks. Really, I'm fine." Chantal bolted up the two steep flights and locked her door. Only then did her breathing begin to slow. The room enfolded her, small and safe and home-like with her teddy bear propped up on a chair and her suitcase sitting in the corner. With hands that still shook slightly she poured herself a glass of water in the bathroom, draining it in a few gulps. Feeling slightly calmer she took Honoré Dubois's rose out of her purse, refilled the glass and placed the flower in the water, then set it on the bureau next to the photograph of her parents.

She had just finished undressing for bed and was reaching for her sleepwear when there was a knock at the door.

Chantal threw on her bathrobe. "Thank you, Madame," she said as she unlocked and opened the door, "it's really kind of you but I don't – " Her voice died in her throat. It wasn't Madame Bernier standing there.

It was her cousin Francine.

"I knew you would come here," the girl said. She spoke in tragic tones, like an actress in a melodrama, her dark eyes welling with tears and angry reproach.

Chantal was too stunned at first to speak. Then with an effort she pulled herself together. "Francine? How did you get in here? And how did you know where I was staying?" she demanded.

Francine looked contemptuous. "I saw you in the crowd at the Palace, and when you ran away I followed you here. There were some boys standing around the hotel door, and they thought I was a guest here too and opened it for me." She stepped forward, her eyes narrowing. "You came to find Yves. You said you didn't want him, but you came here."

Chantal retreated a step. "Francine, that's crazy! I didn't know *any* of you would be here. How could I?"

221

"All of Quebec comes to *Carnaval.*"

Chantal, suddenly weary of the overwrought accusations, turned her back on her cousin. "Look. It's late, and I'm way too tired for all this drama. I'm going to bed now. If you want to argue with me you'll just have to wait till tomorrow."

She made as if to close the door. Immediately Francine launched herself at Chantal, screaming incoherently. She kicked Chantal and pulled her hair, and the older girl slipped and fell over backwards. The door swung shut. Chantal found herself sprawled on her back, on the wrong side of the door; scrambling to her feet she rattled the doorknob, to no avail. The door had latched and automatically locked itself. Then she turned, just in time to seized hold of Francine's wrists as the girl attacked her again. "Cut it out right now!" she yelled.

The younger girl twisted free and backed off, breathing heavily. A group of college-age French boys, no doubt the same ones who had let Francine in, were standing around in the hallway talking. Seeing the fighting girls, they whistled and hooted. But Francine seemed oblivious to their presence, focused solely upon her hated rival.

"I'm going downstairs to get Madame to let me into my room," Chantal told her, struggling to keep her own voice calm. "If you aren't gone by the time we come back, there'll be trouble." She headed downstairs in what she hoped was a dignified fashion, though she was barefoot and wearing nothing but the terry robe.

On the landing Francine pounced on her again and began raining blows on her back and shoulders. "I hate you, I hate you!" she screamed, to cheers from the French boys. "Why do you play games like this? He'll want to be with you again, you know that. Why did you have to come here?"

Chantal tried to pull away, but Francine grabbed her by the hair. "Go on! Show them what you really are!" she shrieked. "Show them!"

And then it happened. She felt the change as an irresistible force seizing control of her. Turning on Francine, she snarled and snapped her teeth. The watching youths laughed no longer: they gaped at her, then yelled. Francine fled down the staircase. With a howl of rage Chantal bounded after the girl, running on all fours, shedding the hampering robe as she went. As she and Francine stormed through the front hallway more people turned and stared.

"Who let the dog in?" she heard someone ask.

"It's not a dog, it's a wolf!" shouted one of the youths, leaning over the upstairs railing.

Suddenly Madame Bernier was there in the hall. "It is all right," she told the astonished onlookers. "The dog sled owners, they sometimes get a bit drunk after the *Grand Viree*. One of them must have let his husky loose."

"It's a *wolf,* I swear to God!" the French youth shouted. "It was a girl, and then it was a wolf!"

"It's true, we saw it!" added another boy. He tossed down the terrycloth robe. "She was wearing this, and then suddenly it was a wolf in the robe instead – "

"It looks like you kids have been drinking too!" retorted Madame, turning brusque. "Or is this your idea of a joke? Anyway, no more shouting if you please: you'll disturb the other guests."

The young men went back upstairs, muttering to one another. Chantal stared after them, then cast her gaze down at her hands – her *paws* – and began to tremble.

*But I'm just hallucinating! This isn't real. So how can they see what I see...?*

"I will care for this... dog, until its owner is found. Come!" Madame took up the robe and gestured to

Chantal to follow her. She obeyed clumsily, stumbling on all fours still. The woman bent down and whispered in her ear. *"Vite!* Back upstairs, before anyone else sees you. Don't be afraid, you're with a friend."

Chantal tried to speak, but all that came out was a wordless whimper.

The proprietress led her up the staircase, unlocked the door to Chantal's room and let her in, replacing the robe gently atop her shivering body. Collapsing to the floor, Chantal held up her hands, and saw to her relief that they *were* hands once more. But she could not stop shaking. Again she strove to speak, and this time was able to form words.

"They *saw,"* she rasped.

"Yes."

"I – I really *changed.* Didn't I?"

"Yes," the woman said again.

The world had altogether ceased to be real. It faded, replaced by sparkling spots that crowded everything else out of her field of vision. She scarcely felt the kindly hands that helped her to her feet and guided her to the bed. When she reached it her knees buckled underneath her and she sank down onto the bedspread, curling up in a ball.

"Rest now," said the soft voice, seeming now to come from a very long distance away. "Don't be afraid, *ma petite.* I know someone who can help you."

Chantal was never afterwards sure if it was a true sleep she fell into, or a swoon of sheer exhaustion. She rose up out of the dim unconscious state some time later to the sound of someone knocking at the door. This time she did not go and open it, but called out fearfully: *"Madame?"*

A deep voice answered. "No, *mademoiselle.* It is I, Honoré Dubois. May I come in?"

Dubois! That name again, like a lifeline being thrown to her… Chantal's eyes strayed to the rose in the tooth-glass.

*"Un moment, monsieur,"* she croaked, and struggled to her feet.

She got dressed with fumbling unsteady hands, and went to the door. She opened it – cautiously, just a crack at first in case of any tricks; but it was indeed Dubois standing there in the hallway, his hazel eyes anxious in his lean, lined face. When he saw her he smiled, and she opened the door wide so he could enter.

*"Mademoiselle* Boisvert." He came in and seated himself on the chair. "Marguerite has told me what happened. My poor child, I am so sorry you have been frightened. Why did you not come to me before now?"

"I – I didn't know then." Chantal struggled to control her trembling voice. "I didn't understand … and later on, when I, when things started happening, I couldn't find your contact information anywhere. I threw out the first card you gave me in Montreal. But you knew where *I* was. Why didn't you –"

"No, I never approach any of … our kind … directly," he said before she could finish the question. "Not at first. I let them come to me, when they decide that they are ready. I did bring my little concert to your town – "

She felt a fresh prickling of fear. "The concert – Yves said you came to Derby Line just for me," she said, sitting down on the bed. "He said you were there because you were trying to recruit me – "

"No! Had I any such wish I could have contacted you while I was in town. But I didn't. I let you decide whether or not to come and see me. And you did come: first to the concert, and then here to Quebec City, so I knew you had a need to talk. Anything about your

225

father you could have learned from the Boisverts. You came here to ask me about – about your other self."

A little pause fell between them, a shared silence, before he resumed. "You must realize now what you are. That the old stories are true. Many of us live in secret here in this province. Yes, I am one myself, and so was your father Édouard. It comes to you through him." He gestured to the framed photograph on her bureau. "He always feared that you would inherit it."

She closed her eyes as the events of the evening replayed themselves in memory. "I thought I was going crazy at first. But tonight, when those boys said that they *saw* me, I knew it had to be... real."

"They did witness your transformation, but according to Marguerite they had been partaking generously of Caribou, and after smelling their breath everyone they talked to either dismissed their account or assumed they were playing a prank. Anyway, even had they been sober who would believe them? No one could take seriously this mad tale of a *loup garou.*" Dubois smiled.

"A werewolf." Chantal's voice had sunk to a whisper.

Werewolves were monsters. She'd seen them in old B-movies: actors in costumes that made them look more like deformed baboons than wolves, hideous unnatural creatures. "But how can it be *possible?*" she cried. "How can a person change their body – turn into an animal?"

He shook his head. "There is no one theory for how this all began. It goes back to a time before recorded history, before science. There are many accounts, though, of wolf-people in ancient writings. They are mentioned in the works of Plato, of Herodotus, of Petroneus and Pliny. *'These herbs and these poisons, culled in Pontus, Moeris himself gave me – they grow plenteously in Pontus. By their aid I have oft seen*

226

*Moeris turn wolf and hide in the woods',"* he quoted. "That is from Virgil's *Eclogues.*"

"Herbs?" Chantal stared. "My grandmother gave me a drink right before I had my first – experience. A kind of herbal tea, a tisane. It tasted strange. I thought later she must have slipped me some kind of drug, and that's why I dreamed of being an animal."

"No, it was a herbal potion she gave you. Those old Pontic herbs of which Virgil wrote still exist, and if ingested they can bring out the wolf-tendency. But the potion only works in those of lupine descent. The *loup garou* strain, you see, is an inherited trait. Only in the movies does one become a werewolf from a bite, and transform at the full of the moon! But sometimes the condition is latent, and must be awakened by other means. There are those who say the mere smell and feel of a wolf's fur is all that is needed to arouse the buried instincts, and in the lore of the Middle Ages one reads of people wearing wolf-skins in order to transform. But herbal salves and potions were more often used. Some men of science identify these as common henbane and nightshade, which are hallucinogenic, and say they merely gave people the *illusion* of becoming a beast. But the *loups garous* know better."

As he spoke she grew slowly calmer. He was so calm himself, so matter-of-fact, speaking of the impossible as if he were a schoolteacher delivering a quite ordinary history lesson. "But why all the secrecy? Why does no one else know about – these things?" she asked in a low voice.

"One simple reason: fear. There was a time when *loups garous* walked openly: when a man like Genghis Khan could boast of his wolf ancestry and command respect for it; when Prince Vseslav of Polotsk roamed the steppes as a giant wolf, and his subjects looked on him in fear but also with awe… In Ireland the clan-chief

227

of Ossory and his sons often went hunting as wolves, even raiding local farmers' herds as the whim took them. For they bore the blood of the first Irish kings in their veins, and took what they considered their due.

"Then in the later Middle Ages there was a werewolf craze, much like the more famous witch burnings which occurred around the same time. You may have heard of Peter Stubbs, one of the most infamous cases. He was executed for confessing to multiple murders and acts of cannibalism, supposedly committed while he was in wolf form. But many innocent *loups garous* were also slain, especially in France which was the very centre of the werewolf frenzy. An entire family, the Gandillons, was burnt at the stake. One woman, Madame Sanroche, was handed over to the authorities by her own husband. In the Franche-Comté region it was legal to hunt *loups garous* as if they were mere animals. We are lucky, *mademoiselle,* that we were not born into those evil times."

Chantal swallowed, but could not find her voice.

"We survive today only due to a quirk of fate. With a very few exceptions, the *loups garous* that died in those purges were peasants. In a little village everyone is aware of what everyone else is doing. A man who steals off in the night, who goes often alone into the forest, will be observed and suspected of being a werewolf. But the nobleman, who watches *him?* He owns vast tracts of land, forests full of deer and boar on which no one dares trespass on pain of death. He can go into these woods of his whenever he pleases, and no one dares question him. This is why the few werewolves now living in the world are mainly of royal or noble blood.

"But even for the aristocratic *loups garous* the end came eventually. In Europe and Britain the forests were cut down to make way for farms and towns. The persecuted wolf-people of France, especially, began to look to the New World with its virgin forests. The French Revolution drove out the last of the old aristocratic wolf-families. Many fled to New France, becoming *seigneurs* or landowners. Others chose to be *voyageurs,* bold frontiersmen who explored the wild lands on foot or in canoe. Still others renounced the human form altogether and went to live as wolves in the wilderness. But they distinguished themselves from the wild Canadian wolves, which they called *bas-loups:* low-wolves. They named themselves high-wolves, *hauts-loups,* because they possessed the power of human reason. There are to this day a few of these *haut-loups* remaining in remote areas of our province. They are a vanishing race, however."

*The Monster Wolves,* Chantal thought suddenly, recalling the McGill lecture. The man-sized wolves that were uncannily intelligent, too cunning to be caught in any trap...

"But those *loups garous* that remained in their human forms prospered. Many became merchants, providing furs to the Hudson Bay Company – for they always knew where to find the wild animals, *naturellement!"* He chuckled. "Some families have dwelt here in Quebec City since the time of the first settlement. That is not to say they lived openly as werewolves. Back in the old days they literally went underground, digging secret tunnels beneath the city so they could pass unseen outside its walls, which were then surrounded by wild woodland. When Quebec was conquered by the British (led by a general named, in one of history's great ironies, James Wolfe) the *loups garous* were more afraid than ever. To this day we still dare not reveal our existence."

She began to shiver again. "I think I can see why."

"But we may yet do so, one day. It's what we all hope for. In the meantime we keep a low profile, while hiding in plain sight. There are powerful *loups garous* who move in the upper levels of Quebec society, in the corridors of power even, unbeknownst to their human colleagues. Businessmen, politicians, even a few members of the Roman Catholic clergy… Some of these have joined forces in a secret clique, a *cabale* that watches over our people and ensures that we are never discovered. Myself, I worry sometimes that they are growing too used to power and may even have some sinister designs. But those *loups garous* do not interfere with our little group for the most part.

"We have a few friends who are regular humans. Marguerite Bernier for instance is a good friend of ours: that is why she was so helpful to you. Her family has known of the existence of *loups garous* for centuries. And the Inuit gentleman whom you met at our dinner, Noah Aglukkaq, is also a secret ally of ours."

"I met someone else," she said, "at Mont Tremblant, a native woman. She said she knew you – " Recalling her meeting with the woman in the shack was like recalling a strange dark dream.

"Ah yes, Josephine Legris; she told me of your encounter. But she is in fact a *loup garou* herself, you know. You shall meet her again, for she is staying here in Quebec City, and I will ask her to come and see you. For many years Josephine has helped young *loups garous* to find their way.

"Our kind can no longer run free in western Europe and Britain: we would draw unwanted attention, for wolves there are either scarce or extinct. Even in your own country of America the wolf population was largely eradicated by the European settlers, and to this day any talk of reintroduction is greeted with hostility and resistance. But in Canada wild wolves are common and accepted as a fact of life, especially in our northern regions. The *Canadiens* love the wilderness. They build summer cottages and cabins deep in the forest, and go there whenever they can to escape the stresses of modern life. So it is that my people are able to retreat into the wilds and no one thinks anything of it. If the normal humans should happen to hear a wolf-howl or two in the night, *eh bien,* that is only to be expected in cottage country! Here we can live as we like, without ever arousing suspicion. This is a land made for *loups garous.*"

He rose to his feet and held his hand out to her. "Now: my home, as you may know, is not very far from here. Won't you come and stay with me and Angélique for a while? We would be glad to have you."

The winter dawn was breaking outside the window, grey tinged with ashen rose. But Chantal knew that even in daytime she dared not stay here alone. The Boisverts and the Lapierres knew where she was. Whoever – whatever – Honoré Dubois might be, she would have to place her trust in him: there was no alternative. And her instincts leaned towards trust. His gentle manner was nothing like the bullying condescension of Yves and Thérèse.

And if what the woman Josephine had said was true, he had been a loyal friend to her father.

"Yes," she whispered. "Yes, please."

The Dubois home was only a short walk away, on the parallel street of St Denys where some of Quebec's oldest buildings stood. The house was built of the same weathered grey stone as the city walls, with a brass plaque beside its door proclaiming its historicity: *Maison Dubois, 1702.* "This house was built by my ancestors. Countless others have sought refuge here," Honoré told Chantal as they entered. "I use it as a safe

231

house for our kind. Your father was often my guest here, in the old days."

"M. Dubois, can you tell me what happened to my father? I was always told he died in some kind of hiking accident."

He hesitated before answering her. "That is what your family told us. We did not believe them. We do know that the Boisverts did not approve of his marriage, and Édouard once threatened to reveal himself as a *loup garou* to the public if his family ever harmed his wife. When she died in the car accident, he blamed the Boisverts even though they swore they had nothing to do with it. A witness to the accident said Helen swerved to avoid hitting an animal that looked like a dog or coyote – or a wolf. Shortly afterwards Édouard went to the Boisvert cottage at Tremblant and denounced them all, saying that he intended to carry out his threat. He ran out the door, and his father went after him; neither was ever seen alive again." Another long pause. "We learned eventually that Édouard and Émile had been found dead in the forest, both in their wolf forms, with many fang-marks to the throat and chest. Some say they must have killed each other in their rage."

"But you don't believe that?" asked Chantal.

"It is hard to accept. For all their personality conflicts, there was real love between Édouard and his father. It need not have been murder. Perhaps they inflicted those wounds on each other in the heat of passion, without truly intending to kill... But we may never learn what really happened."

Somewhere in the house a telephone rang shrilly, an unexpected sound at that early hour. Dubois paused and frowned slightly, but walked on. "Someone else will answer it," he said. He opened a door to the left of the main entrance hall. The room beyond was light and airy, with white-and-gold Toile paper on the walls, and

232

many paintings in gilt frames. Old leaded windows looked out towards the low grey battlements of the Citadelle, rising above the snow-clad slope. In one corner of the room stood a grand piano, in another a tall golden harp. Dubois went and stood next to the latter, running his hand along the strings. "My wife's. Like most *loups garous* she loves music, and she taught me to love it also. The human world knows me as Honoré Dubois, wealthy philanthropist and patron of the arts. But I have another, secret purpose. Encouraging young *loups garous* to cultivate the arts helps reinforce their humanity. Your father was a gifted musician, Chantal. I am sure you are likewise talented."

"Well. I don't know about gifted, but I do play guitar and I like to sing. I was in the Glee Club at my school."

He nodded. "Even wild wolves that have no human blood in them will give tongue for the sheer joy of it. Humans call it howling, but it is singing in the truest sense of the word. Music is the art that most appeals to *loups garous*, for it speaks both to the human and the wolfish side. But all the arts are emphasized here. This painting, now, is particularly important," said Dubois, indicating a large dark oil in a heavy frame that hung over the mantelpiece. It portrayed classically-attired figures in a pastoral landscape, gathered around a tomb with an inscription. "I give it the place of honour here because it holds a special significance for our people. You see – "

He broke off as a tall figure with pale silvery hair came and stood in the doorway. Chantal's heart gave a little leap of recognition. But Raoul Dulac did not look at her. His eyes went straight to Dubois. "It is for you *monsieur,* the telephone," he said in his awkward, halting French. "*Madame* asks that you come at once."

*"Merci."* The old man turned to Chantal. "Excuse me, *mademoiselle*. Perhaps you would like to rest a while? You cannot have slept much last night."

"Not really," Chantal admitted.

He turned back to the boy. "Raoul, will you show our guest to one of the spare rooms?"

*"Avec plaisir.* Please to follow me, *mam'selle,"* Raoul replied. He still did not look directly at Chantal. But it did not seem like a snub to her now. There was a kind of deference, even a polite subservience, in his lowered gaze as he ushered her out of the room.

Chantal welcomed the word "rest". She was beginning to feel the after-effects of shock and nervous exhaustion. As she followed the pale-haired boy up the elegant oaken staircase she felt as though she were in a dream that refused to end. And as she lay down on the spare room bed, still fully clothed, she had a sudden moment of déjà vu. No, more than that, she thought: an actual memory. She was positive that she recalled another similar scene. In it she was also lying down on a bed in some unfamiliar place, and somebody was standing over her. A protective presence, guarding, watching her…

"Don't go yet," she said as Raoul went to the door. "Wait just a moment."

He stood looking shy and awkward, his hands hanging loose at his sides. *"Mam'selle?"* he murmured.

"You're a – a *loup garou*, too. Aren't you?" He nodded, still not looking straight at her. "I have this strange feeling that we've met before, somewhere. Have we?"

He hesitated. "Yes, and no. It was at Mont Tremblant, after you ran from the Boisverts. You were in wolf shape then, and not fully awake. Josephine and I kept watch over you in the shed. So I was there, but I thought you did not see me."

"The memory's kind of blurry... Why weren't you there when I woke up?"

He looked uncomfortable, shifting his weight from foot to foot as he spoke. "Back then I was not able – that is to say, I did not wish to alarm... It was best for you to see just the woman, Josephine, when you woke." He stumbled over the words, as if unsure what to say. "Rest now. I will stay here if you like, until you fall asleep."

"Yes, please." She shut her eyes, glad of his guardian presence.

It was not long before her thoughts blurred again into sleep, but her slumber was not restful. She dreamed that Thérèse pursued her through the night, transforming into La Corriveau and stretching out long bony fingers to seize her. Ahead of her Chantal saw a great river, barring her way. The St. Lawrence. From the centre of its frozen surface, pale under the moon, rose the black shape of an island whose shores smouldered with red flickering fires. As she stood there a canoe appeared – not on the river but in the air. It swept down out of the dark sky, settling on the riverbank. Strange figures sprang out of it, creatures neither human nor animal; they ran towards her, grinning with fanged mouths, reaching out for her with hands that ended in claws.

Thérèse/La Corriveau came striding into their midst, laughing shrilly in triumph, calling out words of command to the monsters. "Seize her! We will take her with us."

They obeyed her, surrounding Chantal. She knew they meant to bear her away with them in that demonic vessel, away to the island of fire and shadow. She tried to scream, yet no sound came from her throat. But even as she despaired, there was a flash of white in the darkness and the blue-eyed wolf was there, baring his teeth at the monsters, placing his powerful body between

235

them and Chantal. As she sank to her knees in the snow her would-be captors retreated. Piling into their enchanted canoe, they rose into the air again and flew away: far over the frozen river, to dance with the damned on the Île d'Orléans.

Hunter waited until she was breathing regularly, then left the room as quietly as possible. He went back down the staircase slowly and with great care. Balancing on only two legs made him constantly afraid he would fall, and descending steps gave him vertigo. Holding the banister was not a solution, for he still did not quite know how to use his human hands with their long supple digits. He leaned instead against the wall, taking one step at a time, and breathed a sigh of relief when he was back on the ground floor. There he paused before the hall mirror.

A human face looked out at him, but he no longer flinched at the sight as he had done at first. He confronted it, taking in the strange features, the patch of pale hair confined to the top of the head, the upright body with its curious coverings that moved loosely as he walked, brushing against his newly sensitive and hairless skin. This was not a disguise, an assumed appearance. This was truly who he *was,* as much as his old familiar form…

A new body. A new life.

"Raoul," said a soft voice nearby. He turned. *And a new name to go with them,* he thought. *I am not Hunter any more. I am Raoul.*

Josephine was standing there in the hallway, watching him contemplate his reflection. "It's still hard, isn't it? I know that everything feels strange and different, but we'll figure this out together." She came up and placed a hand on his shoulder, and they stood looking in the mirror together. "And it all began with a

236

dream… That's what I keep coming back to. You've said, Raoul, that you've had lots of dreams about becoming human before. Why did this one have such a unique effect on you, do you think?"

"It was no dream." It was still difficult to form phrases in wolf-speech when his palate felt so different.

"Perhaps you're right." The *rugaru* woman moved to look straight into his eyes. "I've talked to many people on my travels who have undergone vision quests, as some call them. It's a very old rite, performed by many tribes. A young boy on the verge of manhood would go apart from his people for a time, out into the wilderness, and enter into a trance where he would seek the guidance of the spirit world. The climax of the vision was the appearance of a spirit guide, usually in the form of an animal that would afterwards become a personal totem. This spirit would offer wisdom and advice to the youth, who would then rouse from his trance and return to his people."

He nodded his head slowly in the human gesture for agreement. "It does not sound exactly like what I saw."

"Ah, but you see you were not yet human then," said Josephine. "You went apart from your people, your pack, into a strange place: not the wilderness, for a wolf would feel perfectly at home in any natural environment, but a new, unfamiliar, man-made landscape that was the equivalent for you of a wilderness. A place where you felt cut off and out of your element. And instead of seeing an animal in your vision, you saw a human figure – which again makes sense, because you were an animal yourself and a human would seem otherworldly to you. Chantal became your totem: an apparition in the form of a living creature, who put you on the path to wholeness and personal growth. I believe in these things, Raoul. I've talked to people who have experienced them. What you described to Honoré and me does sound much more detailed than an ordinary dream, and *deeper* somehow. Maybe something, some higher power, is trying to communicate with you. Or maybe your own mind is trying to tell you something.''

Raoul pondered this. It was not unheard of for *loups garous* to shift their shapes in response to duress. Back in the Tremblant forest he had witnessed for himself Chantal's instinctive response to the brutal assault by her relatives, her wolf-self emerging in a desperate bid to save her woman-self. He had undergone a similar change, out of a perceived need to save not himself but another from grievous harm. The true transformation had been in his mind, but that had molded the rest of him in turn, altering his body even as he slept. All this he owed to the feelings she had awakened in him without even knowing it.

He glanced back up the staircase. The Chantal of his vision might be only a shadow, a memory bound within a dream. But the real, living Chantal was here now, in this very house, and it was possible for him to help her in the real world. *She has inspired me,* he thought to himself, *whether she knows it or not. Perhaps I can inspire her in turn, guide her to a greater understanding of her own nature? I can at least try. She has made me human; I can help her learn to be a wolf.*

"Come with me now. There is something we all need to discuss." Josephine led him down the hall and into the large sitting room.

"What is wrong?" he asked when he saw the other people gathered inside. Dubois was with his mate Angélique and the tundra-man Aglukkaq. Raoul had not yet grasped all the subtleties of human facial expressions, but the body language of the figures in the room alerted him that something terrible must have occurred. Dubois sat in a chair, his shoulders slumped, his head cradled in his hands: Angélique was standing

238

over him, murmuring in a low, soothing tone words that Raoul could not quite catch with his human ears. Aglukkaq's head was bent.

"We have had bad news, Raoul," Josephine told him. "Honoré's friend Marc Hébert has been found dead. You remember, he was one of the men you encountered in the north."

"*Désolé*," said Raoul. "How did it happen?"

"His body was found in a place called Algonquin Park," said Josephine. "He was killed by a wolf, according to reports. But wolf-people who are friends of ours have seen the body, and they tell us his wounds were too large to have been made by the small red wolves that live in the park. This was the act of a *loup garou.*"

Dubois raised his head. His face was ashen, and every line in it showed. "*Dieu.* I was so afraid of this. Why did our watchers not protect him? I told them not to take their eyes off him when he was alone in the wilderness!"

"I doubt he was killed in the wilderness," said Josephine. "He made regular trips to town for supplies. A *rugaru* in human form could have lured him to an empty building or other remote place, then transformed to a wolf and killed him. His body could have been dumped in the park afterwards. I would bet you anything it was Jules Lapierre who did it. This business has his paw-prints all over it."

Aglukkaq nodded. "Jules would not hesitate to commit murder. Once he learned that Marc Hébert was the one who fatally shot Guy Lapierre, he would not rest until he had his revenge. But the Lapierres would have murdered him in any case, I think. Hébert was getting far too interested in his so-called Monster Wolves. The Stone Pack are not like you people; they will kill to keep their secrets safe. I am only spared because they know I

239

would never expose the *loups garous,* for the sake of my own wolf-friends."

Josephine put a hand on his shoulder and smiled at him. "And we thank you for that, *mon ami,*" she said in a soft voice. "You've been a faithful friend to us always."

"This is the price of our secrecy," said Dubois, speaking heavily. "Had Marc only known of the existence of *loups garous,* he would have been more on his guard. But we did not tell him about ourselves, and now he is dead."

"We cannot tell everyone, my love," said Angélique. "Not every human could accept the truth. Most would be terrified. They might come to live in fear of each other, wondering if everyone they met concealed a wolf inside. Society itself could collapse from the weight of that fear."

"*C'est vrai,*" he acknowledged, taking her hand in his. "You are wise, *ma belle.* Well. Can we at least hope that the Lapierres' bloodlust is sated, now that they have slain their father's killer?"

"I'm afraid not." Josephine turned to face Raoul. "Guy's sons blame you for his shooting too, pup, since it was you who warned Hébert and the others. They would murder you if they got the chance. I suggest you stay in your human form so they can't recognize you. The Lapierres have no idea that Raoul Dulac is Hunter the wolf." She added, to Dubois: "I'm worried about the girls too, now."

"The girls?" asked Raoul.

"The three Lafontaine cousins," Dubois told him. "They have been trying for some time now to infiltrate Yves and Jules's circle of friends and allies, to learn what they are up to. It seems the Lapierre boys are attempting to form a new wolf-pack of their own by luring impressionable young *loups garous* to their side.

240

The girls volunteered their services as spies. They flirt with the Lapierres and their male friends, and pretend that they are bored with our ways and want something more exciting."

"Very risky," said Josephine, shaking her head. "And in light of what has happened, actually dangerous."

"I agree," said Dubois. "I will tell them to cease their activities. I doubt they will be able to find out anything more, in any case: Manon tells me Yves and Jules are extremely wary and will admit no one to their inner circle unless they are absolutely convinced of his or her loyalty."

"And the Greenwood female, Chantal?" Raoul asked. "She is in danger also, is she not? You said that her own pack might harm her." Thinking of the girl lying on the bed upstairs aroused in him the same blend of tenderness and pity that he had felt at Tremblant, when he first stood watch over her comatose body. Had they saved her life back then only to see her destroyed after all? His mind rebelled at the thought.

Dubois said, "We must persuade her to remain here, where there are many of us to guard and watch over her. Chantal's earlier defiance was bad enough. Now that she has been tricked into revealing herself in public, the pack may turn against her."

Josephine laughed without humour. "That, I am sure, was her cousin's plan."

Dubois got to his feet slowly, his face and voice grim. "I failed to protect Édouard," he said. "I must not fail his daughter. She may be their own blood-kin, but she is no longer safe from them."

## 17

Chantal opened her eyes and then groaned softly. She had endured many such awakenings now, and they had a familiar feel: the weariness, the unfamiliar surroundings, the memories that were too vivid for a dream yet too terrifying and strange to be real. She got up and looked out the window at the view of the Citadelle's low stone wall topping the snowy hill. Old cannons perched atop the battlement of the sunken fort – no ruin, she knew, but an active working base. There were soldiers in there, and officers, and red-liveried sentries like the ones at Buckingham Palace. Thinking of these things helped to ease her fears. She felt secure in this fortress-city, enclosed and protected within its walls that for centuries had sheltered her kind. Her own father included…

She glanced at the digital clock on the bedside table. Four PM! Exhausted and stressed, she had slept the entire day away. The house seemed strangely still. When she went downstairs there was no sign of Raoul or of M. Dubois, but in the Salon she found the Métis woman Josephine. It was even stranger to see her in that elegant setting than in the cluttered shack.

"Hello my dear, so we meet again!" Josephine greeted her. "Honoré is not here just now. He's had some bad news. An old friend has died suddenly. But he asked me to look after you." She stood up. "Why don't you come with me to the lower town, Chantal, and we'll get my truck? There is a place I would like to show you, not far from here, where many of our kind will be gathering this evening."

They bundled up against the cold and walked out together into the Old City. A bitter wind blew off the St. Lawrence, with its drifting pans of ice. But people were still out enjoying themselves. There was a skating rink set up on the Terrasse next to the Château Frontenac, and at the far end of the boardwalk was a giant toboggan run. She watched as the sleds, some carrying three or four people, careened down the wooden track with the riders squealing and clutching at each other. Chantal had not gone sledding since she was a little girl: she recalled swooping down frozen hillsides with her cousins, the wind singing in her ears and stinging her cheeks. It was like remembering another life.

Josephine led her down to the Basse-Ville, the lower town that lay by the riverside, below and outside of the main fortifications. It could be reached by a long zig-zag stair at one end of the Terrasse, which the locals called the *Escalier Casse-cou* (literally the Break-neck Stair), but on feeling the keen edge of the wind they opted for the funicular instead. It descended the cliff's face at a leisurely pace and at its foot passed through a gap in the roof of the lower station; from there they walked out into the Basse-Ville. It, too, was plainly very ancient, its structures all built of grey weathered stone; above its roofs loomed the granite rock-faces of the Cap Diamant, limned with snow and dominated by the huge castle-like façade of the Château. The narrow avenue along which they walked, the Rue Petit Champlain, was according to Josephine the oldest street in all of North America, and not far away lay Place Royale, the site of the original settlement. This was little changed from the days of its initial construction: a broad cobbled square surrounded the little stone church of Notre Dame de la Victoire, and around its perimeter stood the old stone houses of the settlers, converted now to shops that sold everything from jewellery to wood carvings to hand-knit sweaters.

Josephine took her to one that displayed native art and animal furs in its windows. The painted wooden sign hanging over its door sported the carved figure of a northern loon and the words Atelier du Nord. This was the shop where she and her northern native friends sold their wares.

But it was much more than that, apparently. As they went in Josephine said, "This is a safe house for *loups garous*, a backup for when the Dubois place is not available. Upstairs we have spare rooms with beds, clothing and other necessities. We also keep lots of ready cash for those who need it. Many of our kind hang out here." Chantal threw a quick glance at the young native man sitting at the counter, his long black hair caught back in a tidy ponytail. He didn't even glance up from his computer screen. "Oh, don't you worry about Jean-Louis, he's one of us," laughed Josephine, seeing her look.

He glanced up at that, grinning, and Chantal recognized the Métis fiddle-player from Dubois's concert. "Is there anyone in this town who *isn't* a werewolf?" she exclaimed.

Josephine laughed. "Precious few!" she said, exchanging amused glances with Jean-Louis. "But I think I know of one or two. You will be meeting many more of our kind tonight, Chantal. I am going to take you to the Winter Rite."

"What is that?"

"You will see." Josephine smiled in a mysterious fashion. "I'm taking the truck, Jean-Louis. See you tonight, if things don't run too late."

She led Chantal back outside and down another cobbled street into a more modern area by the harbour where there was a large parking lot. There they got into a rusty old pickup truck and drove off through the snowy streets, onto a road that led along the north shore of the river and away from the city. "There is the Île d'Orléans," said Josephine presently. "It is very important to us wolf-people."

Chantal looked at the long hilly island stretching for miles in the middle of the river, and she remembered Manon's tale of La Corriveau, and the tradition that the Île d'Orléans was a habitation of witches. It looked nothing like the island of her nightmare, but presented a wholesome and rustic aspect. Its wintry hills were wooded, but lower down it was cleared for farmers' fields, long and narrow in the *habitant* tradition granting each farmer access to the river. In a new country without roads the St. Lawrence had been a highway both for small boats and for full-rigged sailing vessels, the latter journeying upriver to Montreal or down towards the ocean and France.

"*Île des Sorciers* some called it," said Josephine when Chantal referred to the legend, "the Sorcerers' Island, because the settlers that lived on the mainland claimed they saw mysterious lights on the island at night. They wove tales about Satanic gatherings: witches and sorcerers, *loups garous,* and *feux follets* – will o' the wisps, who are the souls of the damned. The Devil would lead them all in a march right around the island, it was said, before celebrating the black mass with them in a secret location. To this day people still refer to its inhabitants as *sorciers,* and I know one man there – Bernard Lavallée by name – who claims to have strange powers."

"I've heard that name before."

"He is another friend of Honoré's, a gentleman farmer. And something more, it seems… But the truth is, even before the arrival of the French the native peoples of this region called that island the 'Enchanted Place'. It has many secrets, l'Île d'Orléans! One of those is very ancient: I will show it to you some day. But the secret that is most important to us wolf-people is Chapelle-des-loups."

"What's that?" Chantal asked, curious. The words meant "chapel of the wolves."

"It is the home of a small spiritual community, La Communauté des Sauvés, with a chapel dedicated to Saint Francis. It is not open to the public because it has a unique mission. Chapelle-des-loups was founded four centuries ago by *loups garous*, to be a holy sanctuary for their kind. If you are ever in trouble, you can go there and they will look after you."

She turned north off the main road, leaving the river behind. They were heading towards a range of densely wooded mountains – an extension of the same Laurentian mountain-chain Chantal had visited in Montreal. As she drove Josephine chatted, perhaps to put her at her ease. "I grew up in a little place far to the north called Whapmagoostui, on Ungava Bay by the mouth of the Great Whale River. No road leads there, you can reach it only by air. The name is Cree, it translates as Where the Whales Gather – because of the belugas in the bay. Half the people are Cree, the other are Inuit; in fact their half of town has its own name, Kuujjuarapik. But there are fewer than a thousand people living in the place now."

"I grew up in a small town too," said Chantal. "Derby Line, on the border. When did you first learn you were a – a –"

"A werewolf?" Josephine grinned. "That's the word that's scaring you, isn't it? The word you've been taught to fear. And I won't say there isn't a reason for that fear. Some wolf-people are bad lots, as you've learned. But most of us are quite decent.

"Anyway, to answer your question, I first started changing when I was younger than you. I could not believe it at first. I felt as if my own body had turned on me, had changed into something strange and frightening. I couldn't control it, couldn't stop the changes. One

246

evening I felt the change come on when I was out walking on the Inuit side of town. I was all by myself so I ran into an old shed to hide. A young man named Noah Aglukkaq was coming home with a catch of pelts, and he saw a girl go into the shack and a wolf come out. He looked in the shed and it was empty inside except for a pile of discarded clothing. There was no back door, nowhere the girl could have gone. Then he knew. He sat down by the clothing, knowing I must return for it, and waited. I was so scared and ashamed when I saw him there that I ran away. But he wasn't a bit afraid of me, only curious to learn what I was. Aglukkaq kept my secret, and over time he gradually won my trust and my friendship.

"But that's enough about me. Tell me how it is with you. When do you change?"

Chantal swallowed. "It only seems to happen at night."

"Ah! Your wolf-within is clever: it knows better than to emerge during the daylight hours, but waits for nightfall when it knows that it is safe. I only wish that mine had been so careful at first." She smiled, and went on: "It's different for all of us. Nothing to do with the full moon, that's just a lot of nonsense from horror movies. It can be nighttime, daytime, anytime at all… Some begin to turn early in life, others much later. And then there are those who start out their lives in wolf shape, and only learn with time to take the human forms of their ancestors."

"You mean the *haut-loups?* M. Dubois told me about them."

"Ah, yes. He is one of them himself, you know."

"What?" Chantal stared.

"Honoré is a good man, but he was not born a man."

"He… started out as a wolf? No, I can't believe it. He looks so human!"

Josephine's face and voice turned more serious. "Listen. Honoré may have begun his life as a pup in a litter, but he was no ordinary wolf: the *hauts-loups* have human blood in their veins and think and reason as we do. He was never really an animal. And now that he wears the form of his human ancestors, he is no less a human being than you or I. The same is true for Raoul Dulac."

"Him too?" she gasped.

"*Bien sûr!* Have you not noticed the difficulty Raoul has speaking? He is still learning to talk as humans do. We have our own language when we are in wolf-form. Lupine, we call it. It isn't quite like human talk and it isn't quite like wolf-sounds, but sort of in between. Some compare it to Michif, the language the Métis invented which is part French and part Cree. Raoul grew up speaking this tongue of the *hauts-loups.*"

It all made sense now. Raoul's silence and his shyness; his poor French and his failure to understand her when she spoke English; his unease at being looked at straight in the eye – just like a wild animal...

"Raoul is a good and noble person, Chantal, in human and animal form. You can trust him absolutely – which is more than I can say for a lot of people I know, *hélas!* Human-born *loups garous* like to blame their love of killing on their wolf-nature. But wolves are not like that. The wolf-bodies of the *loups garous* only make them more efficient hunters. The blood-lust and cruelty, these come from the human side. It's our humanity, not our animality, that makes monsters out of us."

Chantal said nothing. She sat and watched the wintry scenery go by, and tried to fight her fears. She was aware of Josephine watching her. "Don't worry so, child," she said at length. "My friends and I have a long history of assisting *loups garous* to come to terms with their special nature. We've never failed anyone yet.

Honoré and I helped Raoul by freeing the boy trapped inside the wolf. In your case I have to release the wolf that is trapped inside the girl."

Chantal smiled. "That sounds kind of like Little Red Riding Hood in reverse. You know how the huntsman used his axe to get the girl out of the wolf's belly."

Josephine laughed. "Good analogy. But my task won't be quite that unpleasant, thank goodness!"

Some forty minutes later they finally stopped in a wilderness area. Josephine parked by the side of the road, and together they waded through ankle-deep snow into a dense wood of spruce and fir. "Should've brought my snowshoes," grunted the older woman, kicking her way through a drift.

"What do we do now?" Chantal asked fearfully. "Do we – change?"

"No, not tonight. I will teach you how to control your wolf-self later, but for now I have just brought you here to meet some of our young people. Hopefully being with others about your age will make you feel less afraid. Most of them have only just realized their true nature, like you."

"I just wish I could understand it!" she burst out. "That there was some kind of *explanation*. M. Dubois said no one really knows what *loups garous* are. Where they – we – came from."

"There are theories," her guide said, leading her on through the snow-robed trees. "Honoré will tell you that our Métis term *rugaru* is not a native word, which is true; it is just how we pronounce *loup garou*. Also, that there is no indigenous tradition of werewolves in Canada. But Noah Aglukkaq says that the olden-days *angakuit* – what you'd call the shamans of his people – used to encounter their spirit-guides in visions. These spirits, the *tuurngait*, often took an animal's form: bear, caribou, raven, wolf. Once an *angakkuq* was in true communion with his *tuurngaq,* he – or she – was also able to assume its form. The transformed shaman was human and animal and spirit too, all at the same time. In my youth I journeyed far across this country to talk to the Elders of other tribes, and from them I heard many similar tales of how wolves and other animals took human shapes whenever they wished, and even married into human families."

"So are there people who can take other animal shapes, too?"

"There may well be. In Japan, for instance, there is the tradition of the *kitsune,* magical foxes that can assume human form. In Ireland they tell tales of the *selkies*, the seal-people who transform into humans when they come ashore. And down in South America, along the banks of the Amazon, you'll hear about the *encantados*: enchanted beings who are river dolphins in the water and human beings on land."

"But are those all real, or just fairy tales?" asked Chantal. "Has anyone *really* met one, recently?"

"It's hard to say. If they do exist they may be as shy about revealing themselves as we wolf-people are. But if they are real I think they're probably much fewer in number than our kind."

"Why's that?"

"Because wolves and humans are much more alike, much more *sympathique.* Dogs are descended from wolves, and look how much closer they are to us than any other animal we've tamed. I read somewhere that a dog can read a person's facial expressions far better than a gorilla or chimpanzee, even though those animals share more of our DNA. There are even some wise men of science who say that dogs developed in the first place because wolves and humans actually evolved together, teaching each other how to hunt.

250

"The native peoples I've talked to also have much to say of the special bond that exists between wolf and man. The *Kwakwaka'wakw* in British Columbia told me that their ancestors were wolves who chose to become human. Are all of these stories just myths? Perhaps, and … perhaps not."

"How do *you* explain it?" Chantal asked.

"Me?" Josephine paused, looking thoughtful. "I'll tell you what I think. In the beginning, maybe, all things in Creation were *métis* – mixed together. Beast, human, spirit flowed one into the other, like the waters of the St. Lawrence where they meet the Gulf and blend with the salt waters of the sea. In those days spirit took shape and walked with man; and man became spirit and turned into beast; and beast became man and took a human wife; until in the end one could not be told apart from the other. That is what the old tales say, if you study them closely. In the beginning all things were one.

"So how did we *loups garous* begin? Remember, all of humanity came from the Old World originally: so it's quite possible the werewolf of Europe and the man-wolf-spirit of North America have the same ancestor, way back in the dawn-time when there were no divisions between beings. When I first thought of this I ceased to be afraid. I realized that I was still *myself* no matter what form I took; that I was not cursed but blessed." She stopped in her tracks, her breath smoking on the air. "Ah – here we are, at last!"

Ahead of them lay a clearing in the wood, trampled with many tracks. A number of tents had been raised here, and a pile of logs set for a fire. But there was no one to be seen. Josephine ushered Chantal into the largest of the tents, and from a large pile in one corner she took up two heavy blanket-like cloaks, throwing one over the girl's shoulders and wrapping the other around herself. Then she lit a small fire in a brazier that stood

251

near the tent's opening. "I'll heat up some food for you," she said. "You must be starving! The others will be back before long. They are out looking for their young friends in the forest, I think. When they return, we will perform the Winter Rite together.

"It's not just for the youngsters, you know: it's a celebration of ourselves and what we are. We've never asked that any *loup garou* cease from taking wolf form. That would be to deny our true nature. All those who wish to can avail themselves of this wilderness area, which is a provincial park and home to many wild animals, including wolves. Here those *loups garous* who desire it can run free and hunt as they will. The young ones, those who have only recently learned what they are and are coming to terms with it, we especially encourage to go out into the forest together for a time. But it's also Honoré's wish that in mid-winter we encourage these youngsters to be human again. If we do not, there is a danger that some may turn wild for good and be lost to us."

"Does that happen a lot?"

Josephine paused in the act of opening a tin. "Not a lot... but it happens. There's an old Inuit story Noah once told me, about a woman named Qisaruatsiaq. She was a strange old woman, who shunned the company of her tribe and preferred to live apart from them. One day the other Inuit found her igloo empty, and saw her footprints leading away from it through the snow. As they followed the tracks through the cold and the growing dark, they saw the prints change shape from a human's into a wolf's. Then they were afraid and followed her no more. No one in her tribe ever saw old Qisaruatsiaq again. Unable to relate to her own people, she had abandoned them for wolf-kind." The Métis woman sighed. "There will always be some who reject human society.

"So to encourage our new young friends to rejoin us, we came up with a special ritual. I adapted it from the ancient Winter Dance of the *Kwakwaka'wakw*. See, here are some ceremonial masks that I brought back with me from the Coast." She got up and lifted a tarp in a corner of the tent, pointing to a pile of large brightly-coloured objects beneath it.

Chantal moved closer to examine them. The native masks were carved of cedar wood and covered with bold designs of red, blue and black paint. They were highly stylized, with great blank staring eyes, and on their elongated muzzles tusk-like teeth were painted; were it not for their pointed ears she might have taken them for the heads of lizards or crocodiles, but according to Josephine these were wolf-masks. Chantal also glimpsed piles of clothing set out on the floor. It looked like a rummage sale. But she noticed that they were laid in neat piles, shoes and socks put together with coats and sweaters and pants. Perhaps they were waiting for specific individuals to come and claim them.

Josephine noticed her looking. "The young *loups garous* will need their clothes to return to the human world," she said, confirming Chantal's guess. "We've made all the necessary preparations. Now we just have to wait for them to come to us." She sat down again beside the brazier to cook their food, but Chantal noticed that she kept gazing out the tent's opening towards the forest.

Hours passed. The blue shadows lengthened on the snow, and the sun went down behind the mountains in a low red smoulder. Snow began to fall, in isolated flakes at first and then in soft swirling flurries, luminous in the fire's glow – like swarms of white-winged moths drawn to the light. As night set in Chantal heard at last the sound of voices in the distance, and people began arriving at the camp: native Canadians mostly, though a few looked as though they might be French. In the dim light, and with their muffling hats and scarves, it was hard to tell. Josephine rushed out to greet them, and Chantal followed her. The main bonfire was lit, along with some smaller ones that had cooking pots hung over them. A rich meaty smell soon arose with the mounting steam and smoke. A group meanwhile took some hide drums out of one of the tents. Setting these in a circle by the fire they began to beat on them, chanting.

"First we attract the wolves with music, so they will know we are here," explained Josephine. "Then when they are closer they will smell the food. It will tempt them to come into the camp, to come to us."

And all happened exactly as she said. In the thick darkness under the evergreen trees, like stars emerging in the night, there appeared twinned yellow lights: eyes reflecting the fire-glow. Chantal could not help feeling a little frisson of fear as she saw them. But Josephine and her friends paid no attention: their eyes were on the main tent. Out of its gaping entrance came a procession of figures swathed in heavy cloaks: on their heads were the native wolf-masks, hiding their faces from sight. It was as if the carved and painted things had come magically to life. The figures began to dance around the fire in time to the drums and the chanting. The shining eyes meanwhile watched from the shadows.

At last the drummers fell silent as Josephine stepped forward. "The people of the western sea-coast have a story that they tell," she called in a clear strong voice. "They say that a young boy once became separated from his family and tribe, and wandered lost and alone in the wilderness. There he was captured by wolves, who bore him off to their lair to kill and eat him. But the boy was wily. He showed none of his fear, but spoke to them calmly, and they admired his courage. They decided to keep him alive instead, and rear him as one of their own.

"Through the years that followed they taught him all their secrets: how to be swift and strong and steadfast in danger, how to track the prey, how to work together in the hunt to ensure its success. When he had learned all that he could, the boy thanked his teachers, and returned to his own people. He taught them all the things that he had learnt from the wolves, and they passed them on to their children in turn. And they created the Winter Dance, the rite in which they accept their youths as full members of the tribe.

"And on this night we dance for you, our young friends, to welcome you back into our midst."

The dancers stood still. They removed their wooden wolf-masks, revealing their human faces to the firelight. Josephine walked to the outer edge of the fire's glow, and spread out her cloaked arms. "Our sisters and brothers, we long for your return!" she cried out to the watching eyes. "Our kindred, flesh of our flesh, blood of our blood! For a time you have dwelt in the house of the wolf, learning his ways and wisdom. But now winter is here and snow lies deep. Food grows scarce, and the cold is bitter. Return to our hearths and partake of our food. Live in the house of humankind once more!"

There was a long breathless pause. Then a huge, black-furred wolf came lunging out of the dark, eyes blazing in the firelight. It charged right into the midst of the camp and leaped upon Josephine.

Chantal cried out in alarm. But Josephine showed no sign of fear. She placed her hands upon the great black paws resting on her shoulders and said, "Down boy! Yes, Ti-Jacques, I'm glad to see you too!" One of the dancers came forward with a large red blanket in his arms and wrapped it around the black wolf. The great

255

beast dropped back to all fours. And then – so suddenly that Chantal's eyes barely registered the moment of transformation – it was no longer a wolf enveloped in the blanket, but a man: a young man, not much older than Chantal herself, dark-skinned with a mane of dreadlocks streaming over his bare shoulders. He grinned up at Josephine, showing strong white teeth.

"Told you I'd be back!" he said, and winked.

Other wolves were rushing out of the trees now, into the circle of firelight. From fire-eyed shadows they became live furry forms, yelping and waving their tails like dogs, jumping joyfully into the outstretched arms of the dancers. The latter cast off their cloaks, tossing the great heavy lengths of fabric over the wolves' bodies. Slowly the swathed forms began to take human shape. Faces looked out from folds of fabric: young human faces of all shapes and hues, smiling and laughing. Friends greeted friends with cries of joy.

"*Ma petite,* it has been so long – "

"How was your autumn, *mon cher?* Did you have good hunting?"

"It's so lovely to see you again, my dear! Welcome back!"

The transformed *loups garous* were taken into the tents, and emerged again clad in the clothing that had been brought for them. Everyone moved to the campfires and loaded their plates with the hot stew, still talking and laughing. Chantal stood shyly on the edge of the excited group, moved by what she had seen but also feeling a little left out – like a guest at someone else's class reunion.

"That's Jacques Thibodeau," Josephine told her, pointing to the youth with the dreadlocks. "He's American, like you: he came to us just this past year. He's a Creole from Louisiana, but he also has Cajun ancestors, and some of that race still carry the wolf blood. Ti-Jacques began to change when he was still a child and for years he hid his double nature, fearing that he was some kind of monster. But after hearing rumours that others like him dwelled in Quebec, he came and sought us out. Everyone here has a story much like yours, Chantal."

"Not all of us have returned," said a voice near at hand.

They turned to look at the speaker. She was a fair-skinned young woman, with long brunette hair flowing loose around her face and a native blanket slung over her shoulders: one of the newly-transformed.

"So I see. About half a dozen, no? I hope they haven't come to any harm, Célestine." There was a crease of worry on Josephine's forehead.

Chantal peered inside the main tent at the piles of clothing that remained, looking somehow pathetic as abandoned belongings do. Her gaze moved from a pair of track shoes next to a boy's folded jeans and tee shirt, to a girl's soft rose-pink sweater and matching purse.

"Not any physical harm, no," the brunette replied, moving to Josephine's side, "but those Lapierre brothers have been coming here off and on throughout the fall and winter, trying to lure us away to their side, telling us that the wolf's ways are better. The younger boys especially seemed to be influenced by them. I don't think young Luc Benoit is coming back, and he's not the only one."

Josephine looked annoyed. "Oh, bother those Lapierres! They're always pushing their noses into our business. They're furious if we so much as walk across their territory, yet they've never shown any respect for ours."

The girl Célestine spoke in a low voice. "Even those who came back tonight can't be trusted, Josephine. There's a rumour going around that the Lapierres intend

257

to plant a spy amongst Dubois's people. Tell him to trust only his oldest and closest confidants, and to watch carefully all those newly returned from the forest. Some of them may have been corrupted."

Josephine sighed. "In the old days *loups garous* hung together in the face of human hate; now we fight one another. How can we know friend from enemy?"

As they talked Chantal stood staring at the clothes, wondering who these young people were. Why had they not returned to claim their possessions, and their place in this happy gathering? A feeling of melancholy swept over her, driving out the comfort the Winter Rite had briefly brought to her.

"You see, Chantal," said Josephine, "just as some *loups garous* try to deny their animal selves, others disappear into them. The human self loses its struggle with the wolf, and is devoured by it. Like Qisaruatsiaq."

Chantal turned to face her. "Thanks for bringing me out here, Josephine," she said, trying to keep her voice steady. "It's been great and I really appreciate it, but I – I think I'd like to go back to the house now."

## 18

She was not there.

Raoul looked around the crowded sitting room of the Dubois home. Honoré was holding a *salon* for his out-of-town houseguests and local friends: many voices talked at once, a pleasant sound like the steady rumour of flowing water. He was beginning to enjoy human society. The friends of Honoré Dubois were unfailingly kind and patient with him, and today his host had introduced him to a number of new people, including an elderly white-bearded gentleman who needed a wooden stick to walk: this turned out to be Bernard Lavallée, Honoré's farmer friend from the Île d'Orléans. But to his disappointment the Boisvert girl was conspicuously absent from this gathering. He had hoped to speak with Chantal again, to ask her how she was adjusting to her new life and to offer her his help.

He turned back to Dubois and his friend.

"I feel like something of an oddity at these gatherings," said Monsieur Lavallée with a chuckle, "as I am just an ordinary human."

"But Monsieur, Josephine tells me you are far from ordinary," Raoul replied. "A *sorcier,* she called you. Is that true? Have you special powers that other humans have not?"

The old man smiled, grey eyes twinkling in his weatherworn face. "It's true that I am descended from a noted *sorcier* who lived in the early days of our colony. His father married a native woman, and it's said that he inherited the powers of both the Old Country witches and the Algonquin shamans. He could read the future, so the story goes, and whenever the supply ships were late coming upriver his neighbours would ask him to foretell their arrival date. Some say he could affect the weather too, raising up storms and fogs by making incantations over a magic cauldron. They even claim that he thwarted a British invasion that way! But I cannot vouch for the truth of those tales, and I have no such powers myself, *hélas!* Just the occasional premonition, and mine are not very precise."

"Still, strange accounts have been given me of this island of yours, Monsieur. Tales of *lutins,* and the *feu-follet* – the will o' the wisp that shines in the night? Those cannot be real, surely?" said Raoul.

"What! You balk at the notion of sprites and fairies – you, who are a *loup garou?"* said Lavallée, laughing. "There are some who say the *feux follets* were inspired by fireflies, and we do have a great many of those on the Île d'Orléans. But for my part, I like to think that the world is still full of mysteries we have not begun to grasp – in spite of men of science like René here." He nodded to Leblanc, who stood nearby.

"Even men of science do not claim to know everything," replied Leblanc, entering their group and conversation. "You should talk to people in the physics department at my university. Many think it may not even be possible to know everything about our universe. I don't understand my *loup garou* nature, but just because I have no explanation for it doesn't mean there isn't one. I simply haven't found it yet." He glanced at Dubois. "Is something wrong, my friend?"

Dubois was frowning as he gazed across the room. Raoul looked in the same direction, and saw Suzette and Hyacinthe Lafontaine seated on a couch together. For once their cousin Manon was not with them.

"I hope not," Dubois murmured in reply. "Will you excuse me a moment, gentlemen?"

He walked over to the Lafontaine girls. Raoul also excused himself and followed. "Is there still no word from your cousin?" Dubois inquired of them.

"Not yet," said Suzette. "She said yesterday that she'd meet us here, but she's taking an awfully long time. She's not answering her phone either."

"I hope she is all right," said Dubois. "I think you three had better give up on your little spy operation. I'm growing concerned for your safety."

"Hyacinthe and I couldn't get into the inner circle anyway," said Suzette. "We may have overdone the flirting and giggling thing. Yves seemed much more impressed with Manon because she always acts so serious about everything. They're having a secret gathering this week, somewhere in the forest; but only Manon was able to get an invitation. She told us Yves was trying to get Chantal to come to it, too."

"Was he, indeed?" said Dubois, shooting a glance at Raoul. "I would like to know the nature of this forest gathering. There have been terrible rumours about some of our people returning to the old ways. To rites of pagan times, like the *Lykaia*."

"The what?" asked Raoul. He sensed a ripple of unease go through the others, like a wind disturbing the grass of a meadow. Hyacinthe looked alarmed.

Dubois answered: "A very old, very evil ritual practiced by some of our ancestors in their original homeland. On Mount Lykaion, the Mountain of the Wolf, young men would partake of a dish in which human flesh was mixed with that of beasts. Then they would turn wolf and run off into the wild for a time. It was a test, I think, a way to separate them from the rest of humankind – to make them think of other humans as prey instead of as their own blood kin…"

Hyacinthe said, "We don't really know that anything like – like *that* is going on. I think it's really just wild rumours. There is a rite of some sort, we heard, but – "

"Thank God!" exclaimed Suzette suddenly, springing to her feet and facing the door.

They all turned to face the same way. Manon had returned. Her face looked even more serious than usual, and she acknowledged their greetings with a nod rather than a smile as she entered the room.

"So tell us Manon, did Yves take you to that event in the woods?" Suzette asked as her cousin came over to join them. Hyacinthe made room for her on the couch.

"Yes, he did," Manon replied, seating herself. "It was a place deep in the Laurentides, up on the side of a mountain. They made me wear a blindfold on the way there, so I can't tell you exactly where it was; but it was very wild. There were no houses or cottages to be seen anywhere. Yves and the others introduced the new recruits. I saw that boy Luc Benoit, and a few others whom I didn't recognize; they were all in their human forms at first. There was a sacrifice – "

"Not human!" cried Hyacinthe, her hands flying up to her mouth in alarm.

"No, no! Just a pair of goats: Yves and Jules slaughtered them and smeared the blood on themselves. Then everyone ran off into the woods and stripped, and came back as wolves. And they ate the goat meat, raw." Manon hesitated. "It really wasn't as bad as I thought it would be. I mean, we all hunt animals, don't we, and eat their meat?"

Dubois looked down at her thoughtfully and said, "True. But Yves wouldn't likely let you, an outsider, view the worst of the rite. There may be more to it. Though what you saw sounds bad enough. It seems to be aimed at overcoming the modern human repugnance towards violence and bloodshed."

"So they just made up some ritual of their own then?" suggested Suzette.

"No," said Dubois, "it sounds to me much like another ancient festival: Lupercalia, the feast of the Wolf-cave. A fertility rite where people ran wild in the streets... An ancient Roman practice, it was; though some believe it began long before that, in old Arcadia. It was always held at this time of year, in the month of February. Priests would gather at the cave of Lupercal, where it was believed Romulus and Remus were nursed by the she-wolf. There they sacrificed goats and dogs – to their fertility gods, or so it was claimed."

"Claimed?"

"Killing herd-animals and the dogs that guard them from wolves would be just the sort of ritual a wolf would devise, don't you think? I suspect that it had a *loup garou* origin, and that these other explanations were attempts to hide that fact from normal humans." His gaze returned to Manon. "Are you quite sure you saw all of it? Perhaps the rite continued after you departed, with other things Yves knew you would never approve: the killing of a dog, *peut-être,* or the young *loups garous* being forced to mate with one another by lottery? I have heard disturbing whispers of both things."

"Those may just be rumours," Manon said. "I never heard of anything like that. And they didn't call it a Lupercalia either. Yves Lapierre told me it was simply a ceremony to welcome the new arrivals. He said that eating meat together would help them to bond with one another and form a pack. Maybe that's really all it was."

"Did you join in?" Suzette asked.

"I wasn't invited to. I was just allowed to watch. But if they ask me to join in next time I think I could do it. It isn't as if they were murdering people or anything horrible like that. If I take part then perhaps Yves might confide in me more."

"No, you are in deep enough already," Dubois told her. He bent down and took both her hands in his, gently but firmly. "I don't want you to put yourself in danger.

You're a brave girl and you've done more than enough. Don't go back to them, Manon."

"All right, Honoré," Manon replied. Her expression turned shy and she dropped her eyes for a moment. "I don't really think I was ever in danger, but... whatever you say."

"*Bon,*" said Dubois, looking relieved. He released her hands and stood up straight again. "Now let us enjoy our own gathering... Ti-Jacques, are you leaving us so soon?" he called out to the tall dark-complexioned youth, who was hastening towards the door.

"I must go check on the food," Ti-Jacques replied over his shoulder. "I've got a special treat for your guests. I am making a gumbo for their *déjeuner.*"

"*Excellent! Mais je vous en prie,* not quite so much spice this time!"

Ti-Jacques showed his white teeth in a wide grin. "I will teach you to appreciate Cajun cooking one day, Honoré," he said as he disappeared through the door.

"Curious," said Raoul, looking after him. "I have noticed that you all call that young man 'Ti-Jacques' – that means, *Petit* Jacques or 'Little' Jacques, correct? But he is not little at all. He is extremely tall and strong."

Dubois explained: "It is a joke name that his friends have given him. I must explain the human sense of humour to you sometime." He gazed thoughtfully at the door through which Ti-Jacques had gone. "Just think, before he joined us young Monsieur Thibodeau was very near to ending his own life from fear and despair. Now he lives with Angélique and me and studies the culinary arts."

"Why would he end his own life?"

"In some ways, Raoul, it is much harder for a human *loup garou* to accept his wolf side than it is for high-wolves such as you and I to reclaim our humanity.

Human society is so much more complex. Also, humans have a natural fear of wolves. So many wolf-people are afraid of their animal selves, or believe that other humans will fear them. Some strive actively to deny the inner self, and without herbs or other methods to arouse it the wolf within them never fully wakes.

"But in persons of strong heredity or powerful emotions that is not possible, and they may find themselves shape-changing against their will. Some of these *loups garous* are killed while in their wolf-forms, in accidents or attacks by other animals, so that their human selves seem to 'disappear' and their families never learn what became of them. A few are murdered while in their human form by *loups garous* who fear they may inadvertently betray the existence of our kind: these become unsolved crimes for human detectives to puzzle over. But those like Ti-Jacques and Chantal who have the strength and courage to seek out other *loups garous* are able to explore their nature fully, even embrace it. I think we need not concern ourselves about either of them."

"That reminds me: will Chantal be joining us today?" Raoul asked. "I do not see her here."

"I thought I saw her go outside earlier," said Suzette. "Is she not back yet?"

"Outside the house?" said Raoul. "Is that wise? Perhaps I should go look for her."

"No, let me. I knew her father and she trusts me," said Dubois. He shook his head as he spoke, the gesture used by a human who was troubled. "How like her father she is! She has the same strong, independent spirit. But that means she needs our protection all the more."

"Yes. I am worried for her sake." Raoul leaned close to Dubois and spoke in his ear. "What Josephine says – about there being a spy in our midst – "

"I have not forgotten," said Dubois. "However, her source may be mistaken. I would trust all of these people with my life."

*But not with Chantal's, I hope,* thought Raoul as the older man left the room.

It was the final weekend of *Carnaval*, and the Plains of Abraham thronged with revelers. In a couple of days Bonhomme would preside for the last time over the closing ceremonies, with music and fireworks. Bitter air cut into Chantal's lungs as she wound her way through the outdoor attractions, but it also helped to clear her mind. She needed time to think, and in the midst of these clamorous *Carnaval* crowds she could feel alone and yet not vulnerable to attack. She paused by a sugar shack, where curious Japanese tourists clustered around a man pouring dollops of boiled maple syrup from a steaming pot into a large basin filled with snow. Maple syrup candy: she'd made it herself many times as a child. She remembered waiting with eager impatience for the runnels of amber liquid to cool and congeal on top of the snow, magically transforming into soft gooey strips like taffy. And the taste! She savoured it for a moment in memory; but along with the glimpse of childhood past came a poignant twinge, a sudden awareness of lost innocence. She moved on again, walking quickly as if to leave it behind her.

Would anything ever be the same again? Everywhere she looked she saw happy people, and so many of them were in couples: holding hands, laughing, standing together with their arms wrapped around each other... Valentine's Day was not far off, and she found herself reflecting that once again she would have no one with whom to celebrate it. And likely never would, now. *I can't ever date anyone again. Not anyone normal – not with a secret like this to hide...*

She pined for someone to hold her hand, to pull her close and make her feel warm – and safe.

Her aimless meandering brought her to the site of the international Snow Sculpture Competition; and here she paused, surprised by what she saw. She had imagined something like the snowman competition at her old school, but each one of these sculptures was executed in exquisite detail, the snow smoothed to the consistency of marble and sculpted like a real statue. There was a giant Laughing Buddha; a whole herd of very realistic elephants; a larger-than-life copy of the mermaid of Copenhagen, done by the Danish team, and a scaled-down reproduction of the Stonehenge monoliths (labeled "Snowhenge" on the accompanying sign, which identified it as the United Kingdom's entry). She stood marveling at the craftsmanship of these ephemeral monuments, one tourist among many, forgetting her worries in a brief moment of normality.

A voice spoke behind her. *"C'est magnifique, n'est-ce pas?"*

She started and turned quickly to see Honoré Dubois standing behind her. He bowed.

"I had a feeling I was under surveillance," she said in a tone of resignation.

"My apologies. It's only for your safety."

"I feel pretty safe in a crowd, actually. The Boisverts and the Lapierres wouldn't dare try anything here: too many witnesses. They certainly can't turn into wolves in broad daylight." But she shivered just saying the words, and huddled into her down jacket. "I'm actually more scared of myself than I am of them. Of – of *changing* again. Right now I'm a danger to everyone, my family included. I don't want to leave here until I learn how to control this thing inside of me."

"And so you shall, with our help. I promise." His eyes returned to the snow-sculptures. *"Magnifique,"* he

267

said again. "Such skill! Art is the unique achievement of humanity. No animal makes things of beauty for their own sake. And look, there is Hans Andersen's Little Mermaid! That is one of my favourite stories."

"I thought it was horribly depressing. Didn't the mermaid die at the end?"

"But she gained the thing she wanted most of all, an immortal soul. That meant more to her than anything, more even than her love for the Prince. Because of her noble self-sacrifice, she was not condemned to dissolve into sea-foam when she died like all the rest of her kind, but ascended into the heavens. She evolves in the story from a creature half-animal to a true human, and finally into a pure spirit. It was this idea of the soul that fascinated me most about human civilization: the divine essence that elevates humankind above the beasts. As I was born in a wolf's form it used to trouble me that I might not possess an immortal soul as humans do. My good friend Père Mercier has tried to reassure me on that point, but still I wonder at times..." He sighed.

Chantal shivered again. She still felt slightly uneasy around Honoré and Raoul; despite Josephine's assurances they seemed not quite human now that she knew they had been born as wolves. Dubois saw her shiver, and shook his head. "*Ma pauvre enfant,* but you are freezing! Come back to the house and warm yourself. I am holding one of my *salons* today, and many of my friends are already there. Come and join us."

"Okay," she sighed. "Thanks."

When they got back to the house she heard voices chattering in the main room, and the rippling strains of a harp. Angélique Dubois was playing her magnificent gilded instrument, surrounded by appreciative listeners. Others stood in groups talking. Chantal saw an elderly Catholic priest in black soutane, and a couple of

Franciscan nuns in full habit. Raoul Dulac was there, talking with René Leblanc. As she entered the boy glanced up, and she thought she saw a fleeting expression of relief on his face before he turned back to Leblanc. She also recognized Mme. Bernier and Noah Aglukkaq.

With those last two exceptions, she suspected all present were *loups garous*.

As she glanced around the room her eyes alighted on the oil painting over the mantel. "You were going to tell me about that picture, M. Dubois, when we were interrupted," she said. "You said it was important. Could you tell me now?"

"Ah, yes. This is not the original, alas," Dubois said, "for that would be beyond even my means. It is only a copy, made by a talented artist of my acquaintance, of Poussin's famous painting: *Et in Arcadia Ego.*"

"What do those words mean?" she asked, moving closer to the painting and peering at it. "I'm sure I've read them somewhere before. Is it Latin?"

"It is. The English translation is 'I am in Arcadia also'. A very famous phrase. I have not told you about Arcadia yet, have I? It was an ancient land, located in the Peloponnesus. In French, we pronounce its name *'Arcadie'.*"

"*Arcadie?*" Chantal repeated. "Jules Lapierre did a painting with that for a title. A creepy looking painting, with a ruined city in it, and wolves – "

"No doubt. He would find that subject compelling. Arcadia, you see, was the country of the wolf-people. You can read about it in the writings of Plato, and of Pliny the Elder who learned of it from ancient Greek writers. It was the custom in that land to ritualize one's first human-to-wolf transformation. There were a number of coming-of-age rites, some less … civilized than others. The most common rite involved large numbers of Arcadian youths gathering on the bank of a large river. There they would remove their clothes, hanging them upon tree-branches as a bather might do; but when they swam across the river, they emerged on its far side as wolves. In the wilderness beyond they lived in their animal forms for a period of nine years, after which they would swim back across the river. If they had eaten no human flesh or committed any other crime, they were allowed to change back, don their clothing and live among their fellow men again."

"It sounds kind of like the Winter Rite."

"Yes, I told the *loups garous* here about the Arcadian ritual, and Josephine helped us to establish something similar for ourselves. Unlike the winter rites of Yves and his ilk, ours is meant to encourage the young to come back home out of the woods before… before the waning months of winter."

"I guess that makes sense. I mean, it's harder to find food then, isn't it?" said Chantal.

"Honoré is the soul of tact," put in an elderly man, coming up to join them. "What he is trying *not* to say is that late winter is the mating time for wolves. The homecoming rite is meant to prevent what in English you call the 'hanky-panky'." He winked.

Dubois laughed. "Chantal, this is my friend Bernard Lavallée. Bernard, Chantal Boisvert."

"*Enchanté.*" Lavallée bowed as well as he could while leaning on his cane. His gaze turned to the painting. "Ah, Arcadia. People were much enamoured with this image of a land of virgin woods and hills, where rustic folk dwelled in pastoral tranquility!"

Dubois nodded. "When Virgil and the poets who followed after him wrote of Arcadia, they referred not to the real place but to an ideal: man in harmony with nature. The earthly paradise. But that is only a romantic idealization."

270

"*C'est vrai.* Arcadia was and is a harsh country, with a rough and rugged terrain. As a farmer, I just can't get sentimental about living off the land. It's a struggle sometimes to make a go of it, even in fertile country."

"*Exactement.* It was to counter this romanticization that artists like Poussin took up this new theme: that even in a supposed paradise mortality is still omnipresent and inescapable. It is Death himself who speaks to the viewer through those words carved on the stone tomb." Dubois sighed. "Still, to this day many *loups garous* choose to believe that their Arcadian ancestors had a perfect existence, and they argue that we should all return to those ways."

"Not to Arcadia itself, though," Lavallée said.

"You mean it still exists?" asked Chantal.

"Not as a separate country: it is a part of modern Greece today. But among the *loups garous* that fled to the New World were many whose dream it was to recreate Arcadia in this new and unspoiled continent. If you look at the oldest maps, Chantal, you will see the Canadian Maritime provinces bear the label *l'Arcadie* – Arcadia. That was the original colony founded by the explorer Samuel de Champlain. You know of him?"

"Sure, we learned about him in school. There's a big lake on the Vermont border that's named after him."

"He is also the founder of Quebec, yet there is a great deal of mystery about the man. No written record exists of his birth in France, nor of his burial site here. No one knows exactly where in Quebec Champlain was laid to rest." Lavallée looked amused. "Honoré thinks he may have been a *loup garou.*"

She stared from one man to the other. "Are you kidding me? Champlain was a *werewolf?*"

"It is only a theory of mine," explained Dubois, "but it would explain a good deal. If Champlain was a *loup garou* did he perhaps die in wolf shape, and is that why

271

his burial place was kept secret? And what are we to make of this tale of a fire that supposedly destroyed all record of his birth? Perhaps, like me, he was not born in human form... It would explain, also, why he was so determined to cross the seas and found a colony far away in the New World. Other explorers were content merely to exploit its resources and return home, but not Champlain. He attempted permanent settlement, at a place he named *Arcadie*. A most significant choice of name."

"Some say it was the explorer Giovanni da Verrazzano who named it, not Champlain," put in Lavallée with a mischievous grin.

"Nonsense!" Dubois waved his hand in a gesture of amiable dismissal. "I think Champlain may have been seeking a place where wolf-people would be able to live in peace, far from the suspicion and persecutions of the old country. Unlike the old Arcadia, his New World colony was covered in dense mixed forest: a paradise for wolves. I believe that he intended Canada to be the new country of the *loups garous*, where they could dwell freely in both forms. Over time the maritime colony's name was corrupted to *l'Acadie* – or as the English say, Acadia."

"Acadia!" exclaimed Chantal. "You mentioned the Acadians at the concert, M. Dubois. The French settlers who were driven out of their homes by the British – "

"Correct. Some of them later returned to the Maritimes, while some established themselves in other French territories such as Quebec and Louisiana – your word 'Cajun' is a corruption of 'Acadian'. The wolf-blood sometimes re-emerges in modern-day Acadians, like René Leblanc and Ti-Jacques. And the Lapierres: they are an old Acadian wolf-clan, as are your Grandmère Thérèse's original family, the Valcourts: though unlike the Lapierres they retained their wealth

272

and their influence in both *loup garou* and human society.    Through Thérèse, you and other Boisverts have inherited the old Arcadian bloodline, though in your case it is somewhat diluted.    Pure-bred Arcadians have yellow eyes, the mark of a heritage more lupine than human.    Yours, I see, are brown with a little gold in them: very pretty and unusual, but probably too human for their comfort.    Even in this modern era they wish to keep the old bloodlines pure, so that Arcadia – a land dominated by *loups garous*, ruled by *loups garous* – can one day become a reality here."

Chantal nodded. "That's what Jules Lapierre wants, isn't it? That's what his painting was about."

Dubois shook his head.    "No, young Jules is rather more... extreme... in his desires.    He yearns for humanity to become extinct altogether, clearing the way for *loups garous* to claim all the Earth. But neither he nor his Arcadian kindred will be happy if their wishes do come true."

"*C'est vrai,*" agreed Lavallée.    "What, after all, do we learn of the true Arcadians from the ancient texts? We must remember that the chief of their gods was Pan, who was said to have been born in Arcadia and reigned over its wilderness.    Goat-footed Pan is god of shepherds, but he is also half-beast himself, untamed and fierce; from his name we derive the word 'panic', the fear of wild and solitary places.    An appropriate deity for that race of wolf-people, but not one suited to your civilized folk."

"No indeed, *mon ami.*  Even among the Arcadians, most understood that those who lived as beasts would lose their humanity in the end. And the lot of beasts is suffering and early death.    That is why I hang that picture here for my *loups garous* to see: it is a reminder. *Et in Arcadia ego.*"

The Catholic priest came and joined in their discussion at this point, and a long philosophical debate began which Chantal found hard to follow, particularly in French. She glanced around the room. Raoul Dulac had quietly slipped away, no doubt wearied by the effort of so much socializing. But she saw Manon and Hyacinthe and Suzette sitting in a corner of the main room with Dubois's wife, who was resting from her harp-playing. Chantal went over to join them.

"Are you ready for tonight, my dear?" Mme. Dubois asked her.

"There's something special going on, isn't there?" Chantal asked. "A *Carnaval* thing."

The older woman nodded. "*Bien sûr!* This evening is one of the biggest events of *Carnaval*: the Regency Ball at the Château Frontenac. You must come, Chantal, we have got a ticket for you."

"A ball? I'm afraid I don't know how to do old-fashioned dancing," replied Chantal.

"Very few people do," Hyacinthe said. "They will go over the steps first. Don't worry, you'll do just fine!"

Manon looked at her sidelong. "We three are *loups garous*, but of course you guessed that? We are all from the Lafontaine pack. There are lots of these family packs all across the province: Laroche, Laforêt, Dumont —"

Mme. Dubois broke in: "Now, girls! Honoré does not like us to speak of ourselves as packs."

"Why not?" asked Chantal. "If you don't mind my asking?"

"It is an affectation on the part of many *loups garous*," the older woman explained. "To call themselves 'packs', and to use terms like 'alphas' and 'omegas'. It's a way for them to set themselves apart from other human beings and emphasize the wolf side of their nature. But natural wolf packs are family groups,

274

*vous comprenez*, bound by blood ties. It's different for them. When unrelated wolves are thrown together in captivity, they form a sort of pack but they also fight and try to dominate one another. It just isn't their natural state. Or as Honoré puts it, wolves do not have societies, only families."

"What's wrong with families?" asked Hyacinthe.

"Not a thing – when they are just small groups. But the bigger they get, you see, the more power must be concentrated at the top in order to preserve the leader's authority. When we humans impose a family structure on an entire nation, the usual result is an absolute monarchy or a dictatorship. Honoré's hope for our own community is that we set aside our wolfish desire to be a pack and concentrate on human ideals instead. Otherwise we may end up engaging in games of domination and competition, instead of creating a just and egalitarian society."

Manon bowed her head. "I'm sorry, Madame. It was just a slip of the tongue. But we really have become a sort of family here, with you and Honoré as our head-wolves. Whether he approves or not, we all look to him and to you for leadership – because we love you, not because we fear you."

A clanging sound reverberated down the hallway outside. "There's the gong for lunch," said Suzette, jumping up. "Come upstairs with us afterwards and pick out a costume, Chantal. Angélique and Honoré have rented some for us."

It was wonderfully reassuring to hear these people all talking so naturally of what had been to her a dark and terrifying secret mere days ago. Chantal suspected this was probably the real purpose of these *salons*: to help *loups garous* feel normal and comfortable, supported by the presence of many others who were just like them, and of humans who accepted them for what they were.

That evening Chantal stood looking at herself in the spare room mirror. The girls, after a playful squabble over their own Regency costumes, had chosen for her a Georgian dress with enormous full skirts and fancy lace cuffs to the elbow, creamy-white in colour with a pattern of tiny golden fleurs-de-lys about the neck and hem. It suited her figure perfectly, the puffed sleeves disguising her broad shoulders. She leaned closer to the mirror, struggling to confine her hair in a bun. It was already escaping in rebellious strands.

"No, no, Chantal!" exclaimed Suzette, sweeping out of the bathroom in her long emerald-green gown. "Don't pull your hair back tight like that!"

"It's so messy," Chantal explained, wincing as she pulled out the pins and tried to start over. "And I want a style that goes with the costume. It can't just hang loose."

"Let me," said Suzette. "Sit down on the bed."

Chantal obeyed. "All right – but don't say I didn't warn you! It's a challenge just to brush my hair." Seeing a flicker of amusement cross the other's face she groaned. "Okay, what did I say wrong?"

Suzette's mouth twitched at the corners. "You said that it's a challenge to brush your horses."

"My horses?" repeated Chantal. "Oh, right: *cheveux,* not *chevaux.* Sorry."

"Now, Suzette!" reproved Hyacinthe. "Chantal's French is very good. Others are much worse. An American tourist once asked me in French if I knew the phone number for the chicken of autumn. To this day I'm still not sure what he meant!" she added as the other girls burst into giggles.

Suzette patiently rearranged the masses of dark-brown hair with expert hands, piling them up into a looser style with a few tendrils spiraling down the back of Chantal's neck. *"Voila!"* she said. *"C'est parfait, n'est-ce pas?"*

Manon and Hyacinthe, gowned respectively in rose-red and peacock-blue, stood by and admired Suzette's work. *"Formidable!"* said Hyacinthe. "But it needs one more thing." Reaching up to the rhinestone barrette pinned amid her blonde curls, she removed it and placed it on Chantal's hair. "No, you have it," she said as Chantal protested. "Jewellery shows better on dark hair. There, have a look!"

She held out a silver-backed hand mirror. Chantal peered at the strange reflection in the mirror and could not help smiling a little. Again a miracle had been achieved: instead of attempting to subdue and constrain her hair, the new style took full advantage of its volume. The heaped curls even made her face look a bit smaller – almost delicate. And nestled in their depths the spray of rhinestones glimmered like real diamonds.

*"Bien!* Well, let's go," said Manon, turning towards the door. "They will be waiting for us downstairs."

Honoré Dubois and his wife stood in the foyer. They too had opted for Georgian dress, she in a gown of gold and ivory-white that looked splendid with her white high-coiffed hair, and he in knee-breeches and long blue coat with a wig that made him look like George Washington. Ti-Jacques and Raoul were with them, clad as *voyageurs:* Ti-Jacques all in fringed buckskin with his dreadlocks held back by a leather thong, Raoul in a blousy linen shirt and knee breeches with a red *ceinture.* Chantal tried not to stare at the younger boy, knowing how eye contact still discomfited him, but he looked very striking. His pale hair was caught back in a short period ponytail, revealing the fine modeling of his face, the high cheekbones and square chin. It might have been one of his olden-days ancestors standing there in the hall, an explorer garbed for adventure in the

277

wilderness.  But to Raoul the wilderness would be safe and familiar, she thought; for him it was civilization that was the fearsome unknown.  If she found it a bit intimidating to attend this formal ball, she could only imagine what pitfalls it presented to one who had been human for less than a year.

"*Eh bien,* we are all here then?" said Honoré.  He stooped to kiss his wife's hand in a gallant, Gallic fashion. She beamed back at him. "Let us go!  Our transport is waiting."

They could have walked the short distance to the Château, but it was bitterly cold and windy, especially uncomfortable for the women in their thin costumes and wraps.  Chantal was surprised to see that Dubois had ordered not taxis but a pair of horse-drawn *calèches* for his company.  She shuddered to think what it must have cost him, but the Lafontaine girls said that he did this every year.  "It seems more suitable to arrive this way, in our olden days dress," laughed Hyacinthe.

The carriages were open, but equipped with piles of fur rugs to keep the passengers warm during the ride. Snow was falling as they set out, great feathery flakes that made a misty veil all about them, and through it the floodlit green turrets of the hotel glowed like those of a fairytale palace.

The Château Frontenac is one of Canada's old "castle" hotels.  Only the Château Lake Louise and the Banff Springs Hotel in their Rocky Mountain solitudes could rival it for sheer grandeur of setting.  Occupying the very spot on the Cap Diamant where the original *château* of the Comte du Frontenac stood in the early days of the settlement, the grand hotel crowns the fortress-city with its steep roofs and turrets clad in weathered copper.  The foundations of the count's old residence have been excavated, along with those of the ancient fort, and guided tours are given of the subterranean ruins. But the hotel itself is more than a century old, and has seen its share of history.

Tonight the great building might have been plunged back into a past even older than itself. Its grand lobby was filling up with guests in the garb of bygone eras, mounting the marble flights of the Grande Escalier under the glow of an immense chandelier. At the top the Escalier opened out into the period elegance of the Palm Room, an atrium that in turn opened onto the ballroom. In this antique setting the extravagant costumes did not look at all out of place.

Chantal, climbing the stairs in her turn, felt like Cinderella: dressed in borrowed finery, protected by a supernatural benefactor, filled with awe and self-consciousness at the grandeur of her surroundings. She had never been to any event as formal as this. Her Prom had been a modest affair, held in the school gymnasium, and she had been bored and listless the whole time because Russell Gordon was not there. It had not felt at all like a high point in her life. This was a far grander occasion. In the Palm Room stood a receiving line that included both the mayor and premier of Quebec. Bonhomme was there also, to Chantal's amusement. His costume, clearly designed to keep him warm out of doors, must be sweltering in this indoor venue.

She entered the ballroom just ahead of M. and Mme. Dubois: here were more chandeliers, a stage with live musicians, and a gallery with gilded railings. Costumed dancers were already lined up on the dance floor. It was not like a Halloween dance or a masquerade: the relative uniformity of the period costumes made her feel that she had traveled back in time. She turned around, to thank her host and hostess again for bringing her. But the words died in her mouth.

Through the ballroom doors behind her swept Thérèse Boisvert and Genevieve, each on the arm of a Lapierre brother in matching Napoleonic garb. Her grandmother was dressed in a white Empire gown of almost Grecian simplicity and a royal-blue overgown with flowing train. A period-style pearl comb was set like a tiara upon her upswept grey hair. Genevieve on the other hand looked drab in an ill-fitting beige dress with a lace mob-cap on her head. At the sight of Chantal and her companions, they all stopped dead and stared.

Chantal could not move either; her feet in their dainty slippers seemed to have frozen to the floor. No one uttered a word. The period-clad throngs milled all around them, but the Boisvert matriarch and her attendants had eyes for no one but Dubois's company. The two groups confronted one another, rigid and still, bodies taut with enmity.

## 19

Chantal's companions moved to flank her as the enemy approached, and for a moment the two groups regarded each other with palpable hostility. Thérèse in particular cast a long look of fierce challenge at Honoré Dubois from her darkly glinting eyes. But to Chantal's surprise she and her cohort simply moved on, passing by Dubois's company without incident. When the Boisverts and Lapierres disappeared into the crowd she expelled the imprisoned breath from her lungs.

"*Loups garous* do not call attention to their pack conflicts when surrounded by normal humans," whispered Dubois in her ear. "It is considered bad form."

Chantal turned to him in relief. "So they won't give us any trouble?"

"Not here, no."

"I'm glad. I'd hate to have to leave. This looks like such a great event."

"It is. It was at the Balle that I first met my dear wife, many years ago." Dubois gazed with fondness at Angélique, who squeezed his arm affectionately.

"This ball is very popular with our people," she told Chantal. "All of the old wolf-families attend. Your parents came up to *Carnaval* the year they were married and danced together at the Balle. I will never forget it: so striking they were as a couple, he so tall and dark and she so petite and fair. And so very obviously in love. Many people commented on it." There was the trace of a tremor in Angélique's voice, and her eyes held a sheen that was more than a reflection of light. Chantal felt her own eyes misting over.

"Did my mother – *know?*" she asked in a low voice.

"*Certainement.* Édouard told her everything. It was against the rules, but he loved and trusted her that much, and she accepted it because she loved him too. She was not afraid at all; on the contrary, she thought it wonderful and magical, and said she wished she could be *loup garou* herself and run with him in the wilderness. Can you imagine what it felt like to Édouard to be accepted like that, after years of hiding his true nature from society?"

"But then why did he hide it from *me?"* said Chantal. "Why take me away to America, and never even leave a note to tell me what I was?"

"Because he feared what his family might do to you. He suspected that his family arranged your mother's fatal accident, and so he deliberately left you ignorant of your heritage. He wanted to keep you safe. I only wish he had stayed with you and raised you, instead of returning to confront the Boisverts. But he desired justice for Helen's sake. After he was killed Thérèse, not knowing what he'd said to your family in America, dared not contact you. And Honoré said that we should not do so either, but respect Édouard's wishes that you live a normal life. If you decided of your own free will to contact us, he said, that was another matter. We are so very glad that you did: there is so much of your parents in you, child, that it's almost like having them back with us again." She gave Chantal's shoulder a little pat. "Now. Let us go join the party." She took Raoul by the arm, and Dubois held out his hand to Chantal.

The Regency dances were not really so very complicated, she found; she was reminded of the country dancing she had learnt in school as a child. It was obvious that they were designed as a way for people to meet and socialize, since you danced not only with your own partner, but in a larger group. In many of them you had to pass along the whole length of the set, dancing briefly with each man on the opposite side

282

before returning to your partner. Hand and eye contact were necessary and unavoidable. She was just starting to get into the rhythm of one long dance, mirroring her older and more experienced partner's moves as she made her way down a long line of men, when she made a turn and found herself face to face with Yves Lapierre. She stopped dead.

"How did *you* get into this set?" she hissed.

He smiled at her. "Let us not make a scene," he said. "Keep moving, or you will throw the other dancers off."

Simmering with fury Chantal let him take her hand, but she would not meet his eyes. When he handed her off to the next man she breathed a sigh of relief, and the instant the music ended she swept away without staying to chat with the other dancers, as was customary. But Yves anticipated her move, and followed her.

"Chantal, you look lovely," he said, looking her up and down. *"Ravissant."*

"Give it a rest," she said rudely. "You never cared a rap for me, so why keep on pretending?"

His smile remained fixed. "You're mistaken, Chantal. I admired you always, from the moment I first met you. Will you not relent and dance with me? They are going to do a waltz next, for a change of pace."

"Forget her, Yves," snapped his brother, walking up to stand at his shoulder. "Can you not see that *they* have gotten to her? She is useless to you now. And as for all this frippery, dancing and courting, it is stupid. Human rubbish. Why must we play these games? In the natural world it is better. Animals mate whenever they please."

"Not so," said Dubois's calm voice over Chantal's shoulder. Grateful, she turned to see him and his wife standing behind her. Raoul was with them. "Most male animals must compete fiercely with each other in mating season. In the natural world, you would have to fight for the honour of having a mate – fight, and possibly die."

283

Raoul added, "And among wolves, you might not have the mate ever. The head wolves do not allow it." He moved to stand right in front of Yves. The two youths faced each other for an instant, tension in every line of their bodies.

"I don't believe we've met," Yves said in an icy tone, his eyes riveted on the other's face.

"Raoul Dulac *à votre service,*" the other replied.

Their deliberately formal language and their antique costume gave the whole scene an oddly anachronistic feel. In a moment they would be demanding pistols at dawn, thought Chantal in fascination. But no; this rivalry was of a kind older still. The tension between them was that of two male animals facing each other with teeth drawn, not only ready but eager to shed blood.

Mme. Dubois spoke up. "Perhaps, Raoul dear, you would dance with Chantal?" she said. "It would give you a chance to practice the steps we taught you."

"As Madame wishes." He tore his eyes away from Yves, bowed to Chantal, and offered her his arm as the waltz music began. "Shall we attempt a dance, *mam'selle?*"

"I'm sorry," said Chantal after treading on his foot for the third time, "I'm just not very good at this kind of dancing. And with this humongous skirt I can't see where I'm putting my feet!"

"I do not dance well either," replied Raoul. "Let us go up there – " he pointed to the back of the room – "to that high place, that – "

"Gallery."

"That gallery. Then we can watch instead. Would you like that?"

"I'd love to. Sure."

He offered her his arm again, and they went up and sat in the gallery with a few other ball-goers: elderly people for the most part, wearied by their exertions on the dance floor. From this elevated vantage point Chantal found there was a much better view of the dances: all their intricate patterns were revealed, like the inner workings of a clock. Also, from up here she could more easily spot her enemies. A quick glance, however, showed no sign of either the Lapierres or the Boisverts. She hoped that meant they had left.

She turned to her companion, and spoke to him in a low voice. "Thanks for standing up for me, down there. Against Yves."

"He was bothering you," replied Raoul, as if that were all the justification needed.

"Well – thanks," she said again.

His eyes shifted back to the dance floor, and she stole a glance at him as he gazed at the dancers, his expression curiously focused and rapt. She found herself taking in details, even now finding it hard to believe that he was not what he appeared to be. The hands clasped upon his knee, the veins and tendons in their backs showing in clear relief; the silvery fair hair; the eyes with their deep blue irises and pale lashes and brows; the lips curved in a faint half-smile. She admired the clean pure lines of his high cheekbones, his straight-bridged nose, the strong chin with its pronounced cleft. All of these things said "human" to her. He was not merely a convincing imitation, like a statue or waxwork; he was the thing itself, authentic, alive.

Yet his history was not human. No human mother had birthed him; he had never been an infant or child. This boy had sprung forth fully-formed, apparently mere months ago, from the body of a wolf – that same white wolf of Nunavik which she had seen in the video at the Redpath Museum. Had his lupine form contained its

285

human heritage in the form of some subtle DNA-like pattern, bound within its blood and bones – stamped onto its very cells? Did even *loups garous* themselves understand the mystery of their existence?

The music ended, the orderly patterns of the dance breaking apart into loose knots and pairs as the dancers retired from the floor. *"Formidable,"* Raoul murmured, turning towards her. "I admire these human things very much."

There was something very open and childish about his enthusiasm. That made sense, she reflected, considering he was not as old as he looked. He had lived less than a third of a wolf's brief life before Josephine met him, and so as a human he appeared the equivalent in human terms: a boy of about her age. But he lacked her generation's sophistication and knowledge of the world. Nor had he yet learned to mask his emotions by controlling his facial muscles. She recalled the look of naked aggression on his face as he confronted Yves. He had a very long way to go, still...

Almost as though he had read her thoughts, he continued: "But I find all this hard at times. I cannot walk with ease as a man among men."

She felt a stirring of empathy for him, and something stronger: a kind of tenderness for this waifish being lost in a dazzling but unfamiliar new realm. It was hard enough for her to accept the changes her wolf-side brought to her life, but she at least could live on in the same world into which she had been born. Not so Raoul. She was very glad that he had protectors, experienced and compassionate friends like Honoré Dubois who could guide him through his new life, tell him how to avoid its myriad pitfalls, reassure him when everything became too complicated for comfort. "You'll do fine," she said.

"I hope so. It was you who inspired me, you know."

"I – inspired you? How?"

"I felt for you," he explained, speaking slowly as though considering each word, "back when we found you in the woods – when you were helpless and afraid. Once you returned to your own human world you were happy again. It made me think that this was a world *I* might be able to live in, too. And that one day, perhaps, you and I might meet again and – and help each other. I had a – a dream, one night. Only it was not a dream. That is…" He stumbled over the words. "What I mean to say is, thinking of you put courage in me to become a human being."

His blue gaze was so open, his feelings so plain and guileless, that for a moment she too was at a loss for words. She was still struggling to find something adequate to say in response when a small hand tugged on her left arm, and a voice spoke in her ear, soft and low yet urgent: "Chantal?"

She turned sharply, annoyed at the distraction, to see her cousin Lysette standing there at her side.

The little girl was dressed in a long blue Empire gown, her short dark curls caught back by a fillet of matching ribbon. She looked like a porcelain doll, but her face was contorted as if she were very close to tears. She backed away on seeing Chantal's irritated expression. "Why are you angry with us, Chantal?" she pleaded. "Tell me!"

For a moment Chantal could not find anything to say. She looked helplessly at her young cousin, then at Raoul whose gaze moved from one to the other of them in puzzlement.

"Please," begged Lysette. "*Why* don't you like us any more? Our Grandmère says you won't ever come to see us again. And I waited all these years for the Lost Cousin to come back some day!" The music had temporarily ceased and her high distressed voice pierced

287

the silence. Other people in the gallery were looking, frowning in concern and whispering to one another.

Chantal cursed mentally. "Come with me," she said, standing up. "No, it's all right," she added to Raoul as he too rose to accompany them. She did not want to upset Lysette any further. "You stay here. This won't take a minute. I'll be right back."

Taking her little cousin's hand she led her back downstairs to find a quiet corner. Then she turned and faced the girl, bending down to put their faces at the same level. "Lysette. Please don't think I'm mad at you. Grandmère and I have had a – a disagreement, and I don't think I can come and live with you after all. But I do care about *you*. I really do hope that I can see you again."

Lysette mopped at her tear-filled eyes with the back of one hand. "Then I feel better, a little. I would be sad if I thought you hated me."

"Lysette!" cried Chantal. "Nobody could hate you! You're a sweet kid, and I'm happy to be your cousin. Really and truly."

Someone came up behind Chantal and laid a hand on her shoulder. She turned, expecting to see Raoul, and instead found herself looking up into Yves's face. She sprang back, wrenching herself out of his grip, but checked her angry shout before it left her lips, knowing it would frighten Lysette. Yves stood still.

"Chantal, won't you at least let us apologize?" he said. "Come and see your Grandmère one more time. She's in a room just down the hall. That's all she asks, that you let her say she is sorry. I will stay here, don't fear. Your friend can watch me," he added dryly, nodding to Raoul who was standing at the foot of the stairs. The blond boy's eyes were fixed on Yves, and the warmth was gone from their blue depths: they were cold as sea-ice.

288

"Yes, yes!" Lysette cried, grabbing her hand. "You will come, and everything will be all right again."

Chantal looked down at the little girl, then at Yves. "You swear you'll stay put?" she said to him.

It was Raoul who answered. "He will – I'll see that he does." The two youths exchanged long, hard looks.

"All right, then – I won't be long." She addressed the last words to Raoul before letting her cousin lead her away down the corridor.

There were a number of doors along the corridor, opening into large rooms. Lysette led her into one. It was a large chamber, its rounded shape following the lines of the tower into which it was set, and it had rose-pink walls and creamy trim all softly lit by chandeliers. Once inside Chantal stopped dead. She had expecting to see her grandmother, and possibly her aunt and cousin Francine as well. But the room was filled with people, about twenty or so, all clad in Napoleonic attire. Thérèse Boisvert sat on the round upholstered seat at the base of the room's central column, her blue mantle flowing about her: a queen holding court. To her left stood Genevieve, to her right a tall man in a dark-blue coat and knee-breeches whom Chantal did not know. Francine, clad in a lilac-coloured Empire gown, sat alone by the window looking out on the river. She turned as Chantal and her sister came in, then pointedly looked away again.

"Come in, *ma chère enfant!*" Thérèse called out to Chantal. "This is a lovely room, *non?* It is the Salon Rose – once a favourite of Winston Churchill's. He and your President Roosevelt and the Canadian prime minister Mackenzie King came here often when they were staying in the Citadelle, planning France's liberation from the Nazis." *And how wealthy and powerful must I be, in order to rent such a famous room,* was the unspoken subtext. When Chantal made no reply, Thérèse patted the pink upholstery beside her and flashed a wide, white smile at her recalcitrant granddaughter. "Come and sit by me," she entreated.

*What big teeth you have, Grandmother,* thought Chantal. She remained where she was, several paces away from Thérèse and close to the door. "Thanks, but I'd rather stand."

With a wave of her hand Thérèse introduced the other occupants of the room. Most were older people, Boisvert relatives and members of Thérèse's own family, the rich and powerful Valcourts. The tall man at her side was her brother-in-law, Antoine Boisvert; looking at his heavy brows and thick shock of hair, both now turned iron-grey, Chantal suddenly saw the resemblance to her father and grandfather. In his turn Great-uncle Antoine gave Chantal a long, appraising look.

"I understand now the eagerness of Yves," he said, turning to Thérèse. "Why he cannot wait. I had suspected it was only his impatience for the Boisvert wealth, but no: she is desirable in herself."

Chantal's cheeks burned with resentment. "Are you through discussing me to my face?" she said.

Antoine showed his teeth in a broad smile. "Spirited, too! A credit to her pack. She must be formidable in her other form, Thérèse. A perfect head-wolf – an 'alpha', as the humans put it."

Chantal simmered but said no more. Her grandmother got up and approached her, both hands held out. "Ah, you are still upset! We only wanted to teach you what you really were, to accept and to understand it. Perhaps we were too eager. Will you not try to see things from our eyes? We know how hard and frightening it is to be a *loup garou.*"

"You certainly scared me," said Chantal. "My life has been an absolute nightmare these past few months."

"I am so very sorry. But you would have found out eventually, perhaps in a more unsettling way, on your own with no one there to help and guide you."

Chantal's eyes strayed to Francine's rigid turned back. "And this stupid arranged marriage business – "

Francine abruptly sprang up from her seat and headed for the door, still not looking at her cousin. Thérèse's eyes narrowed as they followed her, then returned to Chantal. "For your own good, child. You belong with us, among your own kind. You must know by now you can never live with your American family again – not knowing what you do now. You are not one of them. Nor can you hope to live with any common man." Her gaze shifted again, to rest on her daughter. Genevieve flushed and looked away.

A brief uneasy silence fell, then was broken by the deep voice of Antoine Boisvert. "Tell me, Chantal, do you know of the *Lai du Bisclavret?*"

"Never heard of it. What is it?" she replied, wondering at the abrupt change of subject.

"It is an old Breton poem by Marie de France. Its hero is a noble knight who is also a *loup garou*. In the story he is betrayed by his adulterous wife, who learns the secret of his double life and steals his clothing while he is in his wolf-form. This curses him to remain a wolf, and he must flee from the huntsmen that his lady and her lover send after him. He is only saved when the king, who is amazed by this wolf's curious gentleness, makes a pet of him. The king ultimately learns the truth, restores the knight's human form and punishes his murderous wife. All Boisvert children are taught the *Lai du Bisclavret* at an early age, to warn them of the perfidy of humankind."

291

"But that's just fiction," objected Chantal. "A fairy tale."

He shrugged. "If you prefer truth, there is the story of Madame Sanroche, the Werewolf of Auvergne. Has Honoré Dubois told you about her?"

"He – mentioned her, briefly. But he didn't go into details."

"I am not surprised. Dubois does prefer to dwell on the benign aspects of human nature... Her story was recorded by Henri Boguet, a French demonologist of the sixteenth century who persecuted *loups garous* in Franche-Comté, though she was not one of his victims.

"Her husband owned a large estate in the Auvergne, a region of France that is mountainous and thickly forested. One day Monsieur Sanroche permitted a huntsman called Fayrolle to chase deer in his private forest. The hunter encountered a huge wolf in the woods, and after a fierce struggle he cut off one of its forepaws. It fled, limping on three legs, while he returned to the *château* of Sanroche to tell him the tale and show him his trophy. But to the amazement of both men, when Fayrolle opened his sack they saw that the wolf-paw had become a human hand. And on one finger was a topaz ring which Sanroche recognized as belonging to his wife.

"He ran at once to his lady's chamber, where he found her moaning in pain, her arm concealed in a swath of fabric. Tearing this away, he saw that her hand had been cut off." Great-uncle Antoine's dark eyes hardened under their heavy brows. "Did Sanroche ask his poor, suffering wife for her side of the story? No! Her offense was simply to be what she was, a *loup garou*. No marriage vow or bond of affection could save her from his fear and hatred. He delivered her to the authorities, and she was burnt at the stake at Riom in

1588. The lesson of Madame Sanroche's fate is clear: humans and wolf-people can never mix."

"*C'est vrai*. Humans are faithless and treacherous to us, always." As Thérèse said these words her gaze once more slid sideways to her daughter's face. Genevieve turned away, but not before Chantal glimpsed the raw anguish in her aunt's eyes.

*Twisting the knife in the wound,* she thought, indignant. *How like Thérèse!* In that moment she knew she could never accept this woman as family, never belong to her oppressive clan. "If you brought me here to apologize, I accept," she said. "But if you just want to try and turn me against my human friends and family, I'll think I'll leave now."

"No, I do not think that you will." Thérèse smiled at her, but her golden eyes were cold now. "We cannot allow it, you see."

"Allow?" Chantal repeated, incredulous.

"Lone wolves are not permitted in our family. We stand united, always."

"I've got a family back home in America, thanks. I don't want to be part of your pack."

Her great-uncle spoke again. "But you *are* a member, by virtue of your birth. Blood will tell in the end, however you try to deny it. And an essential part of living in a wolf pack is – discipline."

Antoine turned to another, younger man, tall and lean and elegant in his Regency attire, with a head of fox-red hair. The young man nodded. "I concur," he said. "This situation has dragged on long enough. An intervention is called for." He, too, spoke as if Chantal was not even in the room with them. She bristled.

"That's it," she snapped. "I'm leaving now."

Genevieve gave a little gasp like a suppressed scream, and Lysette echoed it. Chantal half-turned, but only in time to catch a blurred motion out of the corner of her right eye before something hard and heavy came down on the back of her neck. She staggered and fell to the rose-coloured carpet.

Then everything went black.

## 20

*Not again,* Chantal thought sometime later, as she awakened to a pounding head.

Someone had deposited her on a couch, in a room she did not recognize. Her family had shown her their usual consideration, lugging her unconscious body out of the Salon Rose in full view of everyone before dumping her in here. No doubt they had explained to any bewildered hotel patrons they encountered that she'd fainted at the dance, or taken too much wine... Chantal sat up, feeling groggy and sick, and gingerly put her hand to her head. Her hair had come loose, tumbling down around her neck and shoulders; reaching under it, she probed the tender swelling at the base of her head and then snatched her hand back, wincing. What had they hit her with? It was a wonder she wasn't concussed.

She looked around her. Apparently she was in the Château still: through a nearby window she could see the tapered tip of a floodlit turret, glowing green against a still-dark sky. But this was no ordinary hotel room. She was in an elegant suite, boasting both bedroom and furnished sitting room. She had been placed in the latter; the bedroom must lie behind the door in the wall to her left. In addition to the couch there were three upholstered chairs matching the green-gold leafy wallpaper, a coffee table, a cabinet, and a carved wooden mantelpiece. One side of the room was set into a tower, creating a nook with rounded walls containing a writing desk and chair. Only a person of wealth could afford such accommodations as these. As always, Thérèse Boisvert spared no expense.

She groaned aloud. How could she have been so foolish? She should have known better than to go with Lysette. The Boisverts had succeeded in disarming her suspicions by using the innocent child as a lure. Now she was a prisoner.

As she sat there the connecting door to the bedchamber opened. She tensed, but it was only her *Tante* Genevieve. The woman looked even more haggard and guilt-ridden than usual. Chantal stood and confronted her face to face, and Genevieve's eyes immediately dropped in submission.

Chantal took full advantage of it. "What's the idea?" she demanded, advancing on the woman. "Conking me on the head and carting me around – you people have really crossed the line this time, you know that? This is assault and abduction; you could all go to jail. Anyway, if you don't let me out of this room right now I'll yell until somebody comes."

The older woman did not answer right away. She sank into a chair – almost she seemed to collapse, like a deflating balloon. "It is no use," she said at length. "They will just tell the hotel staff that you suffer from nightmares, which is the truth. Your people at home in America will confirm that. And if you keep it up, they will gag you. There is nothing at all that you can do."

She did not say this like a villain gloating over a victim. Her tone was dull and hopeless, like that of a long-term prisoner counseling a newly arrived captive to despair. But Chantal was so used to fear now that it no longer paralyzed her; it only stoked her anger. "That's it!" she snapped. "I disown this family. You hear me? I won't have anything to do with any of you after this. I'm surprised you haven't ditched them all yourself by now, if they make you so miserable. Is this why your husband left you? Did he just have to give up on you?"

At that Genevieve's eyes flashed, in the first show of spirit Chantal had ever seen in her. "My husband did *not* leave me!"

"Thérèse said – "

296

"What she told you was a lie!" Genevieve sprang up and commenced pacing about the room. "Oh, she was not deceiving you: she believed what she said, but it was false all the same. The lie was mine, not hers. I told her Henri had left me, but it was I who left him."

Chantal stared at her, taken aback. "But – why? I thought you loved him?"

"I left *because* I loved him! She threatened his life, she and her *loup garou* allies. There are so few of us now, they wanted me to mate with another *loup garou* and breed true, adding to their numbers. When I dared to marry a mere human and have his children instead, they were furious." Her eyes filled with tears. "They began to issue threats against our family. I was afraid they would follow through. I might be murdered; or my husband, or my half-breed daughters. Lysette was only a baby... All our lives were in danger.

"So I left Henri, the only man I ever loved; and I brought my children back home to Maman. Once we were securely in her power again there was no reason for her... friends to harm any of us. And I let Maman think that Henri had been unfaithful to me. That way she would not be afraid of him trying to win me back, and would leave him alone. But the truth is he begged me many times to return, for he did not understand why I had left him. He thought he must have done something wrong, when all along I was just trying to save him from them! They would kill him before they would let him discover my secret.

"He did not know, you see, that I was a *loup garou.*"

There was a pause. Genevieve resumed her seat and put a hand to her head. "I never had the courage to tell him. I thought I could hide it from him, suppress the wolf in me and in our offspring. I wanted us to be able to live normal, human lives. They hated that – Maman and the others. It's against their laws. We are not

297

allowed to live apart from the pack, nor mate as we choose; especially with ordinary humans."

It was impossible to see such misery and not feel sympathy stir. "I'm sorry," Chantal said. "But then you should want *me* to be free, right? So I won't have to live the way that you did. You could help me get away – "

Her aunt leaped up out of her chair again. "You don't understand! Haven't you been listening? You *can't* get away from them, not ever. Under their domination you are no threat to them, but once you are free of them they will see you as a threat. Already you have revealed your wolf-self once, in public – "

"That was Francine's fault! She provoked me on purpose!" Anger boiled up in Chantal again. "She has it in for me. It was Francine who hit me on the head in the Salon Rose, wasn't it? What'd she use, a baseball bat?"

"A champagne bottle. It was not quite full," her aunt added feebly, as though this were somehow a mitigating factor. "You must try to understand, Chantal, she is under their control. I tried to raise her properly, but they got to her: Maman, and Yves. He courted her, with Maman's approval. Of course Francine fell in love with him! He is so handsome, and she is only a child. But he never truly loved her. He only wanted a suitable wolf-bride, from a wealthy family, so he was prepared to wait for her – "

Chantal nodded. "And then I came along, and he realized he didn't have to wait for little Francine after all. He sure didn't lose any time: he started hitting on me straight away."

"Yes. Francine knew then that she had not only lost the boy she loved, but that she would be required to wed Jules instead – a boy she dislikes and fears."

"And my grandmother's just fine with all of this!" Chantal shook her head in angry amazement.

298

"Of course she is. The Lapierres may have little money, but they are of pure Arcadian lineage, their blood unmixed with that of lesser humans. One of the few such bloodlines left in the world. All her own grandchildren are half-breeds because of my disobedience and Édouard's. My brother is dead, and I can have no more children. All Maman's hope now lies with the next generation, to restore the Boisvert bloodline to purity. Yves offers her that, and so she gives in to his every demand. If he wants you instead of Francine, then he must have his way."

"Well, I'm not going to be part of any breeding programme! They can't keep me here forever!" Chantal said. She strode towards the door, and was reaching for the locks when her aunt spoke again.

"They do not need locked doors to keep you prisoner, Chantal. Believe me, I know this. If you refuse, if you run away from them, you will live the rest of your life in fear."

Her hand closed on a bolt. "Why? I may not be a pure-bred, but if they're so few in number then the Boisverts can't afford to eliminate me, can they?"

"It is not only the Boisverts you have to fear. The Lapierres are a danger also. So your father found, to his cost."

"What do you mean? My dad and my grandfather killed each other. Didn't they?"

She shook her head vehemently. "No, I never believed that! They had fought before, yes, but for all their disagreements there was real love between Édouard and Papa. My father wanted only to make my brother see reason; he would never have killed or even hurt him, not for anything. But Guy Lapierre was present at the cottage."

"He was?"

"He was visiting us at the time, for the autumn hunt, and it was he who started the fight. Édouard accused him outright of causing the accident that killed your mother. Her car swerved to avoid an animal running across the road – most witnesses thought it was a dog, but some said it was a wolf. Édouard was convinced it was one of our pack, or possibly Guy who would have done anything for Papa and Maman. When he vowed to expose us all and ran away from the cottage, Guy joined Papa in pursuit of him. Later Guy came back saying he and Papa had become separated in their search, and that he'd heard the sound of fighting wolves and come upon their two dead bodies. I didn't believe him then, and I don't now. You see, he was all covered in scratches – from tree boughs, he said, but they could as easily have been the marks of teeth and claws. We keep our injuries even when we change shape, as you may have noticed.

"Guy was Édouard's rival, always trying to supplant him in my father's affections: to be the son that Papa really wanted. They hunted together, both in wolf and human form. But Édouard was still the legal heir who stood to gain the family fortune when our father died. Guy came to resent this, for he never had much money. He courted me when I was a girl, not because he cared for me at all but because as Papa's son-in-law he could replace Édouard in his affections. Maman approved of the match, but I would not agree to it. I suspected Guy's motives even then, and I told Papa I could not marry a man I did not love. Thank Heaven he did not force me to.

"Guy gave up, and married a wolf-woman of Arcadian ancestry. But she was not wealthy and she died after bearing him two sons. Then Édouard married, and had a daughter – an heiress who would be just the right age for one of Guy's sons to wed, one day… Guy used to joke about it to my father, but I believe he had

300

serious ambitions of merging our two packs – passing our wealth on to *his* offspring. Except Édouard would never have allowed such a union. He disliked and distrusted Guy, and he would not sell his daughter into marriage for the sake of a pack alliance. And so, you see, Édouard had to go. Secretly, quietly, in a way no one would find suspicious. But I think my father must have caught Guy in the act, out there in the forest. So of course Papa had to go, too."

Chantal listened, aghast, to this tale of Sicilian intrigue. Genevieve's account carried conviction. She had known these people, understood their passions and designs; and she knew well the ways of the wolf-clans.

"The Lapierres are monsters – monsters!" her aunt cried.

Chantal swallowed hard. "But – but they still want me alive, to get your family's money..."

*"C'est vrai.* But even if they never touch *you,* your loved ones will be in danger: your human family back home in America. And if you dare to love another man – a human – Maman and the Lapierres will threaten his life. Finally you will be forced to give in and return as I did, in order to protect those you love. If you won't protect yourself, Chantal, then think of it as ensuring the safety of others."

"I won't put up with it. I'll – I'll put the police onto them."

"The police will do nothing. Think, child. If you tell them about the *loups garous* they will just laugh in your face. And your enemies are not fools. The police will find no knife or bullet wounds on the bodies, only the marks of fangs. They will blame an animal, a coyote or a mad dog. There will be nothing at all to lead the authorities to the respectable Quebec *familles* Boisvert and Lapierre."

301

Chantal recalled the wolf she had seen in the backyard of the house in Derby Line. It had been Yves, beyond a doubt, sending her a message after she rejected him in the library. He could easily travel to her hometown again... It was true, what Genevieve said: a *loup garou* could kill a human being with complete impunity. She pictured her uncle and Aunt Lorraine and the twins out hiking on one of their favourite nature trails, and she went cold with terror. How could she possibly warn them? They would think she was insane.

"There's Honoré Dubois," she said, grasping at one straw of hope. "He'd know who did it. The Lapierres would have to reckon with *him.*"

"Dubois is getting old. He is not the force he once was. They do not fear him any more."

As she was speaking the door suddenly opened, making Chantal jump back. She expected Thérèse or Yves, but it was Jules Lapierre who entered. He glared at her, then turned on Genevieve.

"Your mother wants you. Go," he said.

Genevieve obeyed without a murmur, shooting one last terrified glance at Chantal. When she had vanished down the corridor Jules closed the door and relocked it. Apparently he had been partaking of his favourite opiate again, whatever it might be. His eyes, with the big black pupils occluding most of the iris, looked dark and cold as two frozen pools. "What did she say to you?" he demanded of Chantal.

"None of your business," replied Chantal.

"Genevieve has been developing a careless tongue of late. If she keeps it up she will have to be disciplined." Chantal remained obstinately silent, and he shrugged. *"Eh bien,* that is not what I want from you anyway."

"Oh?" She eyed him warily, sizing him up. They were of about the same height, and she wondered if she might be able to overpower him, at least long enough to

302

get to the door. He was more muscular about the arms and torso, however: the loose linen shirt of his costume made that plain.

"I want you to tell me which one he is." Jules took a step towards her, his eyes boring into hers.

"What?"

"The white wolf, the one Josephine Legris brought down with her from Nunavik. He walks now in a man's form, among Dubois's household, correct? Which one of them is he?"

"I don't know what you're talking about," Chantal said.

"Oh but you do, I know you do. Is it the Métis, Jean-Louis? He came south with her about that same time. Or that supposed Québecois with the unconvincing accent – Dulac. Is it he? Dulac, *du lac...* 'Of the Lake.' There was a pack of *haut-loups* in the lake country north of Pingualuit..." He was watching her face for a reaction, some tell-tale sign that would betray Raoul. She froze her features into a motionless mask. "Someone else, perhaps? That black guy, Thibodeau: they say he came from Cajun country down south, but that could just be a ruse to throw us off the scent... You know them all by now, don't you? Honoré's precious little *protégés?* But there's only one we care about, Yves and I: the white wolf who helped kill our father. Two contributed to Papa's death: one has paid the price, but the other has not. Yet."

He moved closer still, and Chantal backed away. She hated herself for giving ground, but the menace he exuded was so strong she could almost feel it. "It was you, wasn't it?" she accused, buying time. *"You* murdered that man – Dr. Hébert."

"Murder?" Jules's features twisted as he spoke; his breathing was ragged and heavy. "I call it justice, and

303

long delayed. My father suffered greatly before he died, out there in the wilderness far from any help."

"Dr. Hébert didn't know Guy was a man! How could he? He thought he'd shot an animal – a wolf that attacked him and his students – "

"He fired the fatal shot. That's all that matters. No one harms our pack and gets away with it. We do not spare even the ignorant. But that *haut-loup,* that mangy low-born cur – *he* knew exactly what he was doing when he betrayed us to those men. So tell me which one he is, or I will kill all of Dubois's little pets, one by one, to get him."

"You're wasting your time," she said, with more bravado than she felt. "I'm not helping you commit another murder."

"Not even to save other, innocent lives?"

"What makes you so sure you can kill them all? I'd love to see you go up against Ti-Jacques," she retorted. Just thinking of the tall, strong youth put courage back into her. "I'm not telling you anything. And you're not keeping me here, either."

He glared back at her with apparent distaste, but then said unexpectedly: "No, you are right. You are free to go. Now, before the others come back here to sleep. It is two in the morning already, the party is over."

She stared at him in surprise. "Wait a minute. You'd *let* me escape? Why?"

He continued to glower. "Because I don't want my brother to marry a half-breed. If you were a true *loup garou* you would understand. This is necessary for the integrity of our species."

"That Arcadian bloodline of yours, you mean?" she said.

"You know of *l'Arcadie?"* He gave it the French pronunciation.

"M. Dubois told me."

"I am surprised the old wolf would tell you so much – that he would allow you even to know about *l'Arcadie*. He's always sought to suppress our desire for the land of our origins. My friends and I though, *we* dare to dream of a new world after humankind has gone – after it has annihilated itself. But if we are to master the earth we cannot tolerate any weaknesses in our genome. We are growing inbred as it is, out of necessity, but the impure strains are a greater threat." He was ranting again, the words gushing out of him in a wild torrent. "There are not enough of us pure-breds left. But Yves isn't thinking of the purity of our bloodline; all he wants is the Boisvert money. If Thérèse would allow Yves to have a pure-bred mistress, even – but no, she won't want his bastard offspring competing with *her* descendants. So go then! Maybe he will forget about you, and seek a better match elsewhere." His mouth twisted in a sneer that was almost a snarl. "Go to your weakling friends, and good riddance!" He moved towards the door again, and unlocked it.

"Thank you – I guess," she shot back as she passed through it.

He did not leave her to go on alone however, but shadowed her down the silent empty corridor. They took the elevator together down to the lobby. It too was eerily quiet and bereft of life at this hour, save for one person on duty at the reception desk. A fierce glare from Jules prevented her from calling out.

He led her to one of the side exits of the hotel, giving directly onto the boardwalk. "Where are we going?" she demanded, her suspicions rousing. "Why not go by the front door?"

"No witnesses," he said curtly. "Do you want one of Thérèse's spies to spot you, and come right after us?" It was true that he looked nervous, his dilated eyes darting restlessly to and fro as he walked. "I know a secret way, used only by *loups garous*. There are many of these wolf-ways."

She remembered that Dubois had mentioned the *"chemins du loup"*. They were the catacombs of the *loups garous,* delved in secret by their ancestors long ago for a refuge and escape in emergencies. They were not much used nowadays, since the city walls no longer held the population in and all could go and come as they pleased. But *loups garous* placed high in the local government saw that the wolf-ways were still kept secret.

Jules led her outside the hotel onto the boardwalk. She shivered as they walked away from the shelter of the vast building, out to where the icy wind blew unobstructed. Her thin costume could not protect her, and she had no coat. "It's freezing out here!"

"It is not far. You'll survive."

She followed without another word, walking close behind and using him as a wind-break, her teeth chattering in the bitter pre-dawn cold.

Not far from the Casse-Cou staircase was a kiosk shaped like in iron gazebo, and next to this a short flight of steps led down through a rectangular opening cut into the boardwalk, terminating in a metal door. Jules unlocked it and stepped into the blackness inside. "Hurry up," he said impatiently as she hesitated on the stairs. She followed him down into the dark space, persuaded in part by the subarctic cold. Jules closed the door behind them and flipped an electric switch on the wall, flooding their surroundings in a dull yellow glow.

They stood in a crypt-like space underneath the boardwalk: the archaeological excavation of old Quebec, now preserved as a museum containing all that remained of Champlain's original fort and Count Frontenac's Château St Louis. In summer tourists would be taken through here on conducted tours, but now the place was empty, chill and forbidding. Ruinous, roofless walls of ancient masonry rose all around them; cavernous fireplaces gaped blackly under mantels of fitted stone or brick. The fort's original windows still existed, deep embrasures into which clear modern panes had been placed, and square skylights had been cut into the boardwalk overhead and covered by plexiglass structures like transparent tents: in the daytime these would have admitted light from outside, but now they showed only the ink-black of the night sky.

Jules led her through the maze-like expanse of broken walls, along paths of cracked pavement, past display cases filled with crockery and other historic artifacts, until at last they reached a white-painted wooden wall. In it was another door labeled PRIVE – "Private"; this he unlocked using the same key with which he had opened the main door. It opened onto a stone-paved tunnel with earthen walls and roof.

"The official dig ends here," Jules told her. "This is an old secret tunnel made by our people centuries ago. Only *loups garous* are allowed to know that it exists: we have friends in very high places, *vous savez...* If you follow it, you will come to an opening not far from the Citadelle. From there it is a short walk to the Dubois house. I won't accompany you there. His curs would attack me on sight. Go now, *vite!*"

She went into the tunnel, stooping low. It had been designed more for wolves than humans, by the look of it, and felt claustrophobic. Jules remained behind, and before she had gone far she heard him close the door with an echoing clang. The faint yellow light vanished, leaving her fumbling in the dark. *That was way too easy,* she thought with a twinge of misgiving as she struggled onwards, hampered by her voluminous skirts. *He might have his own reasons for freeing me, but still...*

307

From behind her, like a confirmation of her unspoken thoughts, came the sound of hoarse panting breaths and clawed feet scraping on stone. Her heart seemed to leap up inside her chest and batter against her ribs. "Jules?" she croaked.

There was no reply except for a low, excited growl.

Too late, she understood.

Jules never had intended for her to escape. He had just wanted her out of the Château, away from his family who wanted her alive, in a secret place where he could chase her down and kill her without any interference. She had fallen for his deception, and now there was no one to save her, no one to hear her cries for help.

No witnesses…

## 21

"But how could they have just *taken* her?" exclaimed Dubois. He and his wife stood in the near-empty hotel lobby with Manon and the two boys, the women huddled in their wraps.

"I do not know," said Raoul. "I should have known better than to let her out of my sight, even for an instant. I promised to protect her, and I have failed."

"The Lapierres are cunning," said Angélique. "Too cunning for an honest soul like you, Raoul. The child was the bait, to lure Chantal from your side."

"Honoré!"

They all looked up as Hyacinthe and Suzette came rushing across the lobby. "We talked to the staff in the Palm Room, and one of them he saw an unconscious girl being carried out of the Salon Rose earlier this evening by a young man," said Suzette.

"*Sacré!* I spoke with hotel management earlier," said Dubois. "They told me the Boisverts rented the Salon Rose tonight. The hotel will not disclose where their private rooms are, of course."

"Then we must go have a talk with them before they leave the Salon Rose," growled Ti-Jacques.

"We looked inside it," Hyacinthe told him. "They are not there now: it is empty. The Boisverts are back in the ballroom."

"All of them?" asked Dubois.

"All except the little girl: I think her mother took her up to bed, but Genevieve is back in the ballroom now. There is only one Lapierre brother with them, though. The other is nowhere to be seen."

"Yves?" asked Manon.

Hyacinthe shook her head. "No, it is Jules who is gone."

Dubois groaned. "Did your staff person speak to this young man who was carrying the girl?"

"He just asked if medical attention was needed," Suzette told him, "and the boy said no."

Manon looked doubtful. "But are you sure that this girl was Chantal? It's not unusual for women to faint at this event, with the heavy costumes, and exhaustion from dancing – "

"So the staff person said; that's why he didn't think anything of it. But he said it was a young girl with dark hair, in a white dress that had a big skirt. That sounds like her!" Hyacinthe was close to tears.

There was a ringing sound. Dubois reached into a pocket and took out a cell phone, the sleek plastic device looking incongruous in his lace-cuffed hand. "That might be the staffer now," Suzette said. "I gave him your cell number and told him to let us know if he learned anything else."

"*Âllo?*" said Dubois, and fell silent as he listened to the voice at the other end. The others *loups garous* craned forward in the effort to overhear, wishing they had the keener ears of their wolf-forms. Dubois's face was grave, even alarmed. "*Bien,*" he said a last. "*Merci beaucoup.*"

He switched the phone off and they crowded around him.

"What?" said Ti-Jacques. "What has happened?"

"This staff member says another colleague saw them, perhaps half an hour ago. He said it just looked as though the girl needed fresh air; she was conscious, and walked out a side door with the dark-haired boy – Jules. The side door: that must mean he was taking her to the *chemin du loup*. But why? Why help her to escape from her family?"

He tapped out another number on the phone. "Noah? Is Mademoiselle Boisvert there by any chance? No?"

He turned to them. "Noah tells me Chantal has not shown up at the house. But it should not have taken her so long to get through the tunnel." His face creased with worry.

"What should we do, Honoré?" asked Suzette.

Dubois handed the phone to Ti-Jacques. "Please call for our carriages and accompany the ladies back to the house. Tell Noah everything that has happened. Raoul, come with me."

Raoul followed the older man through the extensive lobby with its many shops, now dark and still, into the outer corridor and out through the boardwalk exit. Dubois led the way to the museum entrance. They found its door unlocked and ajar, and Dubois grunted at this confirmation of his guess.

Once they were down below, in the covered ruin and away from any human eyes, he turned to Raoul. "Take your wolf shape now, my friend. I fear we may have to fight him."

They both transformed, leaving their costumes piled upon the floor, and ran for the entrance to the tunnel. This they also found unlocked. Not far from the entrance they saw Jules's clothing, tossed down in an untidy heap.

"So! Jules wanted to kill Chantal, in a place where she'd not be found by police. And where there was no one to observe his crime."

Dubois began to run through the tunnel and Raoul made haste to follow. A few metres on they came upon her white ballgown, torn and strewn in pieces about the tunnel.

"He has killed her!" exclaimed Raoul, his words blending together into a desolate howl.

"No! There is no body here, and very little blood." Dubois nosed at the ruined bodice and crinoline. "Only as much as would come from a few scrapes or scratches.

She escaped him, and by the condition of the dress she must have assumed her wolf shape. She is no easy prey, our *chère* Chantal! Follow her scent!"

They raced on through the tunnel. After many twists and turns it brought them all the way to the tree-sheltered opening at the edge of the Plains of Abraham, below the Citadelle. The two *loups garous* ran out onto the plain, noses to the ground. It did not take them long to detect the trails of Chantal and Jules. Two sets of wolf-paw prints stretched away across the Plains. The smaller footprints led first in the direction of the Dubois house, and then swerved sharply, the marks blurring. "Yes! See, Raoul, she ran from him towards the house. But he headed her off. Then he gives chase, look. Come with me!"

The scents were fresh, and the wolves had no difficulty following the tracks. The double trail of pursuer and pursued veered back and forth across the Plains of Abraham. At one point the she-wolf had run towards the field of Snow Sculptures, bathed now in a rainbow of many-coloured spotlights, as if hoping the bright glow and the few strolling spectators there would intimidate her enemy. But once more he had successfully cut in front and driven her back into the dark. Again and again Jules had headed her off, and she had sought an escape only to be outmanoeuvred. Dubois and Raoul began to fear that they were too late, and these tracks would very soon come to an end with the slain body of their friend lying in the snow.

But presently they heard in the near distance the guttural snarls of two battling animals. It came from the direction of the Citadelle, where a path ran alongside the deep waterless moat protecting the inner fortifications. "There!" cried Dubois, and hastened to run after Raoul: the white wolf was already speeding towards the sound.

312

Chantal loped along the edge of the moat with her pursuer snapping at her flank. He was trying to pin her between his fangs and the dangerous drop to the icy pavement below: there was no protective wall or railing to save her. He was swifter than she, more accustomed to running in this form while she stumbled in the thick snow, her wolf-paws clumsy and awkward.

Lunging in from the side, he nearly sent her over. She recovered, scrabbling with her claws at the ice-glazed stone of the parapet, then turned on him and bared her teeth in a last desperate stand. Her human voice was gone, along with her woman's body: abandoned like the remnants of the ballgown in the tunnel. But with her lupine voice she sent her opponent a clear message of hate and defiance, feeling it rumble up through her wolf's chest before bursting from her jaws in a puff of steam. He responded in kind, adding a series of high-pitched whining sounds whose meaning she could not fathom. He was speaking in Lupine, the inhuman language of the *haut-loups*. Like her own snarls, though, his wolf-words needed no translation. He sprang at her even as he raged.

They grappled with each other, biting and pawing. Jules struck first, his teeth scoring long gashes in her foreleg before moving up towards her head. Her human instinct was to protect her face with her hands, but now her fingers – *toes* – could not grasp at anything, and using them upset her balance. Her jaws were her sole means of self-defense in this form. Thrusting her neck forward she clamped her teeth hard on the other wolf's ear. He yelped in pain and fury. There was a strange taste in her mouth, bitter and metallic: the iron tang of blood. In the midst of her confusion and terror she felt a surge of something like triumph. She was not a helpless prey-animal. She was a wolf herself, her body naturally armed for battle, her inexperience compensated by the

313

wordless knowledge of instinct. At this understanding, newly assumed along with her lupine form, the last of her fear vanished. The iron taste on her tongue awakened her beast-self and filled her with the desire to savour yet more blood; to rend living flesh; to kill.

The wolves were evenly matched, the male slender and lightweight for his sex while Chantal was big and strong for hers. He yanked his ear from her clamped jaws, tearing it even more in the process, then quick as a striking snake he lunged in and seized her by the throat. She whined shrilly, trying to twist free, but the heavy ruff that provided natural protection for her neck also gave purchase to his gripping fangs. She slipped and fell on her side as he threw his full weight on top of her and bit deep.

As she struggled to free herself the sense of unreality deepened. On the edge of losing consciousness, she seemed to fall into a dream, one that she had experienced before. For with a rush of swift paws and a furious howl, a great white wolf came hurtling out of the dark at her assailant.

Now it was Jules's turn to be taken by surprise. The newcomer flung himself on the black wolf, and they both rolled away in the snow while Chantal lay fighting for her breath. More *loups garous* came running up in a pack. There was another, smaller white wolf, a female; a huge grey he-wolf; a trio of she-wolves whose fur ranged in hue from blond to russet to dark brown; and one monstrous black beast, bigger than Jules, with yellow eyes blazing like flame: *le Diable* himself in lupine form. The grey wolf came padding up to Chantal's side and nuzzled the side of her face gently. At the touch she calmed. This *loup garou* was a friend: perhaps it was even Honoré Dubois himself... She was safe now.

314

She dropped her head to her forepaws and closed her eyes.

"I swore I would kill you one day, white wolf," raged Jules. "But as long as you hid in your human shape I could not find you. Now you have made it easy for me, you fool."

"Not as easy as you think," roared Raoul, and sprang at him.

The two fighting wolves spun around together in a lethal dance. Jules leaned in to snap, but he was too hasty, too eager for the kill. The white wolf ducked and then thrust his own head upwards, fastened his fangs in the other's throat. The black wolf pulled back with all his strength, but still Raoul would not release his hold. Locked together, they staggered backwards.

And then the earth seemed to vanish out from underneath them as they tumbled over the stone rim into the moat. Raoul heard the howls of dismay from his friends as he fell.

Jules was underneath him as they struck the frozen floor of the moat, its paved surface hard as rock under the layered ice. There was a sharp cracking sound, like a tree-branch snapping asunder, and an agonized high-pitched yelp followed by strange wheezing sounds from the black wolf's gaping jaws. Raoul's own jaws were still fastened on the other's neck-ruff. The white wolf wrenched his fangs free of the black fur and stepped back panting with exertion. The other wolf gave a last sickening rattle from his torn throat and was still.

"Enough! Raoul, let him be!" called Honoré from above. The other wolves were all peering down at him over the stone parapet.

"It is too late," he replied. "It is over. He was beneath me as we dropped, and cushioned my fall. I heard his backbone crack when we struck the ground, and my teeth were forced deeper into his throat by the force of the impact. He is dead." Hyacinthe whined shrilly in distress, and Manon raised her voice in a long howl.

"*Hélas!*" cried Honoré. "More blood spilled means more vengeance. There will be trouble for this."

"He would have slain Chantal," Raoul growled back up at him. "Would you rather he had succeeded?"

"I say no word of blame, my friend. You did as you had to do. I am only warning you. Wolves know no malice; you have no idea of the spitefulness of men."

"This is terrible – terrible! What shall we do now?" Suzette asked, looking down at the dead wolf sprawled on the ice. "He did not have time to return to his own form before he died."

"It is what Jules would have wanted," said Angélique. "He hated being human, and would gladly have been a wolf forevermore. In death he has his wish."

"Let him lie there then," said Ti-Jacques. The giant black wolf bared his teeth in disdain. "Whoever finds him can dispose of him. They will see only a dead animal."

"No!" said Dubois. "Jules may have disdained his humanity, but that is no reason for us to do the same. We must return his body to his family, to be mourned and laid to rest as they see fit."

Ti-Jacques looked doubtful. "There is only Yves left now. He will be completely deranged by this new loss. I would not risk approaching him if I were you."

"Nevertheless, decency demands it. He must be told what has happened. But he must never learn *who* it was that killed his brother. He already had a grudge against Hunter for his father's sake."

"Guy is already avenged – by Jules no less," said Ti-Jacques. "Now your human friend Marc Hébert is

316

avenged in turn, and Jules has paid in full for his crime. Yves may mourn for him but no one else will. What happened here tonight was justice."

"Justice!" sighed the old wolf. "But once this cycle of vengeance starts, who can say where it ends?"

"With me, I hope," Raoul called from below. "I would not have anyone else suffer for my deeds this night. If Yves wishes me to face him in a duel, then I will do so."

"No, no! Enough of this!" cried Dubois. "It ends with Jules, as it should. We will leave now, and take his body with us."

"How do we get down there?" asked Suzette. "Go around to the main entrance?"

"No! It will be guarded; the Governor General is in residence for *Carnaval*, so there is extra security on the base. You ladies take Chantal back to the house and tend to her wounds, and tell Noah to come here with some rope. We will have to haul them both up. *Vite, vite!* The rest of us will stay here and keep watch."

Chantal collapsed onto a couch in the sitting room. Noah Aglukkaq had rushed out immediately on hearing of Honoré's appeal for aid, carrying with him rope and also warm clothing so the wolf-men could resume their human forms. The she-wolves had returned to woman form. Tenderly they had wrapped Chantal in a robe before clothing themselves in the costumes which they had hastily discarded upon the floor. At the touch of the terrycloth with its lingering human scent, she felt her body revert, finding its old familiar contours again as it eased itself into the garment. It was like a slow waking, a return to self from out of a dark confusion of nightmare-haunted sleep. She stretched out a forelimb, and saw a hand emerge from the sleeve; looked at the

317

fingers and flexed them. Angélique meanwhile examined her wounded throat.

"It is not so very bad, little more than a graze," she said. "We came just in time, I think. You were very brave, my dear, but Jules was more experienced at fighting in wolf form and would likely have won in the end."

"Where is Manon?" asked Suzette.

"Looking for bandages in the bathroom upstairs," said Hyacinthe. "Chantal, can you sit up?"

"Yes, I'm fine really, just shaken up," she replied. "I'd just like to go lie down for a while. No really, don't bother, I don't need any help. I'll go up to my room."

Angélique said: "I will get you something to help you sleep. That is the best treatment of all."

Chantal drank the draught she brought, and then went slowly upstairs. The gash on her neck still throbbed, and the whole of her body ached as if she had been running a marathon. As she headed for her guest room she heard a soft agitated voice speaking in the master bedroom. Now and then the voice would break off abruptly; then resume. But Chantal could not hear a second voice. Was the speaker on a phone? It sounded like a woman's voice. She did not want to eavesdrop, but something in the voice – a tearful urgency – disturbed her. She went towards it. Soon she could hear the words.

"Yes, yes! I am sure he is dead! I saw his body. Your brother now – first your father and then your brother! And the same person has killed both. The white wolf of the north is the boy Raoul – "

Horrified understanding burst through her brain. Too late, Chantal ran and flung open the door. It was the master bedroom: there was a large canopied bed, and two antique *prie-dieux* against the wall under a crucifix. Manon was there, pacing about in her red ball gown as

318

she spoke into a cell phone. The girl stared at Chantal, then flung down the phone. A man's voice, tinny and small, came from it. "Manon! Manon my love, what is it?"

"Who are you talking to?" cried Chantal, advancing on her.

"No one!"

"You're lying! I overheard you. It was Yves, wasn't it? That's his voice! You told him about Jules – and Raoul!"

Feet pounded up the staircase, and the voices of the other women rang out in the hallway. "What is it? What is all the yelling about?" called Hyacinthe. Her pale face appeared at the doorway to the bedroom.

"Tell them, Manon," shouted Chantal.

"What? Tell us what?" The three other women came crowding into the room.

"She's betrayed Raoul. To Yves," said Chantal, pointing to the cell phone on the floor. "I overheard her just now. Manon told him everything that happened."

"It's not true!" Suzette cried. "Manon would never –"

"Hush, child! Chantal would not lie to us." Angélique's face was pale too.

"Then she has made a mistake!"

"Manon has not denied it."

A tense silence fell as Manon glared at them all. Then with a wordless, inhuman cry she whirled around. Before they could move to stop her, she had yanked the window open and leaped right out of it. As her friends and Angélique rushed to the window Chantal bent and snatched up the phone. There was no one on the line now. Trembling with anger and fear she too went to the window and peered out over the others' shoulders.

"Manon! Manon!" wailed Hyacinthe.

On the ground below the red gown lay, empty and spread out on the snow like a pool of blood. Wolf-prints led away from it into the dark.

*Sister Wolf*

## 22

Raoul sped through the forest. It was spring, and the snow had shrunk away to a few pale remnants in hollows and underneath large rocks. The tree-branches dripped continually as he ran beneath them. In the distance the waterfalls of the Canyon Ste. Anne roared with new vigour, swelled by melt water; louder and nearer, *loups garous* howled to one another as they ran, occasionally communicating in the *haut-loup* tongue about the prey they pursued. They had tracked a deer through the wild Laurentian woodlands, and now they spoke of it stumbling and flagging in its pace as they closed in for the kill.

Raoul did not join in; they were not of his pack, and he ran silent to avoid detection. Upon the fresh mud of the forest floor he presently spotted the trails of pursuer and pursued: the deer's cloven hooves, making only shallow imprints in the mud as it fled at top speed, and the great broad pad-prints left by the wolves. He repressed the urge to howl this information to Josephine. She too ran silent, not wishing to alert the other wolves with the sound of an unfamiliar voice. These were not the followers of Honoré Dubois. They were the rebel *loups garous* who had chosen to remain behind at the Winter Rite, shifting their allegiance to the Lapierres. But the pack that they had formed under the leadership of the Stone wolves was now headless. Josephine had decided to seek them out now, while they still lacked a leader and might be talked into returning to their human homes and lives. They were moving ever closer to the regions of human civilization and activity: she hoped this was a sign that they were growing weary of their wild existence. But both she and Raoul feared the alternative explanation: that they were encroaching on human territory in order to attack human beings, having rejected the kinship of their former kind.

Honoré Dubois had taken Jules's dead wolf-body to Yves, meeting him at a secret location outside the city walls. Dubois returned from the encounter grim-faced. He would say nothing about it, and no one liked to ask. Noah Aglukkaq, who had now returned home to the north, reported seeing Yves roaming alone in wolf-shape on the Stone Plain. He had laid Jules to rest alongside his father's shallow unmarked grave near the Pingualuit Crater and was now living the life of a lone wolf without pack or mate. The local Inuit, believing him to be a shape-shifting sorcerer, gave him a wide berth; the high-wolves of the region were also hostile towards him. In fact, according to Aglukkaq the Lake Pack had begun to encroach on the Stone Pack territory, now that Yves alone remained to defend it, and he would not likely hold it for long. "The last I heard, he'd joined a pack of low-wolves and is now its leader," said Aglukkaq. "Have you ever heard of such a thing?"

"It used to happen sometimes, back in the Old World," Dubois replied. "A lone *loup garou* would command a pack of ordinary wolves, training them like dogs to hunt for his food and to waylay travelers. 'Wolf leaders', these men were called. But it is a sad come-down for M. Lapierre and his once-proud clan."

Of Manon they had heard nothing. A dark-furred she-wolf had been seen by hikers, lingering near Mont Ste. Anne, and this attracted the attention of the authorities as wolves did not usually live in the area. Suzette and Hyacinthe were certain that it was their cousin, for they had often skiied on the hill together. They believed that Manon, like a ghost, was haunting the places where she had been happy as a human. The girls drove to Mont Ste. Anne and searched the woods near the site, crying out her name. But they found no sign of her, though they did see the tracks of many large wolves deep in the forest.

"You will be safer at the wolves' chapel on the Île d'Orléans," Dubois had told Raoul upon learning of Manon's defection. "Ah, what times are these! Shifting loyalties – friendships broken and betrayed…"

"We can't trust anybody, it seems," Ti-Jacques added. "Not even one another."

"Then we are a house divided, and Yves has won," said Dubois heavily. "I told Manon she was putting herself in danger by getting too close to the Lapierre crowd. It turns out she was in far worse danger than I realized – not of physical harm, but vulnerability to temptation."

Chantal had said, "I can sort of see how it happened. Manon's so much quieter than her cousins, and probably not as good with boys; so Yves could easily get around her, flattering her, making her think that he loves her and that he's not such a bad guy. That's why she got that invitation and her cousins didn't: he could see that she really was falling for him. Believe me," she added darkly, "I know how he is with girls."

"It is very charitable of you to see it that way," Dubois told her.

"Oh, make no mistake, I'm still mad at her," Chantal replied. "For one thing, she's put poor Raoul in serious danger."

"That is true, I'm afraid." Dubois turned to Raoul. "Yves already blames you for his father's death. Now that you have killed his brother there is no appeasing him. And worse yet, thanks to his spy he now knows that Hunter and Raoul Dulac are one and the same. You are not safe now either as wolf or man, and can no longer move freely in either world. My home is too public, and there are not enough of us to defend you from the enemy. You must go to the Île d'Orléans with Chantal."

"I will do as you ask for now," Raoul had replied. "But I will not hide from Yves forever."

Now as the white wolf raced through the forest he heard a loud commotion of snarls and worrying noises up ahead, and one thin bleating cry that ended quickly. He halted at the sound. The *loups garous* like any other wolves would be savage and defensive around their kill. He lowered himself to the ground and waited for them to gorge themselves. Josephine no doubt had heard the sounds too.

When he judged that sufficient time had passed Raoul rose again, and followed the trail out of the woods to the canyon's edge. Here the deer had finally turned at bay before the precipice, cruelly caught between one death and another. There its carcass lay warm and steaming, while the wolves clustered around it tearing at it with their fangs. One of the hind-wolves waiting on the perimeter saw him approach, and howled a warning: "Luc, Luc! An intruder!"

A lean wolf with brown-black fur rose bristling and bloody-mouthed from the kill. This was the fore-wolf, no doubt, elevated to temporary prominence in the absence of the Lapierres. Raoul stood with lowered head and allowed the pack to encircle him. These were not true beasts; they retained enough of their original human nature to inhibit them from senseless violence. He spoke to them in a calming tone. "I am not here to make trouble, friends, only to warn you of a possible danger. You draw attention to yourselves in this forest, where there is no low-wolf population to cover for your presence. People will grow suspicious and fearful when they find your tracks and the remains of your kills."

"They had better not come after us," threatened the wolf called Luc, baring his teeth.

326

Raoul made no reply. He looked at the dead deer, its still-open eyes, the sleek brown flank now torn and bleeding. "This doe was healthy and young. If you must be wolves, can you not do as they do and kill the old and sick?"

Another wolf answered. "We are not low-wolves, out grubbing for food in the wilds! We are *loups garous*, and we kill whatever we choose."

"Including humans?"

"Why not?" said Luc. "Did you not kill Jules Lapierre? He was our leader, our head-wolf. He formed this pack, and you took him from us. Murderer!" The other wolves growled in agreement. "He was my friend, the only one who ever understood me. Now he's gone. I hate you, Hunter, and all who run with you!"

The beta male advanced on him snarling, but Raoul held his ground and Luc stopped in his tracks.

"My name is Raoul now," the white wolf said, "and what I did was done to preserve the life of another. I do not judge you. I only ask you to reconsider what you are doing. I have journeyed far, risking my life, to earn that which you now cast aside without thought."

"And what is that exactly?"

"Your humanity." Again he met the eyes of the beta male. "Are you not Luc Benoit? Honoré has told me about you."

The feral yellow eyes glared. "What has he told you?"

"He says that you are only sixteen, hardly more than a child in human terms – is that not so? And that you have a family in the human world, a mother and father and a sister, who all love you. Why did you run away from them, Luc? They are looking everywhere for you. And you others – have you not family and friends also? Where is Manon Lafontaine? Her cousins miss her. They forgive her for what she did, and want only to see

327

her again and know that she is safe." The werewolves glared and shifted their feet, but none answered him. "Why do you remove yourselves from the human world, with all that you have to offer your own kind?"

Still they made no reply, though some growled low in resentment. As they began to advance on him again there was a rustling sound in the forest undergrowth, and Josephine sprang out. With a howl she ran to Raoul's side. "Enough of this! He came here to help you, and so did I. If we'd meant you any harm wouldn't we have come in greater numbers?"

"Yes," said Raoul. "The fact that we have made ourselves vulnerable, does that not prove our good faith?"

"It proves you are fools. Shall we kill them, Luc?" asked one of the young wolves, looking to the beta male.

Luc seemed to consider. "No," he said at length. "I want them to take a message to Dubois. To the one who left the forest years ago and denied his true self, and would have us deny ours also, I say this: if you do not get out of our way, you will be swept aside."

"Swept aside? How do you mean, young one? By what exactly will we be swept aside?" Josephine demanded.

"By us, when we come into our own. When we take back from you what is ours."

"What is this nonsense? We've taken nothing from you lot."

"Nothing but the island!" another werewolf piped up. "It is ours, our birthright as Arcadians. Jules told us so. We must have the island and the – "

"Silence, you fool!" The fore-wolf snarled, and the other wolf cringed and backed away, instantly a submissive omega. The beta turned back to Raoul and Josephine: the latter's sharp ears had pricked up with visible interest when the omega wolf spoke. "Go. Take our message to Dubois. And do not come back to our territory, ever again." Once more he bared his strong young fangs, dyed red with the blood of the deer. "Go, or we will kill you both now."

Raoul and Josephine turned without another word and departed the clearing, leaving the rebel pack to their kill.


"The wolf also shall dwell with the lamb, and the leopard shall lie down with the kid; and the calf and the young lion and the fatling together; and a little child shall lead them."

Chantal pushed her lentils about on her plate with her fork as she listened to the nun read. She would be glad to see the end of Lent and its dietary rules: here at Chapelle-des-loups it was observed with medieval strictness. All around her in the plain rustic dining hall other people – *loups garous* all – sat at the bare wooden tables eating or listening to the scripture reading. Although it was a secular order, most members of the "Communauté des Sauvés" wore monkish robes of a heavy white fabric. The garments were beltless and loose-fitting so that shape-changing could be undertaken with ease and a modicum of modesty, though the residents spent the majority of their time in human form. There were about thirty-five of them here, including some families with young children, but their numbers fluctuated since they came and went as they willed. Several of the children were already able to transform, Chantal noticed, though due to their extreme youth they could only become wolf-pups. They enjoyed play-fighting and other puppyish pursuits, all under the protective gaze of their elders. She envied them. Surrounded by the love and acceptance of this close-knit community, these children would grow up completely unafraid of their wolf-selves.

329

The nun read on: "And the cow and the bear shall feed; their young ones shall lie down together: and the lion shall eat straw like the ox. And the suckling child shall play on the hole of the asp, and the weaned child shall put his hand on the cockatrices' den. They shall not hurt nor destroy in all my holy mountain: for the earth shall be full of the knowledge of the Lord, as the waters cover the sea."

Chantal pushed her plate away. She couldn't stand much more of this drab Lenten fare. It was all they had eaten since *Carnaval,* save for Sundays when the fast was eased. "The word 'carnival' comes from the Latin *carne vale,* 'farewell to meat'," one of the community members had explained to her. "It is called this because it is the last festival before Lent, when for forty days no meat is eaten. Feast is followed by famine. At least, it was always so in olden times. Nowadays people feast both during and after the Carnival, and Lent is just for giving up bad habits. But we *loups garous* here observe a traditional Lent, abstaining from eating meat since it arouses our wolfish instincts. This enables us to concentrate on our human side, on spiritual growth and self-discipline."

*Hence all these tasteless veggies,* Chantal thought without enthusiasm. The rule would be relaxed soon, though. It was April, and Easter was next week. *Easter egg hunts with my cousins in the meadows of Derby Line... Nana's roast ham... No – enough!* Chantal stood up abruptly and took her plate to the kitchen. *Fresh air, that's what I need. To clear my head.* Since it was not her turn to do wash-up duty she was free to depart the dining hall. She went to her room, put on her jacket and walked out of the building.

Unlike the famed basilica of Ste. Anne de Beaupré on the mainland, which had burned down many times over the centuries and been rebuilt in ever grander versions,

330

the home of the Communauté here on the Île d'Orléans was still a humble fieldstone structure of the seventeenth century. Even its stone chapel was tiny and utterly plain within save for a hand-carved wooden crucifix. The dormitories were stark and cell-like, in the monastic style. Chantal had emailed her family members before she left the Dubois home: "I'm leaving Quebec City to go with friends to a beautiful place in the country, a sort of year-round spiritual retreat. No internet access, so don't worry if you don't hear from me for a while. Dad used to visit this place before he met Mom, to get a change from city life in Montreal. Lots of people here still remember him. I've learned so much about him already. Taking this year off is the best thing I ever did." For Uncle Phil's benefit she added: "I've applied to Laval University here in Quebec, where I'm hoping to study French history – in French! I should find out this June if I'm accepted, so everybody cross your fingers!"

It was easier to sound convincingly cheerful and unconcerned in print than on the phone. But it was hard when she had to be evasive about her future location, and dared not give its name in case her email was hacked.

There had been little news of their enemies. The Boisverts were back home in Montreal, and had made no attempts to contact Chantal. She was not sure whether to be relieved or not at this. As for Yves, she pitied him in his solitary bereavement, and hoped that this latest tragedy would be the end of their conflict. But she feared that his self-enforced exile up north would only make him brood over his losses, and perhaps contemplate some means of revenge. Unease filled her whenever she thought of him, twice-removed from the human world though he was, by distance and by form.

The earthen path she walked crossed a large lawn with a barbecue pit and ancient stone outdoor oven, then

331

ran past a row of vegetable gardens and skirted a large fenced-in enclosure. Dozens of husky dogs ran up to the fence, wagging their tails and yelping for attention. She reached through the chain link to scratch their ears. This was Aglukkaq's husky team from *Carnaval*: the community was their summer home. Beyond their enclosure the path led through a dense stand of trees. The inhabitants of Île d'Orléans had preserved a large tract of virgin forest here at the western end of their island, and in it many species of hardwoods thrived, including the northernmost stand of red oaks in all of North America. Chantal whistled softly to herself as she strolled on through the wild groves, her hands thrust in her jacket pockets. It occurred to her that she'd always loved walking in woods, and had put this down to her country upbringing. But had a part of her known deep down that she loved the forest because she belonged there? Back home in Vermont she'd strolled beneath the branches of trees whose ancestors had sheltered her own *loup garou* forebears: the old remnants of the Acadian Forest.

Acadian... *Arcadia.* If ever there was a place worthy of the name it was this island, whose inhabitants steadfastly resisted development. To this day it remained a wholly agricultural society, a bounteous market-garden for the city upriver. There were orchards and pastures amid the island's rolling hills; and in fulfillment of the old name first given it by Champlain, the Isle of Bacchus, it even boasted vineyards and wineries.

The trail branched off to her left: from that direction wafted a heavy sweet aroma, well known to anyone raised in the northeast. The fragrant, steaming vats of a sugar shack. The Communauté tapped their sugar maples for syrup to sell locally, and the sap was now running. As she stood there breathing it in, a wolf emerged from the depths of the maple plantation. At the sight of her it stopped and stood motionless. It was a large male, his fur white as snow in the sun. Unlike all the other *loups garous* in this place he did not salute her with a howl or come closer when she called out a greeting to him. As she drew nearer she saw that his eyes were a deep, clear blue.

"Raoul?" she said uncertainly.

Could it be he? But he did not reply to her hail. There was an intensity in his blue gaze, a kind of terrible innocence. Why, she wondered suddenly, did the word "innocent" always make one think of little children and helpless harmless things? The lion was as innocent as the lamb, with no malice behind his cruelty or the savage rending strength of his claws and jaws. This wolf's eyes held the blazing purity that lies at the heart of nature, and she stared into them for a moment half-mesmerized.

It was the wolf that broke contact. Swerving aside, he retreated back into the trees, white fur dimming to grey shadow and then melting like mist into the dense undergrowth.

A little disturbed by this odd encounter, she walked on.

The path led her to the outdoor chapel: just a few rows of backless wooden benches with a space running up the middle like an aisle, and a low stone altar with an unadorned stone cross. There were no walls, no floor, no roof; the "chapel" was by implication the whole of nature: the trees of the forest surrounding it and the sky showing through their branches, the exposed soil underfoot, the interweaving melodies of birdsong and leaves and the chatter of a small stream in the adjacent ravine. Chantal like the rest of the Vandusens was not religious, but she could understand the appeal of worship in such a place as this. She pivoted on her heel, taking it all in. A little distance to the left was a small grotto containing a bronze statue of a bearded man in monk's habit, a bird perching on one outstretched hand while the other caressed the head of a large dog or wolf standing by his side. A few snowdrops and crocuses grew around the statue's plinth, and floral bouquets had been laid before it: offerings to the saint. A young nun in full habit was kneeling on the ground, planting pansies. As Chantal drew near she looked up and her face beamed. She was almost unrecognizable from the time Chantal had first seen her. The girl had then been wrapped in a blanket, her long brunette hair streaming loose. It was strange to see her now in the neat and orderly habit, her hair confined and invisible under the wimple and black veil.

"I've met you before, haven't I?" Chantal said. "At the Winter Rite."

"I'm *Soeur* Célestine," she replied, getting to her feet. "I'm a Franciscan nun, one of the Pauvres Claires. Their headquarters lie in Rivière-du-Loup where I was born. I was a *loup garou* of the old Larivière pack and joined the *religeuses* at a young age to escape the temptations of my dual nature. But with help from the good people here, I've made my peace with it." She gestured to the statue. "Have you been introduced?"

"No. Who is he?" The Catholic saints seemed to Chantal to exist in bewildering profusion.

"This is the patron saint of Chapelle-des-loups, St. François d'Assise."

"Oh, right: St. Francis of Assisi. The saint who loved the animals."

"Yes. He is shown here with the wolf of Gubbio. You know the tale?" Chantal shook her head. "An enormous wolf once lived in the forest near the town of Gubbio, in central Italy; everyone there lived in fear of its ravenous hunger. But the saint sought it out in its lair, and spoke to it gently. It's said that Francis made the wolf promise not to harm the townsfolk or their livestock, and in return they agreed to feed it whenever it came to their doors. Supposedly the agreement was even drawn up by a notary!"

"Now that can't be true," laughed Chantal.

"Most people nowadays say it's just a fable. But back in 1873 when the church in Gubbio was undergoing repairs, the workers found the remains of an enormous wolf buried underneath its floor. Now what do you say?"

"That's bizarre... unless – Soeur Célestine, do you think it might have been a *loup garou?"*

"Many of our kind believe so. It would explain the creature's intelligence and its burial in sacred ground, not to mention that business with the notary." The nun looked down at the bouquets. "You see these offerings. They are left by wolf-people, who come from all over the country to kneel at the feet of the Saint who loved the birds and beasts, to pray for his guidance and for his help in taming their wild nature. The saint's feet, as you can see, are worn smooth by the touch of the petitioners. On October 4 we celebrate the feast day of St. Francis with a procession through the forest, singing hymns to the beasts and birds. It's so beautiful here in the autumn, when the sugar maples turn all gold and red! Perhaps you will come and visit us then, too."

*Or perhaps I'll still be stuck here by then*, thought Chantal. *Afraid to leave – imprisoned by my own fear...*

"You must be kind but firm with Brother Ass," the nun went on. "That's what St. Francis called his body, as if it were a poor dumb animal that needed his love and guidance. A *loup garou* might call it Brother Wolf. Our bodies really do have a will and a life of their own, compared to those of normal humans. That leaves us

335

with two choices: we can deny our dual nature, slaying the wolf within us; or else like St. Francis we can tame and love it. To me that is the lesson of this image." She waved her hand at the statue, the man with his hand laid tenderly upon the wolf's head.

A woman's voice called out to them, and they both turned to see Josephine striding along the path, clad as always in loose and shabby clothing, her hands stuck in the pockets of her denim jacket. "There you are, Chantal! I was looking for you. They said up at the house that you'd gone for a walk." She came and joined them by the grotto. "Raoul and I just got back from the *Laurentides*. We were trying to reach out to our young *loups garous* who were corrupted by the Lapierres, to talk them into returning to their human lives now that Jules is dead and Yves gone."

"And were you successful?" Soeur Célestine asked.

Josephine made a face. "No. Now that it's spring there's much less incentive for them to leave the forest."

"Where is Raoul now?" asked the nun, glancing around.

"He jumped out of the truck when we returned and took off into the woods."

Chantal said, "I saw a white wolf in the forest just a few minutes ago, but he turned away when he saw me." She had never before seen Raoul's wolf-form in the clear light of day. His blue eyes burned in her memory, like a retinal imprint left by the blazing sun.

"That was he." The Métis woman sighed. "Raoul still suffers in his mind because of what happened with Jules. He has scarcely taken human form since. It's as if he doesn't feel worthy to wear it."

"But it wasn't his fault," protested Chantal.

"So I have told him. But he won't discuss it with me."

336

"Isn't it dangerous for him to be roaming out there alone?"

Soeur Célestine shook her head. "Not here. Our forest is fenced, and the husky dogs would set up a commotion if any unfamiliar wolf trespassed. They know us all by sight and smell."

"So they're an alarm system?" said Chantal.

"That and more. The dogs serve another purpose," Josephine said. "Canadian Inuit dogs are so wolfish-looking that people once thought they were bred directly from our native wolves. Even Charles Darwin himself was fooled! In fact they were brought over from Asia by the ancestors of the Inuit. But the resemblance *is* very strong, so Honoré purchased some of these dogs to provide a cover story for the *loups garous* that live here. Since it's common knowledge that he keeps his sled dogs at Chapelle-des-loups, the other islanders think nothing of it when they glimpse a pack of wolves running about the Communauté's woods and fields, or hear howls in the night. They just say to themselves, 'Oh, it's those husky dogs again!'"

A clamour overhead made them look up. A vast formation of migrating snow geese, white as swans save for the ebony tips of their wings, filled the clear blue sky above the trees. "Speaking of noise," said Josephine, watching them. "Those wild geese make me feel restless. I must go north soon like them, back home to my friends and family. But before I go I will take you into the woods with me one last time, Chantal. I will give you a little lesson on how to deal with your other self: Sister Wolf, let us call her. And – " she looked sidelong at Chantal, "it is time you learned the secret of the Island."

"Not – the Grove? Do you really think Chantal is ready for that?" asked Célestine with a visible shudder.

337

"There's no point in delaying any more. She may be the stronger for it. This miserable business with the Boisverts isn't over yet, I fear. Chantal needs all the help we can give her to fight what lies ahead of her."

Chantal did not much like the sound of this. But she turned obediently and followed Josephine down the path, deeper into the forest, though her unease increased with every step.

*What Grove? What is this secret they all keep talking about...?*

## 23

The two women walked together along the path, following it deeper into the woods. Presently it sloped steeply down into a little dell. There the path came to an end. At the far end of the dell was another stone niche, heavily overgrown so that it resembled a natural cave in the rock wall behind it. Josephine led her right up to the dark cavity, and peering inside it Chantal saw a small stone statue. A man, with the hooves and horns of a goat. She could tell by the weathered condition of the stone that this figure was far older than the St. Francis sculpture.

"This is the old secret of the island that I told you about," Josephine said. "This is an ancient place of worship, for *loups garous* and *sorciers.*"

"It's the Devil!" exclaimed Chantal in revulsion, stepping back. "So the islanders *were* Satanists, then!"

"No," said Josephine, "look harder. What is that in his hand?"

Chantal approached the statue again. There was a long slender shape within the curled fingers of its right hand, an object that was too small for a spear or other weapon. "He's Pan!" she said, recognition suddenly dawning. "The Greek god. He's holding his flute, or pipe, or whatever they call it."

"That's right. Pan *Lykaios*; Faunus; Lupercus… He's been given many names over time, but the god himself is unchanging. That is the old secret of this island: that the worship of this pagan deity continued here until fairly recent times. *Loups garous* brought his cult over the seas from Arcadia. This place is called the Grove of Pan, and it is known only to *loups garous* and their closest friends. They made sacrificial offerings to this idol in olden times. That isn't really as sinister as it sounds. Pan was the god of herdsmen, and many of the *loups garous* that lived on the island were farmers. It was only in later times that the 'Horned One' became confused with *le Diable*. And since in Christianity the pagan gods were regarded as deceitful demons, it would have made no difference even had the truth been known. In the end, the worship of Pan simply died out, just as it did in the Old World; but not before it birthed shadowy legends of Satanic masses on the Île d'Orléans, attended by witches and werewolves.

"Pan may be a foreign deity, but he would feel right at home here. He was a spirit of Nature, and my people believed in such things. I told you this island was called a place of enchantment long before Europeans came here. *Ouindigo,* the native Algonquin tribes named it, after the spirit of the wilderness: the Windigo who dwells in the solitude of the wastelands. All those who wandered the wilderness feared the Windigo, because if he catches you alone he can take over your mind and drive you mad. Those possessed by the wild spirit attacked other humans, even turned cannibal. Does that remind you of anything?"

After a pause Chantal said, "The Arcadians. M. Dubois said some of them ate people when they were in wolf shape."

"*C'est vrai.* Hardly surprising, really, since they were worshippers of Pan. The god of the solitary wild, the father of fear... When you worship cruel and fearsome things, you see, you end by turning cruel and fearsome yourself. It's inevitable."

"Then why hasn't this idol been taken away?" The statue of St. Francis and the wolf had been tranquil, calming; man and beast bonded by mutual love and understanding. Here man and beast were one: Pan had a savage inhuman expression, his horned head flung back, his pointed tongue protruding between his bared teeth.

340

"For the same reason that this part of the island has never been tamed and cultivated. Respect. The wild things have their place in the world, and that is as it should be. The Windigo and Pan are the essence of Nature, a force of destruction as well as of life. That is what the Horned One represents to us: what we were in the beginning, and what we might again become if we don't take care. Do not tread lightly in Pan's domain, or you may never leave it. That is the lesson of the idol. Today you must walk in his realm, and you will walk as a wolf."

Chantal hesitated. "Are – are you coming with me?"

"Not this time. Later you will run with me and other *loups garous*, but today is about self-discovery."

"I'm kind of nervous about being alone."

"You will not be alone," Josephine replied. "Sister Wolf goes with you. She will guide you and protect you. But remember that she needs your guidance also."

With a perfectly casual air Josephine proceeded to strip off her clothes. She motioned for Chantal to do the same. "Don't be shy, there is no one here to see," she said with a smile. "Do as I do, and you will learn how the change should be done. Until now you have only changed yourself involuntarily, as an automatic response to a threat. On those occasions Sister Wolf took charge for you. But you can also command her, altering your shape because you desire to do so. You will continue to fear her as long as you do not control her."

Chantal obeyed, shivering in the damp spring air as she disrobed. Her discomfort was more than physical: she felt vulnerable being unclothed out of doors. Josephine seemed perfectly at ease and unself-conscious, but she was no doubt used to it. And her skin with its golden-brown hue was almost like a garment in itself. Chantal was acutely aware of her own pale, sallow skin which showed every mole and blemish. "I look like a plucked chicken," she thought, watching goose bumps spread across her chilled flesh.

As she watched, Josephine transformed. It was almost instantaneous, too rapid to see. Suddenly there was a wolf – small, dark-furred, lean as a coyote – crouching next to Chantal on the forest floor, a wolf that rose to all fours and turned its head to look at her. The message in its brown eyes was plain: *Now it is your turn!*

Chantal obeyed. For the first time she altered her form deliberately, not in response to drugging or through fear unlocking unconscious instinct. As she concentrated, the familiar tingling warmth spread through her, but it felt pleasant now, driving away the damp chill and icy wind of the April afternoon. She looked down and once again saw paws in place of hands, but this time she felt no fear. She was not going mad. The paws truly were there: no delusion, but a real part of her real self. She moved them, tentatively and then with growing confidence as she saw that they obeyed her will. The wolf-self had not taken her over this time. Instead, it was hers to command.

Chantal stood up on all four feet. She had never taken her wolf-form in full sunlight before, and was somewhat surprised to find that she could still see the full spectrum of colour: a legacy, perhaps, to *loups garous* of their human ancestry. But in every other way this truly was an animal body. Her senses of hearing and smell were keener, and the greyish-brown pelt that clothed her was resistant to the cold: it had both an outer and inner layer, long guard hairs over a dense fleecy undercoat. She felt strong, invincible even, and with that unfamiliar new emotion came a stirring of something like exhilaration.

"Good," said Josephine. She spoke not in French but in the peculiar *haut-loup* tongue that was like a blend of

342

human and canine vocalizations, as close to human speech as a wolf's palate could come. She spoke very slowly, so that Chantal could understand; the latter found that the accompanying body language of ear-twitching and head position made sense to her while she wore her wolf-form. "Go now. I will wait for you here."

Josephine lay down again in the leaves, and Chantal went on by herself into the pathless forest.

Sister Wolf was at home in this environment as even Chantal the country girl had never been. When she stumbled or hesitated it was because Chantal was trying to instruct the wolf-self; when her human self gave way and let the wolf have free rein, she knew where to place her paws, how to run and dodge around roots and saplings. Before long she was bounding with an easy loping gait through a thick debris of leaves and twigs that would have slowed her human feet to a clumsy dawdle. The wind blew towards her, but could not chill her now; her thick pelt kept her warm and its guard-hairs repelled the melt-water dripping from the trees. Her nostrils flared, tasting the wind: there was a wondrous smell on it that went straight to her brain, warm and musky and alive. Not the smell of another wolf. Somehow, without knowing how she knew, she recognized it. She began to salivate.

Deer. There was a deer not far off, and the wind was carrying its scent to her keen new sense of smell. Before she knew it she was sprinting through the undergrowth, kicking up leaf-debris and muddy spray, her mouth agape in eagerness. An excited whine broke from her throat. Prey – flesh into which to sink her sharp teeth, to devour while it still bore the blood and heat of life… Meat! She had been too long without it, and now her whole being cried out for it. She bounded

343

into the forest, questing, tracking the prey-scent to its source.

Several metres ahead the deer broke cover. It had been lying down in the undergrowth, half-hidden from her sight, unable to smell her since she was upwind of it. It was a young whitetail buck. His antlers in their thick velvet coverings were just beginning to grow out again, and his coat to change its colour from the dull grey of winter to summer's rich reddish-brown. At the sound of her approach he burst up from his bed of last year's leaves and bounded away through the trees.

The deer's panicked flight triggered Sister Wolf's chase instinct. Without even thinking she lengthened her stride, speeding after him. Now she felt the sheer thrill of the hunt, the great age-old chase that climaxed in the triumph of the kill. She was a predator, a child of great Pan, and she no longer cowered in terror at the wild god's spell but took joy in claiming her place within his savage realm. This was her right and her privilege: to be an object of fear to others. It would begin now, with this young buck that had unwisely strayed across her path –

Something leaped in front of her, barring her way.

The scent of it told her even before her eyes focused on it that this was another wolf. Not Josephine, but the large white male she had glimpsed earlier. Raoul. Chantal stopped short in confusion and annoyance. She swerved around the other wolf and continued her chase. Already he had cost her valued time by blundering across her path; her swift-footed prey now had a substantial lead.

She ran faster, trying to close the gap. But the white wolf ran after her, caught up to her and again barred her way. No careless blunder, then: his interference was deliberate. Chantal, furious now, bared her teeth at him. Despite his greater size and strength, Raoul did not resist or fight back. He stood aside, but as Chantal moved past he followed her again. She turned on him, and once again he did not meet her challenge but retreated back into the woods. Chantal had pursued him quite far before she realized that he had tricked her into chasing him instead of the buck. She stopped short and cast about her, but could no longer detect her prey's scent.

With the loss of its enticing odour her violent excitement began to subside. Head down, panting with exertion, she slunk back to the Grove of Pan where Josephine awaited her.

They said nothing to each other, but resumed their human forms and clothing. Only when they were fully dressed again did they speak. It was as if, with the resumption of their clothes, they had put on the veneer of human civilization once more. Chantal told Josephine what had happened in the forest.

"Why did Raoul stop me from hunting that deer?" she asked.

Josephine turned and looked full at her. "Are you sorry that he did?"

"No. I've never hunted before. Never killed anything, actually."

"I suspect that is why he stopped you. He recognized you, and guessed that it was your first hunt. You don't understand yet what it is to kill, Chantal. Animals do it from direst need. To kill merely for blood lust is a human thing, and for *loups garous* it's a strong temptation to combine a wolf's fangs with a man's cruelty. The Lapierres gave in to their baser selves long ago. All over this country they have travelled, hunting prey in their wolf-forms, testing their strength even against bears and mountain lions. Killing excites them."

Chantal thought of the trophies in the cottage. "My family did that, too. The Boisverts, I mean. Their cottage is crammed full of animal heads and hides."

345

"Not Édouard. He refused to kill for the joy of it. Now, don't look so miserable!" exclaimed Josephine. "You only responded to instinct, child. There's no shame in that. But had you killed without hunger, without the justification of need, you might have felt differently about it after you returned to human form. Sister Wolf is part of you, but she cannot be allowed to rule you. Once you've mastered her, you'll be ready to go into the woods to live for a time – like those young people you met at the Winter Rite."

"Or like the Arcadians, crossing the river..."

"Ah, yes. The old Arcadians understood that the wolf-within cannot be denied. But the wisest among them knew there must be limits, too, and they would not let any werewolf who killed a human being come back into their society. Such a one might come to view *all* humans as prey... I believe something like this was happening to Jules Lapierre. He was becoming less human all the time, and would eventually have disappeared forever into his Brother Wolf. Not that *you* would ever murder another human being, Chantal. But it's important to remember the extremes to which *loups garous* can be tempted."

Chantal nodded. "I understand. And – thanks," she said. "For everything."

Deep within the woods, on the edge of the Grove of Pan, Raoul lingered. Why he had followed Chantal all this way he was not entirely sure, and he was trying, man-like, to analyze his reasons as Dubois had instructed him. A feeling of combined tenderness and amusement filled him at the memory of the young she-wolf, bounding eagerly through the woods on her strong new legs, pausing with upraised head and working nostrils as strange aromas assailed her heightened sense of smell, cocking her keen new ears. It reminded him of

346

his own early days as a pup making his first half-excited, half-bewildered ventures from his mother's lair, in the company of his equally clumsy brother and sister. She had the same mix of juvenile enthusiasm and imperfect coordination. But she was still deadly, for all that. When she had given chase to the deer he had felt reluctant to see her kill, and lose that engaging innocence and purity. So he had intervened.

He wondered if it was his natural urge to protect the offspring of his own kind that endeared her to him. Or perhaps it was something in Chantal herself? Watching her discover her wolf-self made him appreciate anew the body into which he had been born. There had been no time when he was growing up to appreciate his own speed and strength and youth, so busy had he been kept with scouting and hunting, and caring for Mother Wolf's cubs in order to ingratiate himself with her pack. It was long since he had had another wolf just to play with – not a teacher but a pack-mate, a friend...

He shook himself out of his ruminations. He should not be thinking of such things. He was here to learn to be human, to study their ways. Not to go back to his brutish former existence. He must warn Chantal of the dangers of her animal heritage – dangers to which he himself had already succumbed more than once. It was hard to remember these things with the thawing ground and warming winds bringing out the scents of the earth and traces of animal presences. Small wonder he had failed to convince the rebel *loups garous* to return home, with his own heart so divided.

He entered the Grove, his paws leaving their broad impressions in the earth that bore the she-wolf's smaller prints. Two separate scents hung upon the air here, still fresh to his nostrils: Josephine's familiar aroma and Chantal's, the latter speaking of a more raw and youthful femaleness. When he came to the spot where they had shifted and donned their clothing again he stood still for a time, marking the change in the tracks that led away from the dell, the altered human scents that yet bore a hint of their animal essences. He began to lope uphill, following those tracks with his nose to the earth, breathing them in. They led him past the outdoor chapel and statue, alongside the husky pen where the dogs rushed the fence in ecstatic greeting at the sight of him, tails thrashing the air. Then the tracks disappeared into the community centre.

Raoul took a deep breath. He trotted towards the building and nudged the door open with his muzzle. Human scents assailed him, the aromas of dozens of individuals each with its own individual personality, its unique bouquet of biochemical information. He padded across the floorboards of the main hall and turned down the corridor where his own private accommodations were located. Faint traces of his own man-smell greeted his nostrils as he butted the wooden door open and went in. Once inside his room, he resumed his human form and pulled on the white ankle-length robe given him by the community. It felt strange to be once more in this shape, and clothed, after a month's abstention. He was suddenly dismayed at the ease with which he had set aside his hard-won human nature. Retreating from his friends in shame and confusion, hiding himself in the woods, he had almost reverted to his beast nature and lost what he had gained. Only Chantal's innocent intrusion had saved him. In his desire to preserve her humanity, he had realized the peril of losing his own. Once more he owed her a debt.

He drew another deep breath, to steady himself. Then he left his room, heading for the dining hall.

The two women were there, drinking coffee from the big communal urn. He paused for a moment, contemplating Chantal as she sat there in her human form, as yet unaware of his scrutiny. He had at last begun to learn the unspoken language of the human face, so much more mobile and nuanced than that of the wolf. He admired the young girl's strong features, the way her mouth quirked to one side when she was thinking, the absent-minded gesture with which she pushed back her hair when it tumbled into her eyes. Each of these things, he realized, was Chantal: put together, they created the unique stamp of her personality. Most of all, he loved her steadfastness in the face of the fears that daily stalked and threatened her. He saw this in her level gaze, the proud angle of her raised chin and her squared shoulders.

As he stood there she turned her head and, seeing him standing there in his human form, went still for an instant. He averted his gaze. Even now he had difficulty looking another human straight in the eyes, and Chantal's in particular were overpowering. Unlike Honoré and the other *loups garous* she forgot to keep them lowered when she was speaking to him. Josephine saw her expression and turned too, then she broke into a broad smile and raised her steaming mug in a gesture that he understood meant he was invited to come and join them. His eyes went again to Chantal before he moved. She did not look resentful or angry, much to his relief. She smiled too, and spoke to him before he had a chance to address her.

"Thanks, Raoul," she said, "for helping me back there in the forest. And for – for that other time, too." She hesitated, apparently not eager to remind him of the fight with Jules.

But he found that he wanted to talk about what had happened. He went and sat down at their table, facing them. "It's very strange," he said. "As a wolf I would not hesitate to kill another wolf in a fight, if it was to defend myself or my pack. But I feel sorrow for the life

349

of this young artist that I have ended. For the works he will never now create."

Chantal shuddered perceptibly. "They were horrible artworks. Oh, Jules had talent all right, but his work was ugly and cruel and – and hateful."

"That could well have changed as he grew older and wiser. We will never know now."

Her brown eyes looked straight into his. "Well, I'm not sorry that you came to my defense."

He met her gaze this time, with an effort. "Nor am I, not really. I would do it again, live with any remorse, to keep you safe."

Josephine drained her mug and stood up. *"Bien,"* she said. "Well, I'm off. I'll see you two youngsters later."

"You're not going north now?" said Chantal, turning to her. "This very minute?"

The Métis woman nodded. "Someone needs to help Noah keep an eye on Yves. I'm not easy in my mind about that wretched creature, even way up there in Nunavik. In the meantime, you two can look out for each other. You both have much to learn, but I think you'll be all right. I leave you in each other's hands – and paws!"

They got up and accompanied her outside. She hugged them both before climbing into her rusty old truck. "Good-bye for now! I'll see you both when autumn comes. Look for me before the snow flies!"

"I shall miss her," said Raoul as they watched her drive away down the winding road. Josephine had been his constant companion since he decided to seek out the human race. Already he felt a little lost without her.

Chantal, hearing the change in his voice, laid an impulsive hand on his arm. "She's right. We'll both be fine as long as we stay here," she assured him.

He looked down at her hand, then shifted his gaze to her face. "So you agree, then?" he asked her. "I will teach you how to be a wolf, and in return you will help me to be more human?"

The gentle fingers on his arm tightened their hold. "It's a deal," said Chantal.

## 24

During the month that followed the rhythm of life in the community of Chapelle-des-loups continued serene and tranquil, as it had for the past four hundred years. Dubois's scouts and spies reported no signs of activity on the part of their enemies, who remained scattered and disorganized now that the Lapierres were all dead or gone. As the weather warmed other *loups garous* came to visit, including Honoré and Angélique and their circle. The Communauté set aside its monastic regimen, replacing it with feasting and merriment.

"I love this," Chantal said to her hosts at one outdoor gathering in early May, as meat roasted over the open fire pit and bread baked in the ancient stone oven. "Reminds me of cookouts back home." *Could this place perhaps* become *my home,* she wondered for the first time. *There are much worse places to live, after all...*

"You will always be welcome in our midst," Soeur Célestine assured her.

The meat was bison, donated by Bernard Lavallée. "He knows our tastes," Jean-Louis told her. "We're all partial to bison meat – especially we Métis *rugaru.* Not all our ancestors were trappers, you know. Some escaped the expanding European colonies by moving westward. They lived by hunting wild bison on the prairie – both as native hunters and in wolf-shape. It was their only food for a long time."

After dinner as everyone sat around the bonfire, replete, René Leblanc brought out a guitar and they began to sing old French songs. All *loups garous* had superb singing voices, it seemed. Chantal happily joined in. As she sang along she was reminded of summer camp in childhood, and of Glee Club concerts at school: her voice was clear and pure, rising high above the others'. When Leblanc took a rest she borrowed his guitar and sang some American songs for the company, teaching them how to pronounce the English words. It was a huge success.

As the evening progressed she noticed how, one by one, the revelers began to steal away into the trees beyond the campfire. Before long the human singing was accompanied by a glorious chorus of howls from the depths of the woods.

When nearly all had transformed, they went for a run together in the woods. Leaping and bounding through the trees and undergrowth alongside her fellow wolves, Chantal revelled in the strength of her animal body and the myriad new sensations it afforded her. Night time held no terror for her any more. As a woman she had recoiled from its threatening shadows, the conspiratorial cover that it granted to lurking predators both animal and human. But now it was she who was the force to be feared. Even when she wore a woman's shape Sister Wolf would always be with her, and could be called upon in an instant to deliver her from harm. To walk unafraid after dark was a new and very welcome sensation.

Raoul meanwhile had remained behind, sitting and talking with Honoré Dubois. But he watched as Chantal ran off into the forest in her wolf form, feeling a sudden longing to follow after her. He turned, to find that Dubois was watching him. "Go join her, my friend," the old man said, leaning forward and speaking in an undertone. "Go! I know you want to. Why do you hesitate?

Raoul looked startled. "Can you see my thoughts, Honoré?" he asked. "Are you a *sorcier* like your friend Lavallée?"

*"Mais non!"* Dubois laughed. "But you are transparent as still water. I have seen how you react

whenever she is near. How you look at her, and her alone, even when many other people are present. Why do you hold back? Are you afraid? I understand perfectly if you are. Any lone wolf that dared approach a she-wolf in a strange pack would most likely be chased away. That's what you're thinking, isn't it? But humans are allowed to love whomever they choose, Raoul. There's nothing for you to be afraid of here."

"I'm not afraid," Raoul replied. "At least, not of that. But..." He sighed and looked down at his hands, tightly clenched in his lap.

"Ah. You're afraid she might reject you?" Dubois asked, and Raoul nodded. "We all fear that at first, but there is only one way to find out if a woman is interested or not: ask her."

"Tell me, Honoré," said Raoul, turning to gaze at him earnestly. "You began life as a wolf, like me. Did you never worry that your Angélique might not see you as truly human?"

"A little at first, I confess," Dubois answered.

"Then how did you overcome your fear?"

Dubois looked fondly at his wife, who was talking and laughing with friends a short distance away. "As I came to know her better, I realized that Angélique was loving and accepting and kind. The more time I spent in her company, the more I came to trust in her ability to overlook our different backgrounds. That doesn't mean I was *confident* that I could win her love, mind you. I still had my doubts that she would return my feelings. But I knew that if she were to reject me, it would not be for the circumstances of my birth, or for anything else that I couldn't help. Chantal is the same, Raoul, I'm sure of it. She is a kind, loving girl and will accept you for who and what you are. You don't have to declare your feelings right away if you don't wish to, but neither should you hang back. Be a friend to her first, and see where it goes from there. Go on now! Run with her."

Raoul gave him a grateful look. Slowly he sank down on his hands and knees and shifted inside the loose white robe, shaking it off. As he stepped forward in wolf shape the familiar feel of his old body eased his mind, and he sensed the nervous tension slipping away. He loped lightly across the clearing and into the deepening darkness beneath the trees.

It was not hard to find Chantal, despite the darkness. The wolves were howling, and it was an easy matter to distinguish her voice amid the rest, high and quavering with excitement. He followed the sound until he glimpsed her a short distance ahead. She was running with the swiftest wolves at the head of the pack. *But of course she is,* he thought. That was Chantal's way, embracing with eagerness all that life offered, even a change that would leave other humans terrified and ashamed. He raced along the edge of the panting, bounding throng until he was right by her side. She did not see him at first, so intent was she on her headlong rush, so Raoul ran faster still, pulled ahead of her, and then glanced back. Now she saw him. Her toothy grin widened in acknowledgement of his unspoken challenge and she made to close the distance between them, forcing her supple new body to test its limits, running until her four paws seemed barely to make contact with the ground. The two of them pulled ahead of all the rest, leading the pack in their joyous, preyless chase through the shadowy forest, and for a time Raoul was content with the wordless bond between them.

He made no effort to speak until they had all returned at long last to the clearing. "You are an excellent wolf now," he told Chantal as they lay together by the fire pit, their sides heaving and their tongues lolling out with exhaustion. "But I am still not a very good human being. Perhaps it is your turn to instruct me?"

"All right," she replied. "Let's go visit Bernard Lavallée at his home tomorrow. You can practice making some real human conversation with him."

"That is a very good idea," said Raoul. "Tomorrow, then."

Chantal had brought Minnie with her to the island, and on the following afternoon she drove to Lavallée's farm, with Raoul by her side and a load of maple syrup in the back as thanks for the bison meat. As she drove, she noticed Raoul watching her intently, observing how she handled the steering wheel and the pedals. *I'll have to give him driving lessons next,* she thought in amusement.

Île d'Orléans was divided into half a dozen parishes, each dating back to the seventeen-hundreds; for this was the old original colony from which Quebec City would later spring, and hundreds of modern French Canadian family names traced their roots to the island. Some of the houses were almost as old as the settlements themselves, built in the *habitant* style with sturdy walls and low-eaved roofs. Each town boasted a centuries-old church built of grey stone, topped by a steeple plated not with copper but pressed tin, shining bright as silver in the sun. Between the little towns and silver steeples were large stretches of farmland, narrow ploughed fields lying in furrowed lengths like bolts of brown corduroy. Herds of cattle and horses dotted the landscape, grazing placidly. Here and there by the side of the road they passed a processional chapel: a tiny, whitewashed wooden structure like a miniature church, with just enough room inside for an altar and a statue of a saint.

Bernard Lavallée's property, with its four-hundred-year-old farmhouse, stood at the eastern end of the

356

island where the widening river met the salt flow of the estuary, opening outwards to the Gulf of St. Lawrence and the Atlantic. He kept a few beef cows as well as his small herd of bison, supplying the Communauté with most of its fresh meat. The animals were always dispatched humanely, he assured them; the *loups garous* would not touch the meat otherwise. "They have their own version of kosher, those wolf-people," the farmer told Chantal and Raoul with a chuckle as they walked through his fields together. "They buy only from me because they know and trust me."

He knew everything about werewolves even though he was not one himself. "Wolves and *sorciers,* we have shared this island for centuries," he explained. "And occasionally intermarried also, so a rare few have been born with both kinds of power in their veins."

"This is such a beautiful place," said Chantal, taking in the view. "I really feel as if I could settle here. I've always lived in the countryside, but this is close to the city too. The best of both worlds."

"Ah yes, this whole region is beautiful. The Côte de Beaupré attracts many visitors. Have you been to see Ste. Anne de Beaupré?"

"Not yet," she replied. Many of the *loups garous* had gone to Easter Sunday mass at the basilica, but she had not joined them.

"But you have seen the Chute de Montmorency." She nodded; on the way to the island they had passed the great white waterfall on the mainland, tumbling down its steep cliff. "It is higher than Niagara, as the locals never tire of telling you. And the Bridal Veil, just a kilometre or so to the west, is lovely too. Do you know how it got its name, that smaller waterfall?" They shook their heads. "It's said that a young lady was engaged to be married to a soldier. One day came the terrible news that he had fallen in battle. The poor girl was so distraught that she donned her bridal gown and veil and cast herself into a pool that lay at the foot of a cliff. And so she was joined with her love, not in life but in death. Her gown became the great white cascade of the Montmorency Falls, while her bridal veil floated away on the wind until it caught on the cliff, becoming the second waterfall."

"Wow!" said Chantal. "That's really romantic."

Raoul however wore a puzzled frown. "That story – it is not true?" he asked.

"No, no. It is what we humans call a folktale," replied M. Lavallée.

"High-wolves do not tell such stories amongst themselves. What purpose do they serve?" Raoul asked.

"Purpose? Well, one might say that wonder-tales such as these serve to remind us that the world is wondrous. When we're little we're so full of amazement at everything: trees, clouds, waterfalls. We lose that sense of wonder when we grow older, and our minds and vision become jaded. We forget how to see the magic of it all."

Raoul nodded slowly. "When Soeur Célestine told me about miracles I asked her if she herself had ever seen one. She told me that she sees them every day: seeds growing, birds hatching, rain falling to replenish the earth."

"*Précisément.* Now, *mes jeunes amis,* why do you not take your wolf forms?"

"Here? In broad daylight?" said Chantal.

"Why not? There is no one to see, and there is a wild meadow where you can run – so long as you do not scare my cattle!" He chuckled.

Chantal turned to Raoul. "Okay. Let's do it."

His eyes slipped away from hers. "We were wolves last night. Perhaps today we should be human only."

358

Once again he was denying the other side of his nature: his Brother Wolf. Chantal was sure Josephine would have encouraged him to accept both sides as equal expressions of his true self. "That was just for fun. I need to know how to defend myself properly, if I'm ever attacked again."

Still he hesitated. "You held your own very well against Jules."

"He wasn't as big and strong as you are. Please, Raoul, teach me how to fight," she urged.

Lavallée laughed. "Who could resist such a plea from a lady?" he said, leading them back to the house.

Raoul gave in. He went discreetly into the spare room and shut the door while Chantal and Lavallée walked around the house together. The old stone building sported an eclectic interior décor that reflected the owner's mixed ancestry, with heirlooms dating to *habitant* days as well as native Algonquin artifacts. Some of the latter he had discovered on his property when he ploughed his fields, remnants of vanished pre-European settlements. He had bought more *objets d'art* from the Atelier du Nord, masks and woven hangings and blankets, and they gave the place an aura of mystery. "The French settlers, you see, were not only allowed to intermarry with native women, they were actively encouraged to do so," he explained. "It was a quick way to populate the new colonies. Champlain began it at *l'Acadie,* urging the men to take Micmac brides rather than wait for women settlers to journey out from France. So our history is closely interwoven with that of the indigenous peoples. We fought together against the British, and then again under British command, against the common enemy of our three peoples."

"That'd be us Americans, I guess," said Chantal wryly. "Sorry about that."

359

He bowed to her. "Do not apologize, Mademoiselle. It was the invasion from the United States that forced the disparate peoples of our dominion to forge alliances and grow together in unity. The British realized that they needed the goodwill and cooperation of the conquered French if their newborn nation was to survive; and both of them relied heavily upon the indigenous peoples to assist them in their fight. What else could have united three such different races and cultures? Even now we have only a fragile alliance. Discontent and separatist sentiments are always simmering under the surface in Canada. Perhaps your homeland would be so kind as to threaten us with another invasion?"

He grinned, and she smiled back.

"So tell me, do you really believe your – your powers come from shaman magic?" she asked him.

"Who can say? It is all lost in the past now," he began. Then he broke off, looking behind her.

Automatically she turned her head. Raoul had reemerged from the spare bedroom and stood in the passageway in wolf form. He looked even larger in an enclosed space. He saw her startled expression and his head and tail drooped low, like a dog's when it is unsure of itself. On an impulse she reached out to him and touched the soft snowy fur of his ruff. It seemed important to show him that she felt no fear of him. In fact, his wolf form was oddly liberating to her. Physical contact was perfectly appropriate when offered to an animal instead of a boy, and she did not feel at all shy; it was like petting one of Honoré's huskies. In response, the great white beast leaned his head against her and made the low rumbling sound – not a growl, but almost more like a cat's purr – that a dog makes in response to its owner's caress.

"Come, *mon ami*," the farmer said to him, opening the front door.

360

The wolf left the house with Lavallée, and Chantal went into the spare room.

She felt perfectly relaxed as she slipped off her shirt, jeans and underclothes: she might have been merely changing for a swimming pool party with friends. Raoul's clothing lay on the bed, neatly folded, and as she laid hers next to his she couldn't help smiling at the difference between them. He had obviously taken good care of these garments, unlike her casually ripped and stained jeans and tee. He had no other possessions – had never owned anything before in his entire life. No doubt these pieces of fabric were incalculably precious to him; symbols of his hard-won humanity. Once again she felt a curious tenderness towards the wolf-boy.

When she was completely undressed, Chantal knelt down on the floor and placed the palms of her hands on the bare boards. Once again the transition came to her easily, without the nightmarish feel of her first few transformations. She was just heading for the door when, out of the corner of her eye, she glimpsed herself in the full-length mirror on the wall.

She started and felt her wolf-self grow tense, muscles tautening as she swung about to face her reflection directly. Human unease at the sight of her animal body caused the latter to respond instinctively, as if to a threat from an enemy. She saw the pointed ears go flat, and the fangs spring out from behind the retracting lips. With an effort she mastered herself, looking into her own eyes. They changed more than their shape when she shifted, she noticed: the dark-brown outer rims of the irises retreated along with the whites, and all that remained was the yellowish-amber colour surrounding the pupils. These were true wolf-eyes, the mark of her Arcadian lineage. *I'm in there,* she thought as she gazed into their golden depths. *Somehow that's... me. But then what am I? Who am I?* The answer to that question had always been her familiar human features, her brown eyes, her unruly hair. *But if I'm not those things only, if I can be* this *as well, who am I really? Is Honoré right about the soul? Are we somehow* more *than just our bodies? It's weird: I never used to think about this kind of stuff before. Who'd have thought turning into an animal would make me go all philosophical?*

She found Raoul waiting outside with Lavallée, the old man standing beside the high-wolf as casually as a man with his pet dog. Lavallée smiled when he saw Chantal run up to them, and pointed with his cane towards the woods. "Now then, off you both go!"

They took care to stay away from the cattle, and the great shaggy bison that grazed the woodland pasture with their massive horned heads bowed low. There was a vacant field beyond the trees and they headed for this. It slanted upwards, becoming a steep hill. The sun had set by the time they reached the top, and they lay down panting on the grassy summit to rest. There was an impressive view of the Laurentians on the far shore across the water: Mont Ste. Anne reared up in the foreground, its green slopes scarred with the ski runs that were now snow-free and idle. Eastward the widening river ran, deep indigo-blue in the fading light. Chantal could picture in her mind the sailing vessels that had brought the first colonists here, later giving them a supply line after the settlements were established. The vast stretch of water was still crucial to commercial shipping, but today many leisure craft sailed its blue expanse as well. Presently she and Raoul saw a cruise ship, lit up with strands of white lights, sail majestically downriver. It was departing Quebec City for the Gulf of St. Lawrence and the legendary lands beyond: old Acadia, the Îles de la Madeleine, and farther out in the Atlantic the little lonely islands of St. Pierre et Miquelon

362

that had never been conquered, but remained in the Old Country's keeping to this very day: two little fragments of France.

As she admired the view, Chantal's attention was caught by a faint glimmer of greenish light that sprang up on the darkened shore of the island, then swiftly faded away. She blinked, and looked again. There was nothing there.

Raoul turned to her. "Did you see that? Down by the shore – "

"You saw it too? I thought I was just imagining it. What was that light, do you think? Fireflies?" But it was too early for them. "Or marsh gas, maybe?"

"Maybe. Or … maybe it was a *feu follet,* called up by our friend the *sorcier.*"

"More likely someone walking around with a flashlight, looking for car keys or something that they dropped – "

"No! Do not try to explain it away. Let it be a mystery forever. Years from now we will say to each other, 'Do you remember the evening when we saw the *feu follet* on the Sorcerer's Isle?'"

She gave a barking, lupine laugh. "But why? What's the point?"

"Point? There is none. Except that if we were real wolves we would never think or speak of such things; only humans use the imagination. Perhaps we will start a legend of our own."

His blue eyes shone softly in the dusk as he spoke. The white wolf looked like a creature of legend himself, and so he was: a being from an older and more wondrous age, lingering improbably in the mundane present. In that moment he suddenly seemed to her too beautiful, too magical to be altogether real. He did not belong to this world.

"Raoul?" she said softly, after a moment's silence had passed. "What was it like for you before you came here? You don't talk much about your life as a wolf."

"I hated it," he said frankly. "I was raised in a small den on the shore of Lac du Hibou – the Lake of the Owl, north and east of the Puvirnituq River. After our parents were killed by the Lapierres we three pups were left to survive on our own. We abandoned our den in search of food. After many days we finally came across a musk ox carcass on which a polar bear was feeding. We made the very bad mistake of trying to snatch some scraps of meat, thinking we were too small for the bear to notice or care. We knew no better. The bear attacked us. It killed my brother instantly with one blow from its terrible paw. My sister survived another blow, only to die hours later from the claw-wounds. I alone escaped serious injury. After wandering on my own, starving and terrified, I finally stumbled upon my mother's original pack. The Lake Pack accepted me because they had no pups of their own at that time, and this saved my life. Later, when their Mother-wolf bore her own litters, she looked upon me with less favour. So I learned to be useful, easing her burden by helping to care for the young pups. It was not hard work: I loved those little wolves, and they loved me... until they matured, and were taught by their elders to despise me as a hind-wolf. Josephine says I should not hate my wolf-self, and I try not to; but in that form the life I led was terrible.

"The life of my human ancestors no doubt had its hardships, but it was still better. I do not know why they left it, but I desire everything that they rejected. It reminds me of that story Josephine tells, of the boy raised by wolves who later returned to his tribe. Like him, I can dwell no more in the house of the wolf, for I was never truly at home there. It is to the house of

364

humanity that I belong." He rose to all fours again. "Are you rested? Then let's go back."

They ran down the hill and through the open fields again. The enjoyment Chantal felt now was not like the wild exhilaration she had known in the Grove of Pan when she pursued the deer, nor was it like the thrill of running with the pack. It was more innocent, more playful. She caught up with Raoul and nipped at his hind legs, and they began mock-fighting, lunging and riposting with quick thrusts of their jaws. She sensed that he was holding himself back, though she could still feel his formidable strength every time she closed with him. But Yves was just as large and strong in his wolf-shape, she reminded herself, and *he* would not hold back. She definitely needed these fighting lessons.

Still, the play-fight quickly degenerated into mere play. She could not help herself. The sheer unrestrained physicality of this new existence was so wonderful. Touching Raoul while he was in wolf-form had been a revelation; interacting with him while she too wore animal shape was more liberating still. Again and again she pounced and pawed at her patient companion, howling with glee when one nudge from him sent her rolling over on the ground, springing up again to nuzzle at his face the moment he lowered his guard.

Lavallée was still waiting for them in his backyard and he watched, grinning, as they tussled together and broke apart and closed again. "She is a match for you, *mon ami,*" the farmer called out as the big male finally pulled away and fled, the female in hot pursuit.

"This isn't working!" Raoul called out as he tore past Lavallée. "She is supposed to be civilizing me, but I am only making her more savage!" The old man roared with laughter.

In truth Raoul was not fleeing Chantal, but his own feelings. He had employed with her the skills he developed as a pup-sitter, meeting her awkward lunges with a firm yet gentle resistance. Yet as she sparred with him he began to sense, with dismay, a rising wave of desire. It was inevitable. As Honoré had said, he was ruled by no older dominant wolves here, and so was under no constraint to suppress his natural appetites and yearnings. Shame filled him to find his animal nature so readily asserting itself.

And it was mere foolishness in any case, he told himself. Chantal would likely never love him in that way. Warm and affectionate though she might be, she was still human-born, and in her eyes he was still a wild beast.

*But it is true that Angélique married Honoré, even though he was born a wolf and she was not. If I can only succeed in becoming more human, then perhaps… Until then, though, I am not worthy of her.*

Chantal, finding herself abandoned, ran over to the farmer instead. She admired Lavallée's courage in standing so still and calm while a human-sized wolf gamboled around him. Of course he was used to *loups garous*; but she could feel her own strength and agility, her dangerousness, and the old man suddenly looked frail and small to her. "You're very brave, sorcerer. But I suppose you could always turn me into a frog!" she called out in Lupine.

He clearly understood the language, for he laughed at her jest. "Somehow I feel you would be formidable even in that shape, *mademoiselle!*" he riposted. "But of course I can do no such thing."

"Well then, have you any premonitions for me?" she asked in a teasing tone, going up to him and flinging herself down, panting, by his feet. "Can you read my palm?" Laughing, she held up her enormous paw with the pad facing him.

His smile faded, and a somber look crossed his face. "No. I see nothing clearly, but I do feel at times that there is… something … drawing nearer to you, *mademoiselle.*"

She pricked up her ears, alerted by his change in tone. "What sort of something?"

"I can't tell yet. But I feel…" Suddenly the worn and weathered old face turned pale, and the eyes fluttered and closed. His mouth went slack. For an instant she wondered if he were having a stroke or seizure.

"*Monsieur?*" she said anxiously.

He swayed, nearly dropping his cane, and from the wrinkled old lips there came a hissing whisper. She sprang up and moved closer, trying to hear him.

"*Llla…mmorrr…*"

Her hackles rose up bristling and she backed away. Had she heard correctly? *La mort?* But that meant "death". He continued to rock on his feet, his eyes shut and his lips moving. "Someone close to you," he murmured, "… and to you also… yes it comes, very soon. I see it, I see – "

Yelping in alarm she turned towards the house, calling for Raoul to come and help, that Lavallée had fallen ill. Even as she fled she heard again those mumbled words that sent the blood racing in panic through her veins.

*La mort.*

## 25

The trees around Chapelle-des-loups were approaching full leaf now. As she walked down the long drive leading to the main road Chantal noted the young green foliage on the branches of the ancient oaks, on the slender silver birches and maples and elms. Last autumn's leaves were still piled at their roots, and through these the ferns raised their green coiled croziers; and there were a few lingering trilliums scattered about the forest floor, their pale petals beginning to show a blush of pink. She wanted to pause and appreciate the beauty all around her, but nowadays there seemed to be an underlying menace to everything, a feeling of something sinister lurking always just out of sight.

Her brooding thoughts were interrupted by a voice calling her name.

"Chantal! Hi!"

Chantal stared at the red-haired figure approaching her along the tree-lined avenue, and stopped short in disbelief. "Kath? Is that you? *Kath!*"

Her cousin laughed as Chantal ran up to her. "Warren had to take a business trip to Montreal, so I came along and we made a little side trip. I thought I'd come here and surprise you, just for fun. This place was incredibly hard to find, though!"

"Here, let me take your bag," Chantal offered, still feeling a little dazed. Her cousin – here? How *had* she found the retreat? Seeing the familiar figure in this unfamiliar setting made it seem unreal, as if Katharine were somehow superimposed upon a false background. "There's a common room in the main building where we can sit and talk. They don't usually take overnight visitors here, though." The *loups garous,* though kindly and hospitable, were understandably wary about outsiders entering their sanctuary and she wondered how they would react to this unexpected arrival.

"That's okay, I'm on a tight schedule too. Warren's meeting me in Quebec City." Kath handed over her small suitcase and fell into step beside her cousin. Now well advanced in her pregnancy, she walked more slowly than usual and Chantal kept forgetting to move at a matching pace. The older woman smiled. "You always were a fast walker," she said. "But today you're almost running! What's the hurry, hon?"

Chantal wondered why she was moving with such haste. Was it that being on any woodland trail, even this well-travelled one so close to the werewolf community, made her uneasy nowadays? The undergrowth to either side of the narrow road was so very thick and interlaced: anything might be skulking in there... "Sorry, Kath," she said, trying to sound normal. "I'm just so thrilled you're here, and I can't wait to show you everything. It's great that you decided to visit."

"Such a pretty place," Kath said, glancing around her as she walked. "Reminds me of the forest trails back home. No, really, I'm fine: exercise is good for me, even at this stage. I've been told to walk as much as possible. I'd love to have a stroll in these woods."

"Uh, sure." Chantal did not want to alarm her cousin, but she was finding it hard to hide her nervousness. She was anxious to get Kath to the community centre, safe behind walls and surrounded by people. "But let's go to the main building first, okay? We can get some food, and I can introduce you to everyone – "

There was a swift blur of movement a short distance back and on their right, barely visible to her peripheral vision. Then with explosive speed a dark shape sprang out of the bushes and launched itself at her cousin. Kath gave a cry and fell backwards onto the road, her attacker on top of her.

369

*"Kath!"* Chantal could not seem to move. The black wolf straddling Kath's prone form looked up at Chantal, teeth gleaming in a savage leer, and she thought in disbelief: *But he's dead! How can Jules – ?*

Even as she thought this more wolves burst from cover to either side of the path, converging on her and the helpless Kath. She raised her hands, futilely attempting to fend off their fangs. But she still could not shift from the spot, or change her own shape or do anything at all but stand there paralyzed with terror –

Her own scream woke her.

Chantal's eyes sprang open. She was, she realized, still holding her hands up with the palms facing outwards, in the desperate effort to ward off the attack. She sat up in bed, shaking. "It's all right; I'm all right," she called out, hearing footsteps and concerned voices at her door. "Just another nightmare. Sorry if I scared you." She was relieved to see sunlight seeping through the thin curtains at her window. At least it was morning, and she would not have to try to go to sleep again.

Yet another dream spawned by stress: she'd been having lots of them of late, all relating to her fears for her family back home

"Someone close to you, and to you also... yes it comes, very soon... *La mort.*"

It had all started with the sorcerer's strange pronouncement. M. Lavallée had quickly recovered from his curious fit, professing to recall nothing of what he had said. But still the warning words he had uttered continued to trouble Chantal, a vague but nagging worry at the back of her mind. If werewolves existed, who could say what other things in the old myths might be real? They abounded with tales of seers and oracles. What if Lavallée had truly had a premonition, a glimpse into her future granted him by some unknowable power? If so, its lack of specificity only made it more alarming:

370

she worried about everyone she knew, both here and back in America. The sense of looming tragedy was impossible to dismiss. As May turned to June her apprehension grew, and she tried many times to reason her way out of it.

*M. Lavallée just had a fit or something. He's old and his health isn't too great. Honoré Dubois has been watching our enemies; he's been extra careful since poor Dr. Hébert was killed. He'd let me know if any suspicious activity were going on.*

But when she was alone, or lost in dream-haunted sleep, her confidence evaporated and the fears that she believed she had vanquished stole back into her mind. The enemy, she thought, was being much too quiet.

When she entered the common room Raoul reminded her that she had promised to teach him how to interact with ordinary humans of the outside world. "I have shown you what it is to be a wolf over these past weeks," he said. "I have nothing more to teach you. May I now receive your instruction?"

"All right," she told him. "Why don't we go to the city, then?" *More people around means more witnesses,* she added silently to herself. *We're actually safer there than here, in my opinion. No chance of a wolf attack, anyway...* She still could not shake off the lingering horror of her nightmare.

She drove with Raoul down the winding trail to the main road, which led them away from the forest and along the shore where a panoramic view of Quebec City opened up in the west. Its towers, both old and new, dominated the Cap Diamant even at this distance, overlooking the opposing headland and the great river forced through the narrow gap between. So it had appeared to the first Europeans, Chantal thought, as they sailed down the St. Lawrence seaway from the Atlantic: the narrowing of the river – *Kebec* in Algonquin – that both grants and limits access to the continent's interior. Those that claimed it were keepers of the gate. In that vista all the turbulent history of Quebec City was explained.

They crossed the bridge to the mainland, and at Raoul's request she made a brief stop at Montmorency Falls. The great cascade foamed and thundered over its precipice, fed by the winter melt: in late summer and fall its flow diminished, M. Lavallée had told them, so that from a distance it appeared as light as lace. They walked up to the churning pool at its foot, until they could feel the throb of it in their bones and its spray upon their faces. "Why exactly did you want to come here?" Chantal asked her companion, puzzled. He stood staring at the plunging wall of white water, seemingly mesmerized by it.

"I am trying to see this as a human sees it," he said.

"You're still thinking about that old fairy story of Lavallée's? It's just *water,* Raoul."

"To a wolf it is water. To a human it is – more. It is songs and stories. It is ..."

"Beautiful?" she suggested.

He tilted his head to one side, pondering. "Yes," he said slowly, "that is it. It is beautiful."

"Don't high-wolves have any concept of beauty?"

"No, the word is meaningless to us. Wolves see things only as they are: water and stone, earth and sky, bird and beast. Humans find other, invisible things within them. Real and not real, like the *feu follet.* If I could only grasp such things I feel I would be truly human at last."

"Raoul," she said gently, "you're already there. Trust me. You're as human as anyone I've ever known." *And way more human than some,* she added grimly to herself as they walked back to the car.

372

She drove on to the city and parked in a public lot just outside the Basse-Ville. Its streets, freed of the concealing snow, now displayed their old stone pavements: they might have been the cobbled alleys of some medieval fortress-city in Europe. Feeling energetic, Chantal and Raoul mounted the steep wooden treads of the Escalier Casse-cou to the Haute-Ville rather than wait for the funicular. Raoul paused for a moment by the Champlain monument on the Terrasse, looking up at the bronze statue atop the pedestal.

"This is not a true likeness, they say," he commented. "None of Samuel de Champlain's portraits is, since no one truly knows what he looked like. Do you think Honoré is right about him? That he was of our kind?"

Chantal gazed up at the statue. The sculptor had positioned the famed explorer so that he faced away from the St. Lawrence: his back to France from whence he came, his gaze forever bent upon the colony he had founded. Whoever and whatever this enigmatic man had been, his city had safely sheltered the *loups garous* for four centuries. Would they ever be free to reveal themselves to their human kin? Or were they forever doomed to concealment in the shadows, their true nature denied, their history hidden? "Who knows? Speaking of M. Dubois," she added, "I haven't seen him in ages. Let's go pay him a call."

They found Honoré Dubois alone in his sitting room. Angélique, he told them, had gone out with friends and Ti-Jacques was working as an apprentice chef at a café in the Basse-Ville. The old man seemed to be in an unusually despondent mood, and obviously glad of their company. "The sciatica, it troubles me very much this evening," he said, pointing to his right leg which was elevated on a footrest.

"Is that all?" Chantal persisted, concerned. "You seem kind of down. There hasn't been any bad news, has there?"

"No, no. It is nothing, I am just feeling my age tonight," he said. He picked up a magazine from the table beside him. "Well... there is this. One of the Lafontaine girls passed this magazine on to my wife, and I found it open at this page." He held it out for them to see.

"What is it?" asked Raoul. "I can still only read a little."

"Not the article." He pointed to the opposite page. "What does this picture say to you two?"

It was a perfume advertisement. The female model, tastefully nude, was depicted crouching on all fours and baring a set of perfect white teeth; the feral impression was augmented by black tiger-stripes painted artfully on her well-tanned face, back and limbs. A caption below read *Bring Out Your Wild Side*.

"It's kind of clever, I guess," said Chantal. "The model's gorgeous."

"But the young woman, what is she saying to us?" Dubois asked. "Not the model herself, she is only paid to pose; but the advertiser who conceived this image, what is his message? This woman seems to say, 'I am an animal, nothing more; I am content that it should be so.' It is part of a broader message that modern society is embracing. Souls are not the fashion any more. It is all about the body now, the animal self."

Chantal shrugged. "Times change. I guess people are more comfortable with their bodies nowadays."

"True, this is a very sensual age. A great shift is occurring in our civilization: where once human beings viewed themselves as embodied souls, they are now encouraged to see themselves merely as bodies. But all souls are of equal value; all bodies are not. A young girl

374

may look at a picture like this and say to herself, 'My body is not as beautiful as hers and never will be, therefore as a person I am worth less than she.' The girl will starve herself, perhaps, in an effort to look as thin and elegant as possible; or perhaps she will just hate her body and feel miserable. My wife tells me this happens often with girls today."

Chantal nodded. "That is *so* true," she said with feeling.

"And even the finest body is not young and beautiful forever. All too soon come the wrinkles and the aching joints, the waning of one's strength and desires." He moved his sore leg, wincing. "If life is *only* about the flesh, then I fear someday people will say 'Of what use are the elderly, the disabled, the sick? They are not pleasing to look at, they are weak and contribute little. Perhaps we should do away with them.'"

"Don't say that!" cried Chantal, distressed. "You're important to *us,* Honoré."

He smiled wanly. "Thank you, *ma petite.* But for today's society the new god is Nature, and she is a stern and pitiless mistress. Very few wild animals live to old age. They are killed first, or they die of disease, or they starve. Had I stayed a wolf I would have been dead these many years, instead of enjoying a long rewarding life. Old age is humanity's gift to itself: to live out the last of our days in peace and contentment, passing on to the young all we have learned. I fear that gift may yet be taken away from us, in the name of this new cult of Nature." He shook his head. "It was not for such things that I left my animal's existence behind."

"Why *did* you leave your pack, Honoré?" Raoul asked. "You've never told me. Were you rejected by them?"

"Rejected? No. I did not intend to leave my people forever. I only wished to satisfy my curiosity about the

375

human race. I belonged to the *famille Dubois,* the great Woodland Pack of the *Laurentides* north of Montreal, who long ago turned away from human society. But I was intrigued by the tales I heard from my fellow *haut-loups* about our human kin. There was a wise one of our people, an aged wolf who still remembered the lore of human-kind. I asked him to teach me how to assume a man's form, and instruct me on the language spoken by our human ancestors. When I had learnt all I could, he took me to a house in the woods, the property of our pack, which contained clothing for its members to use on the rare occasions when they still interacted with the human world. I must have looked a sight, for the clothing was *extremely* out of date." He gave a wry smile. "But once I was in human society I had access to the wealth of the erstwhile Dubois family, who had been prosperous merchants. My pack had renounced it along with their human forms, but it supported me as I made my journey of discovery.

"I came out of the forest," Dubois said, speaking slowly as if reliving scenes within his memory, "in the summer of 1967. On reaching Montreal I found myself in the midst of Expo, the great global celebration of human culture and technology. I was both bewildered by it and amazed. I wandered about the grounds and through the pavilions, sometimes alone and sometimes with new friends I had made – for at Expo you could meet many other young people from all over the world. I fell in with a group that was half Québecois, half Anglo visitors, all striving to speak and understand one another's tongues. In such an environment I was able to feel at ease, even though my human body was new to me. What wonders we all saw and shared! In your American pavilion, Chantal, there was an exhibit about the plan to land a spacecraft on the moon. I could not believe that such a thing was possible; I marveled at the sheer audacity of it. But for humans, I learned, to dream is to do. A mere two years later I watched on a friend's television set as men walked for the first time upon the lunar surface. I resolved that day to remain among men, and to use the Dubois fortune to help *loups garous* live in modern society.

"Do you see why I chose civilization? Why to this day I would choose it again, over the hunger and ignorance of the wild? Yet they would still cast it all aside, those young rebels who linger in the forest. They would rather listen to the rantings of maniacs who say that humanity is irredeemably evil. If I could only take them back in time and show them what it meant to be young and human in my day! If I could make them appreciate their great heritage... But you two, you at least understand?" A pleading tone entered his voice. They both nodded, and he appeared to relax, leaning back in his chair. "There, enough of this preaching! It is a beautiful night tonight, *n'est-ce pas?* The city is full of life. Go out and be young, *mes amis!*"

"No, we want to stay. We came here to see you," protested Chantal.

"And waste this perfect evening? I won't hear of it. You are only young once, as they say. Here is some money – no, take it, please! This is part of Raoul's education. And it will make me very happy to know that you are both out there enjoying yourselves. I had my good years; now you must have yours."

At his insistence they said their thanks and goodbyes, and went out into the streets of the Haute-Ville, mingling with the crowds. Chantal still felt a little sad and half-guilty at leaving Dubois all alone. But her spirits began to lift again as she walked. She could not help it: happiness was in the air, omnipresent and contagious. The people of Quebec, with the characteristic French Canadian *joie de vivre,* greeted summer with the same exuberant enthusiasm they showed in their winter celebrations. Flowers frothed down from window boxes and spilled out of sidewalk planters; the outdoor cafés were full; the streets rang with the music of wandering buskers. Down on the river people rode the Lévis ferry back and forth, for no other reason than to enjoy the dramatic view it gave them of Quebec's skyline. She and Raoul sauntered along the Terrasse, went to look at the students' artwork displayed in the narrow little side-alley of the Rue du Trésor that led to the Latin Quarter, then walked back to dine at a café across from the little park of the Place d'Armes.

"You will tell me if I do anything wrong?" Raoul whispered as the hostess led them to an outdoor table next to the street. "I am still not used to eating in public."

Chantal was feeling a bit self-conscious herself. She was accustomed to eating out at cheap chain restaurants with large groups of family or friends; dining in a smart establishment in the company of just one other person felt somewhat intimidating. But it also felt pleasantly grown-up and sophisticated. She scanned the menu and placed their orders, deciding on the day's special for both of them. It was rather expensive, but the money Dubois had given her was extravagantly generous.

Once their waitress had left them Raoul leaned over and said in an undertone, "I understood only a few of the words she used. She talks so quickly! What is 'vegetarian menu'?"

She explained. "Some people don't like eating meat because you have to kill animals to get it, so they eat only plant food."

He looked astonished. "They can do that, and survive?"

"Humans can. Sure."

"I admire that," he said. "I always regretted having to kill to live. The fear and suffering of the prey is so pitiful. I think I would like to be a vegetarian."

"You can be anything you want to be, Raoul. That's the nice thing about being human. I hope you'll have a long happy life."

"It will be long at any rate. Were I still a wolf, I would have but six or seven more years of life left to me. But I am told I will age more slowly now I am human."

They were silent for a time, gazing on the view before them. The trees of the Place d'Armes were in full foliage; the fountain was playing in the Monument de la Foi. Above the treetops rose the towers of the Château Frontenac, like a dream of Old World romance; but Chantal looked away from them, troubled by the memories they evoked. Presently their order arrived: two medium-rare steaks, served with a piquant Dijon sauce and golden wedges of *patates frites* on the side. Nothing more was said of vegetarianism. They attacked the meat eagerly, and Chantal was pleased to see that Raoul was clearly enjoying his meal, though he was still having some difficulty using a fork and knife. After a while he put them down and looked at her. "These are so plainly made for grasping food," he said, flexing the fingers of his right hand. "Tell me, why must we use those metal things instead? It seems so – inefficient."

"It keeps your hands clean. It *is* kind of hard to do at first," Chantal acknowledged. "Humans have to be taught when they're little. Would you like me to show you?"

He pushed his plate towards her. "Please."

She cut up his steak for him, aware all the while of other people in the café looking on and smiling in amusement. No doubt they thought they were looking at a young couple on a date being playful with each other.

Raoul, she couldn't help noticing, was getting a lot of admiring glances from girls. Their eyes lingered on his tall lean figure and well-proportioned features, transparently speculating. Raoul himself was completely oblivious of all this, of course: with no understanding of human aesthetics, he did not yet realize how attractive his new body was. He'd be subjected to feminine advances before long; probably would be right now, were Chantal not there with him. Girls of her generation were not exactly shy. *Great,* she thought, annoyed. *More trouble ahead! How's this poor guy ever going to adjust?* She glared at a blonde who was staring at him openly; the other girl smirked but quickly averted her eyes.

Chantal cleared her throat. "Uh... Raoul, do you ever think about – you know – love, and all that?"

Raoul, in the middle of spearing a piece of steak on his fork with painstaking care, glanced up. "Do you mean courting?"

She laughed. "Courting? That word's way out of date! Even in Dubois's day they were into Free Love. Nowadays people pretty much go at it like animals."

Raoul set his fork down. "I would prefer to court a woman. Honoré courted Angélique for years before he won her. I think that way is better."

Of course: wolves mated for life. Unlike people, they were naturally monogamous. She had forgotten that. It would explain Dubois's old-fashioned ideas, and Raoul's too. He could not be expected to think as modern boys did. "She'll be one lucky girl, Raoul. Hey! Are you blushing?" He was. "Here, tell you what: practice on me and maybe you won't be so embarrassed when you do meet someone. Pretend I'm the girl you want to, uh, court. What would you say to her?"

380

"I would say to this girl," he said slowly, "how much I admire her. That she has what humans call beauty. And spirit. And that I would very much like to be – to be –"

"Her boyfriend," she prompted as he appeared to hesitate.

"Her life-mate," he said. "If she would have me."

He had learnt at last to look someone full in the eyes. His own were so earnest and open, and their deep sapphire colour so beautiful, that they were almost overwhelming. This time it was she who lowered her gaze.

After dinner they walked back out into the teeming streets. The sun had begun to sink behind the roofs, and the light mellowed into the soft refulgence of the "golden hour". They went all the way up the Grande Allée and out through the Porte St. Louis, then paused for a rest, sitting on the edge of the Fontaine de Tourny in the traffic circle before the Legislature. The fountain's tinted underwater lights gave it an emerald glow as twilight deepened. Giant frogs on bronze lily pads spat long jets of water towards the central structure and heraldic dolphins and other mythical figures spouted back, forming an elaborate pattern of luminous green arcs. Raoul seemed fascinated by it. "What is it for, this water?" he asked her. "It is not for the horses?" He had earlier noticed the copper drinking fountains placed here and there along the streets for the convenience of *calèche* horses.

"No, the fountain hasn't got any practical purpose. It's just there to be beautiful. Like the waterfall, except it was made on purpose by people."

"They can *make* beauty then, as well as finding it in things of nature," he said slowly. "I feel... yes, I am sure I am beginning to understand. Honoré has tried to

381

explain to me about these things that humans make. Music and painting, what he calls civilization." He glanced up at the façade of the parliament building opposite, with its towering roofs and rows of statues.

Chantal said nothing. She was aware of a new worry: that the wolf-boy was receiving only an idealistic impression of humanity, seeing its shining ideals but not its underlying darkness. Raoul's assimilation seemed more and more to Chantal like an impossible task. He could pass for a normal human, there was no doubt of that. But try as she might, she could not picture him in her world: going to work on a commuter train, dressed in a business suit with briefcase in hand; coping with the intricacies of office politics. Though he had no desire to return to the wild, would he really fare any better in human society? However would he navigate its complex and baffling maze? His wolf-years gave him physical maturity, but his mind still had an almost childlike naiveté and innocence. He was *too* innocent, perhaps, too good-natured to survive for very long in either world.

"*Bonjour, mes jeunes amis!*" called a voice, breaking abruptly into her gloomy thoughts. She jumped slightly, but it was only the costumed driver of a passing *calèche*. He tipped his tricorn hat as he pulled up beside them and added in English: "You are tourists, perhaps? Would you like to hire a carriage? It's the best way to see the city."

Chantal was about to refuse when she noticed a wistful look in Raoul's eyes, and she sighed. "Okay, maybe just a short ride," she said. "*Merci.*"

She paid the rather hefty fare and together they clambered up into the open carriage. The man drove them back along the Grande Allée and out onto the Plains of Abraham, passing through the Parc des Champs de Bastille. He kept up a steady patter as he

382

went, turned right around in his driver's seat so he could address his passengers directly, and paying little or no attention to the road in front of him. Chantal found this a bit disconcerting at first, but the horse seemed to know the route well and plodded along, seemingly without any need for direction from its driver. Raoul gazed in fascination at its glossy brown back and muscular hindquarters encased in the creaking harness. "Plant-eaters are mere food to my wolf kin," he murmured in her ear. "How clever humans are, to tame another creature and use its strength and speed like this!"

"I guess – but I'm sure the horses are just as happy we invented automobiles," she replied.

Their driver took them deeper into the park, down to the Avenue de l'Ontario where there were fewer signs of civilization, save for an old Martello tower raising up its rounded walls in obsolete defense. The Parc des Champs de Bataille consisted of wide fields interspersed with leafy shrubs and trees: the site of the historic battle that had decided forever the fate of New France.

Suddenly the horse jerked its head up and snorted in alarm. "Steady, Charlot," said the driver. Raoul too was looking around him. He still had a wild thing's wariness, and Chantal saw his nostrils automatically flare as he turned his head, in a reflexive effort to catch a scent. But his weaker human sense of smell could not detect anything, and in the faint light the thick clumps of bushes around them were draped with darkness.

"Would it be okay if we picked up the pace a little?" Chantal asked the driver. "We – we really should be getting back to town."

"As you wish, *mademoiselle*." The driver shook the reins and the horse burst into a more vigorous trot, almost verging on a canter. Chantal turned back, but not before she glimpsed, out of the corner of her eye, a dark shape separate itself from the pool of shadow under a

383

large elm tree and then dart into a low clump of bushes near the road. She turned her head sharply: the shape was gone, but the bushes into which it had plunged were agitated.

She swallowed, her throat gone suddenly dry. "Raoul? Did you see tha – "

She never completed the question. As the carriage drew even with it the bush seemed to explode. Leaves and twigs burst outwards as a dark form hurtled out and straight at them. There was a cry – not a howl, but the savage snarl of a wolf on the attack. With one leap it was in the *calèche*, all fur and fury and bared gleaming teeth.

The horse screamed, rearing up on its hind legs and forcing the carriage backwards. The driver struggled to control it, at the same time twisting his own head around to try and see what had attacked them.

Chantal sprawled on the floor of the carriage, dazed and winded. Her nightmare had come to life. With her bare hands she struggled to hold back the shaggy black head of her attacker, its fangs snapping and dripping slaver into her face. She was dimly aware that she was screaming. Raoul lunged in and grabbed the wolf, wrapping his arms around its neck, his own teeth bared with the strain as he strove to pull the animal away from Chantal's throat.

*"Qu'est-ce que c'est?"* yelled the driver over his shoulder, reverting in his alarm to his native French. *"Un chien?"*

"A mad dog – *oui!"* Raoul shouted back.

He could not take wolf shape himself, not with the man right there to witness it. It was the horse, finally, that took action on their behalf. Unable to free itself from its constraining harness, it opted for the only alternative, headlong flight: the desire to place the greatest distance possible between itself and what

384

instinct told it was a deadly predator. As the *calèche* lurched forward, forcibly dragged by the panicked animal, the driver fell backwards, only saving himself from falling right out by gripping the back of his seat. Chantal, who was trying to pull away from the wolf's scrabbling claws, dropped back to the floor. Raoul and the wolf collapsed together in a heaving heap on top of her.

With an effort Raoul dragged himself up again and, clutching their assailant around its flanks just behind the forelegs, deliberately flung himself backwards. Boy and wolf tumbled over the side of the low-slung carriage. Springing up, Chantal saw the two of them hit the ground and go rolling over and over, still tangled together. The driver, focused on controlling his bolting horse, had not seen. The *calèche* rocked wildly, plunging off the paved path onto the rolling lawn.

Wincing, Chantal gathered herself. She vaulted over the side, hit the ground with a thud that knocked the breath from her, then scrambled to her feet in time see the *calèche* – already yards away – vanish behind a clump of trees. She turned and ran in the opposite direction, crying out Raoul's name. No reply.

After several minutes' hard running she found his clothing scattered about on the grass. Not far away was the nature trail that ran alongside the edge of the Cap Diamant. On its far side the floor of the wood fell away in steep cliffs: the same that General Wolfe's forces had scaled long ago, in their surprise assault on the French colony. It was dark as a mine there, the path steeped in shadow by large elm and maple trees over-arching it. But though she saw nothing, she could hear snarling and yelping not far away. Peering through the gloom as she ran towards the sound, she finally glimpsed a pale glimmer that leaped back and forth: the white wolf, battling something too dark to see in the deep shadows.

The black wolf.   It was as if he were fighting with darkness itself.

"Raoul!" she screamed, and ran towards him.   "Look out!  You're too close to the edge!"

## 26

There was no time for Chantal to change her shape. Just as she reached them, the two battling wolves rolled off the path. Only the line of tree-trunks planted there kept them from tumbling right over the precipice.

She screamed, in wordless warning, and the black-furred wolf turned towards her, distracted. At once Raoul knocked his assailant off its feet and pinned it down, his paws planted on its belly and his teeth threatening its throat. The black wolf howled in impotent rage. "Enough, Luc! Do not force me to hurt you!" cried Raoul in the wolf language.

Chantal stared. It was hard to believe this could be a *loup garou*. Its appearance was wholly feral, animalistic, no trace of humanity to be seen in its glaring yellow eyes. It made no answer to Raoul's command.

The white wolf growled. "Well? What has Chantal done to you, ever?" The savage creature at his feet still made no reply. Then as the white wolf's fangs again menaced it, the dark wolf gave a shrill wordless whine. He looked down at it for long time. Slowly he removed his paws from its belly and stepped back. "Very well. Return to your friends, Luc. Tell them if they wish to live free in the wild they must make no more incursions into human territory. If you do this again you will be punished – not by my side, but by yours. The masters you serve do not tolerate any disobedience. If you expose their secrets, even accidentally, they will destroy you."

The dark-furred wolf rose. Chantal recoiled as it glowered at her, eyes still burning with hate. But its tail was tucked low, and as she watched it slunk away into the night and was gone. "I hope you haven't made a mistake," she said. "He's just taking advantage of your pity."

"I know," he replied.

"Then why –"

"Luc Benoit is only sixteen years old, and has a family that loves and misses him. I will not kill him or anyone else, ever again."

She shuddered. "For a moment there I – I almost thought it was Jules himself, come back from the dead. Crazy, I know, but it looked so much like him..."

"In a way it *was* Jules we encountered here. He poisoned that boy's mind, filling it up with his own evil ideas, teaching him to hate. A part of Jules lives on now in Luc, and all the others he corrupted." The white wolf went up to her, eyes anxious. "Are you hurt?"

She shook her head. "Just a few bumps and scratches. I'll live."

The wolf dropped his nose to the ground and began to retrace his steps. "I must go fetch my clothes. Quick, call Dubois and tell him what has happened."

Chantal pulled out her cell phone and punched Dubois's number. To her relief he picked up immediately. "Honoré?" she said. "Raoul and I were just attacked by a wolf on the Plains of Abraham. He says it was some kid called Luc Benoit."

There was a lengthy pause before Dubois replied. "I do not wish to alarm you, Chantal, but I suggest you and Raoul return to the Île d'Orléans immediately. Things are... happening. The priests at Ste. Anne de Beaupré have been in touch: they tell me one of their number is missing, my good friend Père Mercier. The chaplain who is secretly in charge of ministering to *loups garous* –"

"Missing?"

"Some strangers came to Saint Francis's shrine in the Basilica and remained there until he went and spoke with them. The other priests say he left the church with these people and has not returned. That was this morning, yet he has still not contacted his fellow priests. And now another person has turned up at the shrine of Saint Francis, just within the last hour, asking to see you specifically."

Her heart, still racing from the attack, gave a sharp little lurch. "*Me?* Who is it?"

"I do not know. A woman who will not give her name: that is all they can say. She is still there, apparently."

"That's... disturbing." Chantal felt a prickling sensation on the back of her neck, exactly where a wolf's hackles would be. "I tell you what: we'll drive to Beaupré ourselves and find out what's going on. It's not that far from the island. Let us take care of it, okay?"

"Chantal – "

"Don't worry: I promise I'll be careful. And I've got Raoul." He was coming towards her through the darkness, human now, his shirt still half-unbuttoned. "We'll report back to you as soon as we know anything."

The tiny town of Beaupré was only a little farther up the coast from the bridge to the Île d'Orléans, and they made good time, arriving there in a little over half an hour. They parked in the large lot next to the Basilica and walked across the paved forecourt. The original chapel raised by the settlers in the sixteen-hundreds was long gone, lost to fire. Chantal stared up at a majestic façade, twin spires, a rose window like a circular rainbow: a structure on as grand a scale as an Old World cathedral, incongruously large for the village that hosted it. A candlelight procession was flowing out through its great doors of beaten and sculpted copper. They were heading for the fountain of Ste. Anne with its sacred waters, cascading from the flower-shaped basin below the statue of the saint. As soon as the last of the pilgrims had passed through the doorway Raoul and Chantal hastened up the massive front steps and into the church.

It was as impressive within as without. A muted, golden light illuminated its walls of soaring stone and the ceiling's rounded Romanesque vaults with their Byzantine-style mosaics. Canes and crutches adorned the two columns at the front of the church – props reportedly discarded after miraculous healings. Thousands of the afflicted still came to this shrine every year seeking Sainte Anne's healing miracles. So many tales of sickness and pain, not all of them resulting in cures... *Old Mrs. Ghouley would love this place,* Chantal thought sourly. It was an unwelcome reminder that for many people physical suffering was still an inescapable everyday reality. Medical science had failed them; Nature, indifferent to all pain, offered nothing. So they turned instead to the realm of spirit, to the mystery beyond the knowable that rose up before them in the form of Sainte Anne. Her life-size statue, the infant Virgin cradled in its arms, dominated the nave and the shrine containing her relic was set into the transept beyond.

The ends of the empty pews, Chantal noticed as they walked down the central nave, bore exquisitely carved medallions depicting animal figures: bears, beavers, moose, lynx... and wolves. Saint Francis, she thought, would have approved. And then she wondered if perhaps *loups garous* had had a part in the building of this place, as they had in so much of Quebec's art and architecture. Certainly many had come to the Beaupré shrine over the centuries, appealing to Ste. Anne for deliverance from their wolf nature, which they viewed as a bodily affliction. Over time the Beaupré clergy had even set up a special, secret ministry to care for *loups garous.*

390

Chantal glanced up with curiosity at the image of the robed and crowned saint as she passed it. She remembered what Josephine had told her: "Among my people grandmothers are especially revered, so we embraced Anne the grandmother of our Lord and dedicated many of our own churches to her. We may honour our parents, but when we are little do we not always run to Grandmère who spoils and indulges us?"

"Not me," Chantal had replied. "My Nana wasn't the… indulging type. And the less said about my other grandmother the better."

But she was surprised, now, to find tears welling up in her eyes – tears she had not been able to shed before, loosed now by memory. Nana had loved her: even in her childhood Chantal had sensed that the old woman was strict and controlling only from the desire to protect her. The root of it all was Nana's grief for her adored only daughter, her wish that Helen had never gone to Quebec seeking adventure but had stayed closer to home, and married there, and lived. Nana had clung to her grandchild instead, with a grip all the harder for its fear of loss. Chantal felt a corresponding surge of emotion within herself: love, mourning, understanding… even forgiveness. *Could* it possibly be the influence of the saint? A healing, not of the body in this case, but of the mind?

"Look," said Raoul. "There is the altar of St. François d'Assises."

Chantal wiped her eyes and turned away from the statue. The shrine of St. Francis was located on the opposite side of the nave from Sainte Anne's reliquary: one of many dedicated to the minor saints, it had only a small black marble altar and a bas-relief carving on the wall behind, depicting Francis in the company of the crucified Christ. But by tradition this was the secret meeting-place for *loups garous* who needed help from the clergy here.

As the two of them stood before it, a veiled and dark-clad figure came swiftly up the side aisle towards them.

They stared at her. Head-veils were no longer required in Catholic churches, and this one hid not only the woman's hair but her face as well. She could only be wearing it for reasons of anonymity. The woman moved between them and the altar, and turning to face them she slowly and deliberately raised the black lace curtain of her veil, disclosing her features. Chantal stopped short with a little cry, clutching at Raoul's arm.

"*Tante* Genevieve," she gasped. "Raoul, it's my aunt!"

He scowled. "Why are you here?" he demanded, stepping forward. "Are you trying to make more trouble for Chantal?"

"No. I have left my family," said Genevieve. Her voice sounded drained, exhausted, and her face was pale. "Please, I need sanctuary. They are after me."

Chantal hesitated. "*Tante* Genevieve, I want to trust you, really I do. But the Boisverts have a way of using family members to trick me into traps."

"I understand. I offer you something precious in return for your help: my child."

"Your *child?*" said Raoul.

Gesturing to them to follow, she led them away from the shrine towards a nearby pew. There was Lysette, lying curled up fast asleep. "She did not understand what happened at the ball; she was completely innocent," said Genevieve. "She meant you no harm, Chantal. Neither do I. Believe me, I am on your side. I know what they are planning together: Yves, Maman and the pack. I will not have Lysette used by them again. Will you help us?"

Chantal looked at Raoul. "We can take you both to Chapelle-des-loups."

"Only Lysette. The sanctuary I request is for her, not for me. I am going to go back – to them."

"But why, madame?" Raoul asked.

Genevieve looked him full in the face for the first time. "I have *two* daughters, monsieur. My Francine is still in their power, and … Yves Lapierre has returned from the arctic."

"Yves!" Chantal turned to Raoul. "He must have given Noah and Josephine the slip."

"Yes, Yves is in Quebec City. He's commanded his werewolves to leave the *Laurentides* and join him there. He means to retake the Île d'Orléans with their help – to reclaim the Grove of Pan." Genevieve trembled. "But he has other plans too. Yves is angry over the loss of his father and brother. Both died in wolf form, so he cannot appeal for justice to the human authorities. His only recourse is to take personal revenge on you, Monsieur Dulac."

"Let him try," growled Raoul. "I will not hide from him any longer. Enough!"

"Don't say that! You think Yves Lapierre will fight fair? It's murder he has in mind, not a duel. Stay away from him, I beg you! As for me, if possible I will join the Communauté later with my Francine. If not, they can keep Lysette as a hostage. I know they will not harm my child, but the Boisverts do not know that. My mother especially is always willing to believe the worst of people." Genevieve went and shook Lysette gently by the shoulder. "Wake up *ma petite*, it is time for us to part now."

The little girl sat up, eyes bleary with sleep. "Must we, Maman?"

"Just for a little while, I promise. You are not afraid to go with your cousin Chantal, are you? She will take you to a safe place. I'll join you again as soon as I can."

"*Tante* Genevieve," said Chantal, "let me call Honoré Dubois. He'll know what to do."

Chantal hit redial. Dubois's phone rang several times, but there was no answer. "That's strange," she said, disquieted. "He can't have gone out, not with a sore leg." She handed the cell to Genevieve. "Here, you take this and keep trying that number. M. Dubois can protect you, and he'll help you negotiate with Thérèse for Francine. Raoul and I had better get Lysette to the community right away."

"Should you phone them too, and let them know you are coming?" her aunt asked.

"They have no phones at Chapelle-des-loups. I think it's partly to help them stay secret, and partly because they just don't go in for that kind of thing. It's pretty medieval there. Raoul, maybe you should go with Genevieve to the Dubois place – just in case she runs into the Boisverts on the way? And you can explain everything to M. Dubois."

Raoul shifted his feet uneasily. "But what about you?"

"I'll be fine. It's not that far to the island bridge from here. Once Lysette and I are at the community we'll be safe."


The candlelit procession was still in progress as they left the Basilica, the glow of its myriad little flames spreading throughout the grounds as people walked the old pilgrim paths: one flickering point of light for each person, like a visible soul. In the deep-blue evening sky above the stars shone in their own stately, slow-circling processional. Another time Chantal would have paused to drink in the beauty of the spectacle. But now all was fear and haste. With the other three *loups garous* she headed straight for the parking lot. When they reached the Mini-Cooper Lysette began to sniffle, and Chantal reached into the back seat for Mr. Bear. Clutching the toy in her arms, the child climbed into the passenger seat. Genevieve leaned in and kissed her daughter goodbye, then she and Raoul stood back to watch as Chantal drove away.

"There, now she is safe!" the woman said with an audible sigh of relief.

They crossed the parking lot to Genevieve's small sedan. She was just unlocking the doors when the cell phone rang suddenly in her hand. Genevieve and Raoul exchanged startled looks.

"*Âllo,* who is it?" she asked in a low tremulous voice. "No, Mademoiselle Chantal is not here, she has lent me her phone. It's Genevieve Lalonde speaking." She gave a brief explanation and then listened in silence. Suddenly she gave a sharp little cry and looked at Raoul, her face haggard. "It is Dubois. He wishes to speak with you," she said.

Raoul took the cell phone awkwardly – he was still unused to the device – and talked into it. "Honoré? It's Raoul."

The distant voice of Dubois spoke into his ear. "Raoul! Thank God. Is it true, what that woman says? Did Chantal give her phone to her?"

"Yes, it is all true, don't worry. We have been trying to call you – "

"I am not at home, Raoul. I'm phoning from the car. Angélique and I are coming as fast as we can: there have been some alarming developments. But Chantal, where is she now?"

"She has taken Lysette to Chapelle-des-loups."

"No!" The word was almost a howl. "She cannot go to the island! An informant has just warned us: our enemies are lying in wait there. Chantal is heading straight into their trap."

Chantal and her little cousin drove in near silence across the bridge spanning the river and onto the Île d'Orléans. To either side of the rural road the island's famed fireflies scintillated through field and meadows, like sparks from a wildfire. In the forest they clustered in the trees like fairy-lights. "Look, Lysette!" said Chantal, forcing a cheerful tone. "Isn't that pretty? It reminds me of the pilgrims' candles at the Basilica. What a beautiful night this is!"

Lysette agreed sleepily, still curled up in her seat with the teddy bear. Chantal drove on up the winding private road that led through the woods to Chapelle-des-loups. The lights in the main hall were all on. "There!" she said, switching off the engine. "We're here! You must be ready for bed, Lysette. It won't be long now. Let's go!"

Taking Lysette by the hand she led her up the path to the front entrance. But as she stepped inside the door she stopped dead. The small hand in hers tightened convulsively.

"Ah, there you are, *chérie!*" said Yves Lapierre.

He was standing just a few feet from the door. His right arm was stretched out towards the ranks of robed community members who stood there speechless, held captive by the threat of the gun in his hand – a threat neither wolf nor human could face.

He smiled at her in a mockery of welcome. "I wondered when you would finally get here. Been out partying late, have we? Well, it is a lovely evening," he said.

She made no reply. His face was nothing but a blur to her: all she could see was the gun he was aiming straight at her face. It was a handgun, small and compact, a type of weapon certainly illegal in this country.  He had an accomplice with him, also armed: a teenage boy dressed in a faded tee shirt and jeans. Manon Lafontaine was there also, in human form but bearing no weapon.  At the sight of Chantal the girl blanched and her mouth worked soundlessly.

"How like you to blunder head-first into the snare!" Yves chuckled.  "So clumsy and stupid you are, Chantal, so easy to catch."  His gaze shifted to the child at her side.  "And *la petite* Lysette!  Good of you to bring her along, Chantal.  Tell me, little one: where is your *maman?*"

He was still using a pleasant, conversational tone, no different from his normal speaking voice.  But the child stared at him in obvious terror, her eyes like Chantal's fixed on the handgun, and made no reply.  He shrugged. "No matter.  Now you're back in our hands, she will return to us.  The treacherous bitch has no choice."

Lysette began to cry, not in loud wails but making soft whimpering sounds below her breath.  But it sounded loud in the shocked silence that followed.  Yves grinned, unrepentant.  "What?  She *is* a bitch-wolf, *non?*"

Chantal pointed to Célestine in her black and white habit: in Québecois society a figure of solace and authority, even to a child not raised Catholic.  "Lysette sweetie, go to the Sister," she said, as the little girl's hand gripped hers ever more tightly.  "She'll look after you."  Wordless, Lysette obeyed, walking towards Soeur Célestine as if in a trance.  The nun held out her robed arms.

Yves turned to the younger boy.  "Luc, keep an eye on this lot while I take Mademoiselle Boisvert outside for a little chat."

"Luc?" repeated Chantal, staring at the boy. "Luc Benoit? You're the wolf who attacked us in the *calèche!*"

Yves stared. "What's that? Attacked you when?"

"Only an hour or so ago. It was on the Plains of Abraham. He tried to kill me and Raoul." Chantal glared at Luc, who looked discomfited. He was far less formidable as a boy than as a wolf: thin and lanky, with dull black hair and acne-scarred skin. He quickly dropped his gaze as Yves turned on him.

"I might have known. You stupid kid, so that's why you were so late." Yves suddenly leaned forward and struck the boy with the back of his hand, making Luc stagger and cower. "*Imbecile!* I told you the girl is mine – and only I get to kill Raoul!"

"Jules was my friend –" whined the boy.

"And he was my brother. My flesh and blood. Only *I* can avenge him. Step out of line again and you are out of the pack!"

Chantal tensed, looking for a chance to sprint out the still-open door. But both boys kept a tight hold on their guns, even in the midst of their altercation; there was no opportunity for her to make her escape.

Yves yelled: "Now do as I say: watch these fools, and don't let them get away. Shoot them if you have to." Brandishing his own weapon, the boy Luc forced the community members to back up towards the far wall. His face was still flushed and resentful. Yves eyed him a moment, then turned to Manon. "You stay with him," he ordered.

"Yves, please listen – " the girl began.

"Be quiet!" he barked at her. Manon flinched and fell silent. He returned his attention to Chantal. "Would you be so kind as to accompany me on a short walk, *chérie?*"

398

She dared not resist, not with him waving a gun about in a room full of helpless people. He forced her to walk out in front of him, through the main door and down the path beyond.

At first she could not see her way, and kept stumbling. Fireflies flashed in the night-black depths of the woods; they no longer seemed enchanting to Chantal but impish and malevolent: the *feux follets* of lore, luring lone travelers to their doom. Then she saw other lights moving among the trees: not the phantom glints of fireflies, but sputtering flames of medieval-style torches held in unseen hands. Closer and closer they came, and soon by their red glow she could see long ranks of human figures filing through the maple wood, clad in cowled robes: not white like the Communauté's but deep black, scarcely distinguishable from the shadows in which they walked.

One faceless figure strode towards them and called out to Yves. Chantal knew the voice at once. "You have her! But where is my other granddaughter? What has become of Lysette?"

"She's in the hall with Luc and Manon," replied Yves. "They're keeping an eye on her, don't worry."

"No! I want my grandchild with me, safe and sound. Go back and fetch her at once."

"She is fine where she is. The last thing we need is a crying hysterical child. No, listen to me, Thérèse! After tonight your authority in this pack is over. I will give all the orders now." He shouted to the others. "The island is ours again. We will make our procession now, as our ancestors did in days of old, to honour the memory of Arcadia."

Thérèse stepped back and Yves prodded Chantal forward. He raised his left arm as he walked, its hand curled into a fist. *"Pour l'Arcadie!"* he yelled.

In the darkness others took up the cry: *"L'Arcadie! L'Arcadie!"* In the dark beyond the trees wolf-voices howled, and scores of yellow eyes reflected the flickering torchlight.

The nightmare procession continued. As they passed the husky pen the dogs, roused at the unfamiliar human scents, bayed furiously and charged the fence; but their warning chorus was useless now. On the *loup garous* marched, past the outdoor chapel and the statue of St. Francis – which two of the larger figures toppled over, to cheers from the rest – and down the dark trail that led to the Grove of Pan.

"Why are you doing this?" she asked Yves, not so much in hopes of an honest answer as a need to keep him talking – to keep him *human.*

The youth was silent for so long that she thought he had chosen not to reply to her. Then he said, without looking at her: "It is not so much about you now, *chérie.* All I care about now is drawing Raoul out so I can kill him."

"Murderer!" she cried. "You're as bad as your brother!"

"How is it murder? Tell me, is it a crime for a man to shoot a wolf? I will kill him while he is in his animal form, and no one will be able to do anything about it. This I will do for my father and Jules."

"Jules tried to kill me! Raoul *had* to stop him—"

He glared. "You're not blameless either. In fact, this whole affair is your fault."

"Mine!" she said, forgetting her fear in outrage. "You're pinning all this on *me?"*

"Why not? If you'd just seen sense and agreed to your family's arrangements, none of this would have happened. Jules would have had to accept you in time. But no, you had to be proud and willful, turn your back on me and your own blood kin."

400

"So this is all about your pride?" she said, bitter. "Just because I turned you down?"

He scowled. "Don't think so highly of yourself, *chérie.* I don't want you for your own sake, I never did. You were a means to an end, that's all." The sneering tone entered his voice again. "And it seems I wasn't quite your type, *hein?* Your tastes are rather gross, *ma petite.*"

"What are you talking about?"

"You love the beast. Raoul. Don't you?"

She stared at him, stunned speechless. "Don't play dumb!" he snapped. "You won't have me, a Lapierre of *Acadie*; but you'll take for your mate a filthy brute, whelped in a den in the wilderness! What a fine couple you make. *La Belle et la Bête.*" He leered.

"Raoul is more human than you will ever be." Chantal spoke through clenched teeth.

"I'm not human. I am better: I am *loup garou*, and have the best of two worlds. I never shared Jules's desire to be all wolf. *Haut-loups* are nothing but clever animals. I've hunted them for sport. The true *loup garou* lives in both forms: in the human shape for pleasure, and in the wolf shape for killing."

Chantal had nothing more to say. Her revulsion outweighed her desire to keep him talking, and she trudged on in grim silence. She was still hopeful that her father's family did not want her dead. But what exactly *did* they mean to do with her?

A red glow showed up ahead. It came from the Grove of Pan, where an open bonfire burned. The trees were outlined in the ruddy light and the stone figure of Pan seemed to prance in his shadowy niche. More dark-robed figures stood there; she recognized Francine, her hood pushed back from her face, and her great-uncle Antoine. There was an elderly man, also clad in a black robe but lacking a hood: a Catholic priest in his soutane,

401

held captive between two guards. Père Mercier? Why had his abductors brought him here, to this pagan shrine?

Something else caught Chantal's eye: what looked like a female figure clad in white, standing at the edge of the clearing. But where its face should be there was only a black and featureless void. Her skin crawled. As she drew closer she saw that it was only an empty gown, floor-length, suspended on a hanger from a low tree-branch. Behind it from the same bough hung a great swag of something gauzy and white like a monstrous spider web. Trapped firelight gleamed dully in its pale meshes as it stirred and fluttered in the night breeze.

A bridal veil.

Then at last she understood the purpose of this gathering, and the presence of the priest.

## 27

Raoul and Genevieve sped along the road. By the light of the rising moon, they saw the river to their left and the dark hilly mass of the island against its silvered surface. Raoul looked sideways at Genevieve as she drove. He was grateful for the use of her vehicle, which was taking him to the Île far more quickly than he could run, but he was concerned for the wolf-woman's safety. "It will be dangerous," he said at length, breaking the tense silence. "Honoré sounded afraid, and he does not frighten easily. When we get there you should stay in this car, where it is safe. You are not a fighter, I think."

"No, I will come too. Chantal is my niece. Besides, they have both of my children now." Her voice and expression altered, hardened. "They may believe me harmless, but I will show them otherwise. Any she-wolf will fight for her pups."

He was impressed. "You are brave, *madame.* Very well, let us go on together."

When they crossed the bridge they saw tiny points of light flickering on the extreme western end of the island, near where the Communauté was located. The lights vanished and reappeared, as if occluded from time to time by trees and other obstacles. A candlelit procession of some kind, like the one they had seen at the basilica? Were those lights borne by the hands of their friends, or by their enemies? Raoul looked at Genevieve and saw that her features were contorted with fear, the eyes widened and lips parted and trembling. That gave him his answer.

At they prepared to turn off the bridge onto the island road a large dark van roared up alongside them, attempting to pass. Raoul stiffened, recognizing the vehicle: it belonged to the Dubois household. He called to Genevieve: "The horn! Get their attention – and stop the car!"

She blasted the horn, then slammed on the breaks and swerved to the side of the road. The van also pulled over and halted. "Get in!" a voice shouted from the driver's window of the van as they emerged from their car. It was Ti-Jacques. He got out and opened up the back of the van. "Jump in, quick!"

They obeyed him, springing up into the back. Dubois and his friends were already inside in their wolf shapes. As the van drove off they explained to Raoul what had happened.

"Bernard Lavallée has been saying for weeks that something is threatening the Island." Dubois's teeth showed as he spoke in a low growl. "He could sense that trouble was in the offing, and he regretted being too frail to help us fight it. He saw truly, it appears. We only heard tonight, from an informant on their side: Yves has deceived us all. He wanted us to believe he had given up, but in fact he and his allies have been scheming against us all along. They mean to retake the island tonight. The Boisverts have been joined by their extended clan and some friends, and Yves has summoned Jules's pack from the forest."

"Yes, I suspected when I saw Luc that the others had also returned from the wild. Luc attempted to murder Chantal. But what does Yves want with her?" said Raoul. "*He* would not think to harm her, surely? Would not her family object – "

"Her family!" The grey wolf's fangs were fully exposed now. "Much they care: the poor child is a liability to them now, nothing more. They killed her father for the same offense – "

"No," interrupted Genevieve. "I don't believe that, *monsieur*. It was Guy Lapierre who murdered Édouard, I'm sure of it. You do not know my Maman. To her

404

there is nothing more sacred than the ties of family. We that have her blood running in our veins are safe from her wrath. Chantal will not be killed, only imprisoned and controlled. It is Raoul who must die. That is what Yves wants."

The van stopped, and they all sprang out as Ti-Jacques opened up the back and took on wolf form himself. They were at Chapelle-des-loups. The lights were on in the main building and there were voices.

Dubois was visibly limping. "Are you all right?" asked Raoul, remembering the old man's ailment.

"I can manage," he said, but he winced as his right hind paw touched the ground. Angélique moved to his side to support him. "If it is to be war between us and their wolf packs we can spare no one. We are so few in number."

As they got closer to the hall they moved with caution, keeping to the shadows. Ti-Jacques got up on his hind legs and stole a quick glimpse through one window. "There is a young boy with a gun holding them all in one place," he said. "But I do not see Chantal. Or that *diable* Yves."

"My daughter?' said Genevieve with an anxious whine.

"The little one is there. She seems to be resting; a nun is with her. Manon is there too." His eyes grew hard.

Dubois turned to him. "Manon has repented of her treachery. It was she who phoned and warned us that Yves had returned and summoned his pack. She is afraid for her cousins and for Chantal."

"And you trusted her? How could you be sure that was not more treachery on her part?" growled Ti-Jacques.

"We were not sure, but then we heard from Chantal of the attack by Luc Benoit in the city. That confirmed it."

"Manon wouldn't hurt anyone," said Hyacinthe. "She is really sorry, I'm sure of it. Please, don't hurt my cousin!"

"No one is to be hurt if it can be helped," replied Dubois. "It was to prevent harm that we came here. Now, think: how are we to free those inside?"

"There is a gun in the van," said Jean-Louis. "My hunting rifle."

"No, no guns: not yet. We will try to draw him out first." Dubois sat back gingerly on his haunches. Raising his head, he gave a long deliberate howl of challenge.

At once the door burst open and Luc Benoit rushed out, gun in hand. With him was Manon.

"Who is out there? Are you one of ours? Give the signal!" Luc yelled, brandishing the handgun. The watching wolves were silent. This seemed to unnerve him. When he spoke again his voice was louder and higher, verging on a scream. "I said identify yourself, or I will shoot!" He fired wildly into the dark.

In that instant Manon turned on him. Seizing the boy's arm with both hands, she twisted it back, striving to wrench the gun out of his grip. It went off with another loud crack and spurt of light, but fired into the ground; as he flailed and screamed abuse at Manon the *loups garous* rushed forward. They sprang upon Luc en masse, pulling him down before he could shoot again. Ti-Jacques bit his forearm and the boy dropped the gun, screaming. For an instant he seemed about to take wolf shape, his eyes wild and his teeth bared to the gums. But their own fangs at his throat made him cower back, and his contorted face went white and still. He lay still, raising trembling hands in defeat.

406

"Enough!" commanded Dubois. He turned to the members of the Communauté who had rushed to the open door and stood there staring. "You're free! Tell me quickly, where are Yves Lapierre and Chantal?"

It was Manon, still standing behind him, who answered. "The Grove. You must go there now. Chantal is there, with Yves and the others. Many others: about thirty by my count."

"Thirty? Then we are more evenly matched than I thought. It sounds as though not all of Jules's pack has come. If we bring the dogs with us, that will tip the odds in our favour. Take this boy inside and see that he does not escape," added Dubois to the liberated *loups garous*. "Set a couple of guards to watch over him. The rest of you come with us – in wolf form or human, it does not matter which. Only hurry, or we may be too late."

Thérèse advanced towards Chantal smiling, holding in her arms the ivory-white wedding gown. It was of antique design: its high-collared bodice frothy with lace, its sleeves puffed out above tight wrist-length cuffs, its skirts wide and voluminous. The long trailing train swept the ground behind the old woman as she walked. "This is for you, granddaughter. It is the heirloom wedding gown worn by every Boisvert bride, passed from mother to daughter. Only Genevieve did not wear it, because she ran away to be married. But you shall wear it, tonight – "

"No," Chantal said.

"*Ma chère.* It would mean so much to me."

"Then that settles it. No *way* will I wear that thing."

Yves gestured at Chantal with the gun. He was no longer the boy Yves, but the head-wolf of his pack and soon to be leader of hers. "Put it on. Now," he ordered.

407

There was nothing for it but to obey. It was no use pleading for her privacy, either. With burning cheeks she stripped off her outer clothing and tossed it aside. The priest and a few of those assembled averted their faces, but most – including the fiery-eyed wolves – stood watching as she yanked the wedding gown on over her head. She stood, mute and fuming, as her grandmother fastened the long row of buttons down the back. Despite its age the gown was a perfect, glove-tight fit. Thérèse, of course, must know her measurements from their shopping expedition in Montreal, and had no doubt arranged for the dress to be altered accordingly. How long, Chantal wondered, had this garment been secretly waiting for her, hidden away somewhere in Thérèse's home? Had Francine once believed it would be hers – touched it and tried it on perhaps, imagining her wedding to the Lapierre boy she had been encouraged to love? Chantal could hear Francine sobbing, loudly and melodramatically, and fought the urge to turn and yell at her cousin. Could the girl still want Yves, even now – with the evidence of his selfishness and cruelty so plain to see?

Thérèse put the veil on Chantal's head and pinned it in place. Unlike the dress it was new, a billowing floor-length mass of airy gauze attached to a tiara studded with seed-pearls and tiny diamonds. The impression of a royal diadem was obvious.

Her grandmother stepped back and proclaimed with satisfaction: "You look lovely, my child! A princess of *Arcadie.*"

Yves pointed the gun directly at Père Mercier, sneering. "And now, *monsieur le prêtre*, would you be so kind as to marry us?"

"I cannot oblige you, *monsieur,*" the old priest answered, ignoring the weapon and looking Yves straight in the eye. "This is not a church. And in any case a marriage must be consensual to be valid."

Yves swung the gun back towards Chantal. "Oh, she'll consent all right. She knows what will happen if she doesn't. Don't you, my love?"

She knew. Of course she would give in to Yves rather than risk other people's lives. She nodded, not wanting to speak for fear that her voice would shake. He would so enjoy knowing that he had made her afraid.

"Still you will not be married in the eyes of God," said the priest to Yves.

Yves roared with derisive laughter. "God? Do you think I care about your imaginary friends, fool? What matters is that it will be legal, with respectable witnesses here to sign all the documents. Oh yes, some *very* respectable and important people are our guests tonight." He pointed to the forest depths where many shadowy wolf-shapes stood, anonymous in the dark. "They are here to see that this wayward she-wolf is taught her place, and no longer presents a threat to the rest of us with her careless behaviour."

Yves turned back to the priest. "So: you will do as I say, *monsieur le prêtre,* and shut your mouth about it afterwards, or you too will face... consequences. *Vous comprenez?* Now get on with it." Yves pointed the gun at Mercier's chest.

Still the old man did not move. "Kill me and you will have no one to perform the ceremony," he replied.

How could he have the nerve? Chantal wondered in admiration. But it was no use being defiant now. "Do it," she said to Mercier. "He'll start killing people if you don't; people I care about. I'm willing to go through with this if it saves lives."

And so the nightmare rite commenced: the celebration that every girl dreams and plans for, to Chantal would be a thing of terror and compulsion.

Inwardly she was seething with fury as the priest spoke in a dull flat voice the binding words. She could almost *feel* the wolf within her fighting to get out, to free itself and her. But she strove to calm its rage. A wolf was no match for bullets, and in his present mood Yves might do anything.

"Now repeat after me..." Père Mercier said.

As she spoke the words of the vow something in her hardened. Yves might have his way, make her his property by force and threats; but he would owe his victory to that alone. It must surely be a blow to his vanity that he could not win her any other way. So in a sense it was she who had won today. She intended to remind him of that at every opportunity in the future.

"What is that sound?" Thérèse said suddenly.

The old woman had turned, head cocked, appearing to listen. Chantal too thought she heard a noise in the distance, behind her: her ears seemed almost to be trying to twitch and turn towards it as a wolf's would. At first she thought it was only her wistful imaginings: then it grew more distinct. A baying and yelping, not of wolves but more like hounds in the hunt. Was it the Inuit dogs?

"Don't interrupt," growled Yves. Thérèse gave him a cold look and started to stride away from the assembled *loups garous*. The penned huskies were definitely reacting with excitement to – something. Their barks held the joyous tone of dogs that were not challenging strangers but greeting beloved masters.

Could it be – ?

Then Chantal heard a full-throated howl such as no dog could make, and another and another. She recognized the wolf-voices of Honoré and Angélique, the still deeper notes of Ti-Jacques and – with a leap of the heart – Raoul's clarion-clear howl. He had brought their friends to Chapelle-des-loups and freed the prisoners. They were running together now in a pack.

Yves swore and seized Chantal by the arm, pulling her roughly towards him. She tried to pull away, and he thrust the gun's barrel against her right temple. "Don't move," he hissed.

The black-robed figures turned as one, facing away from Pan's idol and towards the path. The figures appeared to collapse, the dark robes folding and fluttering down to the ground as the human bodies inside them changed. Bared fangs thrust out of drooping cowls; furred paws emerged beneath fluttering hems. Thérèse, a grey gaunt animal with silvered muzzle, stood protectively by the half-grown she-wolf that had been Francine. The grizzled Antoine loped over to stand beside them. The wolves in the wood came forward, mingling with their transformed allies.

Only Yves did not change, for in wolf-shape he would not be able to wield the gun. He stood clutching it in his hand, his other arm wrapped around Chantal, as the attacking force of *loups garous* charged into the Grove.

With a lift of the heart Chantal recognized Dubois's great grey wolf-form in their midst, and the slender ivory-white wolf that was Angélique. With them came many more, including a slight, fawn-coloured she-wolf who flung herself with a howl of fury on Thérèse. The old female staggered and snapped back, but her wiry strength was no match for the rage of the younger animal.

"My daughter!" Chantal heard her cry in the high-wolf tongue. "How dare you!"

But Genevieve made no reply. It seemed that the downtrodden omega of the Greenwoods had at last reached the limit of her endurance. Maddened by fear for her children, she gave free rein to her own "Sister

411

Wolf" and vented years of pent-up rage. With repeated bites and blows she succeeded in driving the older she-wolf back, into the trees.

"Mother, no!" yelped Francine, starting after her. "Stop!"

Genevieve whirled and ran at her wayward wolf-child, colliding with her so forcefully that she knocked her right over. Then she held Francine down with her forepaws and her jaws, not cruelly but firmly, keeping her immobilized as the battle raged around them. Even in the midst of her fear Chantal could not help but feel some satisfaction at seeing Francine finally receive the discipline she sorely needed.

The wolves on Dubois's side were slightly outnumbered, but they had brought the dogs with them. And while one Inuit dog might be no match for an *haut-loup,* a pack of dogs was another matter. The huskies had no fear of the great beasts, having been raised among *loups garous.* They bit at legs, tails and bellies, surrounding their foes.

Chantal recognized one large white wolf at the centre of the melee. He was fighting the great grey-muzzled wolf that was Antoine Boisvert.

"Raoul!" she cried. And then could have bitten her own tongue off, for at once Yves turned and saw the white shape of his enemy, clearly standing out from the rest.

"No!" she screamed, and as he moved the gun away from her head she tried to grapple with him. He struck her across the face with his free hand and she fell backwards, her legs twisted in the satin train.

Raoul, reared upon his hind legs as he fought his opponent, was unaware of his danger. But Dubois saw. He disengaged from his own fight and flung himself at Raoul, knocking him aside.

The gun fired with a deafening report and spurt of light.

The old wolf staggered, blood blooming in a great patch on his chest. Slowly he sank onto his belly, then rolled onto his side, jaws loosely gaping. Raoul ran to him.

"Honoré! No!" wailed Suzette.

"You cannot shoot us all, Lapierre!" roared Ti-Jacques. The huge black wolf advanced on Yves, his eyes reflecting the torchlight with a demonic glow.

"No, but I can shoot *her!*" Yves yelled, jamming the gun's muzzle into Chantal's side and hauling her to her feet. "One step closer and I will do it!"

And as they watched, helpless, he backed away with her into the depths of the wood beyond the statue of Pan.

A quick glance around him showed Raoul the battle was over. A few of the enemy wolves fought on in the dark beyond the firelight, but the majority had fled the Grove as if the gunshot and the fall of Dubois had shocked them to their senses. Genevieve still stood over her daughter, but Thérèse and Antoine had vanished. Raoul turned his attention back to the old grey wolf lying at his feet. Honoré was gasping and blood trickled from his open jaws. Angélique crouched by his side, nuzzling his ruff and whining shrilly.

"We must get him to a doctor," said Suzette uncertainly. "One of ours, a friend – "

"Too late, I think," said Jean-Louis in a low voice as he shifted back to his human form. "What is that he's saying?"

"Something about… mermaids," said Hyacinthe.

"Mermaids? He's delirious!"

The stricken wolf looked up into their faces. "Did I – win my soul – do you think?" he gasped.

413

"Yes, yes, my friend," soothed the priest, bending over him. "Have no fear: you are surely saved." The *loup garou* laid his head down and closed his eyes. Kneeling by his friend's side, Père Mercier began to recite the words of the Last Rites.

"One moment, *monsieur le prêtre*," said Raoul. He put his muzzle close to the old wolf's ear. "Honoré, hear me! You must take your human form. Now, before it is too late."

"Human?" said the old wolf. "Yes, I *would* be a man – at the end."

A convulsion shook the sprawled grey body. And then it was the old man who lay there, naked in the firelight, his chest smeared with blood, his dulled eyes filming over. Raoul seized one of the discarded black robes that lay upon the ground in his jaws and dragged it over the dying man as the priest began to pray over him again. Angélique whimpered, and Dubois reached up his arms, wrapping them around the neck of the she-wolf, burying his fingers in her soft white fur. *"Je t'adore, ma belle,"* he whispered.

The old white wolf flung up her head and gave an agonized howl. Then she too was human, a woman whose long white hair flowed loose all about her back and shoulders as she collapsed upon her husband's body. The arms of Honoré Dubois fell back to his sides, and his eyes stared upwards unseeing.

The *loups garous* clustered around their fallen leader. Raoul covered the lifeless face with a fold of the black robe. One of *loups garous* in human form doffed her own white robe and wrapped it around Angélique as she sat up sobbing, still clinging to Dubois's limp hand. Those in wolf form commenced to howl; the others wept human tears.

Mastering his own emotions, Raoul turned away from the scene. He stared at the dark forest into which Yves had fled with his captive.

*I will grieve for my friend later. It is Chantal who needs me now.*

Lurching and stumbling in the long wedding gown, Chantal knew she could not hope to break away from Yves. She could feel his gun digging into her side with each step. He half-dragged her on through the forest, wading through the dense undergrowth. As she tripped once again over her train she let herself fall to the forest floor, and when he pointed the gun at her she did not get up.

"On your feet!" he shouted.

"What for?" she retorted, glaring up at him. "If you're going to kill me anyway, what's the point?"

"Not you, fool." Yves snapped. "*You're* still useful to me – as bait. Raoul will come after us. He won't be able to resist playing the martyr to save your life. Then I will have him. When the hide of the white wolf hangs on my wall, I will be content."

Yves's eyes held a feverish gleam in the dim light. As always, he was excited by the very idea of killing: it was a kind of stimulant to him, an addiction. But here in the dark domain of Pan he had the look of a man demonically possessed. He bent down to seize her arm in a crushing grip. She yelled, and once more felt the gun jammed into her side. And then she heard the soft thud of approaching footfalls, and turned swiftly in alarm.

*Not Raoul,* she thought as a faint glimmer of white showed through the trees. *Please not Raoul. He'll be killed –*

It was he. But as he emerged from the forest she saw that he was not in his wolf's shape. He was human, clothed in one of the white robes of the Communauté. For an instant he and Yves stood in silence, each taking the other's measure in the manner of he-wolves readying for combat.

Then Raoul spoke. "You can shoot me now if you wish, but while I wear this form you will be punished by the law for your crime. You will be punished in any case for the murder of Honoré Dubois."

*Honoré – dead?* Chantal gave a little anguished moan where she lay.

But Yves was indifferent. "Oh, I doubt that, *mon vieux.* I doubt the Sûreté du Quebec will care very much about a dead wolf."

"Honoré returned to human form before the end," said Raoul.

Yves stared, his eyes narrowing. "You lie."

"I don't expect you to believe me. You can go and view his body for yourself."

Chantal caught her breath. "Well, Yves, you've gone and trapped yourself. That gun's covered in your fingerprints, and the bullet you used to shoot Dubois can be traced to it."

"She is right," said Raoul. "Your *loup garou* allies will not stand by you now that you are a criminal. They fled when you killed Honoré, every last one – for fear that they too will be implicated."

"Yes, somehow I don't think Thérèse will want you in the family any more, Yves," said Chantal. "The Boisvert reputation and all that. You might as well hand yourself over to the Sûreté now and get it over with."

Yves was shaking now – with fear or rage she could not tell – but his gun remained aimed at her. "Surrender? Why would I do that? The evidence is against Yves the man. I can take my wolf form and lie low – for years, if need be. Are they going to arrest a wild animal? Try not to be so dense, *chérie.* Honoré's

416

death does not help you. Nor Raoul, either. If I am already responsible for one man's death, then I might as well be condemned for another." He swung the gun at Raoul and fired.

Raoul dodged to one side, losing his balance in the process and falling to one knee. But his evasive action was not necessary. With the gun finally off her, Chantal exploded into action.

There was no time to think. She leaped up and hurled her whole weight against her captor, knocking his gun arm askew and sending the shot wide. Overbalancing, they collapsed in a heap together and wrestled wildly on the ground. She was in wolf form almost instantly, hardly feeling the transition in the heat of her grief and anger. The antique gown ripped and shredded to pieces as she erupted from it and sank her teeth into her foe's right arm. It was Yves's turn to cry out. He dropped his weapon, tore himself free and ran off without it, deep into the woods.

"Let him run, he has nothing to gain by it. It is over," Raoul said.

"No," she snarled in the wolf-tongue. "It is *not.*"

Still in her wolf shape, trailing tatters of white fabric from her neck and limbs, she hurled herself after Yves.

She was Chantal no longer. She gave herself wholly to Sister Wolf, scenting her prey with questing muzzle low to the ground and running on swift paws. Within a few moments she had overtaken him. He was in the act of tearing his clothes away from his body, to shift his shape. With a deep guttural roar of rage she sprang at him, aiming at his legs, fangs seeking to sever muscle and tendon and bring him down. He fell screaming, and his shape began to alter. But she had the advantage of being already transformed. She dodged his clashing teeth and went straight for the throat that was neither wolf's nor man's, worrying her way through sprouting fur for the pulsing life beneath.

Unable to dislodge her, Yves transformed back to human shape again. Did he think she would spare him in that form? She seized him harder by the throat and shook him, until with a gasp he went limp and ceased struggling. Her teeth broke the fragile human skin of his neck. She tasted blood…

Someone spoke nearby. "Chantal, no!"

It was Raoul's voice – his human voice, gentle and reasonable. "He will not escape punishment. Leave him to the law!" he implored.

But she was beyond the reach of reason now. This was the realm of Pan, and one law alone prevailed here. She continued to bite deeper. Yves yelled in agony.

The voice spoke again, closer, right by her ear. "Chantal, Honoré did not gain his soul so that you could lose yours." A hand was on her ruff, not gripping, just gently stroking the fur. His soothing, familiar scent was in her nostrils.

With a cry she released her hold and crumpled backwards, into his arms. Yves struggled to his feet, bleeding from the neck but not mortally wounded. He fled through the dark woods – where, she neither knew nor cared now. What mattered was Raoul: his arms cradling her, his voice calming her, as she whimpered aloud with pain and sorrow.

"Chantal," he murmured into the soft fur of her neck. He held her name out to her, as a man will hold out a rope to a drowning friend.

*Chantal…*

She seized on the name, clutching it to her. Sister Wolf, sensing that her protective presence was no longer needed, withdrew into the inner darkness from which she had come. Chantal leaned back against Raoul, closing her eyes. It was all over: he was safe, and so

was she. In his gentle, sheltering arms she was herself
again.

## 28

The funeral of Honoré Dubois, held three days later at Chapelle-des-loups, was small and private. Père Mercier officiated at the outdoor chapel along with a native shaman, a friend of Josephine's, who performed a traditional chant of mourning. Josephine herself was there, returned from the north along with Noah Aglukkaq. Angélique Dubois, her face veiled, sat at the front surrounded by friends and comforters: Ti-Jacques, Jean-Louis, René Leblanc, Hyacinthe and Suzette. Bernard Lavallée, leaning hard on his cane, looked even older than before. *Tante* Genevieve sat in the back row, dressed all in black and accompanied by Lysette and a very subdued Francine. It was good at least to see all these familiar faces, Chantal reflected as she sat by Raoul's side. There was some solace in knowing that her grief was shared by many.

Afterwards there was a reception at the Maison Dubois, a sombre cross between a wake and one of Honoré's *salons.* Chantal went and stood by the window with Raoul and Josephine, looking out towards the Citadelle.

"I'm told Manon did not join us because she was unsure of her welcome, but that she has sincerely repented of her treachery," Josephine said. "She was dazzled by Yves's attentions and believed she could redeem him in time, but when she saw the full depths of his cruelty she lost all love for him. Though I hear, Chantal, that your cousin Francine has vowed to wait for Yves to be released from prison."

"We'll see," said Chantal. "Waiting's hard, especially when you're only fourteen, and he hasn't even gone to trial yet. He'll be convicted, of course, with the ballistic evidence and all those witnesses. So: a year for the trial, and then he'll be in for twenty years minimum  – "

Raoul shook his head. "Decades of imprisonment in a cell – and worse, he will not be able to change his form in all that time, for fear of revealing to his cell mates that he is a *loup garou*. It will be very hard for him."

"I'm overwhelmed with sympathy," said Chantal dryly.

Raoul said nothing in response to this. He had learnt by now to recognize sarcasm.

"What about Jules's pack?" she went on. "The *loups garous* who stayed in wolf form?"

"Luc Benoit has gone home to his family, I hear," said Josephine. "As for the rest, they have retreated to the Parc Jacques Cartier, far away from human habitation. There are low-wolves living in its forests, so the presence of *loups garous* will be less noticeable there. We'll leave them alone there, so long as they harm no one."

"I wonder what will happen to them."

"The same thing that is happening to the *hauts-loups* in the arctic. They will retreat ever further and further into the wilds, slowly diminishing in numbers, mating at last with the low-wolves out of desperation. They will raise litters of pups that have no capacity to speak, to imagine, or to dream. In the end their descendants will become true wolves, non-sentient as the life-force, blending back into it. It is what Jules would have wanted for himself, I think: to shed not only his human form but the full consciousness that tormented him so, reverting to a pure bestial state."

"Well, that's their decision," said Chantal. "At least *Tante* Genevieve has left Thérèse. I can be close to her and Lysette anyway – and even Francine someday, if she'll let me. But first I have to go back to America.

421

My cousin Katharine just had her first baby, a girl; she's invited me to come stay with her and be mother's helper."

"Ah! A death, a birth; that is life, no? Always it goes on." Josephine beamed and hugged her. "I am happy for you. Things turned out well for you, after all."

"For me, sure," Chantal replied, with a glance in Angélique's direction. She could not keep the bitterness out of her voice.

Excusing herself, she slipped out of the house. For a time she wandered aimlessly about the streets as dusk fell over the Old City. *Here I am,* she thought, *right back where I started: running away from a funeral.* What was the point of life if it ended in such anguish and heartache? Lavallée had been right when he said death was coming to one she knew. But he'd also said it would come to her as well.

"Pay no heed to my premonitions, child," he had urged her, later on. "I told you, they are not always right." *He was right about Honoré, though. Great. Something else for me to brood about and dread...*

Finding herself on the Terrasse, she descended the sharp angled flights of the Escalier Casse-cou to the Basse-Ville. At Place Royale she joined the throngs of tourists entering the little stone church. There she lit a candle and sat down in a pew, struggling to master her emotions. Her gaze wandered about the exquisite white-and-gold interior and finally settled upon the wooden model of the colonists' ship, *Le Brézé,* suspended on wires from the ceiling. It seemed to sail through the air, its bowsprit pointing towards the sanctuary and the rood screen that was sculpted in battlemented towers, like a heavenly analogue of the fortified Quebec. An enchanted flying vessel, soaring to a celestial city... There it would surely find safe haven for its cargo of souls, and a welcome from those that dwelled amid the white-and-gold towers.

She could no longer hold the tears back. Silently she offered up a prayer for the wolf who had wished to be a man. *If anyone could claim to have an immortal soul it's you, Honoré. Wherever you are now, I'm sure you're right at home. Say hello to my parents for me, and Nana too.*

Feeling a little comforted, she left the church and descended the steps into the square. As she did so, a large white shape rose up from the cobblestones where it had been lying and approached her, tail wagging. A crowd of children straggled after it, petting the soft fur. "Is this your dog, *mam'selle?*" asked one small boy.

"Yes," she said, gazing into the animal's sapphire-blue eyes. "Yes, he's mine."

"He's so big!" said the boy with a laugh. "He looks just like a wolf!"

"But he was very good and patient," added a little girl. "Waiting for you all that time."

Chantal smiled at them and walked away across the square with Raoul following at her heels. "Okay, I give up," she said to him as soon as they were out of earshot. "How in the world did you find me?"

"I have not lost my skill at following a scent trail," Raoul replied in the wolf-speech, falling into step beside her. "Though I had to dodge some well-intentioned people who wanted to catch the big white dog that was running loose in the city without a leash! Now I have located you, I will just slip into the Atelier for some clothing so I can change back to human form again. A dog roaming the streets alone is noticeable enough; a man walking about in public with no clothes would get even more attention!"

She waited for him while he changed in a back room of the shop, emerging presently in an old pair of jeans

423

and a faded tee shirt. They went back out together in silence, walking along the walled streets now plangent with the voices of holiday-makers. It was the festival of St. Jean Baptiste, patron saint of Quebec, and the city was as full of visitors as it had been during *Carnaval*. It hurt her to see these carefree celebrations on a night when she wanted only to mourn. But the world, as Josephine would say, did not cease turning because one life had departed from it.

"Look there." Raoul pointed to the Lévis ferry moored at the docks. Sight-seers were streaming up the gangway. "They ride the boat not to get to the other side, but merely to admire the view. That is very human, *non?* Shall we go too? I have borrowed a little cash from the Atelier's fund."

"Isn't that meant for emergencies?" she asked.

"You are sad," he said. "That is an emergency. The people ride the boat because it makes them happy, and they can forget their troubles. Perhaps it will make you forget, a little."

Chantal doubted that, but he was so anxious to help her that it seemed rude to refuse. They purchased tickets and boarded the ferry, joining the chattering throngs on the upper deck. As the boat pulled slowly away from the docks and swung out into mid-stream the Haute-Ville seemed to float above them, dominated by the illuminated turrets of the Château Frontenac.

"You know, it's funny really," said Chantal as they stood and leaned on the rail together. "Instead of me helping you to be more human, it's you who keep doing that for me. You saved me again from – from my other self, back there on the island."

"While it was you who showed to me the true joy of being a wolf," he smiled. "I can fully accept both of my natures now."

She grinned back at him. "We did it all backwards, didn't we? Oh well, as long as we helped each other *somehow* I guess it's all right."

He looked away again, out over the river. Fireworks launched from the Plains of Abraham exploded high above the city, and the evening sky flowered with flame. Many-coloured sparks fell like a cascade of wind-plucked petals, reflecting in the river below. For some time they stood in silence, watching along with the cheering crowd.

"You are leaving soon?" he said at last.

Chantal nodded. "Yes, Kath needs my help. It's her first child."

"But you will return here one day, *oui?*"

"Oh, yes," she said. "I've been accepted at Laval, so I'll be back again in September."

"Good. I'm glad you will be returning, Chantal. I can't imagine what it would be like if you were not here."

"Even if they'd turned me down I'd still have come back. Quebec is my home now. I've finally found a place where I feel as if I belong."

"I too," he said. Then slowly, hesitantly, he laid his hand on hers.

At his touch a warmth seemed to spread throughout her body. She stared down at the hand enfolding hers, and then raised her eyes to meet his, filled with a sudden wonder. Could Yves, for all his cruelty and selfishness, have managed to see what she herself had not?

And had Yves been the only one? She blinked and gave a little start as a thought occurred to her.

"What is it?" Raoul asked.

"I was just thinking... What if I misheard what old M. Lavallée said to me in his trance? I'd pretty much decided it must have been about Honoré dying. But what if it wasn't *la mort* he said?"

425

"What else could it have been?"

"Well, what if he said *l'amour?* They sound almost exactly the same."

*Someone close to me, that's what he said. He was watching me and Raoul playing, and then he had the premonition that something was coming soon to me and to someone close to me...* l'amour!

"Love," she said aloud, and laughed. "He was talking about *love!"* The last of her sadness lifted from her.

The crowd on the ferry cheered and applauded as yet another firework display lit up the sky. If the two young people embracing at the ship's rail seemed more absorbed in each other than in the spectacle, no one else thought anything of it. They merely smiled indulgently and looked away again, giving the pair their privacy. It was Quebec City after all, and it was summertime; such things were only to be expected.

# AFTERWORD

When I first set out to write this book my specific intention was not to tell a story about werewolves. I knew only that I wanted to pay special tribute to my birthplace of Quebec with a fictional tale set in that province, and that the story would use for its inspiration some aspect of French Canadian folklore. It was an approach I had taken before with other books, such as my young adult fantasies *The Hidden World* and *The Wolves of Woden,* which were based on the Celtic fairy traditions of Newfoundland. Seeking a similarly rich vein of mythology to mine, I settled upon the Québecois version of the werewolf, the *loup garou.* I had already made use of this particular branch of folklore in a short story, "Walking with Wolves", published a few years previously. My favourite books in childhood were nearly all works of fantasy, but I had also come to love the animal stories of Canadian authors Ernest Thompson Seton and Charles G. D. Roberts. I had also read *Never Cry Wolf*, Farley Mowat's semi-fictionalized account of studying arctic wolves in the wild, at a very young age and it had made a deep impression on me. With my short story I saw a chance to blend these two beloved genres in a single work.

I took the same approach with my new novel, blending the fantastic with the naturalistic, but emphasizing the latter wherever possible. In many places where werewolf tales are written and read today, real wolves have long been eradicated from the landscape. Only a lingering trace of their presence still exists, in the form of a mythology that greatly exaggerates the fearsome qualities of these animals and makes them seem like terrifying monsters. In my country, however, they are still quite common: I personally know people who have had harmless encounters with wolves in the wild, and have myself been privileged to hear the thrilling and haunting sound of a pack howling together in the night. So the werewolves that emerged from the shadows of my imagination were not supernatural terrors, but perfectly natural creatures inhabiting an environment in which they felt entirely at home. I read everything I could find on the subject of real wolves, including the latest theories on their pack structure and behaviour. The only difference between my werewolves and true wolves of the wilderness, I decided, was that the former would possess human minds, passions and ideals.

It also became clear to me in the early stages of writing that more research on werewolf mythology would be required for a book-length work, and this led me to many unexpected and fascinating places. The *loup garou* was brought to Canada by the first French settlers, and the European myth made a natural transition to the wolf-haunted forests and fields of this northern land. Edith Fowke, the celebrated Canadian folklorist, suggested that the transplanted myth might have become entwined with the aboriginal lore of the *windigo*, a fierce cannibal spirit of the wilderness. However that may be, the Québecois version of the myth certainly has its own unique character, and I hope that I have conveyed at least some of that in my book. *Loups garous* were in fact linked to the Île d'Orléans (or the "Isle of the Sorcerers" as it was sometimes called) through the local folklore, which made them participants in the Satanic gatherings of witches, demons, and other supernatural beings said to take place upon that storied island. In my book I have substituted the god Pan for the Devil in the tale of the night processions, in order to make a connection with an older strand of the mythology. There is, of course, no Grove of Pan in real life, nor any

Chapelle-des-loups. But the tract of forested land at the western end of the Île d'Orléans does exist, lovingly preserved by the islanders.

I delved deep into werewolf lore, not only from Quebec, but from all over the world. I did not invent the idea of "wolf leaders", lone werewolves who command packs of ordinary wolves: though I barely touch upon it here, this piece of lore fascinates me, and I hope to explore it further someday; but in the meantime anyone else who wishes to write about it is certainly free to do so. The werewolf trials are of course a matter of historical record, and coincided with the more well-known medieval witch craze: another fact of which I had not been aware. Some of the accused, like the infamous Peter Stubbs, are believed to have been serial murderers in real life, but most were probably blameless victims like the unfortunate "witches".

Although our modern werewolf tradition, with all its trappings of infectious bites, full moons and silver bullets, is a recent cultural development, the notion of people who could transform themselves into wolves goes back at least to Graeco-Roman times. I explored its roots in remote antiquity, in the works of classical writers like Herodotus, Petroneus, and Pliny the Elder. The latter's account of the shape-shifting Arcadians, though skeptical, particularly fascinated me: the idea of an entire nation of wolf-people, with its own unique customs and traditions, was so unlike the modern-day image of the werewolf as a lonely and alienated outsider rejected by normal human society. I was also struck by the fact that a portion of eastern Canada, including parts of Quebec, once went by the name of Acadia (*Acadie* in French). Further research into the etymology of the name revealed that some scholars believed it to be a corruption of Arcadia (in French, *Arcadie*). That in turn led to the notion that the Canadian *loups garous* of my

3

fantasy novel could be descended from Pliny's ancient wolf-race. The happy coincidence confirmed my belief that this book was meant to be. Slowly but surely, the story was telling itself.

Some of the traditional stories I have enlarged upon or embroidered. There has never been any lycanthropic element to the story of the Wolf of Gubbio: that is my own invention. And while it is true that Genghis Khan claimed descent from a magical wolf, it was not strictly speaking a werewolf in his case. But the legend about the Irish nobles of Ossory is an authentic piece of folklore, as is that of Prince Vseslav of Polotsk. The fantastical tale of Madame Sanroche comes from the writings of the sixteenth-century French demonologist Henri Boguet, and although it is retold in my own words it adheres closely to the original. Its French setting and the curiously sympathetic female figure at its centre offered, I felt, an intriguing parallel to my own story.

Marie de France's *Lai du Bisclavret* is available in English translation for anyone who may wish to read that enchanting tale.

In closing, I would like to take a moment to acknowledge the support and encouragement of my family and also of my editor and good friend Judy Diehl. I would also like to thank the many readers who read an earlier version of this manuscript on the internet and offered me their feedback and encouragement.

Without the help of all of these people this book would not have been possible.

PREVIEW CHAPTER

# The Way of the Wolf

An excerpt from the sequel to *The House of the Wolf*

The wolf prowled through dense undergrowth beneath towering trunks of giant cedar and fir. Peering through a screen of close-growing ferns, it eyed the small isolated house only thirty metres distant. From the back of the building came a sound of muffled human voices, and then the penetrating cry of an infant. The wolf's ears swiveled forward and it stood for a moment perfectly motionless, one forepaw raised. Then slowly, warily, it stalked ever closer to the house.

It kept to the undergrowth that screened its dark-furred body from sight, blending into the shadows under the trees. Approaching the wooden fence at the back of the property, it paused once more to peer between the railings. Beyond this point there grew a profusion of plant life foreign to the northern rain forest: young fig and eucalyptus saplings, clumps of bamboo, banana plants with their great spade-shaped leaves. From the very centre of the lush alien greenery there rose, ostentatious in its incongruity, a palm tree with a crown of green plumes atop its twenty-five-foot trunk. Through gaps in the mass of cultivated vegetation the wolf had a partial view of the house's back deck, empty now but for two folding chairs and a perambulator. The voices grew louder, nearer: the wolf pulled quickly back into the ferns as the rear door of the house opened and two young women walked out onto the sun deck: a tall brunette and a shorter, plumper redhead. The latter carried the crying baby in her arms.

From behind the green camouflage of fern boughs the wolf's eyes watched, steady and intent.

"I think baby Erin's going to be an opera singer, Kath!" joked Chantal. "She's certainly got the lungs for it!"

"I know!" said her cousin, laughing. "It's a good thing the houses are far apart here and we back onto a conservation area. Otherwise she'd be keeping the neighbours awake all night too!" She patted the baby's back and rocked her gently in her arms. "Hush now, shhh…" The piercing howls subsided to soft, muffled sobs.

"We haven't had time for a really good talk, have we?" Chantal said. "It's been all about the baby these past few weeks. Not that I grudge it to Erin – she's adorable – but we haven't even mentioned your move, and what it's like living here."

"I agree. Time for us to catch up." Katharine stooped to lay her whimpering offspring in a pram. "There, she'll sleep for a bit now, I think. Fresh air agrees with her." She flung herself down onto one of the deck chairs. "*Whew!* A new baby, a new country *and* a new home all within two months' time. I think I've had about as much life change as I can handle for a while."

"Well, it's all good change anyway. How's Warren adjusting?"

"Oh, he's fine. His parents are talking about moving up here too after they both retire, so they can be close to us. Erin's the first grandkid in their family, too. That'll be great: lots of free babysitting! It still feels kind of funny, being in a foreign country. I'm not a born Canuck, like you. But it's not really all that different from Oregon. We'll get used to it. And it's nice and sunny out here on the island, not damp and drizzly like the coast. Warren's got a great garden started, hasn't he? That windmill palm was already here, of course; it's partly why Warren wanted this property. He's planning to plant another one next to it and string a hammock between them!" She chuckled. "And he's planted all those other things. He's thrilled that he can grow some tropicals here. I just hope the deer don't eat

2

everything."

Chantal turned to examine the back yard, frowning. "Isn't your fence high enough to keep deer out?"

"Listen to you! You've only been an urban dweller for how long – six months now? And you're already starting to forget stuff. Deer can jump pretty darned high when they're hungry. We'll probably have to replace the fence eventually."

"Yes," said Chantal slowly. "I'd do that it I were you. Maybe get one of those motion sensor lights too… I love that stretch of forest there at the back of your property, but you don't go wandering around in there, do you? Aren't there dangerous wild animals hereabouts?"

"Possibly. There might be the occasional cougar, I guess."

"A mountain lion, you mean? I've heard about lions attacking people on the west coast."

"Vancouver Island has had its share of those, sure. More than its share actually; it pretty much holds the record for cougar encounters, or so I hear." Kath seemed quite unperturbed. "But I've never seen one, and no one else in this area ever has either."

There was a brief, almost imperceptible pause before the younger woman's next question. "There are… other animals too, though, aren't there? Like – like wolves, for instance?"

"Only in the northern part of the island, where it's really wild. Not down here. Listen to you, girl! You're even more of a Nervous Nellie than I am. And you wouldn't believe what a worrywart you turn into when you have your first kid." Kath leaned back in her chair and kicked her sandals off. She sighed deeply, but it was a sound of utter contentment. "Settling down always sounded so dull when we were kids, didn't it? But I'm loving it so far."

Chantal looked at her and smiled. "I'm glad you're

happy, Kath."

Kath motioned to her to sit down. "Enough about me. What about you, kiddo? Anyone special in your life yet, out there in Quebec?"

Chantal sat in the second chair. "Yes," she said slowly. "Yes, there's someone I like a lot. He—he's French Canadian. His name's Raoul Dulac."

"Ooh, sounds romantic! And...?" There was another short pause as Kath studied her cousin's face. "All right hon, you don't have to say any more if you're not ready to."

Chantal looked away. "It's okay really, it's just … Tell me, Kath, how did you know that Warren was the right one? What made you feel sure?"

"He was a friend of a friend. We met at a party and just sort of clicked. We talked so much he asked me to join him at a coffee shop afterwards, and we went on talking for hours. After that – "

"You went to his place?"

"Well, it wasn't that quick! You kids are so impatient nowadays! No, we met several more times after that, but it was weeks before we started dating officially. We just liked to talk about the same things; we have lots of interests in common. And we both wanted to have families."

"And that was it?"

Katharine smiled. "Not exactly a swept-off-your-feet romance, huh? I don't care. It's real life, honey, not a movie. The point is I'm right where I wanted to be at this time in my life, and so's he."

"Well, Raoul and I are still at that sort of early stage. We haven't known each other all that long. He doesn't want to rush things, and neither do I. That might spoil it."

"Wow, you're taking this seriously." Kath grinned at her. "And here I thought you'd never get over that high school crush of yours. Russell Gordon."

"Who?" said Chantal, and they both laughed.

For a few moments the two women sat in companionable silence. Kath still retained some of the plumpness from her pregnancy: she was a little fuller in the face, a little rounder in the arms. It made her resemble her late mother more than ever, a comforting comparison for Chantal. Aunt Fran had been something of a surrogate mother to her in her early childhood, presiding over a warm and welcoming household just a few doors down from her own. Kath's home would be the same, she sensed, always loving and open as an embrace, available to her if ever she should need it. To Chantal, rootless and roofless at this stage of her life, it was a reassuring thought.

Presently Kath spoke again, her words almost an echo of Chantal's inner musings. "You'll stay in touch, won't you? I hate to see us all growing apart. I guess it was bound to happen after Nana passed away," she added sadly. "She kept all the families together, with those mandatory gatherings at the old homestead. But we're getting so spread out now, with you youngsters going off to college, making new friends... You're disappearing. You especially, Chantal. You spend so much time with your dad's family now, sometimes I almost feel as if we're losing you."

"Hey!" Chantal sprang up and faced her cousin. "Family's forever, Kath. I have to go back to Quebec pretty soon, to start getting ready for university. But I'll phone you, and email and text, until you're totally sick of me! Promise."

"Okay. And you know you're welcome to come out here, any time. I know it's a long way, but we're always glad to see you." Kath stood up too, and they hugged.

The baby began to fuss again, and her mother sighed and let go of Chantal. "Babies! They have to be the

5

centre of attention every minute, don't they? Erin Francesca Fitzpatrick, you are going to drive Mommy mad!" she added in tones of mild reproof as she picked the baby up. "All right, all right, let's take you inside again. And then I'd better see about getting us some lunch."

She carried the still-protesting Erin back into the house. Chantal, left to herself, walked down the wooden steps of the deck and strolled around the yard. She paused by the back fence, peering into the forest. There came a soft rustling sound from the fern bed and she grew instantly tense, every muscle in her body strung taut.

Staring over the fence, she found herself looking straight into the yellow eyes of the wolf.

Chantal relaxed again. "Oh, it's you," she said.

The wolf withdrew into the thick undergrowth. There were more rustling sounds, and the fern leaves shook. Then the bare head and shoulders of a young man emerged from the sea of greenery. His hair was dark, his skin a warm golden hue—not a suntan, but its own natural colour. "Okay if I don't come out any further than this?" the youth said in a low voice. "Seeing as I'm not wearing any clothes?"

They smiled at each other. "I'm glad to see you," said Chantal. "Well, part of you. It's Zachary, isn't it?"

"At your service." White teeth flashed at her in a beguiling grin. "Any friend of Josephine Legris is a friend of mine. Say hi to her for me when you see her again, will you?"

"You bet. And thanks so much for being here. It puts my mind at rest. I don't know if *they* would really try to hurt any of my family, but it pays to be cautious."

"I'll keep an eye on your relatives, and so will my friends from the reservation," the aboriginal boy replied. "You know, it's funny. We always believed in the link

6

between wolves and our people. We do the wolf ceremony, the Winter Dance, every year, and we have loads of stories… But it wasn't till Josephine visited our community that some of us discovered we could actually change our shapes. Wolf-people are still kind of thin on the ground out here."

"But that actually helps," she replied. "It means my enemies will stand out a mile, too. At least that's what I'm hoping."

There was a catch in her voice and the boy looked keenly at her. "We'll keep your family safe from them, I promise. We've learned to look out for each other. Josephine will tell you – uh oh, better go now…"

Katharine was calling her. Chantal turned to see her cousin standing on the back deck, waving. At once Zachary ducked back down into the mass of overlapping green leaves. A moment later Chantal saw the dark-brown back of the wolf reappear, already several metres away and retreating deeper into the trees.

Throwing one last lingering glance towards the forest, she went back to the house. In her head she was picturing another wolf, larger than this one, with a pelt of pure white fur. And strangely human blue eyes… No, she couldn't tell her cousin all about her "special someone". Not now, and probably not ever. How to explain—even if it were allowed—that werewolves existed, and that she was in love with one? That she yearned even now to be running through the fields with Raoul by her side, smelling the enticing smells of the wilderness, feeling the earth beneath her feet?

*All four of my feet…*

Because that was the greatest secret of all, and one that she could also never tell. Not even to Katharine. Not to anyone.

Alison Baird was born in Montreal, Quebec. She started writing at an early age, publishing her first poems when she was twelve. She has since published numerous novels for children and adults, including *The Hidden World, The Wolves of Woden,* the *Dragon Throne* trilogy, and *White as the Waves* which was short-listed for the Violet Downey Book Award. She now makes her home in Ontario.

Her website is www.alisonbaird.net.

www.ingramcontent.com/pod-product-compliance
Lightning Source LLC
Chambersburg PA
CBHW070344260626
47161CB00001B/8